THE
ANGEL
OF
LORRAINE

THE ANGEL OF LORRAINE

Part 3 of the Richard Calveley Trilogy

PETER TALLON

authorHOUSE

AuthorHouse™ UK
1663 Liberty Drive
Bloomington, IN 47403 USA
www.authorhouse.co.uk
Phone: UK TFN: 0800 0148641 (Toll Free inside the UK)
UK Local: (02) 0369 56322 (+44 20 3695 6322 from outside the UK)

© 2021 Peter Tallon. All rights reserved.

No part of this book may be reproduced, stored in a retrieval system, or transmitted by any means without the written permission of the author.

Published by AuthorHouse 10/04/2021

ISBN: 978-1-6655-9371-7 (sc)
ISBN: 978-1-6655-9372-4 (hc)
ISBN: 978-1-6655-9370-0 (e)

Print information available on the last page.

Any people depicted in stock imagery provided by Getty Images are models, and such images are being used for illustrative purposes only.
Certain stock imagery © Getty Images.

This book is printed on acid-free paper.

Because of the dynamic nature of the Internet, any web addresses or links contained in this book may have changed since publication and may no longer be valid. The views expressed in this work are solely those of the author and do not necessarily reflect the views of the publisher, and the publisher hereby disclaims any responsibility for them.

For Jennifer,
my own personal angel

AUTHOR'S NOTE

If anyone wrote a story telling of a humble peasant girl emerging from nowhere to lead the demoralised armies of the most powerful nation in Europe to victory in a few months over a previously unconquerable foe, it would be dismissed as too incredible to be worth reading. Yet this really did happen. The remarkable career of Joan of Arc, as she became known to the English, has no parallel in world history.

It is also one of the best documented events in Medieval Europe; there is a wealth of contemporary records still surviving. Jeanne, the Maid of Orléans, as she was known to the French, personally touched the lives of hundreds if not thousands of people, so in order to prevent a novel becoming a history lesson, I have had to leave out many of the minor characters and merge some of the others into fewer, fictional individuals. But I have remained true to the major players and events in her life.

Norfolk and Suffolk 1429

North Central France 1429

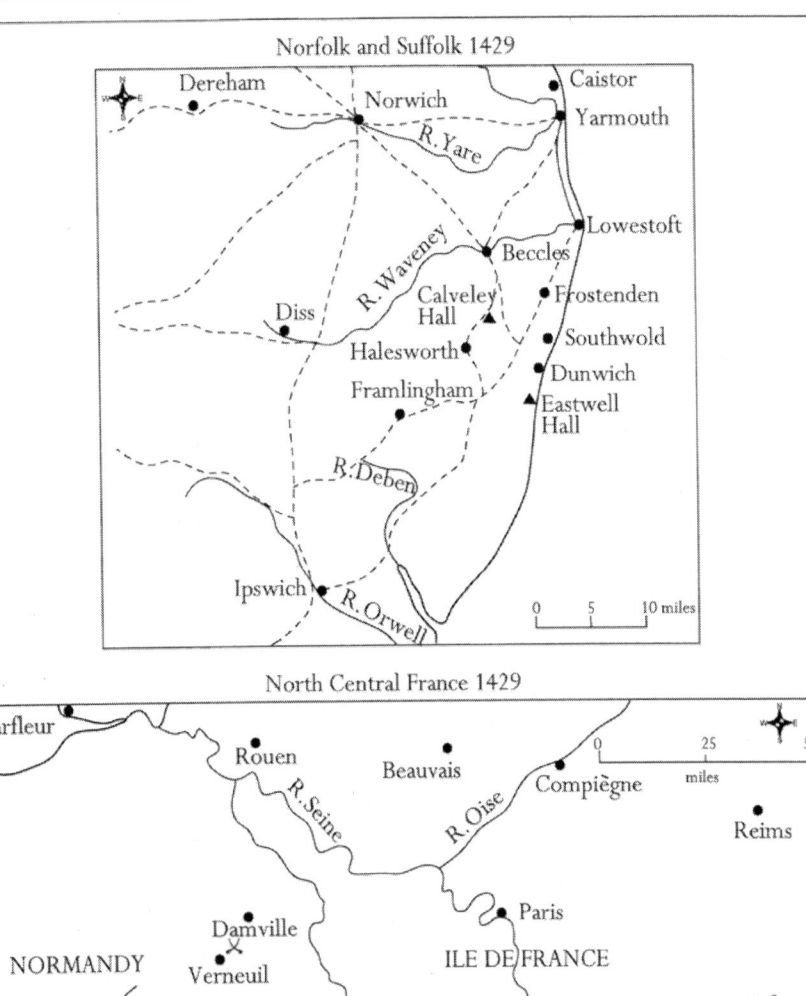

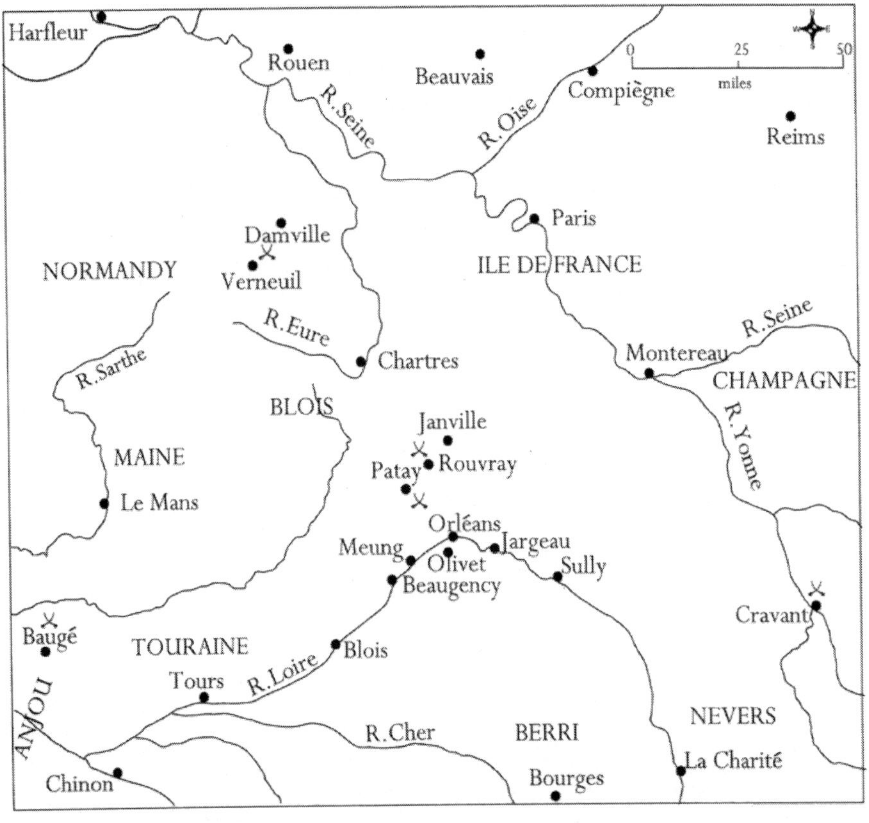

CHAPTER ONE

It was late summer in the Year of Our Lord 1428. In the remote Duchy of Lorraine, the easternmost province of the Kingdom of France, the harvest was well advanced and the farmers could look forward to an excellent yield. On the last Sunday of August, Father Guillaume Front, parish priest of the village of Domremy, sat down at his desk as the bell chimed noon in the church of Saint Remy next to his presbytery. Father Front looked out of his window and glanced at the sundial beside the herb garden. *Late again*, he thought. *I shall have to speak to the church warden about his drinking*, but then he noticed the goblet on his desk, which he had just filled with good Burgundy wine, and admonished himself. *Perhaps I should not be too harsh. I'll leave it till next week.*

He took a sip, dipped his quill into the inkpot, and settled down to write his monthly letter to the bishop, complaining yet again about the dilapidated state of the church roof, which he was certain would let in more rain this winter if nothing was done to fix it. Morning Mass was finished, his congregation had dispersed, so he could count on at least two unbroken hours to compose a stern reminder to the bishop who had ignored his last two letters. But he had only just begun to write his third sentence when there was a knock at his presbytery door.

"Who on earth can that be?" he grumbled to himself, and putting down the quill, he called out, "Who is it?"

"Jacques Darc," came the muffled reply from the other side of the door. Jacques was one of the upper-class peasantry who farmed about fifty acres of his own land close to the west bank of the River Meuse. He was also a substantial benefactor to the church.

"Come in, Jacques," replied the priest, trying to sound as cordial as he could.

A sturdy man of average height entered. He took off his cap, revealing reddish-brown hair, which was receding above the forehead; red hair was not uncommon in Lorraine, where the blood of French and Germans freely intermingled. His round face was weathered from a lifetime of working in the open air, and he was a little stooped for a man of only thirty-eight, the consequence of years of ploughing the fertile soil of the Meuse valley.

"I am sorry to disturb you, Father."

"That's all right, Jacques. Sit down and allow me to pour you a goblet of wine." The goblet almost disappeared inside Jacques's large, farmworker's hand, and the quality wine was consumed in one gulp.

Father Front pointedly took a sip from his own goblet and said, "Jacques, you look troubled. How can I help?"

"It's Jeannette."

"Jeannette! But how can your delightful daughter be a problem?"

"It's those daydreams again, they've become much worse."

"How so?"

Jacques held out his goblet, and the priest dutifully poured more wine into it, but this time only half filling it. "Father, you remember I told you about four years ago that Jeannette said she was hearing heavenly voices?"

"Of course, and I told you not to worry because girls entering womanhood often have flights of fancy which they convince themselves are true. It will pass, it always does."

The Angel of Lorraine

"I pray you are right, Father. Isabelle and I took comfort from your advice, so we allowed Jeannette to tell us about her voices without any attempt to explain to her they were just daydreams. Perhaps we should have been more strict?"

"I think not. It was Saint Catherine the Martyr and Saint Margaret who spoke to her, was it not? They told her to be good to her parents and people less fortunate than herself, say her prayers, and go to church. It is difficult to see what harm can come from that."

"That was true, Father, until yesterday. The voices also used to tell her that God had a special mission for her, but they never gave an indication of what that might be. Isabelle and I assumed it might be a vocation to enter a convent or to go on a pilgrimage somewhere, but all that changed yesterday afternoon when she came home from watching the oxen in the fields."

Father Front now realised that this meeting was unlikely to end quickly, so he put away his letter to the bishop, sat back in his chair, and gave his troubled parishioner his undivided attention. "Very well, Jacques, tell me what happened yesterday—slowly and from the very beginning."

"I was helping Isabelle in the kitchen to prepare the evening meal. Suddenly the back door flew open, and Jeannette burst in panting heavily, for she had been running. Her eyes were alight with excitement, and we had never seen her looking more happy. 'Maman, Papa,' she said, 'the voices have revealed my mission at last. Now I know what I must do, what I was born for!' 'And what is that, my dear?' asked my wife. 'I must go to the dauphin and lead his army to victory against the English. My banner will show Jesus Christ Our Saviour blessing an image of the fleur-de-lis held by a warrior angel. I must go to the dauphin at once, for only then shall the English be beaten and chased back to their homeland.' Father, you can imagine our concern when we heard this. Isabelle, always calmer in a crisis than me, spoke to her quietly. 'First we should speak to Father Front. You cannot just arrive at the dauphin's palace in Chinon and expect him to give an audience to a peasant girl from far off Lorraine. This must be handled carefully. Father Front will know what to do.' And so that is why I am here, Father. The childish dreams have suddenly become a nightmare."

The priest frowned. "You were right to come to me. Such dreams can be dangerous. You and I know that Jeannette is a good, sweet child, but dreams, visions, heavenly messages, or whatever they are could be interpreted another way by those with malevolent intent."

"How do you mean, Father?"

"Witchcraft, messages from the devil, and the like. Jeannette is not the first to claim she hears messages from heaven, and I doubt she'll be the last, but as often as not, such people are sent to the madhouse if they're lucky, or burned at the stake if they're not. We must tread very carefully, or Jeannette could find herself in serious trouble. I will come to see her this afternoon before evening Mass, which, as you know, she always attends."

* * *

II

It was only a few paces from the church to Jacques and Isabelle Darc's residence. As Father Front approached the heavy, oak door clutching his pocket Bible in his right hand, the church bell chimed four o'clock. *Perrin Drappier is late yet again*, thought the priest. *I may have to get another church warden before too long.* The Darc house was a neat, substantial, two-storey building with four windows, front and back doors, and a single sloping tiled roof. Outside was a small, well-kept garden in which herbs and flowers grew and where Isabelle, a slim, brown-haired woman, never tired of working. She was on her knees weeding a flower bed when she saw Father Front approaching.

"Thank goodness you could come so soon, Father," she said as she stood up and brushed specks of soil from her white apron. "We have been so worried. Jacques and Jeannette are waiting for you inside."

"Good, then we can start immediately. Shall we go in?"

Standing next to Jacques beside the kitchen table was the subject of the visit. In appearance, Jeannette was an unremarkable girl of greater-than-average height, though her azure-blue eyes were intense and seemed to look through rather than at you. Her shoulder-length hair was the same reddish brown as her father's, but her angular face and pointed nose were more reminiscent of her mother.

Father Front smiled and pointed to the plain, wooden chairs that clustered around the table. "Shall we all sit down?" As soon as they had settled down, he looked at Jeannette. "My child, I am going to have to ask you some difficult questions which you must answer fully and truthfully. You may choose to have your parents present while we do this or speak to me alone."

"I would prefer Maman and Papa to stay," came the reply in a voice that was surprisingly powerful for such a slim frame.

"Good, I thought you would say that. Now, I have brought the Bible for you to swear on that you will only tell the truth, but I will not use it unless you want me to because I know you would never lie." Jacques and Isabelle smiled at each other as they heard the priest's confidence in their daughter's virtue.

"The Bible is not necessary for this, Father," replied Jeannette.

"Very well, then we can begin. I know you say that for the last few years the voices of Saint Catherine the Martyr and Saint Margaret have been speaking to you. How old were you when you first heard them?"

"I was about twelve I think when I became aware of the voices. I hear them in my mind, not through my ears. The Blessed Virgin has also spoken to me."

"So others could not hear them even if they were standing beside you?"

"I do not think so, Father."

"But yesterday you heard a new voice which gave you a new message. Your father has already told me what was said, so please tell me who this voice belonged to?"

"Saint Michael the Archangel."

"The leader of God's warrior angels! Did he speak his name?"

"No, he did not need to. He just gave me the knowledge. I have no doubt it was he."

"How old are you now, Jeannette?"

"Sixteen years."

"I do not doubt that you believe you heard this voice, but explain to me how a sixteen-year-old-girl from the eastern borders of Lorraine can lead the French army to victory when so many experienced commanders have failed."

"Because it is God's will."

"Is that all?"

"Is that not enough? I do not have to explain or ask questions as you do. Faith is sufficient. It is God's will, so anything is possible."

Father Front scratched his head in frustration. "Jeannette, there are others who claimed to have received similar messages, but they were found to be false. Why should people believe in you?"

"Because it is God's will that they should. I speak only the truth—you know it to be so. I heard Saint Michael's voice as clearly as I hear yours now."

"You have no doubt?"

"None."

"But can you not see the difficulty? Why should Saint Michael the Archangel speak to a peasant girl in Lorraine rather than the king or one of his military advisers?"

Jeannette smiled with the confidence of one who knows rather than believes. "Father, firstly the dauphin cannot be king, as you call him, until he is anointed with the holy oil of Clovis, the first French king, in the cathedral at Reims like all his predecessors. Secondly, why should Saint Michael appeal to those who have already failed? The men of France have been continuously beaten by the English. Perhaps it is time to give the women a chance?"

For the first time, the priest began to doubt himself. Jeannette exuded confidence in a quiet, determined manner. The imposters usually used religious ecstasy or maniacal trances to deliver their messages, but Joan was down-to-earth, conversational, and unpretentious in the way she spoke of her mission. Consequently it was all the more unexpected and uncannily convincing in its impact on the listener. Father Front decided he would have to question Jeannette about her chastity; all the clergy agreed that a message from God could only be delivered through the unsullied body of a virgin. But such an interrogation should not be carried out in the presence of her parents. "Jeannette," he said, "would you like me to hear your confession?"

"Yes please, Father."

Then turning to Jacques and Isabelle, he asked, "Would you give Jeannette and me a little time alone together so I can hear her confession? This kitchen shall have the sanctity of the confessional, and I shall call you when we are finished."

Peter Tallon

The confession took rather longer than the parents expected, but at last Jeannette ran into the front room beaming with happiness. "Maman, Papa, come quickly. Father Front has something to say to you."

When they returned to the kitchen, the priest was still sitting at the table, staring out of the window as if a spirit had suddenly appeared in the herb garden. For a few moments he did not even acknowledge Isabelle and Jacques as he gathered his thoughts for what he was about to say. Then, slowly he faced them and said quietly, "Please sit down." Both did as they were bid. In a measured, unemotional voice, Father Front began, "I find it difficult to accept that the words I am about to say are what I truly believe, but I have examined my conscience, so I speak from the heart even though the consequences of what I shall say may be beyond our wildest imagination. I came here to persuade Jeannette that the voices she hears are the daydreams of a young woman with an overactive imagination, but after detailed questioning both inside and outside the sanctity of confession, it is I who have changed my mind. I am now certain that your daughter speaks the truth and that she really does hear messages from heaven. We are in the presence of a miracle. God has blessed Jeannette to be the messenger who will carry out his wishes on earth."

Isabelle looked at Jacques, tears pouring down her cheeks. "Truly it is a miracle. Our daughter has been chosen by God!"

Father Front continued, "It will be our duty to help Jeannette complete her mission, but the path ahead will be difficult and dangerous."

"How so, Father?" asked Jacques.

"Whilst it is the English who are the objects of God's wrath, there will be Frenchmen with power and influence who will not be pleased when a peasant girl from a remote duchy suddenly appears and subverts what they will see as their inalienable rights as lords of France. The fact that they have failed in their duty to save France will mean nothing to them as they see their power founder upon Jeannette's goodness. She will need protection from those who feign friendship towards her but in fact have malevolent intentions."

"What do you suggest, Father? Should we go to the bishop?"

"Definitely not, Jacques. I regret to say that some of those who will see Jeannette as a threat to their status are within the higher echelons of the clergy. Anyway, the clergy will deliberate forever before coming to a decision, yet I hear that the English are marching on Orléans even as we speak. If Orléans falls, the English will have broken through the line of the Loire, then the heartland of France will be open to them. No, we must go first to the military authorities who truly understand the magnitude of the threat now facing our dear homeland. But before we do that, we must from now on refer to Jeannette as *Jeanne* in public. Jeannette is a child's name, which will not help our credibility amongst the hard-bitten warriors we must convince."

Jacques looked at his daughter who nodded. "It's all right, Papa. I must grow up now and take the place in the world God has ordained for me."

"Jacques, I'm afraid," whispered Isabelle. "This miracle may not end well for our daughter."

Her husband gently stroked her hair like he used to when they were first married. "My dear, the course is set. It is out of our hands now. We should do all we can to help, and then we can worry about the future knowing we have done God's will."

* * *

III

The following Sunday, the congregation of the church of Saint Remy was stunned by a sermon that shocked everyone. Until then, Father Front's orations had been noteworthy only for their long duration, which enabled some of the older parishioners to take a short nap, before the more serious matter of taking Holy Communion. But not this time, for the parish priest gave the sermon of a lifetime, reminiscent of the call to arms by

Pope Urban II at Clermont, which sparked off the First Crusade, three hundred and thirty-three years before. Front breathed fire, extolling the virtue and the mission of the miracle in their midst, Jeanne Darc, at the end of which the older members of the congregation were wide awake and the young men were eager to follow Jeanne in her bid to save France from the hated English.

So even before Father Front, Jacques Darc, and Jeanne set off on the ten-mile journey down the Meuse valley to Vaucouleurs, the seat of the local knight, the Sieur de Baudricourt, word was spreading outwards like ripples of water from a stone thrown into a static millpond that an avenging angel had been sent from heaven to Domremy to lead France to freedom and that this angel had taken the form of an ordinary peasant girl.

Vaucouleurs was a fortified border town awarded to Robert de Baudricourt, a seasoned warrior of France, by Charles Duke of Lorraine. Robert's prime duty was to guard the eastern borders of the duchy against Burgundian incursions, which were becoming increasingly troublesome as the power of France waned. Lorraine had largely been left to fend for itself by the dauphin whose court was three hundred miles away in Chinon, where the English were a far closer and more dangerous threat than the Burgundians. But although Duke Charles was stretched to the utmost protecting his land, he was able to govern from his court in Nancy with almost regal authority and minimal interference from Chinon.

Even before Jeanne arrived at Vaucouleurs, word had reached the town of Father Front's stirring sermon at Domremy, so the unexpected visitors were given quick access to de Baudricourt's sparsely furnished audience chamber. When the three travellers, led by Father Front, were ushered into de Baudricourt's presence, the knight was sitting at a plain wooden table dictating a letter to his secretary. A handsome, black-haired man of about thirty years of age was seated on his right watching the new arrivals with interest; he gave them a friendly smile, which helped put them at their ease.

De Baudricourt, a grey-haired, scarred veteran of fifty, looked up from the document he was answering and pointed to some chairs near a window that overlooked the Meuse. "Pull up some chairs and be seated. I'll be finished shortly. We do not stand on ceremony here."

In fact they waited almost half an hour before the old warrior dismissed his secretary and gave them his full attention. Then, acknowledging the young man to his right, de Baudricourt said, "This is the Sieur de Freuchin, a knight on secondment to our duke from the king's court at Chinon."

"The dauphin's court," corrected Jeanne. "The Dauphin Charles cannot be king until he is crowned and anointed with the holy oil of Clovis at the cathedral in Reims."

De Baudricourt's eyes widened with surprise; he almost smiled. "You are right, young lady, but he prefers to be addressed as Charles VII, King of France. You are, I assume, the paragon we have heard so much about during the last week?"

"I do not understand the word *paragon*. I am but a simple peasant girl bearing a message from God."

"Not as simple as you make out I'll warrant."

"Mon Sieur," interrupted Father Front, "allow me—"

"No, Father. If this girl speaks the truth, she must speak it for herself. Others will expect it, so now is as good a time as any to start. Begin, young lady, by first explaining who you are and who it was who actually gave you your orders to save France."

"I am Jeanne, daughter of Jacques and Isabelle Darc, who are landowning peasants of Domremy. I first began to hear voices from heaven about four years ago, which were those of Saint Catherine the Martyr and Saint Margaret. They told me to be good to my mother and father, help the poor, and go to church often. They also told me God had a mission for me but not what it was. Then two weeks ago, I heard a new voice, a man's voice, who told me what my mission is. The rest you know from the reports of Father Front's sermon."

"And the man's voice, was it God himself?"

"No, Mon Sieur, it was Saint Michael the Archangel."

"And his instructions were?"

"To go to the dauphin's court and lead his army against the English until they are driven out of France."

Now de Baudricourt smiled for the first time since the meeting began, but not with humour. "These are bold and noble orders, and I do not doubt you believe you heard them, but the world is not a simple place. Tell me why the dauphin, as you call him, should spend his valuable time giving an audience to a peasant girl from Lorraine when you are just one of many petitioners who crave a meeting with him to forward their own lunatic ideas. Why should a messenger from God take the form of a peasant when he could have chosen a noble warrior, a bishop, or even the pope?"

"Was not Jesus Christ born of humble stock like me? He came to save the world, yet God could have chosen a king or the high priest of Jerusalem to deliver his message."

"Have you come to save the world, Jeanne?"

"No, just France, the rest of the world I'll leave to others."

De Baudricourt smiled again, but this time with pleasure. "You debate well, Jeanne, for what you describe as a humble peasant girl."

Father Front intervened once more. "Mon Sieur, your questions are unfair because Jeanne has no experience of life outside Domremy. We came here to ask you to provide an escort of ten honourable men-at-arms to guide her safely to the dauphin's court at Chinon."

The old knight's eyebrows knitted ominously. "Father, I am instructed by my liege, Charles Duke of Lorraine, to guard his borders against the treacherous Duke of Burgundy whose lands lie to the south and east of his duchy. Most of my men have not yet recovered from wounds inflicted in the last incursion, but as yet I have received no reinforcements. Yesterday word came that our enemy has started to cross the Meuse in force both north and south of Vaucouleurs. If you were offering twenty men-at-arms or even just five, I would welcome you with open arms, but you are actually asking me to deplete my overstretched garrison to escort a peasant girl all the way to Chinon. I do not doubt that there is something special about Jeanne, but I am afraid that just at this moment, I cannot help you. You are dismissed."

There was no point in trying to argue with such a clear command, so Jeanne, her father, and Father Front left de Baudricourt's small castle and trudged back towards their wagon to begin the journey home. As they walked across the castle courtyard, Father Front said, "Jeanne, I am so sorry. You were doing well until I foolishly interrupted you."

"That's all right, Father. God's will shall not be deflected by one French knight. Our time will come again soon, but for the moment, we must be patient." Suddenly the priest realised that instead of giving advice, he was now receiving counsel himself from a sixteen-year-old peasant girl. *Truly,* he thought, *de Baudricourt was right about one thing: Jeanne is special.*

They climbed onto their wagon, and Jacques had just flicked the reins when a voice from behind hailed them. "Stop! Stop! I must speak with you." It was the Sieur de Freuchin, the young man who had sat silently throughout the meeting with de Baudricourt. Jacques drew rein as de Freuchin caught up with them. "Do not judge Robert harshly, for he is a good-hearted man, courageous, and bold, but the Duke of Lorraine is asking him to do the impossible, and he is too honourable to refuse. Just at this moment, you cannot expect him to welcome a proposal that will make his task even harder."

"Our timing was not good," agreed Father Front, "but even so, we bring the only hope of saving our beloved France. I myself was sceptical when Jacques Darc told me what was happening to Jeanne, but after spending a little time with her, my doubts disappeared like a morning mist in midsummer."

"I understand, and she convinced me too. She was on the verge of convincing Robert until you intervened."

"I know, and I am angry with myself for being such a fool. I shall not make that mistake again. Jeanne is more than capable of delivering her message herself."

Addressing Jeanne directly, de Freuchin said, "I too feel your power. Allow me to introduce myself properly. I am Marcel, Sieur de Freuchin. My land is in Picardy, but it is now in the possession of the Burgundians, the allies of the English, so I am a knight with no land and serve the dauphin directly for payment—not very honourable I know, but it is the only way I can serve France."

Jeanne asked, "Then you hate the English?"

The answer was unexpected. "No, not all of them. There is good and bad in every nation, and I have experienced good as well as bad from the English. Yes, they have stolen my land in Picardy, but I also acknowledge that it was an Englishman who saved my life at Agincourt. But for a common English captain, I would not be standing before you now."

Jeanne smiled. "Then, Marcel, Sieur de Freuchin, you are a true follower of God, for you do not let misfortune blight your judgement. It is brave and thoughtful men like you who will make France great again."

"Thank you, Jeanne," replied Marcel. "It is my greatest desire to help our beloved country to victory, and I am now certain that you are the means to that end. Therefore, I will do whatever I can to support you." Then turning to Father Front and Jacques, he added, "It is clear to me that you have brought with you France's salvation. I will make sure that word of Jeanne's mission reaches the ears of Duke Charles in Nancy. When he hears of Jeanne, I feel sure he will give de Baudricourt the extra men-at-arms he needs to provide an escort to Chinon. I myself must return to

Chinon soon, and when I get there, I will speak to Yolande, the dauphin's mother-in-law. She is a wise and astute lady and wields great influence over the dauphin. She also believes that the power of women is much underrated by men in positions of authority and will welcome the chance to support a female saviour of France."

"Does not a female saviour trouble you, Marcel, Sieur de Freuchin?" asked Jeanne.

"Not in the least. I would welcome any saviour, male or female, who can deliver France out of the hands of the English."

Jacques's eyes watered with emotion as he said, "Mon Seigneur, I am deeply honoured by your faith in my daughter. What should we do now?"

"I am not a seigneur, just a landless knight, but I regret I must ask you to do the most difficult thing of all, which is to wait. Not only must Duke Charles approve your venture, but we must ensure that Jeanne will be received by the dauphin when she reaches Chinon. I will write to you when I have seen Duke Charles. He will almost certainly want to see Jeanne for himself, so you will have to travel to Nancy when the call comes. If all goes well, you will be summoned within the next few weeks when Jeanne shall, I have no doubt, convince Charles of the sanctity of her mission. You must ask him to write a letter of support for Jeanne, which I can present to the court in Chinon, because he will not give de Baudricourt the men-at-arms he needs to ensure Jeanne can make a safe journey halfway across France until he knows that she will be received by the court."

"How will we know how the dauphin responds?" asked Father Front.

"When I have Charles's letter, I shall make it my personal responsibility to convince Yolande that Jeanne is France's true saviour. Once that is done, everything else will follow, including an audience with the dauphin."

Jeanne was not happy with the delay. "How long must we wait? God's command cannot be deferred indefinitely."

"I understand," replied Marcel, "but too much haste will ruin all. We are now nearing the middle of September, so allowing for your trip to Nancy and the time it will take for me to ride to Chinon and get a message back to Duke Charles telling him you will be granted an audience there, you must not expect to receive the call before the end of January next year."

"But that is so long!"

"I said it would not be easy, Jeanne, but it will give you time to pray and prepare yourself. In the meantime, I trust your voices will bring you the comfort of telling you we are doing the right thing."

"We must accept the delay, Jeanne," said Father Front, then turning to Marcel, he added, "I just hope Orléans will be able to hold out until next year."

CHAPTER TWO

Thomas Montacute, fourth Earl of Salisbury, was a small man with a big personality and the darling of the English. Now in his fortieth year, he had fought in every major conflict since Agincourt and, as a commander, could boast an unblemished record of victories over the French and their Scottish allies. With him as their leader, the English believed themselves to be invincible, but Orléans was going to be a tough nut to crack, even for Salisbury.

On a cold, wet afternoon on the twenty-second day of October in the Year of Our Lord 1428, the earl stood with his war council near the village of Olivet looking at Orléans from the south bank of the River Loire. With him were William de la Pole, Earl of Suffolk, his second-in-command, young Lord Scales of Middleton Norfolk, Lord Roos of Rutland, and Sir John Fastolf of Caistor in Norfolk—all were experienced war commanders. They were about five hundred paces from the river, just out of cannon range from the two towers known as the Tourelles, which protected the gatehouse to the bridge of twenty-nine arches that connected the city with the south bank of the river.

Salisbury bit into a chicken leg, chewed, and swallowed, then turned to his council. "My lords, we have almost surrounded the city, but we still need to capture the Tourelles before the French will surrender."

"Indeed," agreed Suffolk, "but we do not have enough men to encircle the city completely. There are still large gaps in our lines which the French can easily penetrate."

Peter Tallon

"Which is why we need a quick victory. If we take the Tourelles, the French will most likely give up."

"But why should they do that?" objected Suffolk. "They probably already outnumber us, and more men join them every day."

"Then the sooner we attack them, the better," interjected Lord Roos. "Numbers did not stop us at Agincourt or Verneuil."

"Our men are hungry, and we have already outrun our supplies," added Lord Scales. "They will fight all the better on empty stomachs, just as they did at Agincourt."

Salisbury, eager that the cautious Earl of Suffolk should not feel isolated, said, "My Lord Suffolk makes a valid point about our numbers as does My Lord Scales about supplies. There is no one better qualified to resolve both of these matters than you, Sir John."

Sir John Fastolf, not a lord but merely a knight, was the oldest in the council and famous for his understanding of the complicated matters of supplies and logistics, which tended to bore the more senior commanders. Like Salisbury, he had been present at all the major battles of the campaign and was held in high regard as a veteran commander. Now approaching fifty years of age, he was still strong in the arm and straight in the back and, at one inch short of six feet in height, taller than most. Addressing Salisbury, he said, "My lord, our lands in Normandy have already been scoured clean of fighting men, though I will endeavour to find a few more, but I should warn you that the Norman French do not have the same heart in this fight as native-born Englishmen. We have already learned that quality overcomes quantity, so it may be necessary for me to cross the Channel to England in order to gather a force you can rely on."

"Then you have my permission to do so," replied Salisbury.

"Thank you, my lord, though I hope it will not be necessary. I will depart early tomorrow. My senior captain, Richard Calveley, will command my men in my absence."

The Angel of Lorraine

"I know Captain Calveley already," acknowledged Salisbury, "and I cannot think of a better man to take your place."

"Thank you, my lord, I shall leave at first light."

Sir John had been gone barely four hours when a breathless messenger arrived at Salisbury's headquarters. "My lord, the French are destroying the bridge between Orléans and the Tourelles."

"God's blood!" swore the earl. "That will mean we'll have to starve them out, which will take months unless we can quickly convince them their position is hopeless. Summon Sir John Fastolf's men and send Captain Calveley to me."

Within half an hour, all the men of Fastolf's companies together with their captain, Richard Calveley, had gathered before Salisbury's campaign tent. Captain Calveley approached Salisbury and saluted. Richard was about the same age as the earl but a head taller. His raven hair was now streaked with grey, and his green eyes shone in the late morning sunlight like stones of polished jade. "Your orders, my lord?"

The earl felt a surge of confidence as he looked at the quietly spoken captain and the battle-hardened warriors behind him. "Welcome, Captain Calveley, it is good to see you again."

"And you too, my lord."

"How goes it with Mary and Joan?"

"Mary is well, my lord, and Joan is growing up quickly. Thank you for asking."

"I have an important task for you, Captain. The two towers yonder guarding the crossing across the Loire are called the Tourelles. I need you to take them before the French destroy the bridge that connects them to Orléans."

Richard turned and looked at the city. "They seem well on the way to completing their task already, my lord. We had better make haste."

"How many men have you?"

"Two hundred and seventy-three fit for duty."

"Then prepare them to attack. I will order a short cannonade to breach the Tourelles walls and soften up the rampart linking them, then I shall speak to the men before they advance. This will be a tough job because the French have cannons in the city which can sweep the open ground you must cross to reach the Tourelles."

"We will not fail you, my lord."

"I know that, Captain. I will be with you shortly."

The English barrage began almost immediately. Twenty-three heavy cannon and bombards pummelled the Tourelles, but the French fired back, and a lucky shot destroyed a cannon less than thirty paces from where Richard stood. The English cannon was already primed, and exploded scattering shreds of flesh and showers of blood over the Norfolk company, which actually contained as many men from across the border in north Suffolk, like Richard, as men from Norfolk.

The company sergeant, John Fletcher, an old friend of Richard's, flicked a piece of bloodstained scalp from his arm and said, "Will we have to stay here like sitting ducks for long, Captain? The men are eager to advance and, the Lord knows, so am I."

"It won't be for much longer, John. Salisbury wants to speak to us before we go. In fact, I can see him approaching now."

The earl, mounted on a fine bay destrier, walked his horse towards Richard and, oblivious to the French cannon fire, called the men to gather round him. Although a small man, he had a powerful voice that all could hear with ease despite the roar of the barrage. "Men, you must take those two towers you can see in front of you. Our success depends on it. It will not be easy, but I know you can do it." This was greeted with cheers. "You are Englishmen, the best soldiers in the world, but you are also Sir John Fastolf's men, which makes you the best of the best." More cheers and hurrahs for Salisbury followed. "But I will not hide from you that it will be dangerous. The French cannon can sweep the open ground between here and the towers, so you must advance as fast as you can because when you reach them, you will be safe. The French will have to cease fire for fear of killing their own men. You already know they will not stand against you when it comes to close-quarter fighting. See! They are already breaking up the bridge behind them, which means they think they're going to lose. Now we don't want to disappoint them, do we!" This was greeted by more cheers and laughter.

"Finally," boomed the earl, "it is so important that you succeed that I have decided to lead the assault myself!"

This was met with silence, then someone shouted, "No, my lord!"

Another voice called out, "Salisbury to the rear!" Further shouts of disapproval followed. Richard, who was standing beside the earl, saw his commander's brow furrow. "My lord," he said, "I beg you to listen to the men. They not only love you but they know, as I do, that you must not take the risk. If we were in open battle, you would be welcome, but cannonballs make no distinction between lord and commoner. We cannot afford to lose you. The men will fight better knowing you are safe. No one doubts your courage, so please, for the love of God, stay behind."

Salisbury frowned. "It is not my way, Captain, to stand back from where the fighting is fiercest."

"I know that, my lord, we all do, but this time, the men are right."

The earl took a few moments to consider, then stood up in his stirrups. "Very well, men, if that is your wish, I shall do as you ask, but I shall be close behind with support if you need it. May God protect you, and give those Frenchies hell!"

Richard could barely make himself heard above the cheers and the cannonade, but the men knew their drill well and quickly formed up three deep with the Yorkshiremen commanded by Sergeant Edward Skippon on the left, the Wiltshire men under one-eyed Henry Hawkswood, Richard's second-in-command in the centre, and the Norfolk men with Sergeant John Fletcher on the right.

Richard placed himself in the centre with Hawkswood, raised his sword, and bellowed, "Advance banners for England and Saint George!"

* * *

II

The companies surged forward with the archers intermingled with the men-at-arms. They had advanced barely fifty paces when some of the French bombardiers found their range, and a huge stone ball swept away four of the Yorkshiremen. The ground was still soft from recent rain, so the men-at-arms in full armour could only advance at a steady walk. Richard suddenly realised that the companies were too bunched up and made an excellent target for the French. He turned to Henry Hawkswood, his most experienced sergeant, who had fought alongside him since Agincourt and, more recently, in the mad venture to the Holy Land four years ago. A strong bond had developed between them.

"Henry, we must advance in open order. Spread the word to extend the line as quickly as possible. The archers may run ahead until they reach that deserted priory just in front of the Tourelles. They should be safe enough there from cannon fire, but they must wait for the men-at-arms to join them before the attack on the towers begins."

"Understood, Captain." Hawkswood did not need to say more; Richard knew his orders would be carried out in full. Just then another huge cannonball swept close overhead with a rushing, howling sound that chilled the flesh to the bone. Everyone within earshot involuntarily ducked, but quickly recovered except for a young man-at-arms with hair the colour of ripe wheat. Richard saw he was shaking violently as if he had the ague, but in truth, the lad was terrified.

Marking time so that the line could catch up with him, Richard spoke to the fair-haired youngster, "What's your name, and where are you from?"

"John Hook, Captain, and I come from Willingham."

"Willingham near Beccles in Suffolk?"

"Yes, Captain."

"That's less than three miles from my home. I come from Westhall. But what are you doing marching with the men from Wiltshire?"

"I don't know. Everything happened so quickly after the earl's speech, I got mixed up and joined the wrong company."

"Then you may march with me if you wish. Is this your first action?"

"Not quite, Captain, but it's the first time I've faced cannon."

"How old are you?"

"Seventeen I think."

Richard glanced at Henry, who said, "Shall I return him to Sergeant Fletcher's company?"

"Not yet, sergeant." Richard walked a few more paces with Hook at his side. "Well, Master Hook, you need not fear cannon. The chances of one of those cannonballs hitting you are remote. Also the ground is wet, so they will not bounce. The worst that will happen is you might get splattered with mud, but in the unlikely event that a cannonball does indeed have your name written on it, there is nothing you can do to avoid it. But I can tell you that if you do get struck, you won't feel a thing. It will not be like a

Peter Tallon

crossbow bolt or a spear thrust. You'll never know what happened, and you will be with your maker even before we reach the Tourelles. Those cannon make a lot of noise, but they are nothing to worry about. Now would you like to march with me or return to the Norfolk company?"

John Hook had stopped shaking and answered, "I'd like to march with my company now, Captain."

"Good man! Sergeant Hawkswood, take John Hook to Sergeant Fletcher's company if you please."

When Henry returned to march beside Richard again, he said, "That was well done, Captain, he seems to be settled now."

"Thank you, Henry, let's hope what I told him is proved right!"

Ten minutes later, all three of Richard's companies had reached the shelter of the priory walls at the cost of only a few more casualties, none amongst the Norfolk men. Richard was pleased to see John Hook was still safe and chatting amongst his comrades. The archers were already shooting at the French sappers, who were working like demons to lay the gunpowder that would destroy the last arch of the bridge. But despite the archers' best efforts, a huge explosion erupted just as Richard was about to lead a sortie of men-at-arms to drive the sappers away. Once the smoke began to clear, it was obvious that the English were just seconds too late; the last arch was smashed, and the link to Orléans was broken.

"What now, Captain?" asked Henry Hawkswood quietly.

"We came to capture the Tourelles, so we'll complete our task. We at least forced the French sappers to hurry their work, so there may still be some Frenchies on our side of the river. Give the order to take prisoners where possible and bring them to me. I'll send them on to Salisbury for interrogation."

The sun was low in the sky and the shadows lengthening when Henry returned dragging a terrified young crossbowman with him. "The French

The Angel of Lorraine

had already abandoned the Tourelles before we attacked, Captain, but I found this in a cupboard on an upper floor. I think he may be a deserter."

"Very well, keep a tight grip on him while I talk to him." Then turning to the Frenchman Richard, who spoke French almost as well as he spoke English, asked, "What is your name?" There was no answer until Henry shook him roughly by the collar.

"Henri Montbrun, Mon Sieur."

"Henri, I am not a *sieur*, only a captain, and do not be frightened. No one will harm you if you answer a few questions."

"Thank you, Mon—er…Captain."

"Good. Who commands in Orléans?"

"The Sieur de Gaucourt."

Henry, who knew enough French to understand the answer, spoke in English to Richard, "Was it not de Gaucourt who held Harfleur against us back in '15?"

"Indeed it was, Henry, he's one of their best." Then speaking French again, Richard asked Montbrun soothingly, "And who is in command of all the French forces in the Loire sector?"

"Jean Dunois, Bastard of Orléans."

For Henry's benefit, Richard added, "Dunois is the illegitimate son of the Duke of Orléans, who we captured at Agincourt, and still languishes in prison in England until his ransom is paid. According to the laws of chivalry, we should not be attacking his city while he seeks to recover the funds for his release."

"Then why are we here, Captain?" asked a perplexed Henry.

Peter Tallon

"I neither know nor care. We are not knights, so we just follow the orders of our betters until the war is won. But one thing I do know is that Dunois is also one of their best commanders. This is not good news, so I bid you to take this prisoner at once to Salisbury for further interrogation. See he is not molested, and report back to me as soon as you can. I shall be with the Norfolk men."

Henry departed with his prisoner, and Richard went over to the Norfolk company, where he found Sergeant Fletcher. "John, how goes it here?"

"We lost six men in the attack, Captain, but the good Lord knows we expected to lose many more."

"I think we have the mud to thank for that John. The cannonballs could not bounce." Then seeing a hunched frame bending over a corpse fifty paces away, Richard asked, "What's going on over there, John, near the priory wall?"

"It's Will Potter, Captain, searching for teeth."

"I know Will Potter, he hasn't a tooth in his head! What's he up to?"

"Best ask him yourself, Captain. It's an unusual story."

Richard and the sergeant walked towards a figure on its knees, bending over the corpse of a large Wiltshire man. Richard shouted, "Potter! What are you doing!"

The hunched figure slowly got to its feet and answered cheerily in a broad Norfolk drawl. "Good day, Captain. Oi'm searching for good teeth from those who've no further need for 'em." Potter, who was not the most beautiful of God's creations, smiled a toothless grin. "This here Wiltshire man has a fine set which will help me with moi quest."

"What quest is that, Will?"

"To win moi Margaret back. Oi got news she's run off with a saddlemaker from Wrentham."

"But, Will, I distinctly remember you saying your Margaret would remain faithful because she's well, er…"

"*An ugly old rooster* was moi exact words, Captain, which is why Oi had no fears she would stray while Oi was in France."

"Then what happened?"

"Turns out she wasn't as ugly as Oi thought."

Sergeant Fletcher whispered, "Captain, Will's eyesight is not what it was. Margaret is quite a handsome woman in fact."

"Very well, Will," said Richard, "but what's that go to do with a Wiltshire man's teeth?"

Will scratched his bald pate and sighed. "Well, it looks like Oi'm going to have to woo moi Margaret all over again. She's a determined woman, so Oi can't force her to come home."

The idea of Will wooing was a startling thought, so Richard continued, "But I still don't understand what the teeth have got to do with it."

"Well, you see, Captain, Oi knows Oi'm no beauty myself, but if Oi go back home with a full set of teeth, Oi'll be irresistible, so she's bound to want to come back to me then."

"But, Will, the teeth need to be in your gums, not a bag."

"Oi already knows that, Captain. Oi've found a surgeon in Rouen who says he can slit gums and insert teeth that will stick as long as they're fairly fresh."

Richard glanced at Sergeant Fletcher, who was trying to smother a smile. "Sounds a painful procedure, Will," said Richard.

"That's true, Captain, but it'll be worth it to get moi Margaret back, and Oi'll drink a pipkin of wine before the surgery, so Oi don't expect Oi'll feel much anyway."

"How many more teeth do you need?"

"Only two or three, Captain."

"Well, there are some French corpses you could use in the towers, Will."

Potter spat, "Gawd no, Captain. Those there Frenchies eat strange fodder. Oi hear tell that they eats snails and frogs and such like. Oi can't put teeth in moi head that's chewed on stuff like that!"

This was too much for Fletcher, who burst out laughing. "God's teeth, Will, you'll be the death of me."

"Never mind God's teeth, Sergeant, it's mine Oi'm thinking about."

Richard just about managed to contain his own mirth as he pointed back towards the English camp. "Of course, Will, I should have realised. Yonder are five fresh English corpses, but make haste. They are Yorkshiremen, and their comrades may not take kindly to seeing you pillaging their remains."

"Thank you, kindly Captain. Oi'll be on moi way then if you'll excuse me."

"Of course, be off with you."

As they watched Will trot off towards the English camp, Richard asked, "What do you make of all that, John?"

Fletcher replied, "I've known Will all my life. He's one of a kind. There'll never be another like him. I just hope he wins his wife back after all the trouble he's taking."

"You said he's shortsighted. What are we doing employing a shortsighted archer?"

"He's more than shortsighted, Captain, he can hardly see ten paces ahead in full sunlight, though that wasn't so when he was first taken on. In fact, it's well-known in the company that when Will is practising at the butts, the only safe place to stand is right in front of the target! But in battle, accuracy is not too important because the French always attack en masse, and we shoot back en masse."

"True, so I suppose he's got as good a chance of scoring a hit as anyone else."

"And when it comes to close-quarter work, Will's at his best. He's as strong as an ox."

"Well, I wish him well then. With Sir John away, I have the authority to give him leave when he has collected all his teeth."

Sergeant Fletcher laughed again. "Just as well, Captain, because nobody else would believe the story we just heard."

* * *

III

Eight days before the English attacked the Tourelles, eleven-year-old Jean Pierre and his little black and white dog, Elly, sat just below the great battlements of Orléans close to the Bridge Gate, which guarded the bridge that connected the city with the south bank of the River Loire. A warm, afternoon sun gave no comfort to the citizens, who went about their business in an atmosphere of foreboding, because the English had, in the last few days, captured Beaugency, Meung, and Jargeau—three strong fortresses dominating the Loire, which meant that Orléans was now cut off from support from the river. And today, worse still, news had come that the hated islanders, commanded by the formidable Earl of Salisbury, were marching on Orléans itself. Everyone knew that if Orléans fell, the heartland of France would be open to the invaders.

None of this was of the least interest to Jean Pierre and his dog, for they were enjoying watching eight tough bombardiers assembling a large cannon on the southern wall of the city a few paces from the Bridge Gate, which would surely drive away the insolent English. The cannon was one of many sent to Orléans by the dauphin's generals to bolster the city's defences. Jean Pierre had heard of course what a cannon could do, but he had never seen one in action; these new weapons of war fascinated him. The long, black tube made of cast iron, reinforced with iron bracelets to hold the dreadful power created when fired, looked the very image of malevolent danger. The large solid wheels with steel rims spoke of weight and power, while the huge stone balls neatly piled beside the cannon warned of the havoc that would be created when this huge creation of man's ingenuity was used in anger.

Every day for a week, Jean Pierre had been watching the bombardiers slowly assembling and preparing the cannon for its destructive work until this morning, when the sergeant in command at last noticed him. Jean Pierre had Elly to thank for this exciting turn of events because it was noon, and the little dog had already worked out that now was the time when the men took their midday break. Anticipating this moment, Elly took up a position close to the cannon's long barrel and locked her large, brown eyes upon the man who had pork in his lunch pack; she loved pork, especially when it was accompanied by crispy crackling, and it did not take long for the moist, brown eyes to work their magic.

The sergeant in charge of the cannon threw her a piece of crackling, which she eagerly devoured, then he saw Jean Pierre sitting on a step a short distance away. "Hey, boy! Is this your dog?"

"Yes, sir," answered the boy.

"What's her name?"

"*Elly*. It's short for *Eleanor*."

"And yours?"

"Jean Pierre at your service, sir."

"How old are you?"

"Eleven but almost twelve."

"And what do you want to be when you grow up?"

"A soldier, sir, and I shall fight for France."

The sergeant smiled and handed Jean Pierre a piece of pork from his lunch pack. "You seem like a good boy. And what sort of soldier will you be? A crossbowman shooting the English from two hundred paces, or a dashing man-at-arms charging the enemy on horseback with a couched lance?"

"Neither, sir. I wish to be a bombardier like you."

"Really? Well, in that case, you can begin your training by helping us now if you like. It will only be fetching and carrying, but at the same time, I can show you what it means to be a bombardier."

The next few days were a sheer delight for Jean Pierre. Not only did he run errands and make friends with the rest of the gun crew, but the sergeant, true to his word, explained in simple terms how the cannon worked and the different roles of all the gun crew team. Jean Pierre's mother was not at all sure about her only son being exposed to coarse, ill-educated soldiers, but his father, Gaston, a junior city clerk who had never experienced warfare but wished he had, encouraged him on condition that he would remain at home when the fighting started.

On the day the cannonade of the Tourelles began, Jean Pierre reluctantly took his leave of the gun crew and returned home with Elly, but after the Tourelles were abandoned and the bridge linking the towers to the city was broken, there was a pause in the fighting while the English decided what to do next. This enabled Jean Pierre to secure permission from his father to return briefly to the gun crew. All the bombardiers had got through the fighting unscathed and gave him and Elly a fine welcome, but although all was quiet for the present, the men were on full alert because the English might order an escalade at any moment. Full alert meant that the cannon was primed, and the slow match for firing it was burning.

Just before the noon meal, the sun, which had remained hidden behind cloudy skies for the last few days, reappeared. At the same time, the sergeant received orders that he and his crew should attend a short meeting in the Bridge Gate office because the Sieur de Gaucourt, the city's commander, wanted to reposition some of his cannon to cover other sectors now that Orléans was no longer threatened from the direction of the Tourelles bridge. The office was only a short distance away, so the sergeant, who had grown fond of the boy and his dog, called John Pierre over to him.

"Now listen carefully, Jean Pierre, I have an important task for you and Elly. My men and I must go to a short meeting, so I am leaving you in charge until we get back. Can you do that?"

"Yes, Sergeant!" answered Jean Pierre, overwhelmed at being entrusted with such responsibility.

"Very well, we won't be long. My only order to you is do not touch anything, anything at all. This cannon is ready to fire. Is that clear?"

"Yes, Sergeant, very clear."

The gun crew departed, but the sergeant forgot to order the slow match to be extinguished.

The Angel of Lorraine

Jean Pierre peeped over the battlements where now only the Loire separated the French from the English. He could not see the enemy, but he knew they were near. He had heard the English were human monsters and extremely ugly; he hoped never to see one close to, but he could only marvel at how brave the French must be to confront such horrible creatures. He glanced back at the huge cannon, which pointed between the battlements towards the English in the Tourelles. The cannon gave him comfort, for he knew that even English monsters could not withstand the mighty power it would produce when handled by brave French bombardiers. He also knew he must not touch anything, his orders forbade it, so he stepped down from the parapet below the battlements and walked back to the rear of the cannon. But he did not reckon with Elly. To her, the brown pole, which was attached to the slow match, looked just like one of the sticks her master would throw for her to retrieve when he used to take her for walks outside the city in happier times. The pole was set into a socket in the battlements where it stood vertically with the slow match on top. No wonder she gripped it in her mouth and dropped it at Jean Pierre's feet ready to play.

"Elly, what are you doing!" But when he tried to grab it, she picked it up and ran off to the other side of the cannon waiting to be chased. He ran after her, but she doubled back to where she had been just seconds before, delighting in this new game. Panic seized Jean Pierre. What would the sergeant say if he saw this breach of his orders! After three more hopeless attempts to catch the agile dog, Jean Pierre feigned disinterest hoping this would entice Elly within range. Soon, curiosity got the better of her, and she quietly crept up behind her master. Despite a desperate desire to grab her, he continued to stare at some imaginary scene outside the city walls, but all the time looking out of the corner of his eye as her shadow got closer. He made his move a second too soon lunging at her, but instead, sprawling onto the battlement floor as she turned and ran. He managed to get his fingertips on the slow match pole, and Elly released it, but it was just too far away for him to grip it properly. Instead he knocked it towards the cannon, and struggling to his feet, he watched in horror as he saw the burning slow match land beside the touch hole of the cannon. He began to walk nervously towards the cannon, but there was still some unburnt black powder residue around the touch hole caused by the firing earlier in the day. He was only two paces away when the powder crackled into life.

"Elly! Quickly!" Fortunately the dog sensed the fear in his voice, and they both turned to run just as the cannon roared into life. The sound was like a thousand thunderbolts exploding inside a small chamber. The ground shook under Jean Pierre's feet as the recoiling gun missed Elly by a finger's width. There was no time for explanations. Boy and dog fled homewards as if all the devils in hell were after them.

Although Jean Pierre might not have altered the course of history, he had just given it a severe jolt.

* * *

IV

On the twenty-fifth day of October, the day after the capture of the Tourelles, the Earl of Salisbury called a noon conference with his senior commanders in an upper floor of one of the towers. Present were the Earl of Suffolk, Lord Scales, Lord Roos, and Captain Calveley, who stood in for the absent Fastolf. In peacetime, a commoner would never have been permitted to sit at the same table as such elevated company, but the needs of war were such that none present, except Richard, gave this a second thought. Richard decided to write to Mary that very evening to tell her about it, but upon reflection, he changed his mind because she was not the sort of woman to be impressed by status and men of war. She came from the Lollard sect who believed in absolute equality between all men and women; status had no place in the Lollard form of Christianity. Needless to say, the Lollards were soon condemned as heretics by the English governing establishment, which was why he and Mary were obliged to dwell in France, where no one knew or cared about Lollards.

The chamber where the war council sat still smelled of garlic; the French had left so quickly that the commander's lunch of yesterday had only just been cleared away and replaced by bread and beef, but Salisbury had retained the elegant Burgundian wine to wash down the traditional English fare. He sat with his back to a large, open window which provided an excellent view of the broken bridge that now separated the English from Orléans' southern gate. Suffolk and Roos sat on his right while Scales and Richard were on his left.

"My lords and Captain Calveley," began Salisbury as the meal ended, "the French have frustrated us. Behind me you can see for yourselves that the access I had hoped to use to capture Orléans has been destroyed. We cannot restore the bridge under the noses of the French because they have cannon and crossbows at the ready to foil any such attempt. I now see no alternative to a long-drawn-out winter siege."

"Could we not attempt an escalade from the north side of the city?" suggested Scales.

"Too costly," replied Salisbury. "The walls of Orléans are high, and we don't yet know how many men the French have in there. From what little we can glean, they probably outnumber us already, and more men join them by the day. What we do know from the prisoners taken yesterday is that the city's commander is Raoul de Gaucourt, who gave us so much trouble at Harfleur back in '15. More worrying still, Jean Dunois, who is in my opinion their best general, is in overall command of the Middle Loire sector. Unlike some of the others, he won't run at the first sight of a serious assault."

"But, my lord," interrupted Suffolk. "We have barely four thousand men. How can we hope to starve out a city when we cannot even surround it through lack of numbers? The circumference of Orléans must be at least three miles, perhaps four. It has more than thirty towers. We need double the numbers we have to invest it properly."

For the first time in a week, Salisbury smiled. "I am pleased to be able to tell you that only this morning, I received a dispatch from the Duke of Bedford advising me that Philippe, Duke of Burgundy, is sending two thousand Burgundians to support us here. They will arrive in about two days."

Suffolk shook his head in frustration. "By which time at least another two thousand Frenchmen will probably have joined their comrades in the city. And I do not believe Philippe's men will be of much use to us anyway. They did not fight well at Cravant and would rather fight us than the French."

Salisbury grimaced; he hated negativity. "The Burgundians will at least be able to guard the eastern approaches to Orléans, which will free up our own men to reduce the gaps in the cordon round the city, and remember, Sir John Fastolf has gone north to gather reinforcements. No one could garner more good men than he."

"But that will take months! You recall he said just before he left that he would probably need to go to England to get men of the quality we need. The men of Normandy feel no ties to England anymore. In terms of quality, they are not much better than the Burgundians."

Salisbury was trying his best not to show his irritation with Suffolk's pessimism, but it was obvious to Richard that his restraint was close to breaking point. "Then what would you suggest, my lord?" asked the earl quietly.

Suffolk was a little older and more corpulent than his commander, but he did not lack experience. "My lord, winter will soon be upon us. We do not yet have the numbers for a siege, and supplies are running short. I suggest we retire to Paris, regroup, recruit, and build up our strength there so that we can return in the spring fresh and strong enough to complete our task quickly."

"But we cannot retire now!" exploded Lord Scales. "We only just got here! The French will think they've won a victory. All our good work this year will have been a waste of time!"

Suffolk responded acidly, "Would you rather see us starve and give them a real victory?"

Lord Roos of Rutland intervened, "Surely there must be a middle way. Can we not offer the French terms generous enough to allow them to leave Orléans with their honour still intact?"

Salisbury sighed. "That would probably have worked with some of their leaders, but de Gaucourt and Dunois are made of sterner stuff. They would interpret such an offer as a sign of weakness on our part." Then turning to Richard, Salisbury said, "Captain Calveley, you have said nothing yet. What is your opinion?"

"My lord," answered Richard, "I do not think it is my place—"

"Nonsense, Captain!" responded the earl. "You have as much knowledge and experience of war as anyone here. What do you say?"

"My lord, I do believe as Lord Roos suggests, that there may be a middle way. We cannot retire to Paris for fear of giving the French the encouragement of an unwarranted victory, but perhaps we could consolidate for the winter months in the fortresses we captured along the Loire this autumn and, at the very least, block supplies to the city by river and maybe capture a few French knights worthy of a good ransom while we await Sir John's reinforcements."

Salisbury smiled again. "Captain, that is close to my own thinking, though somewhat less ambitious. Although we cannot prevent isolated groups slipping through our lines at night, we can at least prevent large supply convoys reaching the city, so I propose we set up small fortresses all round Orléans, seven on the north bank of the river and four on the south, which will be capable of containing up to three hundred men. These fortresses will be simple in construction, just earth walls topped by wooden palisades. The French have a name for them, 'bastilles.' They will be set up on all the approach roads to the city so if the French try to bring heavy equipment like cannon to bolster their defences, they will be obliged to abandon the roads and travel across fields and through forests. The wet autumn has already soaked the ground, so we should have plenty of time to intercept them. If we get on with this work diligently, we could even see a French surrender before Christmas. I think—"

It sounded like a thunderclap but magnified tenfold, accompanied by a storm of wind that blew the assembled company clean off their seats. The crack of splitting rock rent the air, and sharp shards of stone rained down upon them all, cutting flesh and tearing hair. The window lintel behind Salisbury blew inwards, smashing the conference table and spinning goblets of wine in all directions. Richard was covered in grey, plaster dust that seemed to fill every orifice of his body. For a few seconds, he lay quiet, trying to comprehend what had happened.

Then Scales's voice rang out, "Anybody hurt?"

"What the hell was that!" swore Roos.

"A cannonball," answered the calm, mature voice of Suffolk. "The French have scored a direct hit on the leaders of the English army. What of My Lord Salisbury?" There was no response. All stayed quiet until a throaty, gurgling noise came from the direction of Salisbury's seat. Richard was on his feet first and clambered through dust and rubble to where Salisbury had been sitting. His eyes were watering, he could hardly see, his nose was blocked with dust, and he could feel warm blood trickling down the side of his face near his left ear. Frantically he began pulling shattered lumps of lintel and rubble to one side; he was soon joined by Scales, who helped him to uncover first Salisbury's left shoulder then his face, or what was left of it. Richard had seen war wounds of many sorts during his time as a soldier, but nothing to compare with poor Salisbury's blast wound, for the right side of his face had been blown away. The left side, including the eye and nose, seemed to be untouched; but there was only blood, torn flesh, and unrecognisable fragments of bone on the right. Richard could not understand how the earl could still be alive with such terrible wounds, but he was still breathing. Scales and Richard did their best to clear the rest of Salisbury's body from the rubble still covering it, while Suffolk staggered

The Angel of Lorraine

down the winding tower steps to call for help. Roos, who had been struck on the forehead, lapsed into unconsciousness.

In Orléans, the clock in the half-built Cathedral de Sainte Croix struck twelve thirty.

Salisbury's strong constitution enabled him to survive for a while, but mercifully he departed this life eight days after the unforeseen cannon strike. The command of the English army now devolved upon the Earl of Suffolk, who dutifully proceeded with the building of the bastilles, which, despite interference from the French, were largely completed during the month of November. But supplies to Orléans still managed to evade the English because the soldiers, who were nearly all experienced warriors, seemed to sense that their new commander's heart was not really behind this siege. The isolation of Orléans now became a farce, but everything changed on the eighteenth day of December when the Duke of Bedford's newly appointed commander arrived to take charge.

John, Baron Talbot, had already gained a reputation as an aggressive, skilful leader that had been won by the capture of many important French cities and nobles of high ransom value. At thirty-eight he was still young for such a senior command, but his fame preceded him, and the army was ready to welcome this new, charismatic leader who would be such a contrast to the dull, cautious Earl of Suffolk; he had done nothing since Salisbury died except build bastilles.

Talbot's arrival matched his reputation. He cantered into the English camp wearing superb plate armour of the latest Greenwich fashion with a white, ostrich feather plume placed in his helmet, which flowed in the wind like a victor's trophy at a tournament. Behind him was his personal entourage of sixty knights and men-at-arms who were also clad in the best armour money could buy.

Standing beside Richard and watching this cavalcade was Edward Skippon, the Yorkshire sergeant and a man of few words. "Well, if looks have anything to do with it, we'll be in Orléans tomorrow."

"Come now, Edward," chided Richard, "there's nothing wrong with a bit of showmanship. The men seem to like it by the sound of the cheering they're giving our new commander."

"Aye, Captain, but a blind beggar would be an improvement on Suffolk, and it's not the armour that matters but the man inside it."

"I may agree with the sentiment, but be careful of voicing opinions like that, or you may find yourself in trouble."

"We speak our minds in Yorkshire, Captain."

"Yes, Edward, so I've noticed. That is one of the reasons I have recommended to Sir John Fastolf that if anything happens to me, you would be the right person to succeed me as captain. You care nothing for popularity and always speak the truth. Now come on, let's take a closer look at our new leader."

Talbot's first act after his arrival was to summon his war council to which Richard was not invited, but late in the afternoon, he called another meeting for all the lower-ranking officers to discuss with them the next steps of the campaign. Such a thing was unheard-of, and all the captains and sergeants arrived at army headquarters in Olivet eagerly anticipating what this remarkable commander was going to say to them. Richard and his three sergeants were there—Hawkswood for Wiltshire, Fletcher for Norfolk, and Skippon for Yorkshire. The weather had turned cold, and there were snow flurries on this bitter, December afternoon, but nobody seemed to notice as Talbot stepped up onto a hastily built platform and began to speak to the men who were the backbone of his army. This was a risky thing for the new commander to do because his experienced audience would soon sense if Talbot was all that his reputation justified. *He's certainly got guts,* thought Richard, *or might it be overconfidence?*

Talbot had the advantage of being taller than average and handsome. He did not sport the fashionable short beard of most of the English leaders, but was clean-shaven like the men under his command. He was also helped

The Angel of Lorraine

by his rich, powerful voice, which easily carried to all of the two hundred or so who waited to hear him with baited breath.

"My noble lads!" he declaimed, immediately reducing his words from a speech to a friendly, personal chat. "I know there have been disappointments here, but all will now be well. Your previous leaders were slow to grasp the opportunities that came your way, but all that is now about to change." Some in the assembly, including Richard and his sergeants, did not appreciate this opening because the criticism seemed to include Salisbury, which was entirely unjust. "This means," continued Talbot, "that we must draw the cordon round Orléans much more tightly. The French are coming and going as they please. This must stop!" There was no cheering, just a few murmurs as these veteran warriors wondered what was coming next. Talbot sensed this too; he had hoped for at least a few shouts of support. "The sooner Orléans falls, the sooner we can rest, so there'll be no more skulking in the rear round warm fires. We will all take our turns, including me, patrolling day and night between the bastilles to make sure the French no longer enjoy being supplied with food and men while we live on short rations outside the city. Once they realise they're cut off from outside help, they'll begin to think about handing us the keys to Orléans without more serious fighting. If they don't, starvation will do its work, and they'll be too weak to withstand a determined assault. Either way, there'll be plenty of loot for all of us!" This at last broke the stony silence as the cheers reverberated around the camp. Talbot had won them over, but not quite all.

"That man's not after loot," grumbled Edward Skippon, "he doesn't need it. It's personal glory he's after, and we'll be his means to achieve it."

"Aye," agreed Henry Hawkswood, "he won't think twice before shedding our blood for his own glory."

John Fletcher, whose heretical Lollard background inclined him to fairness whenever possible, said, "We should not judge too quickly. Talbot's reputation alone should make us think twice. Is that not so, Captain?"

"Er, yes, John," agreed Richard none too fervently, for his instincts inclined him more to the opinion of his Yorkshire and Wiltshire sergeants, "we must give Lord Talbot the benefit of the doubt."

Talbot wisely ended the meeting while his men were still cheering the prospect of easy loot. The new, tough regime began next morning, but not for Richard, who was summoned to Talbot's headquarters after breakfast. The man Richard saw now was quite different to the dashing presence he beheld the previous day. Huddled over a campaign table in a spacious tent, the English commander was scratching notes on a piece of parchment like a worried secretary. With his head bent over his quill, Richard could see that Talbot's brown hair was thinning at the back and his face was prematurely lined, but even so, the ingrained arrogance was still there. "Ah, Captain Calveley," he said as he put down his quill, "you are Fastolf's man, are you not?"

"Yes, my lord."

"Well, I am not satisfied with the length of time Sir John is taking garnering our reinforcements. He is claiming they need more training before going into battle."

"Then assuredly they do, my lord."

"I would expect you to say that of course. I have your war record here in front of me. A man of your experience would certainly know when men are ready to fight, so I want you to go to Paris immediately and assist Sir John to bring his reinforcements to Orléans, fit for battle, as soon as possible."

"Yes, my lord, but who will command Sir John's companies in my absence?"

"I have plenty of men who can do that."

"I would recommend Sergeant Skippon of the Yorkshire company."

The Angel of Lorraine

"No need, there are at least three experienced captains in my entourage already."

"But Sir John's companies are not just any companies, my lord. On the day we captured the Tourelles, the Earl of Salisbury described them as the best of the best."

"I understand the Tourelles were abandoned before you took them?"

"No, my lord, they were abandoned during the attack, which was being pressed home fervently."

"Perhaps so, Captain, but just obey my orders and return here by mid-February at the latest with my reinforcements. Look upon this as a period of leave. Your home is in Rouen, is it not?"

"Yes, my lord."

"Then you have my permission to go home first and spend Christmas with your family. But make sure you get to Paris by New Year's Day and help Sir John complete his task by my deadline."

The prospect of spending a few days with Mary and Joan sweetened the pill of leaving his men for a short while. Talbot certainly knew how to get the best out of his men.

"Thank you, my lord."

"I will send Fastolf a letter to expect you in Paris on the first day of January. Now I wish you God speed, Captain. Dismissed."

Richard took leave of his companies at noon, then set off on the road north. But as he rode past Janville, he passed a detachment of Burgundians heading the opposite way. So much for the Burgundian duke's two thousand men, thought Richard, there were barely twelve hundred of them.

* * *

V

It was Christmas Day in the Year of Our Lord 1428. Father Hugh sat in his cold, bare room looking out of his lead-lined window in the Franciscan priory at Dunwich, close to the Suffolk coast. The early morning sunlight sparkled like crystals on the snow that had fallen on Christmas Eve, which added to the excitement in the priory anticipating the great day. But Hugh's spirit remained unmoved and sullen. It was now more than four years since he had returned to the monastic world at Dunwich, but try as he might, he could not settle to the cloistered life of prayer, penitence, and servitude. His vocation, which was never very strong, had faded away and left a void that could not replace it.

Four years! He thought. *Four boring, pointless, wasted years!* The trouble was he had experienced too much in the outside world to accept the introspective existence, which now confronted him for the rest of his life, and he was only thirty-six! In 1415, he had been confessor to Sir John Fastolf's company as they battled their way through northern France; he had been swept up in a dramatic cavalry charge in Normandy and was present at the battle of Agincourt. Later that year, he had helped his good friend Richard Calveley rescue Mary Hoccleve, Richard's future wife, from a heretic's death in Beccles for Lollardy and, with Millicent Fastolf's assistance, saw them safely off to Normandy just in time to escape the clutches of the Beccles sheriff's men. For the next few years he managed Calveley Hall as Richard's steward where he met Annie Mullen with whom he had a tempestuous affair, but after managing to make her pregnant, he weakly abandoned her and fled back to Dunwich Priory instead of standing by Annie and facing her large, formidable husband. He would never forgive himself for that. *Coward! No backbone!* he scolded himself. *You ran instead of protecting her, so you well deserve the life that now confronts you.* But it was some compensation to know that big Will Mullen accepted his wife and the unborn baby back into his household. More than that, he abandoned his violent ways because the baby, a girl, was the only child they ever had and became the apple of big Will's eye, so Annie found contentment in the end.

Which is more than you'll ever have if you do nothing about your sad life in Dunwich, Hugh told himself. Now he sat alone, his brown hair shaven off and his large, brown eyes staring at the kitchen garden he tended for the priory, which to him seemed the sole purpose of his life.

The noon bell chimed calling the Franciscan brothers to their Christmas lunch. Hugh could hear the excited chatter as they hurried down the cloister corridors to their roast goose meal. *How sad,* he thought, *that this is the pinnacle of their year. For the next three hundred and sixty-four days, they'll fast and pray living like prisoners until next Christmas.* It was at that moment that Hugh finally resolved to do something positive about his inadequate life instead of wringing his hands and quietly moaning about his misfortune. He would seek an appointment with the prior, Father Simon, to have his vocation revoked, his ordination annulled, so that he could go out into the real world and lead a normal life. He had been trained as a notary before becoming a Franciscan, wrote well and could speak French and Latin; he felt sure he could make his way in secular society. Yes! He would speak to Father Simon after lunch.

Unfortunately, Simon was far too busy to see him during Yuletide, so the much needed interview was delayed until the day after the Epiphany, the seventh day of January 1429.

As he stood outside the heavy, oak door to the prior's office, much of the fire had gone out of Hugh's stomach, but it had been replaced by a cold determination that would enable him to put forward his case more lucidly and logically. A reasoned argument was likely to have a greater impact on the cold, dispassionate prior than an emotional plea. He knocked at the door.

"Enter," came the aristocratic, rather bored response, suggesting that this was an annoying intrusion on the prior's valuable time. Father Simon was the third son of a wealthy East Anglian merchant. The first was destined to manage the family estate, the second had joined the army to fight the French, which left the third, Simon, available to the priesthood with the aim of moving swiftly through the ranks to the post of bishop or even archbishop. Physically he was small and lean with a pinched, foxlike face, but a slight widening of the waist revealed that his hunger for advancement had slowed somewhat to be replaced by a more basic form of hunger as his career progression stalled while others were promoted over him. Hugh glanced round Simon's palatial home. Rich tapestries adorned the walls, crystal goblets sat on the dining table, and, most impressive of all, there was, on the floor, a multicoloured, geometric patterned carpet woven in the eastern lands beyond the domains of Christianity. *Whatever happened to the Franciscan vow of poverty?* wondered Hugh, but he kept his thoughts to himself.

"Welcome, Father Hugh," said the prior without looking up as he continued to scratch at some parchment with his quill. "I am extremely busy so I would be obliged if you would make this meeting as short as possible."

Hugh, who did not lack courage despite his own opinion of himself, replied, "Father, it will take as long as is needed."

Simon sighed. "Very well, Hugh, proceed."

Hugh was not asked to sit down, which only served to harden his resolve. "Father, my vocation is lost. I am not sure why, but it is probably to do with the life I led before I finally returned to the priory four years ago."

"Almost certainly," agreed Simon.

"Then I need your advice as to what I should do now."

Simon put down his quill and closed his eyes as if he was communing with a higher being, or was it just boredom? "Then tell me in specific terms how the loss of your vocation manifests itself."

Hugh already realised he was probably wasting his time with this frustrated, ambitious cleric who obviously thought he should be a bishop by now, so he did not trouble to clad the truth with fine words. "Father, I am wasted here. I have tried to concentrate on prayer and penitence for the many sins I have committed, but despite that, there seems to be no purpose to my life. I cannot go out into the world to preach because I would be a laughing stock and a hypocrite in the eyes of those who know of my past, and there are many that do. But the thought of staying here for the rest of my life praying for forgiveness does not enthral me. I joined the Franciscans so that I could go out into the local community to preach the word of God. Had I wanted to be a cloistered monk, I would have joined the Benedictines."

"I doubt the Benedictines would have you now, so I take it you are not asking for a transfer to another order."

"No, I wish to abandon the priesthood altogether."

This was more serious than Simon expected. "God may have a purpose for you that you do not yet understand."

"But I can't fritter my life away hoping for a sign that may never come."

"Yet your prayers have value, a value you may not appreciate now but may become apparent in time to come."

"Father, how can I know that? I have seen the world. There is so much in it I could make better, but not as a Franciscan. I need to abandon my clerical state to go forth and do my best for people as a free man. I have skills that would serve a purpose in secular society which I cannot use locked up in this priory."

"You speak as if this is a prison. It is not."

"Well, it is to me. Please release me from my vows so I can leave this place and lead a life worth living!"

Simon had heard enough; his limited reserves of patience were gone. He could not contemplate the loss of an ordained priest by allowing this insolent friar to do whatever he wanted; the effect on the rest of the priory community was unthinkable. So to save wasting any more time, he cut straight to the quick. "Hugh, what you ask for is not only beyond my power, but outside the gift of all the bishops and archbishops in England. Only the holy father himself can grant such a dispensation."

"The pope!"

"Exactly, you would have to travel to Rome, wait for an interview, and persuade the holy father of your case."

"I have heard that Pope Martin is a fair and reasonable man."

"That may be so, but he will also expect a contribution to the papal funds, which will be an added expense to the costs of your travel. Do you have money in your family?"

"I have no family and certainly no funds or means of earning any. But if the priory would lend me the money, I could pay it back over a period of time after I am able to find paid work."

Simon feigned sadness as he damned any hope Hugh may still have had. "And what if Pope Martin refuses your request? How would you pay us back then? We are not a bank. We do not have the means to subsidise you for a trip to Rome."

Hugh pointedly looked at the rich furnishings in the prior's office. "So I see. Is there no way out for me then?"

"Alas, no, unless you can find a benefactor who will pay for your needs, but you say you do not have one."

"No."

"Then you must make the best of your life here, much as it disagrees with you now. If you pray hard enough and listen hard enough, God will speak to you."

Simon felt well satisfied as he watched the deflated Hugh depart. He was pleased with the way he had handled what could have been a difficult matter, and smugly picked up his quill again.

Hugh slowly walked back through the dark, priory corridors to his little room. The interview with the prior went much as he had expected, but he still felt heart-aching disappointment. He had thought that Simon might be glad to be rid of him, but his last hope of escape was now dashed. He looked through his window once more at the orderly priory grounds containing vegetable plots, a herb garden, dormant flower beds, and a flock of sheep; but this view, pleasant though it might be, was curtailed by the grey, flint-and-mortar curtain wall that formed the hard boundary of his existence. Outside, just out of sight, lay the exciting world he had once revelled in.

He turned and looked at the small, oak chest beside his bunk, which contained his spare, grey Franciscan cloak. Slowly he opened it and moved the grey cloak to one side. Beneath lay the things that still connected him to the outside world, which he had smuggled in those four long years ago when he returned to the confines of the priory. The black leather tunic, breeches, and stylish shoes he had worn when he was steward of Calveley Hall were the clothes that made him a man instead of a priest. He picked up the tunic and held it to his face, imagining he could still smell Annie Mullen's perfume on it. He determined there and then, he knew not when or how, to escape the purgatory he was living through before the year of 1429 was ended.

He did not have the consolation of knowing that his visceral desire would receive a response even sooner than that.

CHAPTER THREE

The great castle of Chinon stands on the north bank of the River Vienne, just a few miles upstream from its confluence with the Loire, the river that drains most of central France and divides the realm between north and south. It was here that the dauphin, who was King Charles VII in the eyes of most French people, set up his court, which was near enough to Paris to remind the rebellious citizens who was their true king, yet far enough from Bourges, the temporary capital of free France, to be above the petty squabbling of the day-to-day demands of governing a divided kingdom.

The war with the English was going from bad to worse, so on the sixth day of January in the Year of Our Lord 1429, the Dauphin Charles summoned his military leaders to the castle to debate the future strategy that would preserve the "most Christian country of France" from the onslaught of the hated island nation. The Military Council assembled outside the great audience hall of Chinon, which was bedecked with flags bearing the coats of arms of the noble families of France, many of whom, including the Duke of Orléans, the dauphin's uncle, were still languishing as hostages in England after the disaster at Agincourt fourteen years before, waiting for their ransoms to be paid before they could return home.

Fate seemed to have treated the Dauphin Charles harshly. Short, coarse featured, and lacking the physical presence a leader should have, he hardly seemed a worthy contender for the French throne compared to the great Valois kings of old or the recently deceased warrior King Henry V of England, who had claimed the throne for his son by marrying Charles's sister Catherine. His closest family adviser, Jean Dunois, the bastard son

The Angel of Lorraine

of the Duke of Orléans, sat beside him as they prepared for the audience that must shortly take place. Being a royal bastard had not hampered Jean's progress up the ladder of French society. Unlike the dauphin, he was tall and good-looking but at the same time totally loyal to the man he saw as Charles VII of France. Dunois was well aware of the dauphin's shortcomings, but there was something about him, a sort of steely, inner determination, which gave him hope that the young dauphin was the man who would eventually send the English home with their tails between their legs.

Charles muttered, "Jean, must we really deal with those glorified brigands waiting outside? They should all be hanged for the crimes they've committed in our name."

"But they're winners, Your Majesty," replied Dunois. "They have risen to their present positions because of the failure of our more noble families to beat the English. Can we afford to ignore such men when those whose flags now fly above our heads have let us down time after time?"

"But you are of noble blood."

"I am a bastard, so I do not count."

"Yes, you do. Without you, Jean, I would be in exile by now or worse. Call them in."

Three men entered the audience hall. All wore their black hair long and sported the fashionable long moustache favoured by most of the French military commanders of the day, but apart from that, they could not have looked more different from each other. The first to enter, Jean Poton de Xaintrailles, a minor noble from Gascony, would have been every woman's image of the perfect, heroic knight. Tall, lean, but muscular with hazel-coloured eyes and a smile that could melt the hardest heart, he had the intelligence and humour to match his striking appearance. Following him was Etienne de Vignolles, more commonly known as La Hire, or to the English, the Wrath of God. Also from Gascony but not of noble blood, he was a huge man overtopping his friend de Xaintrailles by almost a head. His short temper was well-known, but he was even more famous for his swearing, which, some claimed, he had raised almost to an art form. He walked with a slight limp caused some years before at an inn when a fireplace collapsed on him breaking his leg. The last to enter was Gilles, Baron de Rais, who was descended from an ancient and noble Breton family. He was of medium height, but his most distinguishing feature was his eyes, which were so dark as to be almost black and unfathomable. He was fifteen years younger than the other two and stood a little apart from them, the outsider of the three, when they presented themselves to their uncrowned king.

"Mes Seigneurs, please sit," said the dauphin pointing towards three seats. "You are most welcome. There will be no standing on ceremony today."

"Thank you, Your Majesty," replied de Xaintrailles in his rich, cultured voice tainted only slightly by the trace of a Gascon accent. "Except for Mon Seigneur Dunois, we three are surprised to see no princes of the blood or the Constable of France in attendance today."

"Then, Jean Poton, you do not realise how badly my court has been fractured by personal jealousies and rivalries. We cannot allow such internal differences to influence our strategy. Time is not on our side. Today we must decide what to do about Orléans." Then turning to Dunois, the dauphin said, "Jean, please summarise the situation."

"Yes, Your Majesty. My friends, we are now at a critical juncture which could well determine the outcome of this endless war. Last month Baron Talbot took command of the English army. He is their best general. Since then, the siege of Orléans has been pressed more vigorously, and we are finding it much more difficult to get men and supplies into the city because of the aggressive English patrols. We have now reached a point where we can still reinforce Orléans with men, but we cannot supply the extra provisions needed to feed them. The city commander, Raoul de Gaucourt, is not given to exaggeration, so we may believe the dispatches he sends us from time to time. He says that evidence of malnutrition is becoming clear amongst the citizens, and fights are starting to break out in the bread queues. Our bombardiers are now running low on powder and shot, and already our rate of fire has slowed down. Therefore, if we allow things to take their course without further intervention, Orléans will fall."

"Thank you, Jean," said Charles, "you have made the position very clear. So, Mes Seigneurs, if we do nothing, the city will open its gates to the English. Some of my advisers in the Royal Council say, 'Let it be so,' then we can regroup further south in Berri or even Provence and counterattack when we are stronger. Others say we should hold Orléans at all costs because if the English break the line of the Loire, France is lost. I would welcome your views."

La Hire answered first. "Your Majesty, there has been far too much talk and not enough fighting. Let us gather all our men together and attack the English from outside Orléans while de Gaucourt sallies out from the city and takes them in the rear. We can wipe out the English army in a day."

Dunois disagreed, "We have tried to take the English head-on before, and you well know what happened. We have never succeeded."

"But the English are not invincible! Only last month I personally sent two of them to the next world in a skirmish near Janville."

"Not quite, Etienne," corrected his friend de Xaintrailles. "They were Norman French in the pay of the English."

"Well, they're all the same to me. If they fight for the English, then they're English!"

The more measured de Xaintrailles addressed the dauphin. "Your Majesty, La Hire makes a fair point in so far as we must not permit Orléans to fall. All France is watching this battle. If we abandon the city, the undecided—and there are many of them—will conclude that your cause is lost, and they will finally commit to the English king Henry. He is only a boy, but he has Valois blood in his veins from his mother, and his advisers have already announced that he will respect French laws, customs, and language. In other words, there would be nothing to lose by supporting what would appear to be the winning side. Only victory at Orléans will stop the rot."

The dauphin asked, "Then what action do you propose, Jean Poton?"

Before de Xaintrailles could answer, Gilles de Rais, who had said nothing so far, interjected, "May I make a suggestion, Your Majesty?"

The dauphin nodded. "Of course."

"Your Majesty, it is true that we must be careful about taking on the English, whatever our numerical superiority, because their archers dominate the battlefield, but they have only one field army in France, and that is concentrated around Orléans. We have many times their number, but instead of trying to beat them with overwhelming force in a pitched battle, we could simply contain them and accept the ongoing losses we are taking while continuing to supply Orléans. Meanwhile we could equip three or even four armies of at least eight thousand men each and use them to attack English-occupied France. They have nothing to stop us in Maine and Anjou and almost nothing in Normandy. We could take back our towns and cities at little cost to ourselves. We might even recover Paris. As we reconquer our land, we will hang all collaborators as a warning to others who may be thinking of joining the English. Then the English will have to decide whether to keep their only army in France tied down at Orléans and watch all their conquests fall into our hands, or to abandon the siege and fight for what they already have. Either way, for this strategy to succeed, we must hold Orléans."

De Rais's proposal was greeted with silence, but then de Xaintrailles, who was always generous with praise when praise was deserved, said, "Your Majesty, de Rais has just put us older and more experienced commanders to shame. His strategy is brilliant, and I am embarrassed and annoyed that I did not think of it."

"And I," agreed Dunois.

The Angel of Lorraine

"And what were you going to propose, Jean Poton, before de Rais came up with his plan?" asked the dauphin.

"It concerns a possible answer to the English archer's dominance in battle. There lives in Paris a certain Jean Bureau and his brother Gaspard. Both are loyal to Your Majesty despite the English occupation of their city. They have developed new techniques for casting stronger gun metal and mixing more powerful forms of gunpowder which can increase the range of shot. This has enabled them to produce a small, lightweight cannon which can be pulled by a single draught horse. The Bureau brothers have written to me asking if they may be permitted to give you a demonstration of its effectiveness."

Charles raised a sceptical eyebrow, "All this under the noses of the English? Do the Bureau brothers expect them not to notice a cannon passing through the gates of Paris?"

"They will not see it, Your Majesty," replied de Xaintrailles, "because it is easily dismantled and reassembled. It will be transported in an ordinary cart just like hundreds of others that go to and from Paris every day. The English are now so confident, they only carry out superficial searches on a few of them."

The dauphin glanced at Dunois. "What do you think, Jean?"

"Well worth giving these brothers a chance, I'd say. Depending on range and accuracy, Jean Poton could be right. This might alter the balance of power on the battlefield."

"Very well then. Jean Poton, go ahead with your demonstration as soon as you can, and we shall judge this masterpiece of French ingenuity." Then addressing all three of the commanders before him, the dauphin's voice took on a sterner tone. "I know of your successes in war, but I also know of your tendency to pillage and plunder our friends as well as our enemies. The English are fair game, but you must stop this behaviour in the Duke of Burgundy's lands and loyal French lands under English occupation and that, de Rais, includes hanging so-called collaborators without a trial. Remember, Burgundy will ultimately return to France as will Normandy,

Anjou, Maine, and Paris and," he hesitated and glared at de Xaintrailles and La Hire, "and yes, Gascony too. You are now paid by my treasury, so you can no longer justify plundering our own people for want of money. I want your word before you leave this room that this will stop!"

De Xaintrailles beamed one of his irresistible smiles. "I believe I may speak for us all, Your Majesty, when I say we will do all in our power to prevent such behaviour reoccurring."

"That is not quite the same thing Jean Poton, but I suppose it will have to do for now. Now all of you return to your men while Mon Seigneur Dunois and I consider how best to put de Rais's strategy into action."

"And pray for a miracle," added de Rais under his breath.

When they were alone again, Charles asked Dunois, "Jean, did you notice anything odd about those three?"

"Do you mean the way de Xaintrailles and La Hire seemed to distance themselves from de Rais?"

"Yes. Could it be they were jealous because the youthful de Rais came up with the best strategy?"

Dunois paused, as if he was bracing himself before answering. "Your Majesty, people say there is something dark about de Rais, something unsavoury within his character. Rumours are starting to circulate about his sinister private life, but I do not know if there is any substance in them."

"I see. Well, for the present, let us not enquire too deeply about them. We cannot afford to be choosy about our commanders, especially the only good ones we have. Today I have overlooked their past, which includes murder. There can be no worse crime than that, can there?"

"I hope not, Your Majesty."

* * *

The Angel of Lorraine

II

Just as the dauphin and Dunois were about to leave the audience chamber, a servant entered and bowed low. "Your Majesty, the Lady Yolande asks if she may see you."

"Of course, the queen's mother is always welcome. Ask her to come in." A few moments later, the heavy, double doors to the private royal apartments opened and in walked, or rather glided, a remarkable woman. Now in her midforties, Yolande of Aragon, mother of Marie of Anjou, Queen of France, still retained her slim figure despite having borne five children. Once called "the prettiest woman in the kingdom" by no less than the Bishop of Beauvais, Yolande was now handsome rather than pretty and oozed noblesse in her elegant manner, but beneath that womanly exterior lay a personal mission to ensure her bloodline inherited the French throne. This could only be accomplished through her six-year-old grandson, Louis, who was the new dauphin in most French minds even though his father, Charles, had yet to be crowned king in the cathedral at Reims, where all his predecessors had been anointed with the holy oil of Clovis, the first king of the French.

But another powerful woman, Isabeau of Bavaria, Charles's mother, was equally determined that her own son would not be anointed king but would be replaced by his sister, Catherine, widow of Henry V of England, whose son Henry VI united the Valois and Plantagenet bloodlines as approved by the Treaty of Troyes. Isabeau now resided in Paris under English protection, scheming to dislodge Charles with the help of the English and their Burgundian allies.

"Please sit, Mother," said Charles, who used this term when speaking privately to Yolande. Like most French children, he used to refer to his own mother as Maman, but now he did not speak of her at all if he could avoid it.

"Would you like me to leave, my lady?" asked Dunois.

Peter Tallon

"No, Jean, please stay, we are all Valois here. Remember, I am King Jean, the Good's granddaughter."

"Then how can we be of service, Mother?" asked the dauphin.

"There is someone I want you to meet, but first I need to give you a sense of the importance of the news this young knight brings. Strange, possibly wonderful things seem to be happening in Lorraine. Already people are talking of a gift from God. A young maiden has appeared in Domremy who claims to have heard voices from heaven telling her she must raise the banner of France and drive the English out of God's most Christian country, the leader of the crusades, our own dear France."

Charles looked upwards as if asking heaven for help. "Oh no, not another one! If I had a ducat for every religious maniac who promised to save France, I could pay for the war for a year and still have money left over."

"I knew that would be your response, Charles, which is why I have the Sieur de Freuchin waiting outside. He is a knight who has lost his lands in Picardy to the Burgundians and is now based in Lorraine as a soldier of France paid by you. You know I am not easily fooled by charlatans, so I ask you to listen to him before rejecting out of hand what may be our only means of beating the English."

Charles sighed. "I do respect your judgement, Mother, so bring him in."

A young, fresh-faced knight entered the audience hall and bowed low before the dauphin, Yolande, and Dunois. "Who are you?" asked Charles in a neutral tone.

"I am Marcel, Sieur de Freuchin, Your Majesty. I am landless since the English and Burgundians conquered Picardy, and now I serve you as a paid soldier in Lorraine. I have fought in many battles including Harfleur, Agincourt, and Verneuil. I have the scars to show for it. I fight for Valois France."

"And the return of your land."

"Of course, Your Majesty."

"Then tell me about these extraordinary events in Lorraine."

De Freuchin glanced at Yolande, who gave him an almost unnoticeable nod of approval to respond. "Your Majesty, late last year a maid called Jeanne, daughter of Jacques Darc who dwells in Domremy, was brought before the captain of Vaucouleurs Robert de Baudricourt by the Domremy parish priest, Father Guillaume Front. Jeanne told de Baudricourt of the voices from heaven that speak to her saying she must lead France to victory over the English. The voices are those of Saint Catherine the Martyr and Saint Margaret. De Baudricourt questioned her in depth, but she answered him well and confidently with none of the religious ecstasy so commonly used by charlatans. I was there and heard it all myself. There is something about this girl, who is only sixteen, which I cannot explain well. She is only from peasant stock, yet she has an aura, a kind of light about her which forces you to listen. I have never seen anything like it before, nor would I believe it unless I'd experienced it myself. I could see de Baudricourt was beginning to feel the same way, but the spell was broken when the parish priest unwisely intervened thinking he was protecting Jeanne from unfair questioning."

"Mon Sieur," interjected Charles, "you use the word *spell*. May not this strange power emanate from hell just as easily as from heaven?"

"Your Majesty, that question has been asked by others who have not met Jeanne but by none who have. This is why I ask only that you might give her an audience. If you are not convinced, then she can be sent home, but if you do not even see her, you may throw away France's best chance of winning this war."

"Is that all you have to say?"

"Not quite, Your Majesty. Since the visit to Vaucouleurs, Jeanne has been interviewed by Charles Duke of Lorraine, who believes in her. He has sent a letter of support which I have with me."

"Have you read it?"

"No, Your Majesty, it is addressed to you. The seal is unbroken."

"Then give it to me."

Charles broke the seal and unrolled the letter. It was not long and soon read. He rolled it up again and expressed surprise. "I know Duke Charles well enough to be sure he is not given to exaggeration, yet from the tone of this letter, Jeanne sounds almost like an angel sent from heaven to help us." He handed it to Dunois whose eyes widened as he read it.

"And what did de Baudricourt say as he interviewed Jeanne?" asked Dunois.

"Not much. He listened carefully but said he could not spare any men from his already depleted garrison to escort Jeanne halfway across France through enemy territory without help from his duke."

"That sounds like de Baudricourt," acknowledged Dunois. "Has this help been requested?"

"I do not know, Mon Seigneur, but I think not. I believe Duke Charles will do nothing until he knows what His Majesty's response will be."

Charles looked at his mother-in-law, who smiled sweetly at him. "Well, I know what the queen mother thinks, but what about my wife, the queen?"

"Marie agrees with me, Your Majesty," answered Yolande, adopting formality now that the Valois family was in the presence of an outsider.

"No surprise there then. And what about you, Jean?"

The Angel of Lorraine

Dunois rolled up Duke Charles's letter and handed it back to the dauphin. "Your Majesty, I think we should at least give this Jeanne a hearing. We have nothing to lose. If she is like all the other seers and soothsayers, we can just send her back home. If not, then we can put her to the test, though we will need some clerical brainpower on hand to do that."

"Very well," said the dauphin. Then addressing de Freuchin again, he gave his instructions. "Mon Sieur, ride with all speed back to Lorraine and tell Duke Charles that Jeanne will be received at Chinon, and that he should send her here immediately."

* * *

III

It was the end of the last week in January, and yet another day dawned in the freezing weather that dominated that terrible winter. The ground was hard with frost, which refused to melt even in the daytime, and a biting wind blew down from the northeast. Under a cloudless, early morning sky, three men walked across a vast, open plain north of Chinon towards two more men who were waiting for them beside a horse and cart; all were shrouded against the cold. As they walked, their boots cracked open the ice covering half-frozen puddles, splattering their breeches with muddy water, but mercifully the wind was beginning to ease, which made the cold a little more bearable than it would otherwise have been.

The smallest of the three, the dauphin, grumbled, "Was it really necessary to leave our warm beds so early on a Sunday morning? Every civilised man is now abed with his wife, or maybe someone else's at this time."

"Exactly, Your Majesty," answered de Xaintrailles, who did not seem to feel the cold like the other two. "There will be no prying eyes about. What we are about to witness must remain a state secret for as long as possible."

"This won't take too much time, Your Majesty," added Dunois soothingly, "just as long as is needed for the Bureau brothers to prove, or fail to prove, the effectiveness of their new field cannon."

They were met at the horse and cart by Jean Bureau, the elder of the two brothers, who was a small, craggy-faced man with an unusually long nose. "Welcome, Your Majesty, Mes Seigneurs, we are truly grateful to you for sparing us some of your precious time. May I introduce my brother Gaspard, who will demonstrate our new cannon."

"Just get on with it," muttered the dauphin ungraciously. Jean Bureau took them to the other side of the cart where something was hidden beneath two grey horse blankets. He nodded to Gaspard, who removed the blankets with a theatrical flourish to reveal the smallest cannon Charles and Dunois had ever seen.

"What is this!" demanded the dauphin. "It's tiny! Have I been dragged out of bed to view a child's toy?"

"It is anything but that," replied de Xaintrailles. "Just hear these men out, Your Majesty."

"This cannon is small and therefore easy to move," explained Jean Bureau. "It is not big like the siege cannon you are accustomed to seeing because it is not designed to break down walls, but it will certainly break human bodies, armoured or unarmoured, at a distance far greater than any longbow can reach." Then pointing northwards with the rising sun on their right, he continued, "Your Majesty, observe the white sheet suspended between two poles near that barn yonder. Do you see it?"

"Yes, yes, I see it," answered the dauphin irritably.

"Well, that is six hundred paces away. What is the effective range of the English longbow?"

De Xaintrailles replied, "A powerful archer can achieve three hundred paces, but in battle conditions, between two hundred and two hundred and fifty paces is more usual."

"Very well. Gaspard, prime the cannon if you please. Is the slow match alight?"

"Yes, Jean."

"Then proceed."

The cannon had a short, stubby barrel no more than half the height of a tall man in length, set upon a rectangular, wooden frame supported on either side by two large, spoked wheels. Gaspard placed the gunpowder charge, which was contained in a small, linen bag, into the mouth of the cannon and pushed it to the back of the metal tube with a ramrod. Then, he carefully placed a heavy, cast-iron cannonball into the cannon and rammed it home so that ball pushed the linen bag of powder snugly beneath the touch hole at the back of the tube.

"Take aim," ordered Jean. His brother squinted along the top of the cannon and adjusted the range finder, which was a brass quarter circle of cogs set at the back of the cannon. This altered the angle of elevation of the tube.

"Prepare to fire." Now Gaspard used the pointed spike at the far end of the ramrod to poke through the touch hole until the linen bag containing the gunpowder was pierced. Then he sprinkled some more powder down the touch hole so that there was a direct connection with the powder in the bag.

"Your Majesty, Mes Seigneurs, please stand well away from the cannon and cover your ears with your hands," requested Jean Bureau. All three stepped back, but the dauphin grumpily ignored the order to cover his ears.

Jean looked at Gaspard. "Fire!"

Gaspard blew on the slow match and held it to the touch hole. There was a brief fizz, then a flash as the powder in the touch hole caught hold. Suddenly the cannon jerked backwards. There was a mighty roar that stunned the dauphin, who fell to his knees. De Xaintrailles and Dunois had been present at many cannonades, but even they were shocked by the noise made by such a small version of the cannons they had seen before. Only the Bureau brothers and the draft horse seemed unmoved by the explosion.

Dunois ran to Charles. "Your Majesty, are you all right?"

"My god!" swore the dauphin as he struggled to his feet. "What a terrible noise! I've wet my goddamned breeches!" De Xaintrailles turned away to hide a smile.

"The bombardiers soon get used to it," said Gaspard, "though many suffer premature deafness."

"I'm not goddamned surprised! Must we see any more of this?"

"I'm afraid we must, Your Majesty," answered Jean Bureau. "If you will look at the target, you will see a man with a red flag. He is waving it twice, then stopping, then waving it twice again and so on. That means we have overshot by two hundred paces. Gaspard! Signal the acknowledgement and then a second firing. Use a little less powder this time."

The signal was duly made, and the cannon prepared for firing again. Jean Bureau said, "Your Majesty, Mes Seigneurs, please prepare yourselves for another round. Gaspard, fire as soon as you are ready."

The small cannon roared again, but this time the audience was ready, and even the dauphin held his hands over his ears. Then close to the target, a man appeared waving a green flag. Both brothers jumped for joy and hugged each other. "A direct hit!" shouted Gaspard. "A direct hit at six hundred paces at only the second shot! I'll signal the recall."

The Angel of Lorraine

Ten minutes later, two red-faced assistants arrived holding a crumpled sheet and poles.

"Unwind the sheet!" ordered Gaspard. The two exhausted men, who had just run six hundred paces, stepped away from each other unwinding the sheet as they separated. A perfect round hole about a handspan in diameter was revealed close to the centre of the sheet.

Jean Bureau, trying to control the elation he felt, said, "You can see, Your Majesty, a direct hit at six hundred paces. Now consider this. English archers shoot their arrows from parallel ranks sometimes twelve files deep. Each man steps forward, shoots, then runs to the rear rank until his turn comes to shoot again. This way they can keep steady volleys of arrows shooting at five-second intervals at their enemy without tiring. They call it the portcullis formation, and so far, it has proved to be invincible. But now imagine twenty cannon like this one firing into their massed ranks from six hundred paces, each cannonball taking down an entire file. It would be a slaughter because we can fire one of these field cannon every thirty seconds. So if the English decide to attack us, they will be destroyed long before we come within range of their arrows."

"Most effective at six hundred paces," acknowledged Dunois, "but what if the battlefield is not an open plain like this? Most aren't. Usually they are studded with hamlets or forests and hedgerows like Agincourt. How will your bombardiers cope when they are within arrow range?"

"We will show you," replied Gaspard. He ordered the two flag holders to retire one hundred paces and unfurl the sheet again. Then he turned to his brother. "Small bore?"

"Of course," came the reply. The previous procedure of loading the cannon was followed, except this time four handfuls of small, lead balls were rammed in behind the powder bag instead of a single, large cannonball. "Ready to fire," commanded Jean Bureau. The audience, including the dauphin, placed their hands over their ears, and the flag men ran for cover.

"Fire!" Instead of producing a single, round hole, the sheet was shredded, torn to pieces. Jean smiled and addressed Dunois, "Does that answer your question, Mon Seigneur?"

"Indeed it does. How soon can you deliver twenty of these little monsters with crews trained to fire them?"

"Ten days for the cannons, Mon Seigneur, but the bombardiers will need a week's training before they can operate them safely and effectively."

"A week, is that all! It takes the English twenty years before they can produce a competent archer. They train from childhood, gradually building muscle, until they can fully draw the great longbow. Yet we can train a bombardier in a week! I do believe that we have today seen a weapon that can change the course of history."

"There is still the matter of price to be discussed," said Jean Bureau hesitantly.

"Of course," agreed Dunois. "The Sieur de Xaintrailles will deal with that, will you not, Jean Poton? I am sure you can drive a harder bargain than I can."

"I will do my best, Mon Seigneur, but perhaps we should order just six to start with in case they do not all work as well as this one."

"I leave that to you, Jean Poton."

The dauphin, whose treasury would have to pay the bill, added, "And don't forget to agree a price for the powder and shot until we can manufacture them in our own foundries. A low price for the cannon is no good if we can't afford to use them."

"I will not forget, Your Majesty," smiled Jean Poton.

Finally, and despite the discomfort of his wet breeches, the dauphin also allowed himself a rare smile. "I think today has been a good day for France."

* * *

IV

Marcel Sieur de Freuchin rode hard and reached Domremy in only nine days. It was already getting dark, and a frost was forming as he trotted his tired horse into the little village. Candles had been lit in most of the cottages, casting an inviting light to anyone unfortunate enough still to be outside. Not knowing which house belonged to the Darc family, Marcel called in at the presbytery of Saint Remy where the parish priest, Father Front, had just finished his evening meal and was quietly enjoying a goblet of red Burgundian wine. A loud rap at the door startled the priest who was about to doze off in front of his log fire. He had given his housekeeper permission to leave early because of the cold night, so he was obliged to open the door himself.

"Sieur de Freuchin! Welcome! What brings you here on such a cold night?" Marcel accepted a comforting goblet of wine, sat down by the fire, and told Father Front about all that had happened at Chinon.

"So you see," he concluded, "we must present Jeanne to de Baudricourt once more and, with the dauphin's authority as well as Duke Charles of Lorraine's, persuade him to release enough men to escort her back to Chinon as soon as possible. Orléans will fall to the English without urgent help, so there is no time to lose. Can we see him tonight?"

"Mon Sieur," replied the priest, "how far have you travelled today?"

"I'm not sure, about forty miles maybe."

"Vaucouleurs is yet another ten miles from here, and both you and your horse are exhausted. May I suggest you stay here at the presbytery tonight as my guest, then early tomorrow we shall collect Jeanne and ride to Vaucouleurs together. No time will be lost because de Baudricourt will certainly not see anyone tonight, and in any event, you will present your case far better after a good night's sleep." De Freuchin frowned, unsure of what to do, so Father Front took the empty goblet from his hand, filled it up again, and handed it back. The young knight took a sip, looked at the warm fire, and relaxed. Tomorrow morning would be soon enough.

Jeanne, her father, de Freuchin, and Father Front arrived at de Baudricourt's castle just as the church bell at Vaucouleurs chimed eleven o'clock in the morning. They had no appointment, but nonetheless, de Baudricourt agreed to see them at once. This time he did not keep them waiting, and they were taken to the audience hall immediately. The old warrior was alone apart from his secretary and stood up to greet them.

"Welcome, I did not expect you so soon. Ah, Marcel, I see you are now standing before me instead of at my side."

"Robert, I am both before you as well as at your side, but I cannot be in two places at once."

"No, of course not, but I think I can guess why you are here."

"An escort to Chinon," answered Jeanne.

De Baudricourt's stern face suddenly broke into a disarmingly broad smile; he had been a handsome man in his younger days. "Well, I am pleased to tell you that an escort is now possible. Duke Charles has sent me twenty crossbowmen and eight men-at-arms, so I can spare two men-at-arms, Jean de Metz and Bertrand de Poulengy, plus their servants, and a royal messenger, Colet de Vienne, who happens to be here at the moment. I assume the Sieur de Freuchin will accompany you back to Chinon?" Marcel nodded. "Very well," continued de Baudricourt, "I will also write a personal letter of recommendation to the dauphin for you to deliver. Jeanne, you will need more practical clothing for the journey than the red dress you are now wearing, so I will arrange for something suitable to be prepared for you to take away with you. Are your voices still speaking to you?"

"They are, Mon Sieur, and they are becoming impatient at the delay, but all will now be well, thanks to you."

"Jeanne, I have but a small part to play in your story. You are the main character. I pray your voices protect you in the world you are about to enter."

"They will, Mon Sieur, I am certain of it."

"Good, then I shall personally escort you as far as the boundary of my land and wish you Godspeed. Is there anything else I can do for you?"

"Yes, Mon Sieur, pray for me."

CHAPTER FOUR

Richard sat contentedly staring into the log fire in his warm, comfortable home in Rouen. Christmas had passed four days before, and on the morrow, he would have to depart for Paris to join Sir John Fastolf. The evening meal had been consumed, and his fourteen-year-old daughter, Joan, was visiting friends for the evening, so he was alone for a while with Mary.

"You're smiling, my dear," she said, "it's good to see. Will you share your thoughts with me?"

"Of course. I was thinking how fortunate I am to have a beautiful wife and daughter who I have been able to enjoy Christmas with this year."

"It has been even more wonderful because it was so unexpected. How gracious it was of Lord Talbot to release you this year."

"Perhaps, Mary, but it suited his purpose too. That is why I must leave for Paris in the morning."

"We shall both miss you and your stories. Joan especially loved the one about Will Potter's teeth."

"Ha!" laughed Richard. "And all absolutely true. I couldn't have invented a story like that one."

"And I was pleased to hear that John Fletcher is doing well."

"John has turned out to be an excellent sergeant, though you may rest assured he has not given up his Lollard beliefs. There are now many in his company who share his views. Lollardy seems to suit the East Anglian mentality."

"Hurrah for that! Equality before God, sharing of wealth, promotion on merit, not birth or patronage. One day it will become the mentality of all England."

"No need to preach to me, Mary, I'm more than halfway there already, but while I'm a soldier, I cannot agree with all your Lollard principles."

"Your first wife did."

"Ann never told me."

"She knew you would disapprove."

"Perhaps, perhaps not. Sometimes I could surprise her."

"And me too. Your bluff exterior conceals a gentle heart and an original mind. Ann and I would have become good friends had we known each other longer."

"A formidable combination that would have been. Even the Archbishop of Canterbury might have been a Lollard by now!"

"Now you're being silly. On a more serious note, have you given any thought to Joan's future? She is fourteen now and reminds me of Ann more and more each day. Should we not be thinking about a suitable husband for her?"

In truth, Richard had not given it a thought. The war was preoccupying him too much since the English advance on Orléans had been thwarted. "Plenty of time to think about that after Orléans has fallen, and we can all take some leave. Joan is only a child as yet."

Mary shook her head. "Typical of a father. Have you looked at her lately? She has become a fine-looking woman and already has many admirers."

"Has she indeed? Anyone you would approve of?"

"Not yet."

"Pleased to hear it. All right then, we'll set our minds to it as soon as I get back from Orléans, I promise. Now come and sit closer to me, let us enjoy our last night together."

Mary cuddled up beside him and rested her head on his chest. He stroked her long, fair hair, which still had no signs of grey in it, but she had not finished yet. "Richard, do you realise you will be forty-one years old next year?"

"Yes, my dear, and so will you."

"Is that not rather old for a frontline warrior?"

"Well, it's certainly above the average, but I'm still fit and healthy, and there are many others on the front line older than me."

"But could you not at least request a less dangerous role, now? You have done more than your fair share of fighting."

"What had you in mind? A storekeeper? A clerk maybe?"

"Now you're mocking me. I thought a trainer or perhaps an adviser. Men listen to you, and are you not about to go to Paris to assist Sir John Fastolf to turn men into soldiers?"

He kissed the top of her head. "I did not mean to mock. I could be a trainer I suppose, but there would be no booty or ransom money."

The Angel of Lorraine

"Do you need more? We already have two houses in Rouen besides the one we live in, as well as your eighty acres in Suffolk."

For this first time since he joined the army in 1414 as Fastolf's man, Richard was forced into thinking seriously about his future. The rents coming from his Suffolk land and the Rouen properties covered all his family's needs with plenty to spare. He was a commoner, and the chances of being knighted were vanishingly small, which meant there was no incentive to carry on for the sake of promotion because he had already got as far as he could go. Although he was physically fit, he had noticed that heavy duties tired him more easily now, so why indeed did he continue to put his life at risk when he had Mary and Joan to consider? Could it be that he would miss the comradeship in the army too much, or was it, he thought darkly, that he just loved the thrill of fighting? Like many of the English, he had not yet tasted defeat. If ever that happened, he might feel differently, but one thing was certain—there was no trace left in him of that young farmer who joined Fastolf's company almost fifteen years ago.

"Richard! Have you fallen asleep!"

"No, my love, I was thinking seriously about what you've just said. You make a great deal of sense, though it is hard for me to come to terms with. Can we talk about it again once the Orléans campaign is over?"

"Are you serious? I have never heard you speak like that before. Every time I have even hinted at such a thing, it has been instantly dismissed."

He kissed her again. "Maybe so, but not this time. Orléans can't hold out much longer, and then we can decide what's best for our future together."

That night, when they made love for what would be the last time in many months, Mary was as passionate as she had been when they first came together. Richard's last thought as he drifted off into a contented sleep was, *There's no going back, my lad, you've committed yourself now, so have no regrets.*

Peter Tallon

The next morning, after he had endured a sorrowful parting with Mary and Joan, Richard called in at army headquarters, which was located close to the great cathedral near Rouen's market square. He was still surprised at what he had agreed to the previous evening and astonished he felt no regrets on this fine, frosty morning. In fact, he felt more at peace with himself than he had done for years. But sadly, all that was about to change.

The retired sergeant who worked as the receptionist at headquarters was known to Richard from the Agincourt campaign.

"Ah, Captain Richard," he said cheerily as he picked up a box from beneath his desk with his left hand; the right, together with the arm attached to it, lay somewhere beneath the soil of the great battle. "We came across a sack of intercepted correspondence when we captured Meung last October. There is a letter addressed to you somewhere here. The Frogs opened it, I'm afraid, but did nothing with it. They just left it with a load of other stuff in a cellar and forgot about it."

He fingered through some scrolls of varying sizes and selected one of the smaller ones. "Here it is, Captain. As you can see, the seal is broken."

"Thank you, Michael, I'll read it when I have reported in."

Within five minutes, Richard was back on the road, and after he passed through Rouen's east gate, he drew rein and unrolled the letter. He looked first at the signature; it was from Ruth! His stomach churned. Then he looked at the date; the tenth day of June 1425. But that was more than three and a half years ago! He started to read, but his hand was shaking too much, so he dismounted and held the letter firmly against his horse's saddlecloth.

My Dear Richard, 10/6/1425

You have a son. The premonition I had at Pilgrim's Castle proved to be half correct. The child I saw in my dream was ours but you are not with us. When we parted at Ancona I thought I might be carrying your child but it was too soon to be sure. Perhaps I should have told you, but what if I had been wrong?

My father's response when I told him I was pregnant was not what I expected. Instead of scolding me he put his arm round me and said, "Have no fear, I shall be at your side. That is what your mother would have expected." He was disappointed but not angry and knew you were the father before I told him. He did not even seem surprised.

Another surprise was Captain Paolo Dandolo. When he was told he immediately offered marriage. I had not heard from you, I still do not know if you were alive or dead, so I accepted. I know he will always be a good husband and treat Enrico, your son, as his own. We were married in a Christian church before my pregnancy showed, so Enrico was not born a bastard.

After you left we soon felt Doge Foscari's hatred of Paolo when the two assassins he sent from Venice to murder him were arrested by the Ancona authorities for getting drunk and aggressive on the night before they were due to complete their mission. That is why I am writing this letter to you from Genoa, where we now live and run our business. It is the one place where we are beyond Foscari's evil reach.

Richard, I still love you and I forgive the deception which misled me into thinking you were unmarried because I know you really did love me. I am sending you this letter because I believe it is your right to know you have a son. I shall be a good wife to Paolo but I shall never stop loving you.

I suppose it would be for the best if you do not reply to this letter, but I would truly like to know if you are well. If you decide to respond use my married name, and address the letter to the Jewish quarter in Genoa. Your letter will find me because I am the only Jew in this city who bears a married Christian name; Dandolo. If you do not reply I shall understand.

Ruth

By the time he finished the letter, Richard's hands had stopped shaking, but he felt he was going to vomit. The unprecedented feeling of well-being and contentment he had enjoyed before calling in at army headquarters had lasted barely an hour. Now his life was in turmoil again. He loved Mary deeply, but the passion he felt for Ruth was on an altogether different scale. With the passage of time, he had managed to accept he would never see her again, but the knowledge that she had forgiven his deception and that he had a son changed everything. His mind was in chaos, but one clear fact stood out amidst all the confusion: he must see Ruth and his son Enrico, even if it was only once, whatever the cost. But first he must reply. He stowed Ruth's letter safely inside his tunic pocket, mounted his bay palfrey, and returned to army headquarters where Michael was still at the reception desk.

"Hello again, Captain. I thought you were on your way to Paris. Have you forgotten something?"

"Not exactly, Michael, but I do need to answer the letter you gave me immediately. Have you a spare room, a quill, parchment, and ink where I can write a response?"

Michael laughed. "It's Yuletide, Captain. Everyone is at home except you and me. You can choose whichever room you like."

A few minutes later, Richard sat down in an office at the back of the building and began to write.

Dearest Ruth, 29/12/1428

I have only just received your letter of 10th June 1425!! It was intercepted by the French and reached me this very day a few minutes ago. I cannot tell you how sorry I am for misleading you about being unmarried but, equally I am delighted you have forgiven me. And to add to my joy I now know I have a son. I promise you there will be no more deception. I never intended there to be but somehow events moved so quickly and I really believed we would die at Pilgrim's Castle. Had it not been for Paolo and his brave sailors we most *certainly would have been left to the tender mercies of the vengeful Turks.*

I write in haste because I am on my way to fight yet more battles in the never ending war with France, but you must know that I will come and see you and Enrico as soon as I can. I have only just read your letter so I am not thinking sensibly at the moment, but I will do my utmost not to cause a problem with your new life. But I MUST see you both.

It is unlikely to be soon because things are not going too well for us in France, but do not be surprised because it will happen. Take great care of yourself and Enrico.

My love to you both,

Richard

"Michael, is there any wax you can heat up so I can seal this letter?"

"Certainly, Captain, it will only take a minute or two."

"Good. Now can you tell me how I can have this letter delivered to Genoa?"

"Genoa, in Italy?"

"The very same."

Michael pondered for a moment. "Well, I know there's a cog that docks here every two or three months. It does a regular route taking in Lisbon, Cadiz, Rome, and Genoa. I don't know where it is now, but I could make sure your letter is on board the next time it arrives here. Is it urgent, Captain?"

"Yes, it is." Richard felt in his pouch and took out two silver Venetian ducats. "I don't know what the cog's captain will want for delivering this letter to Genoa, but two ducats will be more than enough, and you may keep whatever is left over because the letter is important to me. And here is a third just for you because this morning you changed my life."

"But, Captain, this is too much."

"Then give it to charity or whatever else you would like to spend it on. Just accept my gratitude and make sure this letter gets to the cog's captain next time he docks here."

"Thank you, Captain. I'll go down to the dockyard personally as soon as my shift is over, find out when the cog is due back in Rouen, and take it from there."

"Thank you, Michael, and I will see you again when Orléans has fallen."

"I hope so, but from what I hear, that siege is not going too well."

"True enough, but I am here to make sure we will win early in the New Year."

"Then the best of luck to you, Captain, and may God go with you."

Richard swept out of the office, mounted his horse, and kicked on for Paris. Michael was left wondering, *I don't know what was in that letter, but I'll make sure Captain Calveley's reply gets to Genoa, whatever it takes.* The veteran sergeant was as good as his word.

* * *

II

It took five weeks to complete the training of Fastolf's force, which consisted of seven hundred native-born English archers, fifty Parisian crossbowmen, one hundred mostly Norman French men-at-arms, and two hundred light cavalry known as hobelars, recruited in Norfolk and Suffolk. Hobelars were normally used for scouting and lightning raids, but occasionally they could be used as formal cavalry when conditions were right. Fastolf had a particular fondness for them because they cost less than a third per man of a fully armoured man-at-arms.

On the tenth day of February, Fastolf gathered his entire force just south of Paris ready for the march on Orléans. With them were four hundred wagons laden with bows, arrows, cannon, powder and shot, as well as victuals for Lent consisting primarily of barrels of salted herrings that would substitute for meat, which was forbidden during the forty days before Easter.

"Well, what do you think, Richard?" asked Fastolf after they had completed their morning inspection.

"The men look in good heart, Sir John, though I wish I knew them better."

"I had to scour most of the English shires to find enough volunteers. We don't want pressed men, do we"

"Of course not, pressed men desert, but only one thousand is not many, bearing in mind how few we are at Orléans."

"True, but this is only the advance guard. There will be four thousand more before Easter, by which time we shall be joined by an old friend of mine, Sir Thomas Rempston of Bingham in Nottinghamshire, who will bring another thousand after he has finished mopping up in Brittany. The Duke of Brittany needed a reminder of whose side he's on, and Tom was just the man to deliver it."

"Are they all English?"

"Almost all, the rest will be Norman French."

"You are confident in our French allies?"

Fastolf shrugged. "Not really, but they will be adequate for occupying trenches and bastilles as long as they believe they're on the winning side. Well, it's almost nine o'clock and high time to be on the march. Give the order."

The area between Paris and Orléans is known as the Beauce. It consists of open, rolling countryside ideal for cavalry warfare and easy for unfriendly eyes to observe military activity. Consequently, the movements of a large English force were soon reported to the dauphin's commanders, who began to assemble a considerable array to intercept Fastolf's column. The long winter refused to release its grip, and so the English marched under a clear, blue, winter sky and bitter cold. Soon, some of Fastolf's wagons were occupied by more than forty men suffering from fever or frostbite, but even so, the soldiers made good progress, and after just two days, they had covered fifty miles and were within a day of Meung on the Loire, the headquarters of the English field army.

But unknown to Fastolf, two French armies were closing in on his little force. The first, coming from the west, was commanded by the Count of Clermont, one of those nobles of the blood who had failed France so badly in the past, but his troops had taken no part in the fighting around Orléans and were fresh and eager for battle. His army contained around four thousand men. News of the English approach had also reached Orléans, and a second force of fifteen hundred men, including eight hundred hardy Scots, managed to slip past the English blockade and unite with Clermont's army ten miles south of Janville. The Orléans array included Dunois, de Xaintrailles, La Hire, and the Scottish commander Lord Darnley, as well as six of the Bureau brothers' field cannon, which were ready to engage the English for the first time. Unfortunately Clermont had seniority and therefore took command when the two armies united.

It was a few minutes after midday on the twelfth day of February; Richard and Sir John were riding at the head of the column when a hobelar scout came galloping back over the crest of a low hill just ahead of them. He pulled his horse up in front of the Norfolk knight. "Sir John," he panted, "Frenchies! Swarms of them!"

"Steady now," replied Fastolf calmly, "and there is no need to tug so hard at your horse's bridle, you may damage a valuable animal."

"Sorry, Sir John."

"Now, first tell me your name."

"John Stebbings, Sir John."

"And where are you from?"

"North Walsham, Sir John."

"A fine town, I know it well." By now the hobelar had calmed down somewhat, so Fastolf continued, "Now, Master Stebbings, we have plenty of time, so tell me how many French there are, and how far away are they?"

"Their leading outriders are half a mile away, but their main body is at least a mile from us. I saw maybe three thousand, but there must be more because they are still coming over the next ridge."

"Thank you, Master Stebbings," said Fastolf, "you have done well. Now go and call the other scouts in, then you may rest until the action starts. Off you go."

Fastolf and Richard cantered their palfreys the five hundred paces to the crest of the hill and halted at the top. They had a fine view of the surrounding countryside, which was studded with copses and some larger areas of forest, but mostly the land was well-tended farmland, which at this time of year was bare, brown soil except where the farmers had left green pasture to graze their animals. To their right, nestling close by a small stream half a mile below them, was a hamlet of perhaps eight cottages together with a barn and a small chapel whose polished bronze cross reflected the noon sun like a beacon.

Fastolf shaded his eyes as he looked at the French. "You have better sight than me, Richard. What do you think?"

Peter Tallon

Richard, who had a good eye for numbers because of his work as a military surveyor, answered, "Stebbings was right about the number in sight, but I would say the head of their main body is more like two miles away rather than one. A mixed force of footmen and cavalry in a ratio of about three to one, but they are still too far away for me to identify any banners as yet."

Fastolf looked from side to side. "Well, there's going to be a battle today, and where we are now is as good a place as any to fight. Go down to that village and, without frightening the villagers, find out its name. We shall name our victory after it."

Such was the confidence of the English at that time.

By the time Richard returned, the supply wagons were being formed into a large circle on the crest of the hill where he had last seen Fastolf. He searched for his master and eventually found him near the rear of the column urging forward the laggards; the French were now only a mile away, so there was no time to lose. When he saw Richard, Fastolf beamed a cheerful smile. "Ah, Richard, this is going to be interesting. It seems we are facing between four and five thousand Frenchies, so we must protect the supplies for Orléans before we take them on. Therefore, I'm forming our supply train into a defensive circle on the top of the hill, inside which we'll station all the civilian drivers, horses, men-at-arms, and hobelars. Outside, the archers can plant their stakes as usual to protect themselves against a cavalry charge and wait for the French to come into range. If they're pressed, they can fall back behind the wagons and shoot from there. What do you think?"

"Very sound, Sir John, but I'll be amazed if the French will do us the favour of launching a cavalry charge after what's happened in the past."

"True enough, but if they do, the chance of securing some ransomable knights will improve."

"Indeed it will, Sir John."

"What is the name of that village you've just visited yonder?"

"Rouvray Saint Croix."

"Well then, Richard, prepare to engage in the Battle of Rouvray Saint Croix."

Fastolf's men were ready and waiting for battle as the French and their Scottish allies slowly made their way up the hill towards the English position on top. The banners were now clearly visible, and the Scots took up their post opposite the English left, while the more numerous French faced the English centre and right. The Scottish men-at-arms now dismounted and assembled their ranks; clearly they had decided to fight on foot, but many of the French remained mounted, seemingly unaware of the devastating effect the longbow had on cavalry.

It was now nearly two o'clock. All seemed ready, yet there was no movement from the Franco-Scottish army. Richard stationed himself with a company of Welsh archers. In the last five weeks, he had got to know most of the men in Fastolf's array, but the Welsh tended to keep themselves to themselves. Beside him stood the Welsh company sergeant, Owain ap Griffith, a man of medium height and sturdy build whose heavy, black eyebrows met over the bridge of his nose.

Richard asked, "Have your men seen action before, Owain?"

"A few, Captain, but most are straight from the farm. Mind you, they're all good marksmen, I can vouch for that."

"Good. Do they all understand English?"

"Of course, man! The men of South Wales aren't barbarians see. We're not the same as those half-naked savages from up north round Bala."

The lilting Welsh accent was pleasing on the English ear. Richard smiled. "I did not mean to offend you, Owain, I just want to make sure there'll be no misunderstandings when the fighting starts."

"Don't worry about that, Captain, my boys know what to do, and I have already told them to aim low when firing downhill."

"And was it not the Welsh who gave the longbow to the English?"

"Indeed it was, Captain, in the days of the first king, Edward, the one called longshanks, and not before you English had felt its power from the sharp end."

Half an hour passed, and still there was no sign of an attack. The English could not know that there was a blistering argument taking place amongst the French leaders regarding tactics, but a few minutes before three, the Scots became tired of waiting for their allies, so Lord Darnley gave the order to advance. A rousing cheer went up from the English as the enemy at last moved forward, but the French remained motionless.

Fastolf galloped across to Richard. "Looks like the Scots are attacking on their own. Send two companies over to me. I'll return them to you if you need them."

"I will, Sir John."

Fastolf stood up on his stirrups and squinted towards the French array. "Have you noticed those tubelike things in the French lines?"

"Yes, Sir John, they look like cannon but are much smaller than anything I have seen before. I don't think we need fear them."

"Don't be too sure, Richard. As you know, I've made a study of artillery warfare. The French are years ahead of us both in metal casting and powder technology." As if to comment on the Norfolk knight's statement, six small cannon opened fire in quick succession, hurting no one but disabling one of the supply wagons by smashing two of its wheels.

"God's balls!" swore Fastolf. "That's good shooting. Get the men to lie down until the French make their move."

The Angel of Lorraine

"Certainly, Sir John," answered Richard, shaken by the accuracy of the first round. "I never thought such small cannon could have such an impact at that range. They must be at least five hundred yards away."

Fastolf turned his horse around and set off for his sector of the line, calling back to Richard, "God be with you, and get those two companies over to me as quickly as you can!"

The Scots advanced silently and menacingly, spurred on by the banner of Saint Andrew, the diagonal white cross on blue that they called the Saltire. By contrast, the English, as was their custom, shouted insults and profanities, some of which were witty enough to cause ripples of laughter, especially when referring to Scottish kilts. When the Scots were three hundred paces away, the English sergeants ordered silence so that Fastolf's orders could be clearly heard.

"Archers, ready!" Three hundred and fifty one-yard arrows were notched into their bows.

"Remember to allow for the slope! Aim low!" Each man selected his target.

"Draw!" A lifetime of practice built the muscle that enabled the archers to draw their longbows to the full length of the arrow; a normal man could manage only half of that.

"Shoot!" The snakelike hiss of arrows flying from their drawstrings was a comforting sound to the English but always chilled the ardour of the unfortunate victims on the receiving end. The brave Scots were no exception, and even at this extended range, many in the front rank fell screaming in pain as the lozenge-shaped arrowheads pierced their outdated armour. Only the high-ranking officers could afford the latest plate design, which was proof against the longbow except at close range.

But the Scots were undeterred and continued their inexorable advance. The English were too few in number to use their favourite portcullis formation, which ensured constant volleys of arrows at five-second

Peter Tallon

intervals, so Fastolf gave the order, "Shoot at will!" This was greeted with a stirring cheer. Now a steady stream of arrows descended on the Scots, but bravery alone was not enough to keep them going, and gradually their ranks began to disintegrate. Still the French made no move while their allies were being massacred.

Nearly half an hour after the Scots began their attack, the French at last joined the battle. Their first line consisted of a thousand mounted knights and men-at-arms drawn up in ranks four deep. About two hundred paces behind them came the dismounted men-at-arms, about three and a half thousand strong, advancing in an unwieldy mass.

Just as Richard was about to shout his orders, Fastolf rode up with a small column of archers trotting behind him. "Richard, the Scots are done for. I've brought three companies to reinforce you. When you've beaten off the French, come and join me in the wagon park with the hobelars as soon as possible."

"Thank you, Sir John. This won't take long, so I'll be with you shortly." Then taking a deep breath, he shouted, "Archers, ready! Await my next order!"

The French cavalry broke into a slow canter on the frozen ground; they would be in effective range in about half a minute. The impact of thousands of hooves on the hard ground could be felt rumbling through the archers' feet.

Richard said to his Welsh sergeant, "Owain, if anything happens to me, you are in command here."

"Understood, Captain."

Richard waited a few more seconds, then, estimating the French to be within one hundred and fifty yards, gave the order, "Archers, draw!" A short pause, then, "Shoot!" Five hundred deadly arrows were loosed with the familiar hiss of death. A moment later, the entire front line of the cavalry seemed to crumble. Wounded and dying horses shrieked in pain;

The Angel of Lorraine

almost as many were brought down unwounded as they stumbled over their kicking comrades, sending their heavily armoured riders plummeting to the unforgiving, frozen ground. The charge was stopped in its tracks.

"Shoot at will!" Richard hated giving that order. The cavalry was no longer a threat to the English; it was now a massacre, but there were still three and a half thousand dismounted Frenchmen coming up behind. But the panic-stricken horses did the work of the English for them. The terrified creatures behaved in the only way that came naturally to them and bolted back the way they came. The riderless horses galloped full belt into their own advancing infantry while those with riders still in place ignored the desperate tugging of their masters on their reins and did exactly the same. The infantry assault came to a shuddering halt as men were crushed under hooves or against each other. It would take many minutes for the chaos to be sorted out, but Richard made sure those precious minutes would not be afforded to the French.

"Owain, advance the line fifty paces and keep the French in range. Do not allow them to reorganise."

"Understood, Captain."

"I am going to see Sir John. I expect I'll be back shortly."

When Richard reached Fastolf, he found the hobelars and the men-at-arms already mounted and his own horse saddled and prepared for him. "We're going to charge!" boomed Sir John with delight. "The Scots first, then the French. They're all in confusion. They won't stand if we press home hard."

Richard quickly mounted and trotted up beside Fastolf. "Then let's be at it, Sir John!"

Fastolf stood up on his stirrups, raised his sword, and bellowed, "Cavalry, charge!" Some of the wagons had already been pulled aside to create a gap for the horsemen who thundered through and headed for the demoralised and debilitated Scots. There were less than two hundred and fifty English horsemen, but the effect of a well-timed cavalry charge on disorganised infantry was out of all proportion to the numbers involved. Now the bold northmen turned and ran leaving their Saltire banner to be crumpled under the hobelars' hooves. There was no organised resistance, but even under these terrifying circumstances, no Scots surrendered; they all fought to the death or until so badly wounded they could resist no more.

With the Scots beaten, the hobelars wheeled to their right and headed next for the confused mass of Frenchmen who were still recoiling from the English and Welsh arrow storm. Owain gave the order to cease shooting just before Fastolf's horsemen smashed into the flank of the panic-stricken French. There was no more fight left in them; they turned and ran for their lives. Now, the English horsemen and their mounts were exhausted, so the command not to pursue was obeyed; the Battle of Rouvray Saint Croix was over.

* * *

III

Being mid-February, night came early, so once the French and Scottish corpses had been stripped, they were left where they lay for burial until the following day. Richard and Fastolf sat by a campfire near Fastolf's tent and discussed the eventful day over some wine purchased in Rouvray, where the English army made camp for the night.

"Four English dead against more than seven hundred," ruminated Fastolf. "I never heard of such a thing before."

"Nor I, Sir John," agreed Richard. "You have won a most remarkable victory."

"How did the Welsh company perform?"

The Angel of Lorraine

"I was impressed. They are all marksmen as far as I could judge. Very few arrows were wasted. Can we get more of them?"

"Perhaps, but not this year. I only took them on because I was struggling to find enough willing Englishmen, but now they've proven themselves, I think I might go to Wales myself when Orléans has fallen and recruit some more."

"But you said four thousand more men are coming this year, did you not?"

"Yes, they'll be ready in the spring, and my agents are still scouring Normandy for some more suitable Norman French."

"Lord Talbot will be pleased with that. He'll at last be able to draw an unbroken cordon around Orléans."

Fastolf frowned. "Yes, but hopefully the city will have fallen before then. Our victory today will have disheartened the French."

Richard poked the fire with a broken arrow shaft. Bright sparks and smoke billowed up into the night sky. "They were badly led today, Sir John. Do we know who was in command?"

"One of the prisoners said he thought it was the Count of Clermont, one of the Valois family."

"That would explain it—another high-ranking noble of royal blood. Dunois or de Gaucourt would never have led an army like that. Clermont let the Scots, his best troops, attack alone before he did anything to help."

"Aye, Richard, which allowed us to concentrate our forces where the most danger lay and beat the French and Scots piecemeal."

"And you and I got through it all without a scratch yet again."

Peter Tallon

Fastolf did not respond immediately, but when he did, there was a note of concern in his voice. "Richard, did you glean anything else about today that we should be thinking about?"

"You mean the field artillery?"

"Exactly. If the French had been well led, we might have been sorely pressed, but consider this. If they had, say, thirty of those nasty little cannons and we had no wagons to hide behind, what then?"

"They might have won without attacking at all! The threat of their superior numbers would have forced us to stay concentrated in a tight-knit group, which would have made us ideal targets for their field artillery. We would have been obliged to attack or be blasted to pieces by cannonballs."

Fastolf nodded. "And there you have it. Today was a great victory for England, but we must not let our present superiority blind us to the technical advances that are taking place in France. Did we capture any of their cannon?"

"I'm afraid not, Sir John. They were withdrawn as soon as the attacks began."

"A pity. We must try and do better next time. Although we won today, I think we also had a glimpse into the future."

Richard had no answer. He took another pull from his goblet, but before he had finished, Sergeant Satterthwaite, one of the trainers who had worked with Fastolf in Paris, arrived out of breath and agitated. He spoke in a broad Yorkshire accent. "Sir John! Captain Calveley! There's trouble brewing."

"Then spit it out, man!" said Fastolf, annoyed that his private discussion with Richard had been interrupted.

"There's a Welshman taunting the English. He's challenging any Englishman to a wrestling match, and he's knocked over three of our men already."

"Oh, really!" snapped Fastolf. "There's nothing wrong with a bit of friendly competition."

"This is far from friendly, Sir John. The companies are gathering behind their champions, and if that Welshman keeps winning, I fear blood will flow."

Richard intervened. "Sir John, let me deal with this. It's the sort of thing that needs to be nipped in the bud, but it should not require the presence of a knight of the realm."

"Are you sure about that, Richard?"

"Not entirely, but if I fail, we still have your authority to fall back on."

"Very well, but we don't want to spoil a great day, so call me if you need me."

As they walked towards the scene of the trouble, Richard asked, "Sergeant Satterthwaite, you are with the Northumberland men, are you not?"

"Yes, Captain."

"Then you have big Will Armstrong with you?"

"Yes, Captain, but you know what he's like. He's as docile as a lamb until he sees the French."

"All right then, let's take a look at the problem."

Peter Tallon

The problem was soon apparent. Beside a blazing campfire stood a Welshman bawling a challenge to the English having just knocked over his fourth victim.

"Come on, you English! Is that the best you can do? My grandmother can fight better than that! Call yourselves soldiers! You're no more than a bunch of fairies!" Ominous growls and mutterings came from the English ranks born out of frustration, for the Welshman was indeed a formidable opponent. Five feet tall sitting down but barely five feet six inches standing up, he had the low slung physique every good wrestler needs. His legs were as thick as tree trunks, his shoulders broad and heavy, and knocking down Englishmen was his stock-in-trade.

"Sergeant Satterthwaite," said Richard. "Send Will Armstrong to me."

While Richard was waiting for the arrival of Armstrong, Sergeant Owain ap Griffith appeared at his side. "I don't like the look of this, Captain. Llewelyn earned his living as a wrestler before he joined the company. No one without formal training can beat him at his own game."

"Thank you, Owain, but I hope to end this here and now without calling on the help of our commanding officer." Then out of the shadows, big Will Armstrong appeared. "You want to see me, Captain?" he said in his barely understandable English, for he came from Corbridge in Northumberland.

Armstrong was the biggest man Richard ever met in his life. At over six and a half feet tall and muscular with it, he was a man of mountainous proportions. Yet as his sergeant had warned, he was as docile as a lamb probably because he had no need to fear anyone.

"Will, that Welshman shouting by the campfire is stirring up trouble that is likely to end in bloodshed. I need you to challenge him."

"But I have no quarrel with that man, Captain. Why not just let him shout his mouth off? He'll soon get bored if everyone ignores him."

An angry murmur came from the nearby English companies as a fifth Englishman was bowled over like a fairground skittle. "Will, I will not order you to do this, but for the sake of peace in our ranks, I ask you to."

"Has it not occurred to you, Captain, that I might lose?"

"Then you will have done all you could to help."

The big Northumbrian sighed. "Away then, let's get on with it."

A rousing cheer went up from the English as Will stepped forward to challenge Llewelyn. The Welshman turned to his countrymen and laughed. "Don't worry, boys, the bigger they are, the harder they fall, see. This boyo won't last one minute against me."

The two men faced each other for a few seconds, then Llewelyn, crouching like a cat about to strike, began to circle round Will. Will watched him but made no move. The Welshman was more than a foot shorter than Will and looked hopelessly outmatched, but he soon proved that to be an illusion. Suddenly he sprang forward, and keeping one leg on the ground, he launched a brutal kick with the other, which smashed into Will's shin. No one could have resisted a blow like that, and to groans of horror from his supporters, big Will sank to his knees. With a whoop of victory, Llewelyn followed up in a flash and gripped the Northumbrian in a strangulation headlock. It now seemed it could only be a matter of time before the Welshman claimed his sixth English victim.

Richard began to rue what he had done and decided he must stop the fight, but then, to everyone's astonishment, not least Llewelyn's, Will slowly got to his feet with his opponent dangling round his neck still with the headlock in place. He walked slowly, strolled almost, to the small stream that separated the camp from the hamlet and stopped beside its bank. A sharp punch to the bone behind Llewelyn's ear immediately broke the headlock and momentarily stunned him until Will tossed him into the freezing cold stream.

The icy water soon revived the Welshman. He stood up in the water, which was only thigh deep, and shouted above the cheers of the English, "You cheated! That was a foul move, see! Punching with a clenched fist is not allowed. I wasn't expecting it, see!"

"Away, man, nobody told me. I don't know the rules of wrestling."

"But you cheated. You're disqualified. I win!"

"Doesn't look like you've won to me. You're the one in the water."

"But you still cheated!"

"Let's call it a draw then. Here's my hand on it." The Northumbrian held out his huge, bearlike paw. Llewelyn flinched, unsure if this might be a fiendish trick, just the sort of thing he would do.

"Away, man!" said Will. "Take my hand, it's over now. A draw?"

Llewelyn drew breath to complain again, but thought twice as he saw the huge frame towering above him. "Well, all right then, it's a draw, but I would have beaten you in a fair fight, see."

"Of course you would. Now take my hand, and I'll pull you out of the stream." Will lifted the Welshman as if he was no weight and clapped him on the shoulder. "You dry out by the fire while I go and fetch some ale to celebrate our draw with." Llewelyn did not argue.

Richard said to Owain, "Sorry about that, but at least we've avoided something far worse."

"No need for sorry"—Owain chuckled—"you've done us a favour, see. Llewelyn's got too big for his boots, become a bit of a bully, see. The boys will be delighted big Will brought him down a notch or two."

"But it was a draw."

The Angel of Lorraine

"Only in Llewelyn's eyes. Everyone else knows he lost."

Will and Llewelyn drank long into the night. In the army, getting drunk together was considered a sign of friendship, and it brought the Welsh and English closer together. There were no more wrestling challenges after that.

And so ended the twelfth day of February 1429, the day of the Battle of Rouvray Saint Croix, which later became known as the Battle of the Herrings because of the victuals in the supply wagons that would feed the English army at Orléans throughout Lent.

But neither the elated English nor the dejected French yet realised that this day would mark the high tide of the English invasion of France. In less than two weeks, the ebb would begin.

CHAPTER FIVE

When the news of Rouvray reached Chinon, the dauphin's court was thrown into a black depression. A chastened Clermont arrived soon after the battle, blaming everyone but himself for the disaster, but the dauphin was not taken in by this and decided to wait for a report from Dunois, who had been wounded in the foot by an arrow. Along with de Xaintrailles and La Hire, Dunois returned to Orléans to assist de Gaucourt to prepare the city's defences for an imminent English assault, which seemed the most likely outcome of the battle. When it became clear that the dauphin would take no action until he had heard from Dunois, Clermont left in a huff with his entourage and remained a campaign spectator for the next few weeks, but he did learn from his mistakes and became a better leader for it.

Soon Dunois, still limping from his wound, travelled to Chinon to report in person to Charles, who met him in his private dayroom overlooking the River Vienne. It was early afternoon, and a steady drizzle seemed to mirror both men's subdued spirits. "Welcome, Jean," said the dauphin. "I am sorry to see your wound is troubling you."

"It is healing slowly, Your Majesty. The cold weather does not help."

"Thank you for making the journey from Orléans. I apologise for putting you through it, but I must know what really happened at Rouvray."

"You have received Clermont's account?"

"Yes, but it was full of bluster and self-justification."

The Angel of Lorraine

"I'm not surprised, Your Majesty. He was the problem. Not only was our attack badly directed, but we French discredited ourselves by allowing our brave Scottish allies to attack alone and unsupported."

"How so?"

"Clermont took command of our united army because of his rank and the fact that he brought twice as many men with him as we did. He ordered us to attack as cavalry, but I disagreed and reminded him of the many occasions that has led to disaster. La Hire and de Xaintrailles agreed with me, but Clermont insisted on a mounted charge."

"He's learned nothing from Agincourt then?"

"I'm afraid not. I could not accept his decision, and we had an argument. Meanwhile, the Scots became tired of waiting and attacked alone, so I was forced to follow Clermont's orders. But even then, he took so long arranging the order of battle ensuring his own men went in the first line so they could gain the glory from what he thought would be an easy victory, that by the time we advanced, the Scots had already been beaten with heavy losses. When we attacked, the inevitable happened, and most of the mounted men in the first line were brought down by the English longbowmen. The wounded horses turned and broke up the ranks of the following infantry as they fled, and before we could reorganise ourselves, English horsemen charged and swept us away. Before the day ended, I came across some Scottish survivors, no more than a handful of them, who had started to make their way back to Nantes to board ships for their homeward journey. They were disgusted with us. I was insulted and accused of cowardice. I cannot blame them for that. The twelfth day of February 1429 will always be remembered as a day of shame for French arms."

The dauphin remained silent for a while then asked, "And what of Orléans, Jean? Can the city hold out?"

"Not without a miracle, Your Majesty."

"But we cannot surrender to the English."

"No, but we could to Burgundy. We could offer to hand the city over to Duke Philippe on terms which would save face for us and look less like a defeat, especially if Philippe can be prised away from England."

"You recommend negotiating with Philippe?"

"Yes, Your Majesty, before the city falls to the English."

"But, Jean, you are in no fit state to travel to Burgundy, your wound has not yet healed."

"Then send de Xaintrailles with a clear mandate. You can rely on him, and if anyone can sweet-talk Philippe into a satisfactory arrangement, he can."

"Very well, send him to me."

Two days later, de Xaintrailles left Chinon for Duke Philippe's palace in Bruges, but when the dauphin offered him a companion for the mission, he made the surprising choice of Gilles de Rais rather than his good friend La Hire, saying he needed intellect for this task instead of a mailed fist. Seven days hard riding took them to Bruges, which was a very different city to its counterparts in northern France. Spring had just arrived, and as the two travel weary riders and their squires entered the city in the early afternoon, it was market day. The cobbled streets were lined with stalls overflowing with valuable ornaments, skilfully woven tapestries, and victuals of all types but especially fish because Bruges was also a port. There were no signs of the ravages of war in this Flemish city, just prosperity and contentment. The Frenchmen rode to the palace but were told that Duke Philippe could not see them that day but would make time in his very busy diary to meet them at half past the hour of eleven the next morning. Having ridden three hundred and fifty miles in just one week, the French emissaries were content to wait until the following day.

They arrived at the palace at the appointed time and were greeted by Burgundian servants who ushered them through the audience hall; clearly, the meeting with Philippe was going to be elsewhere. De Xaintrailles looked at the rich tapestries that adorned the walls and whispered to de Rais, "This makes our king's palace at Chinon look like a beggar's hovel. Clearly Duke Philippe is prospering from the war."

"Then when we have beaten the English," replied de Rais, "we shall call to account this treacherous duke who burns the candle at both ends. He will end up being scorched himself."

"Perhaps, but for the time being, we need him, so we must play an intelligent game. That is why you are here."

The French emissaries were taken to a private chamber where Philippe was waiting for them. Leaving their squires outside the door, they entered on their own; Philippe was taking no chances where the French were concerned, because in attendance were two large soldiers who stood guard either side of him. There was no one else in the room. The Duke of Burgundy cut an extraordinary figure. Everything about him was insect-like. Dressed entirely in black including a large, round, black hat, his pale skin seemed deathly white compared to the weather-beaten faces of the French. He had the long, aquiline nose characteristic of the Burgundy lineage, but most noticeable of all were his long, thin legs. They were so thin that his kneecaps stood out where they bulged beneath his tight, black hose. He seemed to have no muscle at all, so the thin, black sticks jointed at the knee looked to de Xaintrailles for all the world like large spider legs.

"Welcome," said Duke Philippe in a clear, high-pitched, nasal voice that, though quiet, was easy to hear because of its clarity. "Please forgive the delay in my seeing you."

"That is of no matter, Mon Seigneur," replied de Xaintrailles, "we are very pleased you have agreed to meet us."

"I could not see you yesterday in open court because my sister, Anne, was present. I am sure you know she is married to the Duke of Bedford, so her first loyalty is to England now. She is the mortar that binds Burgundy and England together, so I thought you would prefer to see me alone."

"Most astute, Mon Seigneur," acknowledged de Xaintrailles. "Our mission is confidential in nature."

"And what is your mission?"

"Mon Seigneur, Orléans may fall quite soon. We are still well stocked with armaments and soldiers, but the people are suffering. Supplies are getting through but not in enough quantity to feed the troops as well as the citizens. We must continue to nourish the fighting men, so it is the civilian population which is beginning to starve. We will never surrender, at least not to the English, but we hope we might reach an accommodation with you."

Philippe's eyes widened, though he tried to mask his surprise. The prospect of a choice morsel like Orléans falling into his hands without serious fighting was attractive indeed. It was not far from his home duchy and might, perhaps, pave the way to a considerable westward expansion of Burgundy. But of course, he must not appear to be too enthusiastic.

"But is not Orléans part of the hereditary territory of Louis of Orléans, the dauphin's uncle?"

"Who has been held hostage in England since Agincourt," countered de Rais, "and can do nothing to protect his own land or raise enough money for his ransom. Your English allies have broken the rules of war by attacking his land, so he cannot raise the money he needs. Under the present circumstances, he seems destined to spend the rest of his life as a prisoner in England."

Philippe's hooded eyes flickered with irritation; the implication was clear. He too had broken the rules of war because his own soldiers were alongside the English at Orléans. "Perhaps, perhaps not," he said stiffly.

De Xaintrailles was pleased de Rais had made the point, but ever the diplomat, he quickly stepped in to diffuse the tension. "Mon Seigneur, we would be prepared to surrender Orléans to you on certain conditions."

"Which are?"

"You will hold the city on behalf of Louis of Orléans if—or until—he pays his ransom in full. Half of the city's revenues will be paid to the English, but the other half will be reserved to build up the money for Louis's ransom. You will oversee these arrangements and ensure the terms are carried out properly."

This was beyond Philippe's wildest dreams. True, he would only occupy the city on behalf of his cousin Louis, but he would be in full control of the flow of revenues, and as long as the English were satisfied with their share, he could take as long as he liked finding enough money to pay the ransom; in fact, there might never be enough! Where property was concerned, the English had a saying, "Possession is nine-tenths of the law." Maybe now was the time to introduce this concept to the French. Extending the boundary of Burgundy westwards was now a real possibility.

Ignoring the prickly de Rais, Philippe addressed de Xaintrailles. "If I accept, you must understand I will need to persuade the English. You may have to be flexible with regard to their portion of the city revenues."

"Mon Seigneur, our mandate does not allow us to exceed what has already been offered, but I cannot believe a small but necessary change will affect the French view of this offer."

Philippe paused as if he was struggling with himself to decide on this matter, but at last he said, "Very well, I accept. Tell the dauphin that I will need a little time to consult with the Duke of Bedford, who is now in Paris, but I should be in a position to confirm my acceptance, perhaps with a minor change or two, by the end of March or early April at the latest."

De Xaintrailles frowned. "I am not sure. Another five or six weeks might be too long."

"Then what if the Burgundian contingent has a bout of blindness and deafness regarding your supplies during that time?"

"That would certainly help."

"Then I think we understand each other, Mon Seigneur," smiled Philippe.

The French emissaries returned to their hotel in Bruges and had lunch sent to de Xaintrailles's room. While they were eating a typical Flemish meal of smoked fish and bread, de Rais asked, "Do you think that meeting was a success?"

"Yes, in so far as our offer was accepted, but I have doubts about the attitude of the English. You and I know they have done all the hard fighting at Orléans while the Burgundians have done little more than cheer them on from the safety of their trenches."

"But unless the English can find more men, they will not dare to attempt an escalade on the high walls of the city. It all comes down to supplies."

"Indeed, and we can now tell Dunois and de Gaucourt to concentrate on resupplying the city through the east gate, where Philippe's soldiers are stationed. At least that is something definite we have achieved from this mission."

De Xaintrailles pushed away his plate even though not all the fish had been eaten, for he had lost his appetite due to what he felt he must say. "De Rais, I think we have spent enough time together on this mission to dispense with formality. You may call me *Jean Poton* if it pleases you."

"Thank you, Mon Seigneur, and you may call me *Gilles*."

"Excellent! Excellent! Then you will understand that what I am about to say is borne from friendship and is not intended to be judgemental. It concerns your private life."

"How does my private life concern you, Jean Poton?" asked de Rais guardedly.

"Are you aware of the rumours circulating the French court about your private life?"

"What rumours?"

"Rumours to the effect that you have sexual preferences for young children." De Rais was silent, so Xaintrailles added, "If the rumours are false, then I implore you to forgive me, and I will challenge any man I hear spreading them."

Still de Rais did not answer, so de Xaintrailles feared that the rumours were true. "You understand, Gilles, that the penalty for such a crime is death by hanging, irrespective of rank or family?"

Finally de Rais spoke. "I thank you, Jean Poton, for your honesty, and I know you have my interests at heart—"

"And the children's," interrupted de Xaintrailles.

"Of course. I shall think on what you have said and give you no further cause for concern."

De Xaintrailles was not quite sure what to make of that response, so he contented himself with another, "Excellent," and hoped de Rais had really taken notice of what he had said.

De Xaintrailles's reservations about the attitude of the English to the Burgundian acquisition of Orléans turned out to be fully justified. Duke Philippe visited the Duke of Bedford in Paris to discuss the proposal, but Duke John flatly refused to consider it because the idea of giving away part of his dead brother's inheritance was unthinkable. Philippe departed for Bruges angry and humiliated, and in order to save face, he gave orders for the withdrawal of the Burgundian contingent from Orléans, thus, at a single blow, nullifying the effect of the reinforcements Fastolf had brought in February after Rouvray. Now the English were more stretched than ever as they took over the vacated Burgundian sector, so the mission to Bruges had not been a waste of time for the French. For the present, the English somehow managed to continue the siege, but what would happen if the defensively minded French, who outnumbered them by two to one, suddenly decided to attack?

* * *

II

Jeanne and her escort of six managed to evade all enemy patrols as they crossed the hostile territory between Vaucouleurs and Chinon, and on the twenty-third day of February, they arrived at Chinon, saddle sore and weary. They found accommodation in a hostelry in the lower town where, after washing and eating an evening meal, Jeanne dictated a letter for Marcel to write announcing her arrival. The letter was sent to the castle; then they waited.

The very next morning, Yolande of Aragon, the queen mother, came to see them. The owner of the hostel, a portly man with a red face, the result of drinking too much wine, knew who she was and hurriedly prepared a room where she could meet his customers, but Yolande made it clear that she only wanted to speak to Jeanne. So while politely acknowledging Jeanne's escort, Yolande took her into the room provided for them where they could be alone.

Yolande spoke first. "You are Jeanne, the maid from Domremy who hears voices from heaven?"

"I am."

"Do you realise what a stir you have caused here?"

"No, but I am pleased to hear someone has listened to my words."

The Angel of Lorraine

"That someone is me. I am Yolande, the mother-in-law of the king."

"The king, as you call him, will not truly be king until he is crowned and anointed at Reims. Until then, he is the dauphin in God's eyes."

"Then tell me, Jeanne, why are you here?"

"To save France from the English."

"And how will you do that?"

"By defeating the English in battle with the army the dauphin will give me and taking your son-in-law to be crowned in Reims."

"But what makes you think you can do that?"

"I do not think, I know, because the voices from heaven have told me so. Charles will be the true King of France. He comes from the line that goes back to Jesus Christ himself. I have been sent to place him where he rightfully belongs—on his throne."

Yolande sat quietly for a moment considering what had just been said. This bold, teenage girl impressed her mightily. Her confidence was irresistible; she was well prepared for an audience with Charles. "Very well, Jeanne, I will arrange for you to meet my son-in-law. It is also important that some of the high-ranking nobles of France witness this meeting. Do not be overawed, they are only men. You and I know that it is women who truly make history."

They laughed together at that remark; the quiet but powerful sisterhood of women was beginning to make itself felt. Jeanne asked, "How should I address you?"

"In private, call me *Yolande*. In public, I do not know, because you do not accept that Charles is king yet, but after his coronation, *Your Highness* will do."

"Then I pray that will be soon. As for the high-ranking nobles you spoke of, I shall treat them with respect but not fear."

"That is more than most of them deserve." They both laughed again. "Jeanne, I am also here to tell you what to expect. First, there will be a delay of a few days before you will be granted an audience. Charles is waiting for the return of two of his close advisers who are on a mission to speak to the Duke of Burgundy."

"Good. Making Duke Philippe see his error in supporting the English must be one of our top priorities."

"An astute observation, Jeanne, but I fear we may still be a long way away from achieving that particular task. Now, when you have given Charles your message and convinced him it comes from God, as I am sure you will, you will be subjected to some of my senior ladies-in-waiting testing your virginity."

"I can cope with that."

"Finally, before you are given the army you need to accomplish your mission, you will be interrogated by the best clerical intellectuals and theologians in France to confirm that your voices come from heaven and not hell."

"I look forward to it."

"Good, but be careful. These are clever men. They will interrogate you with seemingly innocent questions, but if you give wrong or inconsistent answers, your credibility will be impaired."

"I do not fear that. I speak only the truth. Let them ask whatever they want."

Yolande smiled; her confidence in this peasant girl was strengthened still more. "Jeanne, have you any questions for me?"

"Yes, just one. Why are you helping me?"

"The answer is simple. You are the saviour of France and will place our rightful king on his throne."

Although greatly encouraged by Yolande's visit, Jeanne chafed at the delay, but at last, two days later, the call finally came. The royal messenger arrived just after six o'clock in the evening. It was already dark, which made the events about to take place all the more memorable than they would otherwise have been. Accompanied only by Marcel, Jeanne followed the messenger up the steep path, which was lit on both sides by torches, to the royal castle of Chinon. When she was shown into the great audience hall, her eyes were momentarily blinded by a blaze of light, the like of which she had never previously experienced after nightfall. The hall had been cleared of furniture except for a long table on one side bearing sumptuous food laid out in rows and patterns: a hog's head with an apple in its mouth; cuts of beef arranged round it in a style of petals around the centre of a flower; game birds placed in little clusters; and brightly coloured fruits, some of which Jeanne did not even recognise. Large silver bowls contained wine blended with fruit and spices that the guests could ladle into their goblets whenever they wished. Servants dressed in colourful hose and tabards bearing the royal coat of arms of France Moderne, large golden lilies on a dark-blue background, moved quietly among the assembly checking that everyone's needs were being met. The whole scene was illuminated by braziers lining the walls and huge chandeliers adorned with many scores of candles suspended above the heads of the gathering by long, black chains attached to the vaulted ceiling.

A tall, handsome man clad in a scarlet doublet and hose approached Jeanne and bowed. "Are you Jeanne the maid who has come to visit the king?"

"Yes, Mon Seigneur, though he is but the dauphin until he is anointed in Reims. Who are you?"

"Who do you think I am?"

"You are not the dauphin, though you pretend to be. You are one of those emissaries just returned from a mission to the Duke of Burgundy."

"But how can you possibly know that? Is it a miracle?"

"Nothing so grand, Mon Seigneur. I can tell you have only just returned because I am a peasant girl and can recognise the smell of fresh horse sweat on you."

The knight threw back his handsome head and laughed. "Jean Poton de Xaintrailles at your service, mademoiselle. Would you like me to escort you to the king?"

"That will not be necessary, Mon Seigneur, I shall find him without difficulty."

Even Marcel, though a knight himself, felt overawed amongst this exalted company, but he could not stop himself smiling as he followed Jeanne's little figure clad in a dull grey tunic and black hose, the clothing of a peasant man. He recalled that somewhere in the Old Testament, one of the books described a woman dressed in a man's clothing as "an abomination to the Lord," but no one here seemed to mind. The Old Testament scribe would have been even angrier had he been able to see Jeanne's hair, which was cut short in the style of a young boy. But she walked through the crowd as confident as a lion inspecting its pride until she caught sight of a small group of men standing a little apart from the rest near a great, wooden door. This group, which consisted of four men, two quite portly, one very fat who wore the grand chamberlain's chain, and one short and thin, seemed to Marcel more like advisers or clerks rather than knights of France, but as soon as Jeanne saw them, she quickened her pace and stopped in front of the thinnest of the four. She bowed and then curtseyed, an incongruous act in a man's clothing.

"Who are you?" asked the thin man.

"Very noble Lord Dauphin, I have been sent from God to bring aid to you and your kingdom."

"What if I am not the man you seek?" Then pointing to de Xaintrailles, he said, "That man is the king."

"In God's name, my dauphin," answered Jeanne, "it is you and none other, but you will not truly be king until you are anointed at Reims like all your predecessors. I shall take you there."

"What is your name?"

"I am Jeanne, the maid from Domremy in Lorraine. The King of Heaven commands that through me you shall be anointed and crowned at Reims as the lieutenant of the King of Heaven, who is King of France. You are the true heir of France and a king's son. I shall take you to be anointed and crowned if you wish it to be so."

"Jeanne, I do not doubt your sincerity, but how can I know your message is truly from God and not from the devil, who is capable of deceiving even the most worthy of people?"

Jeanne glanced from side to side then said, "Is there anywhere we can go and speak privately? I can prove to you that my message comes from God, but not without revealing some of your most secret thoughts."

The dauphin asked his three advisers to move away then beckoned Jeanne to follow him to a corner of the audience chamber and speak behind a curtain where there was no danger of being overheard. "Is this suitable, Jeanne?" he asked.

"It is, noble dauphin."

"Then you may proceed."

Jeanne touched the dauphin on the back of his hand in reassurance, something none of his nobles would presume to do. "What I am about to tell you has been revealed to me by those same voices which have given me the messages from God."

"I understand."

"Then I shall tell you what nobody on this earth knows except God and yourself. You have begun to doubt yourself, and because of that, you have asked God what you should do if Orléans falls. You have suggested going into temporary exile in Scotland or one of the Spanish kingdoms who are old allies of France, but you have received no answer. This is because God has now sent his answer to you through me, and Orléans will not fall if you give me the arms and men I need to save the city. Forget Scotland and Spain, France will triumph if you let it."

The dauphin did not respond for fully a minute. Slowly tears came into his eyes, and he clasped Jeanne's hand, which still lay on his. "I thank God and you for this day," he whispered hoarsely, his voice full of emotion. "You have indeed reported accurately my private prayers which no one else knows because I dare not give voice to my doubts, for if I lack confidence, it will spread through my supporters like the plague. But thanks to you, I doubt no longer. You are indeed a messenger from God."

"Then when do we march on Orléans, my noble dauphin?"

"It must wait a week. It is not enough that I believe in you, I must also convince my nobles and, above all, the Church. The senior clerics have had no part in your mission so far, but it is important that their approval is secured too. So after the queen's ladies-in-waiting have confirmed you are still a maid, which I am sure they will, you will be escorted to Poitiers, which is a day's journey from here, where you will be questioned by the leading theologians in France. They will vouch for your sincerity provided you answer them with the boldness and honesty you have just afforded me. While you are away, I shall have weapons and armour forged for you and a banner prepared to your design so that on your return to Chinon, you will be able to lead the French army to the relief of Orléans."

"Thank you, noble dauphin, I shall not disappoint you."

"Finally, tomorrow you shall meet one of my cousins, Jean, Duke of Alençon. He is only twenty-three but has already proven himself in battle and is not one of those royal nobles who thinks of his status before anything else. He will be in command of your army when his ransom has been paid, but he will take advice from our experienced generals in tactics, though in strategy he will defer to you. I believe you will like him because he is closer to your age than I am, and I know he will like you. He will also tutor you in handling weapons, which you must understand if you are to lead men in battle. Tomorrow I will arrange for you to move into the Coudray Tower, here in the castle. The men in your escort may then return to their duties, and I will ensure all your needs are met here."

"Noble dauphin, I would like, if it pleases you, to keep Marcel Sieur de Freuchin near me. He was the first knight who believed in me and helped Robert de Baudricourt to change his mind about providing me with the escort I needed to make the journey here."

"Then it shall be so. Now it is time to return to the main hall."

When they rejoined the gathering, many of the guests commented on the change in the king. He was observed to smile "radiantly," something none had seen before in this shy, retiring, and rather dull monarch. Clearly the maid from Lorraine had enthralled him, and this in turn astonished all those present except Yolande, who already knew the truth.

The interrogation at Poitiers took almost three times as long as the dauphin expected, but when the report reached him at Chinon, it was unambiguous and conclusive. For Charles, the wait had been particularly difficult because reports of his uncharacteristically fulsome response to Jeanne had circulated well beyond the court and had even reached Orléans itself. Rumours, as rumours do, became added to each time they were repeated, so that by now, stories of an angel sent from Lorraine by God to aid the French in the form of a humble peasant girl were causing excitement and anticipation in the towns and cities along the Loire. But what if the claims of this angel were rejected by the theologians in Poitiers? Then Charles's credibility, already at its lowest ebb since Rouvray, would never recover, and his hopes of retaining his throne would finally be at an end. If the Church turned its back on Jeanne, she would just be sent back to her obscure home in Lorraine, but for Charles, it would be as bad as Orléans falling to the English. His hands trembled as, in the privacy of his own dayroom, he picked up the letter he had just received from Poitiers and broke the seal of Regnault de Chartres Archbishop of Reims, who was the chairman of the committee that had interrogated Jeanne.

Ten minutes later, Yolande received a visit from a court official asking her to attend upon the king as soon as possible. The court grapevine had already informed her that a letter had arrived from Poitiers, so she guessed this was the cause of her sudden summons. She relaxed when she found her son-in-law sitting at his desk with a broad smile across his face.

He handed her the letter. "Mother, read this." She started to read the neat and precise script that had been written by a well-trained clerk. There was a great deal of tedious religious argument to wade through setting out the pros and cons of Jeanne's mission, but the conclusion was clear enough. "It was concluded by the investigating clergy after their interrogation of Jeanne, daughter of Jacques and Isabelle Darc, that there was nothing evil in her, nothing contrary to the Catholic faith, and that given the great need in which both the king and his kingdom found themselves, the king should make use of her assistance.'

Yolande handed the letter back to Charles. "Well, it looks like our angel from Lorraine has won over the Church!"

Charles jumped up from his desk and hugged his mother-in-law. "This would never have happened had it not been for you. France will be saved!"

"Charles, please put me down! You are squeezing me too tightly."

"Forgive me, Mother, but my elation is difficult to control."

"So I see. What will you do now?"

"First, I must calm myself. Miracle or no miracle, this is all about confidence. Two months ago, our soldiers ran away from a quarter of their number of Englishmen at Rouvray. Why was this? How could it be that men of the same stock as the Crusaders could behave in such a way? Confidence! The English knew they would win, and the French knew they would lose, and so it turned out. Yet the Crusaders, who were predominantly French, conquered the Holy Land and held it for two hundred years against appalling odds before the armies of Islam finally won back their homeland. How could this have happened? Because the Crusaders expected to win, for they knew God was with them. Now, thanks to Jeanne, that confidence will return to our men, and they shall drive the English from Orléans and eventually from all of France. This will not happen in weeks or months. It may take many years, perhaps not in my lifetime, but it will undoubtedly happen. I am certain of it."

Yolande smiled. "And the Bureau field cannon may have some say in the matter too."

"You are well informed, Mother"—laughed Charles—"as always!"

"You must prepare a great reception for Jeanne when she returns from Poitiers and publicly acknowledge her for what she is, the angel sent by God to save France."

"I shall do that and, at the same time, present her with her armour and banner with which she will lead our army to victory."

"What will the banner show?"

"It is Jeanne's own design with the gold fleur-de-lis of France set on a white background and Christ sitting in judgement over the world flanked by two warrior angels."

"Men will certainly follow that."

"They will, and now Jeanne will be able to prove the miracle by raising the siege of Orléans, which has dragged on for seven months, and chasing the English devils back to their foggy island."

"Charles, we must not rush this. Orléans should be enough for this year. As you already said, this may take some time. The foggy island may have to wait for a while."

Jeanne the Maid, as she was now known, left Poitiers in the third week of March. Word of her approach had got out, and crowds of ecstatic Chinon townsfolk lined the streets to welcome her back. A fair number of nobles were also present, though Dunois and his officers had returned to Orléans to help de Gaucourt. But young Jean, Duke of Alençon, a noble of royal blood, was there standing by Charles's side as he welcomed Jeanne back to the castle. This was to be a very public event designed to show to all Charles's approval of her mission and committing him to support her with the arms and men she needed to complete her work. As if heaven also approved, she arrived on a glorious spring morning that fuelled everyone's optimism on this day, the twenty-second day of March 1429.

The king, as he was known to everyone except Jeanne, received her in the courtyard of the castle where nobles as well as humble folk watched her dismount from the fine bay destrier given to her by Alençon and bow low before the king. Wild cheering broke out when, against all court protocol, Charles stepped forward and embraced the peasant girl from Lorraine. Jeanne had passed all the tests; now her mission could begin.

To many observers, this started there and then with yet another apparent miracle. Jeanne was presented with her armour and banner, but like any other great army leader, she needed a special, named sword; Arthur had Excalibur, Charlemagne had Joyeuse. When the king asked her what he should do about her sword, she immediately responded, "Please bring me the sword of Sainte-Catherine-de-Fierbois. You will find it behind the altar not buried too deeply. It has five crosses engraved upon it, but it will need cleaning for it is rusted now." An armourer from Tours, who was present in the crowd, was ordered to fetch it immediately because Sainte Catherine's church was only twenty-five miles from Chinon. The sword was exactly where Jeanne said it would be, and the clergy declared another miracle. The English, when they heard about this, said more prosaically that someone must have told her.

Jeanne did not stay long in Chinon because her army was assembling on the south bank of the Loire between Tours and Blois. There were many practical matters to consider, not least training her in the skills of war and becoming accustomed to wear armour for extended periods of time, which she would be obliged to do when on campaign. The Duke of Alençon took on this responsibility, and their friendship strengthened as the two youngsters practiced jousting and swordplay together while their more mature officers dealt with the important but mundane matters of supplies and logistics.

By mid-April, Alençon judged Jeanne was ready for combat. On the orders of the embittered Duke Philippe, the Burgundian troops had just withdrawn from Orléans, leaving the English lines stretched to breaking point, especially on the east side of the city; so on the twenty-sixth day of April, Jeanne left Blois and led her army to war.

CHAPTER SIX

By now the English were well aware of what was happening in Chinon, Tours, and Blois, but remained mystified as to how a low-born peasant girl could have captivated the court, the nobles, and the common people in the way reports suggested. This Joan, to use her name in English, even had the gall to send a letter to the Duke of Bedford and all his senior commanders threatening them with death and destruction if they did not immediately leave France and abandon the claim of Henry VI to the French throne. This was, of course, ridiculous because Henry, the son of the victor of Agincourt, had been accepted as the royal heir by no less than King Charles VI of France at the Treaty of Troyes in 1420. His mother was, after all, the daughter of Charles VI and sister to the false claimant now calling himself Charles VII.

But it was nonetheless discomforting to the more superstitious within the English ranks, who blindly accepted that God's will directly affected the affairs of men on earth, and who could, if he chose, change the fortunes of war. The desertion of the Burgundians from Orléans seemed to presage this possibility. For now, all the English could do was watch and wait and let starvation do its deadly work in the city. No one even considered that after seven months of siege, the French might suddenly go from defence to attack.

* * *

II

Leading the French army alongside Jeanne as they left Blois were La Hire and Gilles de Rais. The Duke of Alençon could not join them because the ransom he owed the English for his release after his capture at Verneuil had still not been fully paid. But Jeanne at once noticed that someone else was missing. "Where is de Xaintrailles?" she asked. "I met him at Chinon and expected him to be here."

"Jean Poton was wounded in a skirmish with the English," answered de Rais. "The injury was quite serious and enough to make him avoid action for a while."

"How long for?"

"The surgeons say at least till the end of May, but if I know Jean Poton, he will return to the front line well before then."

"I hope so. Where is he now?"

"In Orléans with Dunois and de Gaucourt."

"Good, then we shall meet him soon."

Progress was slow because of the numerous supply wagons attached to the army that were destined to provide relief for the starving people of Orléans, but by the evening of the twenty-eighth day of April, Jeanne realised something was wrong and called her commanders to attend on her when the army made camp for the night. De Rais soon felt the steely side of the warrior angel in their midst. "Where is La Hire? I ordered all my commanders to come to me."

"He is posting the sentinels. We are in enemy territory now and must be on our guard."

"But we have been travelling for two days, and we have seen nothing of the English."

"We have made a detour to the south to avoid their outposts on the south bank of the Loire. We shall cross to the north bank tomorrow at Checy."

"But that is upstream of Orléans, so we have passed the city already! We came here to fight the English, not creep round them. All this talk of avoiding the English, making detours, and so on is unnecessary. God has already told me we shall win. Do you not believe me? Have you no faith?"

"Of course we believe in you, Jeanne," answered de Rais, "but by waiting until tomorrow, we shall gain the benefit of a diversionary attack on the Bastille Saint Loup, which blocks our way."

"Diversionary attacks! Wait, wait, wait! Pah! Is that all you can say? God has promised us victory, yet still you hesitate."

"Jeanne, would you just listen to me for a moment?"

"Naturally, Gilles, but please do not speak of detours and delays."

"I shall not, but consider this. No one doubts you, and we are all certain of victory, but victories can be won cheaply or expensively. Just because God has promised France victory, that does not mean we should abandon basic military common sense. If we had attacked today, we would have been obliged to storm prepared, entrenched English defences, which would have been costly. But by fighting tomorrow in conjunction with Dunois and the garrison of Orléans, we shall secure victory at less cost to ourselves and much greater cost to the English. That means many more French mothers will see their sons come home after our campaign than would otherwise have been the case."

Jeanne frowned and was silent for a while, but then the frown disappeared and was replaced by a heartwarming smile. "When I was being interrogated by the theologians in Poitiers, one of the things they told me was that, for an ill-educated peasant girl, I could debate remarkably well. Today it seems I have met my match in you, Gilles, but from now on, please do not exclude me from the decision-making debate. I am capable of listening to reason, and anything that means more French sons will come home to their mothers will please God as well as me. We march to Checy tomorrow!"

The action on the twenty-ninth day of April was a skilfully coordinated affair managed by Dunois. The Bastille Saint Loup, one of the largest English fortifications, stood a mile and a half to the east of Orléans astride the road to Burgundy, but since the departure of Duke Philippe's men, it was now isolated from the rest of the army being the only English presence east of the city. From there, the English could interfere with French troops and supplies approaching from the east but could never entirely block off access to Orléans with just the three hundred and fifty men who occupied the bastille. But though this was not ideal, it was still enough to ensure that the citizens, and eventually the soldiers protecting them, did not have sufficient food to sustain them.

Half an hour before dawn, the French were ready. Dunois had decided to lead the garrison troops in person so that he could judge the moment when the English were fully stretched. Then he would leave the fighting under the control of de Gaucourt, gallop to Checy where Jeanne would be waiting on the south bank, and guide her and her soldiers and supplies into the city.

Dunois looked eastwards from his place above the Burgundian Gate. The sky was now just light enough for his men to see the ground they must cross before reaching the Bastille Saint Loup. In full armour, it would take at least half an hour to traverse the land between Orléans and the English, but the French would be approaching out of the dark from the west, so there was a reasonable chance of surprising the arrogant islanders. A silent advance was imperative; each one of the thousand men designated for the attack knew there must be no shouting, no cries of Vive la France!, no warning to the English.

His mouth now dry with tension, Dunois whispered the signal to his captains. The Burgundian Gate, which had been well lubricated with olive oil and goose fat, swung open silently. The French formed up in two lines: the first with handpicked axemen in the centre who would smash down the wooden palisades on top of the steep, earth ramps that protected the defenders; and the second consisting of men-at-arms led by de Gaucourt. There was no bugle, no resounding call to charge. Instead the French moved forward silently, determinedly, realising that this was the moment of truth. Dunois well knew that the French had failed in every attack they had made against the English for the last fourteen years. Only the inspiration of Jeanne the Maid gave him the hope that this time they would succeed.

Incredibly, they got to within a hundred paces of the bastille before the alarm was sounded, and by the time the English had awoken from their confident slumber, the French axemen had already hacked a path through the wooden palisades. The French managed to force their way into the bastille, but the English, now fully alive to the danger they faced, counterattacked and pushed the French out of the bastille after a short but bloody gutter fight.

But now de Gaucourt's second line arrived, and the struggle swung back in favour of the French. Dunois, his experienced instincts as his guide, knew that now was the moment to bring Jeanne across the Loire. Dawn had broken, and he easily found de Gaucourt at the base of the bastille rampart urging his men forwards.

"Raoul, hold the English as long as you can. I am going to bring Jeanne and her men across the river and into the city. Capture the bastille if you can, but don't worry if you can't; we will take it another day. Just keep the English in play until you see Jeanne's banner enter Orléans."

"I understand, Mon Seigneur," growled de Gaucourt. "The English are still trying to recover from our surprise assault. They will not trouble you for at least four hours."

The Angel of Lorraine

"That will be enough. Good luck and take care of yourself, my friend." And with that, Dunois galloped to the crossing at Checy.

* * *

III

By the time Dunois had crossed to the south bank and passed the Church of Saint Pierre and Saint Germain on his left, it was just past noon. He allowed his tired horse to walk up to the hilltop overlooking the town where a group of horsemen was waiting for him. He had not yet met Jeanne or seen her banner, but he knew she would be there. When he saw the white flag with the gold fleur-de-lis and Christ sitting in judgement of the world, he walked his horse towards the small figure in shining new armour beneath it.

Jeanne spoke first. "You are Jean Dunois, the bastard son of the Duke of Orléans?"

"Yes, and right glad I am at your arrival here."

"Was it you who decided that I should avoid the English and come to Checy?"

"Yes. I and my advisers agreed it was the safest and most prudent thing to do."

"Well, Dunois, Bastard of Orléans, do not presume your counsel is wiser than God's who advises me."

Dunois had expected something like this and was not angered by Jeanne's criticism. "Then now you are here, I shall make sure you will always be informed of matters as they happen, and your counsel shall be sought for all decisions. Now I beg you to cross the river and come with me to Orléans where the people deeply desire to see you. It is only their belief in you that has helped them to survive the last few weeks, which have been very hard. The way to the city is open, but not for long."

De Gaucourt did not manage to take the Bastille Saint Loup, but he succeeded in containing the English long enough for Jeanne and her vanguard to enter Orléans unmolested. By now it was getting dark, but the reception in the city was overwhelming. Torches had been lit and placed all the way along the main street from the Burgundian Gate at the east end of the city to the Renard Gate at the west end where the house of Jacques Boucher, the treasurer of the captive Duke of Orléans, was located. Boucher's home had been selected as the only suitable dwelling to accommodate the war angel from Lorraine and her entourage, but before she could get there, Jeanne, with Dunois at her side followed by her vanguard and the desperately needed supplies they brought with them, was obliged to parade along the main thoroughfare in Orléans where the people went wild with joy. It was as if the city had already been saved from the English.

Because the reaction of the citizens was spontaneous, the authorities had made no arrangements to manage their enthusiasm. Consequently, the relief column with Jeanne and Dunois at its head was frequently forced to stop when the press from the crowd became too great. Many wanted to touch "the Maid" to see if she was real while others were satisfied just to touch her horse. An abiding memory of many present that evening was the sight of the stonemasons and carpenters on the half-built Cathedral Saint Croix who had scaled the scaffolding to return to their workplaces to get a better view of the astonishing events taking place in the streets below. They had lit torches to see their footholds on the scaffolding, but to the crowds in the street, the torches seemed like lights in the sky reaching up to heaven. It all added to the magic of that unforgettable evening.

The noise was tremendous, even for Dunois, but the peasant girl from Lorraine took it all calmly and waved to the ecstatic citizens as if she had done this sort of thing many times during her young life. Nobody present ever forgot that evening, but at last, Jeanne and Dunois reached Boucher's house, dismounted at the stables, and went inside.

The Angel of Lorraine

Jeanne was not pleased and turned on Dunois as soon as the door was shut behind them. "Where is the rest of my army? I could see only the vanguard behind me."

"The king's orders were that as soon as you were safely inside Orléans, the main army must return along the south bank of the Loire to Blois."

"But how am I expected to beat the English with only my vanguard?"

"You also have six thousand men in Orléans."

"Earlier today you said I would be consulted on all decisions."

"And so you will be, but the army is obeying the king's orders, not mine."

"You have deceived me."

"I have not, and I do not agree with the king's decision either. Tomorrow morning, I shall ride to Blois and implore the king to change his mind. If I am successful, you shall have your army back in three days, but in the meantime, please assure me that you will not attack the English until I have returned."

"Why should I agree to that?"

"Because if you do not, more Frenchmen will die than necessary. If you wait for me and the rest of your army to return, your losses will not be so heavy."

Jeanne's anger subsided a little. She well knew that Dunois wanted only the best for her and France. She spoke more softly. "That's strange. De Rais said something similar to me only yesterday. I suppose I have the impatience of youth. Yes, of course I shall wait for you, Jean Dunois."

The next three days passed excruciatingly slowly for Jeanne. She did her best to occupy herself by meeting as many citizens as she could, including Jean Pierre and Elly, who had become famous as the slayers of the terrible Earl of Salisbury, and inspecting the English bastilles around Orléans, but she was not here to be a figurehead; she was here to fight. On the same day as Dunois departed for Blois, La Hire led a raid on the Bastille de Paris, the largest bastille to the north of Orléans. It achieved nothing and served only to arouse Jeanne's anger again because it was ordered without her consent. But on the fourth day of May, just before noon, Dunois, with Gilles de Rais alongside him, returned with the rest of Jeanne's army behind them. They had manged to persuade Charles to change his decision, and the battered English in the Bastille Saint Loup did not try to stop them.

The following four days changed the course of the war. The French were eager for battle with Jeanne as their leader, so an attack on the Bastille Saint Loup was planned to take place as soon as Dunois and de Rais returned. For the first time, Jeanne was going to experience the brutal truth of combat. Dunois, La Hire, and de Rais stood with her beside the Burgundy Gate. All were in full armour. De Freuchin stood a little behind Jeanne carrying her banner. Two thousand French soldiers were crammed into the small square behind the gate and all the streets and lanes leading to it.

Jeanne looked at them admiringly. "They have the light of battle in their eyes, do they not?"

"They are inspired by you, Jeanne," answered de Rais.

"Have they all been shriven and blessed?"

"All as you ordered," answered Dunois. "We will attack in two waves. The first will be led by Etienne and Gilles. You and I will lead the second."

"But I should be at the front where the men can see me."

"No, you should not," countered Dunois. "You are no longer just an 'ill-educated but inspired' peasant girl, you are the leader of the army of France. Every soldier here knows that the leader should be at the head of

The Angel of Lorraine

the second wave so he, or in this case she, can determine where and when it can be most effectively used. Their lives depend on you making the right decision."

"That is true," whispered Marcel, Sieur de Freuchin from behind her. "He is trying to help you lead properly. It's what the soldiers expect."

"Very well then, sound the advance."

War horns echoed around the city walls as the first thousand men spilled out of the Burgundy Gate and began the advance in column formation across the flat plain that led to the Bastille Saint Loup, a mile and a half away, where the English were waiting for them. This time they would not be taken by surprise. Two hundred paces behind, Jeanne and Dunois led the second column. The remainder of the city garrison under de Gaucourt stayed on alert ready to intercept any attempt by the English to send help to the Bastille Saint Loup.

The approach to the bastille took half an hour because all the French, except for the officers, advanced on foot. The damage to the palisades caused by the fighting on the day Jeanne arrived at Orléans had been repaired, and the English seemed well prepared for the dance of death, which was about to take place. Neither they nor the French were in the mood to give quarter.

At four hundred paces from the bastille, La Hire gave the order for the first wave to deploy into line, then waited for the second column to do likewise behind him. At just after four o'clock, all was ready. The banners were raised, and La Hire shouted, "For King Charles, France, and the Maid, forward!" The French cheered and charged as fast as their armour would permit. As soon as they were in range, the English let loose a hail of arrows, but the French held their shields high and kept going. Many fell, pierced by the dreaded one-yard shafts, but inspired by Jeanne, and La Hire's threats and swearing, they scrambled up the earth wall and began trading blows with the English at the palisade.

Jeanne and Dunois watched from the second wave, which had halted a bowshot behind the first. Jeanne could not contain herself. "Look! The attack has been held! We must go and help!"

"Too soon, Jeanne," answered Dunois calmly. "We must watch and wait until we see where we can be of most value. It is difficult I know, but before we move, we must understand where the English are really holding and where they are breaking."

It took some minutes before the action began to clarify, and on the left, some of the French began to fall back into the ditch below the palisade. Dunois began to consider supporting the left, which was starting to crumble; but then on the right, a surge led by La Hire, wielding a huge battle-axe, broke through the palisade and forced its way into the bastille. But the English could be seen running from other parts of the line to plug the breakthrough; it would only be a matter of time before La Hire was pushed back.

Dunois had to shout to be heard above the din of battle. "Now, Jeanne! Unfurl your banner and charge up there on the right. That's where the battle will be won!" Marcel handed Jeanne her banner, and with a mighty roar, the second wave rushed forward following Jeanne and Marcel up the rampart and through the broken palisade just as La Hire's men were beginning to falter. The arrival of the second wave was decisive. The English did not run, for there was nowhere to run to, and they knew no prisoners would be taken on this day, so they fought to the death or until they were too wounded to fight any more. The flag of Saint George in the centre of the bastille was torn down and replaced with Jeanne's banner while the English were cut down, pummelled, and slaughtered. The victory was complete, the English annihilated. Only one man escaped under the cover of darkness.

The French set fire to the Bastille Saint Loup and returned to Orléans in triumph. Here they discovered that a second battle had been fought when de Gaucourt led part of the garrison out of the city to intercept a relief force, which had been sent from the Bastille de Paris to support

Sainte Loup. The relief force was turned back, so the day was a double victory for France. Years of unbroken defeats were avenged at last.

That evening, in contrast to the wild celebrations going on in Orléans, Jeanne sat quietly in Jacques Boucher's house trying to eat a small meal. She had now experienced battle for herself, and it affected her deeply. She drank some wine, excused herself from the presence of Dunois, La Hire, de Rais, and de Gaucourt, and went to bed. All four men understood.

* * *

IV

With nothing to fear from the east now that the Bastille Sainte Loup had fallen, the French turned their attention towards the English garrisons south of the Loire. But in the hour before dawn on the fifth of May, a wounded and exhausted English soldier staggered into Talbot's headquarters in the Bastille Saint Laurent on the west side of Orléans. Talbot was already awake; in fact, he had not slept all night due to the loss of Saint Loup. He gave orders for the wounded soldier to receive medical attention and then called his war council together to hear the survivor's report.

The sun was just rising on another beautiful spring morning, but there was nothing beautiful about it for the shocked English. The war council was waiting when the fugitive from Saint Loup was escorted into Talbot's tent. Present were the second-in-command, the Earl of Suffolk, Lord Scales, Lord Roos, and Sir John Fastolf.

Talbot, sitting at the head of the campaign table, addressed the exhausted soldier who bore the stripe of a sergeant on his arm. Like his commander, he had not slept for twenty-four hours. "Your name, sergeant?"

Peter Tallon

The sergeant, a swarthy, black-haired man who looked as though he had been carved out of solid oak, answered, "Alfred Hayhurst, my lord. I am—er was…a sergeant in one of Sir Michael Sheldrake's Cheshire companies."

"Sit down, Sergeant Hayhurst. Are you well enough to give this council your report?"

"Yes, my lord. My wounds are less serious than they look."

Talbot looked at the cuts and bruises on Hayhurst's face and the trails of dried blood on his brigandine jacket. "You seem to have been through a hard time, Hayhurst. What happened?"

"As you know, my lord, we drove off an attack five days ago without too much difficulty, but even then we noticed the French fought more aggressively than usual. Yesterday they came at us like lions. We held their first line for a while, but then they managed to break through the palisade on our left. I could not see much because I was on the right, but we seemed to be pushing the French back when their second line hit us. It was led by that Joan woman we've all heard so much about. She waved her banner and encouraged her men with no fear of the arrows shot at her. How they all missed, I'll never know. It was as if she had an invisible protector."

"Then what happened?" asked Talbot.

"The second line broke through in many places. There was no way we could drive the French out this time. There were too many of them. The struggle broke up into small knots of Englishmen fighting for their lives against many more French. The French were taking no prisoners, so we knew we just had to fight it out and take as many of them as we could with us to the next world. The last thing I recall was my company being reduced to about twenty men, then I was confronted by a large Frenchman, and everything went black."

Talbot said, "You mentioned that the French fought like lions. Why do you think that was so?"

"We all believed it was because of that Joan woman. Some said she is a witch. I don't know about that, but she did seem to cast a sort of spell over the French."

"And how did you manage to find your way back here?"

"When I awoke, I couldn't move because I was under a pile of bodies. The French must have thought I was dead. I could smell burning flesh and guessed they were burning our bodies instead of burying them, so I wriggled my way out of the heap of corpses and, by the light of the flames, saw Frenchmen moving about setting fire to our camp inside the bastille. I crawled to the edge of the rampart and rolled down the outside slope, then, crouching low, I ran to a group of trees nearby and hid until the French went back to the city. When all was quiet, I walked back here."

"My lords, does anyone else have questions for Sergeant Hayhurst?" No one did, so Talbot continued, "Your information is most valuable, sergeant, you have done well. Where are you from?"

"Chester, my lord."

"Do you have family?"

"Yes, my lord, a wife and two fine sons. They say they want to be archers when they grow up."

"And right good ones they'll be if they grow up like their father," smiled Talbot. "I shall write you a two month pass, Sergeant Hayhurst, so you can go home to your family and recover there. Now go back to the medics and have your wounds dressed again. I can see blood still oozing from some of them. Until you leave, you shall be temporarily attached to one of Sir John Fastolf's companies. Dismissed."

"Thank you, my lord." Hayhurst stood up, wobbled slightly, and left Talbot's tent.

"Well, my lords, what do you make of that?"

As second-in-command, Suffolk responded first. "My lord, things have changed. The French have gone on the offensive, which is something we did not anticipate. Their success at Saint Loup will only encourage them to try again. We are now down to less than three and a half thousand men fit for duty. We can no longer seriously hinder the French from sending men and supplies into Orléans using the Burgundy Gate, so I propose we withdraw to Paris, link up with Sir John Fastolf's reinforcements, and resume the offensive in June."

"Thank you, my lord," said Talbot coolly. "Are there any other views?"

"Yes, my lord," replied Fastolf. "Let us stay here, hold what we have, and await my new army. We can reduce the garrisons at Beaugency, Meung, and Jargeau to the bare minimum to make up our losses here and still make life difficult for the French when they try to resupply Orléans even though we cannot stop everything."

Talbot asked, "How many, and when will your new army get here?"

"Early to mid-June, though I am not yet sure about their numbers. At worst, there will be four thousand, but if Sir Thomas Rempston quickly concludes his campaign in Brittany, that number will swell to nearer five thousand."

Young Lord Scales, always looking to attack, intervened, "My lord, with Sir John's five thousand and the three and a half thousand we still have here, we will be able to take the offensive again. Surely we should stay here and wait as Sir John has suggested? We must not abandon our positions."

There were no more comments, so Talbot said, "My lords, we will stay here, dig in, and wait for Sir John's new army. Then we will end this interminable siege even if we have to escalade the walls. With eight thousand Englishmen at our backs, we shall show the French who are the true masters of war!"

Talbot received spontaneous applause from all present except Suffolk, but if the English thought they would be allowed to wait in peace, Jeanne had other ideas.

* * *

V

While Talbot was holding his war council meeting, Jeanne with two thousand fresh soldiers from the Orléans garrison was crossing the Loire to attack the Bastille de Saint Jean le Blanc, the easternmost English bastille south of the river. But when the attack went in, there was no fighting because the English had abandoned this position and concentrated their forces at the much stronger Bastille des Augustines, the deserted priory, which was less than two hundred paces from the redoubt protecting the Tourelles. This alone showed how the English had come to respect the new fighting prowess of the French; a week earlier, they would never have walked away from a fortified position.

The French were encouraged and built up their forces during the rest of the day for an attack on the Bastille des Augustines, which both sides knew would take place on the morrow, the sixth of May. Fastolf's companies were based in the bastilles called Rouen and London, which were on the northwest side of Orléans, so Richard was spared what was to come.

As dawn broke, Jeanne, in an attempt to avoid further bloodshed, rode with de Rais and Marcel waving a white flag of truce up to the Augustine bastille and asked to speak to the English commander whose name she already knew, Sir William Glasdale. The shadows were still long, and Sir William did not appreciate being woken sooner than was necessary. A crusty, experienced commander, he had no patience with the so-called Maid of Orléans and refused to speak in French, which he could easily have done.

Glasdale stood on top of the priory wall that formed part of the bastille rampart, arms folded, and glared down at the group of three below him. "What the hell do you want!" he demanded.

Marcel, who had learned the coarse language at home in Picardy because English-occupied Calais was not far away, replied for Jeanne, "The Maid of Orléans, who is beside me now, wishes to prevent further bloodshed. Your position is hopeless, but she offers you a truce, during which you will leave Orléans to its rightful owners, the French, and depart from France with the promise that you will never desecrate our country again."

"Bollocks!"

"I am sorry, but I do not understand the meaning of the word *bollocks*."

"Then tell that peasant girl that the English never surrender, and even if they did, it would not be to that whore you call the Maid. What she needs is a damn good rogering, and if the French can't do it, we will!"

Marcel said to Jeanne, "Glasdale refuses your offer."

"But he said more than that. Tell me the unvarnished truth."

"I cannot. He said something which casts doubt upon your virginity."

"Then tell him that the offer comes not from me but from God in heaven, who speaks through me."

Marcel did as Jeanne requested, only to be rebuffed again by Glasdale. "That whore does not speak for God, who is an Englishman as everyone knows. Any spiritual message she has heard must be from the devil, and we shall burn her as a witch when we catch her." This brought cheers from the English and raucous laughter when an archer pulled down his hose and waved his bare backside at the French.

De Rais growled menacingly, "They shall all die for that."

Jeanne said, "But, Gilles, do they not understand I am offering them their lives?"

"They are too stupid to realise they have no hope. We are wasting our time here." And with that, they galloped back to the French lines, and Jeanne ordered the assault to begin.

With de Rais, La Hire, and Dunois at her side, as well as the ever faithful Marcel, Jeanne led the attack in person. But Glasdale had a surprise in store for her, and instead of waiting, he led half of his garrison out of the bastille and took the French head-on. The English and the French had not fought in the open since Verneuil five years before. Jeanne, who had yet to fight in close combat, was almost unhorsed when an English man-at-arms riding a large, black warhorse bumped her much smaller mount, knocking it momentarily to its knees, but the natural balance she had acquired from riding farm horses at an early age enabled her to stay in the saddle though at the cost of dropping her banner. The Englishman raised his mace for a killer blow, but de Rais and La Hire saw the danger and chased him away before he could strike while Marcel dismounted and handed the banner back to Jeanne.

"You must be careful in battle, Jeanne," he said. "Never allow yourself to become isolated. Did not Alençon tell you that?"

"He might have, but I forgot. I shall be more careful in future."

The fall of Jeanne's banner disheartened the French, who began to withdraw under the determined attack of Glasdale's Englishmen. As soon as she saw this, Jeanne called to La Hire and de Rais, "Why are we retreating? We must go forwards! The English are exhausted. Follow me!" Then raising her banner again, she called out to anyone near enough to hear, "All is well! God is with us, he will give us victory today! Have faith and follow me!"

Despite what she had said to Marcel only seconds before, she rode her horse straight into the middle of the English with her banner fluttering above her like a beacon of hope to the French. La Hire, de Rais, and

Marcel charged after her fearing she would put herself in danger again, but those French who heard her turned and followed while Dunois rode to the others, who were still hesitating, waving his sword above his head and urging them to help the Maid to victory. It was enough, just. Two thousand counterattacking Frenchmen cheering loudly for the Maid was too much for the English. They fled back to the cover of the bastille, but the French began to slow down as the English disappeared behind the priory walls. La Hire and de Rais trotted their horses back to Jeanne. "Well done, Jeanne!" exclaimed La Hire. "You've saved the day!"

"No! No! We haven't finished yet. We must keep going until we've taken the bastille! The English will not stand if we attack now!" De Rais and La Hire looked at each other. They were both tired and wanted the fighting to end for the day, but Marcel dismounted and handed his horse to a squire. "Mes Seigneurs," he said, "Jeanne is right. Now is the time, we must keep going!"

There was no place for mounted men when storming a fortified position, so the French men-at-arms dismounted and followed Jeanne's banner up to the priory walls where they began to exchange blows with the English on the other side. The walls were designed for enclosure, not war, and were only the height of a tall man. The English had built a fighting platform inside the wall and so had the advantage of being able to rain blows downwards on the French, but they had been shaken by the unexpected counterattack. La Hire, the most athletic of the French commanders, saw a low point in one of the walls, where a few courses of the stone masonry had fallen away, and headed straight for it. Covered by crossbowmen from his personal bodyguard, he scrambled over the wall and began to trade blows with three Englishmen on the other side, but the men of his bodyguard were close behind him, and soon enough Frenchmen had managed to get over the wall and form a small enclave that was rapidly being reinforced from behind. It was clear that the bastille was falling. Suddenly, without orders, the English broke and ran to the safety of the Tourelles enclosure, leaving behind almost a hundred dead and wounded. The Bastille des Augustines was back in French hands once more.

The fighting had lasted all day; the losses were heavy on both sides, but Jeanne and the French were elated by their greatest victory yet. She had received a small but painful wound in her foot from a mace blow, so she missed the evening war council meeting while she was having medical treatment back in the city. This meeting, which would last more than two hours, was held because the next target, the Tourelles, would be the toughest objective confronting the French since the siege began. It took place within the Bastille des Augustines in a hastily erected campaign tent because the fine spring weather had broken and a heavy downpour of warm, early summer rain had just started. Present were Dunois, the army commander, La Hire, de Rais, de Gaucourt, and an almost recovered de Xaintrailles. Also invited was Marcel, Sieur de Freuchin, as Jeanne's representative.

"Mes Seigneurs," began Dunois, "let me first allay any concerns you may have about Jeanne. Her foot was badly bruised by a mace blow when she was climbing over the priory wall today, but no bones were broken, and she says she will be with us for tomorrow's assault. I also welcome back Jean Poton and congratulate you on the speedy recovery from your wound, but with your arm still in a sling, I fear you can only be an onlooker tomorrow."

De Xaintrailles replied, "One more week, Mon Seigneur, and I shall be in the saddle alongside you and the other brave knights present here."

Dunois smiled, delighted that the darling of the ladies of France would soon be in action again. "Excellent! Now, I know our men are tired, but so are the English. They must also be dispirited after today because the Bastille des Augustines was considered to be a formidable obstacle. The Tourelles towers and the rampart linking them will be an even tougher assignment, but if we can take them tomorrow, we shall have gained control of the south bank of the Loire, which, when added to the fall of the Bastille Saint Loup, means we can resupply Orléans at will. The siege of Orléans will in effect have been lifted."

"How many English are in there?" asked de Rais.

"We believe about six hundred," answered Dunois.

"But we can bring six thousand to this party if we choose," said La Hire.

Dunois shook his head. "Not really, Etienne. The English also know that the Tourelles are the key to the city, so we must keep a substantial reserve available to cut off the reinforcements that will inevitably be sent to assist the defence. I believe we should attack with three thousand, no more."

"But last October, the English overran the Tourelles in just minutes," said de Gaucourt. "Surely we only need half the number you are proposing to drive out six hundred English dogs."

"But remember, Raoul, we chose not to defend the Tourelles," answered Dunois. "Things were different then. We did not yet have Jeanne with us. It is certain that the English will contest every pace of ground. They expect no quarter and will be fighting for their lives. We know the Tourelles defences are strong because we built them. The Tourelles stand on a small island separated from the south bank of the Loire by an arm of the river, but linked to it by a short bridge. On our side of the bridge is a heavily fortified rampart which extends in a half circle from the Loire with each end touching the riverbank and the middle facing us here in the Bastille des Augustines. This rampart forms a redoubt that protects the southern end of the bridge to the Tourelles. So not only must we capture the redoubt, we must also force our way across the bridge before we can assault the Tourelles themselves."

No one spoke for a while as the council digested the magnitude of the task confronting them. Then the thoughtful de Rais asked, "Mon Seigneur, once we have taken the redoubt, do we actually need to assault the Tourelles? Would it not be sufficient just to occupy the redoubt because then the English will be cut off on the Tourelles island with no hope of resupply or escape? We could just starve them out, and meanwhile there is nothing they could do to interfere with our troops and supplies coming and going from the city as we please."

The Angel of Lorraine

"You make a good point, Gilles," acknowledged Dunois, "but there are two problems. First, the redoubt is in easy range of English longbows shooting from the Tourelles, but I suppose we could cope with that, and without resupply, they will eventually run out of arrows. But second, and far more important, our agents in Paris tell us that the English are building a new army to send south to join Talbot at Orléans. It is said to be many thousands strong, so we must make sure all resistance here is ended before they arrive. We simply do not have enough time to rely on starvation achieving our aims."

"Then we have no choice," agreed de Rais, "the Tourelles must fall, and quickly."

"And we have one more weapon available to us," continued Dunois, "one the English will not expect: the armed militia of Orléans. When we have captured the redoubt, at a signal from us, the city militia will attack the Tourelles from the north bank of the Loire."

"God save us from the militia!" exclaimed La Hire. "They're an undisciplined rabble and more a threat to themselves than the English! And may I point out that the bridge linking the city to the Tourelles was destroyed by us last October."

"That is true," said Dunois, "but the supports are still in place. Wooden planks have been prepared, which are long enough to span the broken arches and allow the lightly armed militia to cross. I do not expect them to engage in heavy fighting, but when the English see they are being attacked from both north and south, they may choose to surrender."

"But we'll be taking no prisoners," said de Rais grimly.

"We may have to take a few," replied Dunois. "We are French and know the meaning of mercy."

"It is what Jeanne would want," said Marcel.

And with a touch of steel, Dunois added, "And you will obey orders, de Rais."

The discussion then concentrated on tactical details, in particular how de Gaucourt would stop English help reaching the Tourelles while Dunois led the attack from the Bastille des Augustines, but at the end of the debate, Dunois concluded by saying, "My friends, tomorrow will be hard and bloody, but with God's help, we shall prevail. I know you are all concerned for Jeanne's safety, so I ask you, Marcel Sieur de Freuchin, to persuade her to rest tomorrow and give her wound time to heal."

Marcel replied, "I will try, Mon Seigneur, but you know what she is like. She believes it is her God-given duty to lead her men into battle."

"Well, do your best, that is all I can ask. Now all of you get a good night's sleep. It is possible that some of us may not come back tomorrow night, so I would like you all to know that I am honoured to have served with each and every one of you, and may God protect you tomorrow."

"And you too, Mon Seigneur," they all replied.

* * *

VI

The seventh day of May dawned misty and damp. The heavy rain had stopped, but a steady drizzle had set in, which kept the ground slippery and wet, but at least the poor visibility favoured the attackers. Jeanne, of course, refused to countenance, missing the battle, and joined Dunois in the second line while La Hire and de Rais led the first. But before the assault began, Jeanne insisted on speaking to Glasdale once again to try and avoid unnecessary bloodshed. As on the previous morning, she rode forward with de Rais and Marcel under a flag of truce. They stopped at the base of the earth rampart, which was the height of four men, and

Marcel called out in English that the Maid of Orléans wished to speak to Sir William Glasdale.

Seconds later, the tall, bearded knight appeared and stood on top of the rampart glaring down at them. "Not you again! Well, what is it this time!"

Marcel answered for Jeanne. "The Maid wants no more bloodshed. You are cut off from the rest of your army and have no hope of help, but if you lay down your arms now, your lives will be spared and you will see your families again when this war is over."

"So there can be no misunderstanding or alterations in translation," replied Glasdale, speaking in French, "I shall now answer you in your own effeminate language." Then addressing Jeanne directly, he said, "If you want our arms, then come and get them if you dare. Otherwise, go back to that dark witch's hole you crawled out from and leave the fighting to the men, you peasant whore!"

De Rais could not contain himself. "Glasdale, I am Gilles de Rais, and I shall personally cut off your head and rip out your disgusting entrails!"

"Better men than you have tried, you strutting French cockerel. Now piss off before I order my archers to give you the sharp end of fine English ash!"

De Rais seemed confused by the answer, so Marcel whispered, "He means an arrow when he talks of ash."

"English pig!" shouted de Rais.

"Oink, oink, ha haah!" roared Glasdale to the delight of the English.

"Well, we tried," muttered Jeanne as she turned her horse to face the French lines. "Glasdale is a brave man, but what a stupid waste of life."

"All the English are stupid," growled de Rais angrily.

Marcel, casting his mind back to that day at Agincourt when an Englishman saved his life, responded, "Not all Englishmen are stupid, Mon Seigneur." De Rais raised his eyebrows, shrugged, and galloped off after Jeanne.

The horses were taken to the rear; the assault, entirely on foot, began just after nine o'clock. From the beginning, it went badly. The rain during the night had turned the front of the rampart, which was constructed of clay, into a slippery surface. Even had it not been defended by a determined foe, it was still a formidable obstacle to men in heavy plate armour. Under a hail of arrows, the French struggled to keep their footing as they tried to climb the steep bank, but by the time they reached the top, most had been obliged to sheath their weapons so they could use their hands to help them climb. So when they finally confronted the English at the top of the rampart, not only were they exhausted and defenceless for a vital few seconds until they could draw their weapons again, but their difficulties were augmented because the rain clouds had gone and the sun had begun to bake them inside their armour.

The first assault was driven off with ease, but Dunois noted that instead of pursuing, the English halted at the base of the rampart and collected spent missiles from the battlefield. They had not been resupplied since the fighting on the south bank of the Loire had begun; were they running short of arrows?

The French needed time to recover, so the second assault did not take place until the afternoon. This time Jeanne demanded to lead the first line. Dunois reluctantly agreed and joined her there alongside de Rais and La Hire. When all was ready, Marcel unfurled Jeanne's banner and handed it to her. She raised it and watched it flutter above her head for a few seconds, relishing the cheers from the inspired French soldiers behind her. She was oblivious to the crude insults coming from the enemy because they were all in English. Then she called out in that remarkably loud voice for such a small frame, "Forward in the name of Saint Catherine and France!"

The Angel of Lorraine

The French surged forward again. The clay in the rampart had dried out since the morning attack, and although they were still hot inside their armour, the first wave scaled the slope much more easily this time. A brutal struggle began along the top of the rampart with the English fighting with the desperation of knowing that no quarter would be given if the French broke through. But even so, they began to give ground before the ferocity of the French assault.

Suddenly everything changed. The attack faltered as word quickly spread along the French ranks. "The Maid has fallen!" "The Maid is down!" Jeanne, with Marcel at her side as always, had stopped at the foot of the rampart to urge forward the second wave when she was struck by an arrow. It was a lucky shot because it penetrated the join between her helmet and the left shoulder plate of her armour. Fortunately the arrow was at the end of its range and almost spent, so that it was falling to the ground having lost its initial velocity. But it was enough to knock Jeanne off her feet and stun her. Marcel called a passing soldier to help him carry her to the rear.

When the English saw this, they quickly regained the top of the rampart from the disheartened French. Glasdale, breathing hard and covered in blood, yelled, "It's all right, boys! The witch is dead! The day is ours!" There was nothing Dunois could do. All the hard-won gains were lost as the French withdrew, shocked by the loss of their leader. Even de Rais and La Hire seemed to lose heart, but once again, instead of pursuing the French, the English stopped and collected spent arrows.

"There is nothing to fear, Mes Seigneurs, the wound is only superficial," said the surgeon to the French commanders who crowded round the hospital tent. "I have washed and bandaged the wound. All Jeanne needs now is some rest."

"Thank God for that!" replied de Rais. Then with some emotion, he added, "We are nothing without her."

"Indeed," agreed Dunois, "I will call off the assault until tomorrow. Today has not been a complete failure because de Gaucourt beat off an attempt by the English to send help to their comrades, and we know Glasdale's men are running short of arrows because—"

"We must attack now!" came a voice from inside the hospital tent. A moment later, Jeanne, unsteady but upright, appeared. She was still in full armour, apart from the left shoulder plate, which the surgeon had removed, and clutched an English arrow in her right hand. "This is the arrow the English believe killed me. Well, they're in for a surprise! I have just received a message from the Kingdom of Heaven. 'Attack now, and France will win.' It cannot be clearer than that!"

But the decision belonged to Dunois, who hesitated. "The men are exhausted, Jeanne. We should wait for tomorrow."

"Mon Seigneur," said de Rais, "Jeanne and her voices have never failed us yet. Surely we must have faith in them."

Dunois turned to de Xaintrailles. "And what say you, Jean Poton? Should we resume the assault now?"

The latter day, Sir Launcelot beamed one of his winning smiles. "Mon Seigneur, I am with de Rais on this, but I have a few suggestions which will, shall we say, enhance our impact on the English."

It was about half past five in the afternoon when the English heard the French bugles call their men to arms again. Glasdale was surprised because he thought the fighting had finished for the day, but he was not concerned; the myth of Joan's invincibility had perished along with Joan herself. His own men had regained their confidence, and things would get back to normal with the English victorious as usual. Once more he led his men to the top of the bastille rampart and watched the approach of the French, who had abandoned a first and second wave and instead advanced in a single, dense phalanx, which was, he assumed, a sign of desperation. The phalanx halted just within range of the English longbows, but Glasdale had ordered there should be no shooting at long range because arrow supplies were low and the prospects of getting more soon were not good.

The Angel of Lorraine

For three minutes, the two sides faced each other in silence, then at a single word of command, a gap appeared in the middle of the phalanx as the men in the centre files moved sideways to left and right. English eyes widened as through the gap rode Joan the Witch carrying her banner aloft accompanied by her senior commanders. Handing her banner to one of her knights, she held an English arrow above her head and shouted in that unmistakeable voice, "See! Your arrows cannot harm me." Then, so all Glasdale's men could understand, she added five words in English, which de Xaintrailles had just taught her. "De witch is not dead!"

The impact on the English was huge. Now they really believed they were confronted by supernatural forces, except Glasdale of course. Jeanne dismounted along with her commanders, took back her banner, and called to her own men, "For France and King Charles. Forward!"

For the third time on that bloody day, the French surged forwards, fired up by de Xaintrailles's piece of theatre. The English were devastated; their confidence so high just minutes before, drained away through their boots. This time there was no holding the rampant French. The clay in the rampart had completely dried out; there was no more slipping and sliding, and following the Maid's banner, they were soon trading blows with the English.

Glasdale could see the bastille was about to fall. "Back! Back!" he shouted. "Get back to the Tourelles. Hurry!" The English needed no further encouragement, but the bridge linking the bastille to the Tourelles was narrow, and being made of wood, it was still slippery from the rain the day before. Funnelling more than five hundred frightened men into this narrow bottleneck had not been anticipated, and soon some of those unfortunate enough to be on the outside of the fleeing mass were inadvertently pushed into the Loire.

Amongst the last to cross was Glasdale himself, swinging a huge, two-handed battle-axe that threatened to split in half anyone who came too near. Manfully he did his best to cover the retreat of his men, and when a bold French man-at-arms tried to get inside the swing of the axe, he was cut almost in two, falling at Glasdale's feet and spilling blood over the already saturated wooden beams of the bridge deck. Then de Rais stepped forward.

"No, Gilles!" shouted Dunois, who had already ordered some crossbowmen to finish off the English captain from a safe distance. But de Rais either did not hear or ignored his commander amidst the clamour of battle. He calmly walked towards Glasdale, who drew back his axe ready to swing it in a horizontal, waist-high cut. De Rais feinted as if to take the last step that would bring him within range of the axe, but just as Glasdale delivered the strike, he quickly stepped back and allowed the huge axe-head to miss him by inches. This time the power of the blow was not absorbed by another French body; instead, the momentum continued to swing its arc onwards, taking Glasdale by surprise and twisting him almost off his feet. Inevitably he lost his footing on the slimy surface of the bridge, toppled backwards, and fell into the Loire, which had already claimed the lives of many Englishmen that day. But before he disappeared beneath the water, he grabbed and held desperately on to the edge of the bridge deck with his right hand. De Rais stepped forward, stood over him, and smiled as he kicked the hand away. In his heavy plate armour, Sir Willian Glasdale, knight of the English realm, sank to the bottom of the river, never to be seen again.

The dispirited English survivors were now bottled up in the two towers either side of the gate leading to the city. As the French began crossing the wooden bridge under a half-hearted barrage of arrows, Dunois gave the prearranged signal to the city garrison, who were waiting behind the Bridge Gate, which faced the long, multiple-arched bridge across the Loire linking the city to the Tourelles that had been broken by the French seven months before. But although the arches had been destroyed, the mighty stone piers were still there.

The English watched as the Bridge Gate swung open for the first time since October. Members of the city militia emerged carrying freshly cut wooden planks long enough to span the broken arches. Behind them followed a contingent of de Gaucourt's city garrison. But even though they had lost their charismatic commander and were under attack from north and south, the English held on until it was almost dark. By then they had shot their last arrow, and the city cannon were blasting holes in the Tourelles walls.

Eventually the eastern tower collapsed, and the few English still alive inside were slaughtered, but before the western tower fell, Jeanne called a halt to the fighting and, much to de Rais's disappointment, offered the remaining English their lives. This time the offer was accepted, and the French took possession of the burning wreck of the Tourelles and seventy-four mostly wounded Englishmen.

The bitterly contested siege of Orléans was over at last.

CHAPTER SEVEN

"Burn everything you can't carry, we're leaving for Meung tomorrow morning." Richard was giving his orders in the sergeants' mess in the Bastille de Rouen, northwest of Orléans. News of the fall of the Tourelles had just reached them.

"Have we given up the siege then, Captain?" asked Owain, the Welsh sergeant.

"It looks like it for the time being at least."

"That's a pity, isn't it? We're comfortable in these lodgings, see. It's a damn shame to burn them."

"No point in leaving them for the Frogs," said Edward Skippon of the Yorkshire company.

John Fletcher of Norfolk sighed. "The Lord knows, I would dearly love to have another crack at them before we leave."

"You may be in luck, John," replied Richard, "because the word is that Talbot will offer battle to the French tomorrow morning. If they accept, Orléans could still be ours by tomorrow afternoon."

"That's a big *if*, Captain," said Henry Hawkswood of Wiltshire. "Why should they risk a battle when they know they have already won?"

The Angel of Lorraine

"Gallic pride perhaps, or maybe their success might have gone to their heads. Anyway, we should plan on marching to Meung tomorrow."

By ten o'clock the next day, the English were drawn up ready for battle opposite Orléans's Paris Gate in the north wall of the city. They were in the usual Agincourt formation; archers on the flanks and dismounted men-at-arms in the centre. The French came out to meet them and deployed with their backs to the city walls but made no move to attack. For an hour, nothing happened, then at last, Talbot, impatient for action as always, ordered the Earl of Suffolk and a bodyguard to ride under a flag of truce across the five hundred paces separating the armies and formally offer battle. The bodyguard selected to accompany Suffolk was Richard because of his excellent knowledge of French.

As they rode together, Suffolk said, "I have heard good reports about you, Captain Calveley. When we reach the French lines, I want you to watch and listen. The French will assume you don't speak their language, so they may talk freely in front of you. I understand you are also a surveyor?"

"Yes, my lord. I learned geometry with the friars at Dunwich priory where I was brought up."

"You were an orphan?"

"Yes, my lord, the plague took my parents."

"I am sorry to hear it. Well, I want you to assess our enemy's numbers. Talbot thinks there are about six thousand, which is only double our number, but I think there may be more than that."

"I will, my lord, but I shall need time, so the longer you talk, the more accurate I shall be."

The French opened their ranks, and under heavy guard, the two Englishmen were escorted to the French commander, who was stationed in the centre of his army. There, Suffolk and Richard were permitted to dismount. Suffolk spoke first. "Mon Seigneur, I am the Earl of Suffolk and deputy commander to My Lord Talbot. To whom do I have the honour of speaking?"

"I am Jean Dunois, bastard son of the Duke of Orléans. With me are my three senior commanders—Jean Poton de Xaintrailles; Etienne de Vignolles, known as La Hire; and Gilles de Rais. May I offer you some refreshment?"

"Thank you, Mon Seigneur. After we have spoken perhaps? Is the Maid not present today?"

"She is at Mass."

"I see. Well, My Lord Talbot offers you battle today, or if you prefer, a combat of champions to determine the fate of Orléans once and for all."

"I regret that will not be possible, my lord," answered Dunois. "As you know, today is Sunday. The Maid does not wish blood to be shed on Our Lord's day, so we will make no move to engage you. If, however, you choose to attack us, we shall defend ourselves with the utmost vigour."

This answer was unexpected. Suffolk, knowing Talbot's desire for battle, tried again. "But, Mon Seigneur, we are offering to complete this long-drawn-out struggle in a single day. Is that not what you want too?"

Dunois smiled, for he knew he had the upper hand. "My lord, it is my belief that the struggle was decided yesterday with the fall of the Tourelles, but stay where you are until tomorrow, and we shall fight then. That is our final answer."

"Very well," said Suffolk, "I thank you for that, Mon Seigneur, and I will take your answer back to my commander, and may God be with you."

Suffolk made his glass of lime juice last as long as possible to give Richard the time he needed, and as they rode back to the English lines, he asked, "Well, Captain, what do you think?"

"I believe the French are expecting more men to arrive by tomorrow, my lord. When we turned our horses to leave, I heard one squire say to another, 'The English are in for a surprise tomorrow,' which leads me to believe they will be reinforced later today or during the night."

"And your estimate of the numbers they have today?"

"More than eight thousand, less than nine, my lord."

"I thought so. Good work, Captain, now you may return to your companies."

At noon, the English army began its withdrawal from Orléans, leaving behind materials and supplies, including most of the siege artillery, a sure sign of a beaten army. At last the citizens could relax and enjoy the fruits of victory. They devoted the rest of the day to thanksgiving and the celebrations they richly deserved.

* * *

II

News of France's unexpected victory at Orléans reverberated around Europe. The French and their sickly dauphin were thought to be on their knees and on the verge of surrender, yet suddenly, under the leadership of a peasant girl from Lorraine, they had given the English a thorough beating. Jeanne's reputation swelled as the stories about her were told and retold. The skilled Milanese armourers were particularly pleased because Orléans meant the war would go on and, therefore, so would the demand for their products.

For a few weeks the two armies disengaged. Jeanne and Dunois left Orléans on the ninth of May and went back to a grateful dauphin to ask for more men and supplies to finish the job. Men were already flooding in to join the army and serve under Jeanne; everyone loves a winner, but the cost had to be met by Charles and his exchequer. The French had also learned that quantity is no substitute for quality, so time was needed to assess the volunteers and select only the best recruits.

Meanwhile, the English marched back to Meung, their regional headquarters, to lick their wounds and wait for Fastolf's reinforcements. Although reduced in numbers because of the heavy losses at Orléans, the army was still far too large to be billeted on the townsfolk of Meung, so a forest of tents appeared outside the town boundary where the rank and file camped, while the knights and commanders occupied the castle just outside the town.

As a captain, Richard did not have to share a tent, so he was able to write to Mary in peace assuring her that whatever rumours she may hear, the army had only suffered a setback, not a real defeat; he remained in good health, and as always, he was being careful not to put himself in any unnecessary danger. But on the sixteenth of May, the gloom afflicting the English camp lifted a little when a small convoy of supplies from Rouen managed to avoid the marauding French patrols and arrive intact at Meung. With it came a certain Will Potter.

Richard had almost finished checking the morning roll call when John Fletcher arrived at his tent.

"Come in, Sergeant. What is it?"

"Captain, Will Potter is back."

"Is he indeed? So our lost sheep has returned to the fold. Well, put him under close arrest and bring him here at once."

Five minutes later, Sergeant Fletcher returned with a bemused Will Potter in tow. Potter began to speak, "Captain, Oi don't understand why Oi'm under arrest—"

"Shut up, Potter! You've been absent without leave."

"But Oi'm only a few days late."

"Five months!"

"As much as that? Well, it took longer to woo moi Margaret back than Oi expected, Captain."

"Potter, at the moment, you have been branded as a deserter. You know what the penalty for that is, so you had better give a good explanation for your absence, or you'll be facing the gibbet."

"No need for that, Captain. Oi'm no deserter, Oi just overstayed moi leave a bit."

"A bit!"

"Well, maybe a bit more than a bit, but you see, Captain, Oi thought when Margaret saw moi new teeth, she would fall into moi arms, but it didn't happen like that."

"Did it not? Well, show me your teeth then."

Potter grimaced to show off his new teeth then asked, "What do you think, Captain?"

"None of them match! None of the colours are the same. They vary from dark amber to perfect white, and I swear to God that your upper left tooth is a canine, not an incisor. You look like something that's just woken from the grave!"

"Well, the surgeon couldn't be too fussy because he had to make do with what Oi brought him. At least Oi can chew mutton now."

"And what of the saddlemaker from Wrentham? He put up a fight by the looks of that gap in your teeth on the right hand side."

"Lord, no, Captain! He ran off when he saw me coming. Moi Margaret did that. She packs a good punch when she's a mind to. It took me a long time to persuade her to come home, but in the end, she did."

"Why did she change her mind?"

"Oi think it was when Oi mentioned moi prize money. She became interested then, especially after Oi promised to buy a new house and frocks for her to wear every day of the week. Now she's the envy of every wench in Frostenden, and Oi was a happy man till you arrested me."

"But, Will, you overstayed your leave by five months! You had a two month pass but stayed away for seven. It's clearly written on the pass I gave you."

"Captain, you know Oi don't read too well, and in all the excitement, Oi clean forgot about the time limit."

Richard looked at his sergeant. "What's your opinion, Sergeant Fletcher?"

John Fletcher knew full well that his captain would never really allow Will to go to the gibbet, but with some difficulty, he managed to maintain a serious face. "I don't think Will appreciated the effect his new teeth would have on Margaret, Captain. Instead of charming her, they frightened the life out of her as they do me. But he did his best and won her back in the end, and I don't suppose his absence for the last five months will make a difference to the outcome of the war."

"I see." Then turning back to Will, Richard pronounced sentence. "Will Potter, in order to save your skin, I shall fill in your absence as compassionate leave, but you'll receive no pay for that period."

"Thank you, Captain," replied a relieved Potter. "Oi'll be more careful next time."

The Angel of Lorraine

"There'd better not be a next time, and find some more teeth to fill that gap Margaret made. Dismissed!"

* * *

III

The lull in the fighting since the eighth day of May abruptly ended on the eleventh day of June when the French launched a surprise attack on Jargeau, the only English-held fortress upstream from Orléans. The English fought well and held the French at bay until the next day, but eventually numbers and the presence of Jeanne told: Jargeau fell on the twelfth day of June; the English commander, the Earl of Suffolk, was captured and one of his younger brothers killed. In all, five hundred Englishmen were lost, of whom two hundred were taken prisoner. When the news reached Meung, Fastolf was immediately sent to Paris to bring his reinforcements, ready or not. The crisis was looming.

Next, Jeanne led the French to Meung, but she did not attack the main English army there. Instead she led an assault on the bridge crossing the Loire and left a garrison to guard it, thus cutting off the English from the river and making their occupation of the castle on the north bank pointless, for they had now lost control of the river traffic. Now Jeanne led her army to Beaugency, ten miles further downstream, and laid siege to the town. Talbot's decision to divide his forces in the face of a superior enemy by holding on to three fortresses was proving to be disastrous.

But on the morning of the fifteenth day of June, a ray of hope appeared for the English. A rider arrived at Meung with an urgent message for Talbot. He had just ridden from Janville, twenty five miles to the north where Fastolf and his new army were due to arrive later that day. Talbot decided to ride out to meet Fastolf, but now the French were roaming almost at will in the area, he was obliged to take an escort of three hundred men that included Richard and the Norfolk company. They arrived at dusk and found Fastolf in a large farmhouse just outside Janville, and from the number of tents pitched outside the town, it seemed that he had indeed brought a large army with him. Talbot and Lord Scales went in while Richard posted a guard outside and waited.

"Welcome, my lords," said Sir John, "I have the honour to present Sir Thomas Rempston of Nottinghamshire, who was able to join us after a very successful campaign in Brittany."

"Good to meet you, Sir Thomas," replied Talbot. "Your reputation precedes you, and you are especially welcome now that we have lost Lord Roos, who has been called back to England to deal with family matters."

Sir Thomas, a man of middle height and a cheerful round face, who looked more like a merry farmer than a soldier, answered, "It will be an honour to serve with you, my lord."

Fastolf pointed to a large, oak table. "My lords, we have simple but hearty fare to offer you." On the table were platters of smoked ham, cheese, wine and just-baked bread. All four men sat and helped themselves. After a few mouthfuls, Talbot said, "I am sorry to inform you, Sir John, that since your departure, the French have captured the bridge at Meung and laid siege to Beaugency. Their army grows by the day. How many men have you brought?"

"At this morning's roll call, there were four thousand seven hundred and eighty-three fit for duty and nineteen sick. This figure includes the seven hundred and forty men brought back by Sir Thomas from Brittany."

"Excellent! How many have experience of battle?"

"Only about a quarter, but they have all been selected for their health and vigour. I am sure they will give a good account of themselves when the time comes, but from what my scouts have reported, we need to be cautious."

"Why so?" demanded Talbot. "With your five thousand and my two and a half, we can engage the enemy at once."

"But have you not heard that another French army is forming between Tours and Blois under the command of Constable Richemont? He will soon march to join the Orléans army."

"Hah! Richemont is so treacherous he may be coming to join us! He was on our side not so long ago."

Rempston said, "My lord, my information from Brittany confirms that Richemont is now definitely against us. He has patched up his differences with the French court, thanks to the dauphin's mother-in-law's influence."

"Yolande is as wily as a fox," acknowledged Talbot.

Scales asked, "How many does Richemont bring with him, Sir Thomas?"

"A little over a thousand we believe."

Fastolf added, "We don't yet know how many more are joining Richemont, but there are likely to be many because Joan the Maid is said to be with him."

Talbot shook his head. "I cannot believe I'm hearing this! We now have seven and a half thousand men at our disposal, yet you cast doubt upon what we should do. Is it not obvious? We must attack at once!"

Fastolf frowned. "Who exactly? Richemont? The army at Orléans? And how many men will we face? Also remember, my lord, we have just been beaten at Orléans. The men in your army have their heads down while the French are on the crest of a wave."

Now Talbot raised his voice as his temper began to fray. "I care not about French numbers when I am accompanied by seven and a half thousand stalwart Englishmen, but the longer we wait, the more likely it is that our enemy's numbers will grow. If we attack now, we will hit them before they can unite, but if we sit here fretting about numbers, our task will be harder. As for my men's heads being down, just the sniff of battle is enough to raise an Englishman's spirits, especially when the enemy is the French!"

Lord Scales predictably agreed with Talbot, but Rempston, who was a similar age to Fastolf, remained silent.

Fastolf, who had no more patience than Talbot, would not be put off. "My lord, you say you have seven and a half thousand Englishmen with you, well, you have not. A third of your army is Norman French as are five hundred of my own. They fight well enough while we are winning, but how do you think they feel now? Do you think that your talk of the sniff of battle will apply to them?"

"Then what do you suggest, Sir John?" replied Talbot angrily. "Should we run like beaten dogs!"

"Is not one defeat enough for you, my lord! Must you go searching for more! The first thing we should do is find out where the French are and in what numbers. I suggest we send out scouts tonight who will bring us this information tomorrow. Then we can decide whether to head south or retire to Paris."

"And abandon Meung and Beaugency? Never! We faced greater odds at Agincourt and Verneuil and won through."

"But there was no Joan at Agincourt and Verneuil," said Rempston quietly.

That statement lowered the temperature slightly, and as leader, Talbot tried to ease the tension. "My lord and knights of the shires, we must not weaken our position by disagreeing on strategy, but as the ranking officer, I must make the final decision. We shall follow Sir John's advice and send out scouts tonight, but we will not wait here for an answer. The scouts will be ordered to bring their information to us at Meung because we shall march there with all speed tomorrow. At Meung, we will be between the French at Orléans and the new army assembling at Blois. We shall strike at each separately and put the defeat at Orléans behind us with a double victory. Sir John, I will leave you to organise the scouts. Is there anyone you can trust with the Identification Ledger?"

Fastolf had received a direct order from his senior officer, so he had to obey. "Yes, my lord, I shall see to it at once."

It was almost the solstice; the night sky did not really get dark like it does in winter, so Richard and his two companions from the Norfolk company, Sergeant Fletcher and John Hook, were able to ride for most of the night. Their orders from Fastolf were crystal clear: "Ride straight for Blois, speak to no one, and stay north of the Loire. When the job is done, return to Meung, where we will be by noon tomorrow."

They took about four hours' sleep, wrapped in their cloaks as a heavy dew formed around them during the cold, clear night, but as soon as the predawn greying in the sky appeared in the east, they resumed their journey westwards. They gave Beaugency a wide berth where part of the army of Orléans was laying siege to the English garrison, but after that, they reduced their speed from a steady canter to a trot because they were now entering territory unknown to them.

"How much further, Captain?" asked Sergeant Fletcher.

"I'm not sure, John, but less than eight miles, I would guess. A large army takes up a lot of space, so we could easily come across outlying pickets in the next hour or so. We'll slow to a walk soon. It's essential we see the French before they see us if we are to have enough time to form a reliable estimate of their numbers."

By the time the sun flooded golden light above the eastern horizon, the three Englishmen had covered another four miles. The landscape was fairly flat, and a line of green pasture mixed with willow trees on their left marked the position of the Loire.

Sensing the proximity of the enemy, Richard spoke in hushed tones, "We'll walk the horses from here. We must be near Blois now. One of us will be the advance guard and go four hundred paces ahead of the other two. A single rider walking his horse will attract less attention than three, but it will be dangerous, so we'll take that job in turns. Now remove your white surcoats with the cross of Saint George on them. We don't want to make it too easy for the French to identify us. And stay alert!"

They travelled this way for about an hour. Hook was in front and had just disappeared over the crest of a ridge when Richard asked, "Sergeant, how is Hook developing?"

"Coming along well, Captain. He's got his confidence now, and as you know, he's a fine specimen physically, which helps to give him presence. In a few years, he could be sergeant material."

"I'm pleased to hear it. Perhaps we—"

"Captain, look ahead!" interrupted Fletcher, "Hook's coming back, and he's mounted. He must have seen something."

The young Norfolk soldier cantered his horse towards them giving them the circular mount up signal, which Richard and Fletcher duly did. Hook drew rein just in front of them and panted, "The French army is just over that ridge, their pickets are less than a mile from here."

"Were you seen?" asked Richard.

"Difficult to say, Captain, but there was no visible reaction, so I think we are safe to go up to the ridge and take a look." Richard thought back to John Stebbings, the scout who reported back after he sighted the French at Rouvray; he was so excited he could hardly get his words out, but the calm assessment he had just heard from John Hook was impressive. Sergeant Fletcher's opinion of him seemed accurate.

"Very well, Hook, we'll follow your advice. Sergeant Fletcher, how is your eyesight?"

"Better than Will Potter's but only average, Captain."

"And yours, Hook?"

"Perfect I think, Captain."

"All right then, here's what we'll do," said Richard as he opened the satchel strapped to his saddle and pulled out the calf-bound Information Ledger. "This is a record of the coats of arms of all the lords and knights of France. There is nothing special about that, and the French are sure to have a similar record of ours. But thanks to our agents in Bourges, Chinon, and elsewhere, this copy has an addition, which is the number of soldiers each one is obliged to bring to the service of France in time of war, so it is obviously of great value to us. This is one of only three copies, and we are honoured to have been entrusted with it. So while you, Sergeant Fletcher, will stay out of sight with the horses and keep watch, Hook and I will go forward and count the enemy numbers. I shall do that by eye first, then using Hook's sharp eyesight, we shall identify as many banners as we can and use the numbers in this ledger to cross-check my visual count. That way we should be able to take a reliable estimate back to our commanders. Is all that clear?"

Hook frowned. "But, Captain, I don't know anything about coats of arms, gules, argent, sable and such like."

"You don't need to, Hook. All you have to do is describe in plain English what's on each banner to me. Here, look at this." Richard opened the ledger and picked a coat of arms at random. "Now tell me what you see."

"I see a flag divided into four equal parts. Top left is a lion."

"Sitting or prancing on its back legs?"

"Prancing."

"Colour?"

"White."

"Colour of background?"

"Red. There is another exactly the same bottom right. Top right and bottom left is a red cross on a white background just like our Saint George's cross."

"Well done, Hook, you have just described the coat of arms of Poton de Xaintrailles, one of the best French commanders. He brings to the army eight hundred men."

Hook smiled. "Now I understand, Captain."

Sergeant Fletcher asked, "Captain, what's the difference between a flag and a banner?"

"*Flag* and *banner* are usually interchangeable words and are often used to mean the same thing, but a banner can also be a rigid flag made of thin wood or a normal flag stretched open between two wooden rods so that it can be placed outside a campaign tent and identify its owner even if there is no wind blowing. Now let's get started."

Richard and Hook crawled the last few yards so they would not be silhouetted against the skyline while Sergeant Fletcher remained a hundred paces behind with the horses. In the distance, chimney smoke from thousands of hearths identified the city of Blois, but in the foreground, covering all the fields between the Englishmen and Blois, was a large army. It was an impressive sight. Thousands of men, the sun glinting on their armour, were assembling for morning inspection. Equerries were running to and fro on missions for their masters, while in a huge paddock to the north of the camp, many thousands of horses of all sizes and colours were quietly grazing, their peaceful, relaxed ambience contrasting with the bustle and activity in the camp alongside them. There was a great deal of cheering going on as if something good had happened; morale seemed sky-high.

"Hook," said Richard, "you can see the banners outside the large campaign tents, so make ready while I do my visual count. I won't be long."

The Angel of Lorraine

The fact that the French were assembling in groups ready for inspection made Richard's counting easier, so in only fifteen minutes, he was ready for Hook's banner descriptions. Drawing a line in his notebook under his visual estimate, which came to seven thousand eight hundred, he said, "Hook, I'm ready. Start now."

The young Norfolk man systematically began to work through the banners, describing them tent line by tent line from left to right to avoid missing any, but it was going to be a long process because most knights brought just ten men or less, so there would be many banners to describe. First there was the banner with the gold fleur-de-lis on blue, the royal banner, which meant a prince of the royal bloodline was present. Then, quite soon, Hook described a banner with a broad red rim all round it containing golden, prancing lions within the rim. Inside the rim was a chequer pattern of alternating blue and gold squares. "Well, that's interesting," said Richard. "That's the banner of Arthur of Richemont, Constable of France, who is worth twelve hundred men. He must have been reconciled with the dauphin. That will anger Talbot."

Later Hook described a white banner with angels and a Christlike figure beside a fleur-de-lis. Richard thumbed through the pages of his ledger. "Well, I can't see anything like that here. I've not seen it, but my guess is that's Joan's. If so we, now know where the leadership of all the French armies is."

Hook had just started on the last line of tents on the far right of the camp when they heard pounding hooves coming up behind them. Richard turned round. "Sergeant Fletcher, what are you doing! We'll be seen!"

"Too late, Captain, we already have been."

"Wait, we're nearly finished."

"If we wait, Captain, we'll be taken. The Frogs are already behind us. We must go now!" Fletcher had brought their horses with him, so without further debate, Richard and Hook sprang into their saddles and headed east for Meung. Less than a quarter of a mile on their right, and slightly

Peter Tallon

ahead of them, twenty French horsemen were riding on a converging course hoping to cut them off. Richard thought of the precious ledger in his saddle and prayed his mount would not choose this moment to go lame. But at least the horses were fresh. The French were all men-at-arms, so in their heavy plate armour, they were unlikely to be fast enough to catch the Englishmen, none of whom wore armour for a scouting mission.

Soon the pursuit was abandoned, and Richard could allow the horses a short rest before continuing the journey to Meung. He quickly checked his figures, and even though they had not managed to complete the banner count, the numbers corresponded well to his visual estimate. He was confident that they had seen around eight thousand men.

They reached Meung in the early afternoon, and Richard went straight to the castle outside the town where he was immediately taken to Talbot's quarters. He handed the precious ledger back to the army commander and gave his report.

"Thank you, Captain," said Talbot when Richard finished. "So the Frenchies have eight thousand men at Blois, not counting those who will be freed up now that Beaugency has fallen."

"I had not heard about Beaugency until now, my lord. That means we only have Meung left on the Loire frontier."

"True, and the latest report from Orléans is that there are now at least nine thousand French in the field there. By contrast, we have suffered some desertions by the Norman French, which, added to our losses at Beaugency this morning, leaves us with less than six thousand in all. I think you may safely tell your sergeants to prepare to leave at daybreak tomorrow."

"In what direction, my lord?"

"We'll abandon Meung and head north for Paris. I can't afford to lose more men by leaving another isolated garrison here."

Richard wanted to say, "So you have taken Sir John's advice at last," but that would only have fanned the flames between the two men, so he confined himself to a simple, "Very well, my lord," and turned to go.

"A moment, Captain Calveley."

Richard turned back again. "Yes, my lord?"

"Your scouting mission to Blois was good work. You are also a surveyor and a notable captain. I can always find work for men like you in my service. Would you consider joining my retinue?"

"My lord, it would be an honour to serve you, but I cannot leave Sir John. Fifteen years ago, when my first wife and two sons were cruelly murdered, I was on my knees. But Sir John was there when I was in need and helped me back on my feet again. I don't know what would have become of me without him and his wife, Millicent."

"I understand, Captain, and loyalty is one of the prime virtues. Still, I suspect you have paid that debt many times over, so if you should ever change your mind, my offer remains open to you."

"Thank you, my lord."

"And I am sorry to hear about your first family. It was a damnable thing. Was the murderer caught?"

"The man who committed the act is dead, but the man who gave the order still lives. That debt has yet to be paid."

"Then I wish you well, Captain, and hope you find the justice you deserve in due course. May God go with you."

"And with you too, my lord."

* * *

IV

The English left Meung at dawn in the usual marching formation of vanguard, main guard, and rear guard. The French did not follow until midmorning because they waited for Jeanne and the new army from Blois to join them; but the vanguard, commanded by La Hire and de Xaintrailles, left earlier in order to harry the English rear guard. Constant skirmishing slowed the English down, so Talbot himself joined the rear guard to take direct command, leaving Fastolf in charge of the main guard. Nobody thought to order the vanguard to slow down; as a result, the gap between it and the rest of the army grew wider than it should have been.

Meanwhile, the united French army under the nominal command of the Duke of Alençon, now released from his parole, caught up with its own vanguard in the early afternoon due to Jeanne and Dunois constantly urging the soldiers forwards. Everyone wanted to engage the English as soon as possible, and the opportunity came at last four miles south of the village of Patay where the Paris road crosses the Chateaudun to Orléans road.

After yet another vicious little skirmish, the English and French temporarily lost sight of each other. Talbot could see the rear guard was weary and called a brief conference with his senior commanders.

He spoke first to Lord Scales, the rearguard commander. "How are your men, my lord?"

"They need a rest. We've been fighting more or less continuously since this morning."

"Well then, I think it's time we gave the Frenchies a bloody nose."

"That would be just the tonic we need, my lord."

Talbot pointed to the crossroads just ahead. "See that cluster of trees on the far side of the crossroads. We'll deploy your rear guard in there while the French are out of sight so that every archer has a clear view of the road. Then let the French get to within a hundred paces of the forest eaves before you shoot. That will give them something to think about."

"It will indeed, my lord," smiled Scales.

"Sir John, I would like you to deploy the main guard on top of that low hill behind the trees where it will be in full view of the French, so the last thing they will expect is a fight in the woods below, but hurry, this needs to be a surprise."

Fastolf turned his horse and galloped back to the main guard to carry out his orders, but Rempston did not follow, hoping to join in the action. "My lord, may I stay here with Lord Scales?"

"Certainly, Sir Thomas. I'm sure Sir John will be able to manage without you as I do not intend the main guard to become involved. I shall return to you shortly."

With that, Talbot followed Fastolf up to the top of the hill to ensure his intentions were clearly understood. "Sir John, spread your line as wide as possible to make the French think we are more numerous than we are. I have given Sir Thomas permission to stay with the rear guard because I do not intend this fight to be anything more than a holding action. Are you comfortable about taking direct command of his men?"

"Certainly, my lord. They are all veterans and need minimal supervision. Shall I recall the vanguard as a precaution?"

"No need, Sir John, you will not be engaged today."

"I understand, my lord, I will see to the deployment immediately."

Under these circumstances, Fastolf did not think too hard about the details of his deployment, so Richard's four companies found themselves at the extreme left of the line facing the woods but separated from the rest of the main guard by a small stream that was lined with willow and alder trees. The fact that they were effectively out of sight of the rest of the army was of no consequence because there was no intention to give battle here.

Talbot's plan would have worked had it not been for one of those unforeseeable accidents that can change the course of events. One of Lord Scales's archers needed to relieve himself and so walked a little way away from the rear guard into a thicket of young trees. But before he could begin his task, he almost stepped on a large, brown stag, which had been hiding from these unwelcome intruders into his domain. The frightened creature bolted and ran straight through the middle of the men of the rear guard, who were busy preparing themselves for the arrival of the French. The archers scattered, some yelling shouts of alarm, others making hunting calls as the stag broke cover from the woods and galloped down the road towards Meung.

The French vanguard was approaching the crossroads from the southwest. La Hire and de Xaintrailles had already seen Fastolf's men fanning out along the top of the next hill but suddenly realised they were but a bowshot from an English force in the wood below. They did not wait for their men to form up but instantly gave the word to charge, leading the attack themselves. Fifteen hundred armoured horsemen surged forward cheering wildly; they were amongst the English in seconds.

Scales and Rempston were caught by surprise. Scales's men were in the middle of planting their stakes while some of Rempston's had not even strung their bows yet. There was no resistance, just blind panic; there was not even time to mount their horses—the English just ran. Talbot had only just returned to the rear guard and, together with Scales and Rempston, was taken prisoner at the beginning of the action.

The sight that confronted Fastolf from his position on top of the hill in the middle of the three thousand strong main guard was shocking. Hundreds of fleeing men burst from the woodland eaves running up the hill as if all the devils in hell were after them. Intermingled with them were French knights and men-at-arms hacking down the fugitives at will.

There was no time to plant stakes or line up properly, but Fastolf kept his head as always.

"Archers, face your front and make ready!" he bellowed. There was not much time, only enough for two volleys at most, but Fastolf knew he could not give the order for volley shooting, the deadly trademark of English archery, without endangering the lives of the fleeing rear guard.

"Archers! There will be no volley shooting. We must avoid hitting our own men. Aim well and fire at will!" That order, essential though it was, emasculated the effect of massed archery. Hitting individual, fast-moving targets was hard enough at fifty yards, never mind two hundred, so very few French saddles were emptied. The archers knew this too; it was obvious that the French would be amongst them in seconds. Most did not wait. Without orders, the main guard turned tail and ran except for Rempston's veterans and a few hardy souls amongst the rest, who had seen action before. Wild-eyed with panic, the fugitives grabbed any horse they could find in the stabling area and galloped headlong up the road to Janville and safety, oblivious to Fastolf's stentorian threats and swearing.

By now Richard knew something was badly wrong. The customary cheers and jeers he expected to hear echoing towards his position were absent. Leaving Sergeant Hawkswood in command, he ran to the willows and alders blocking his view, crossed the stream, and looked westwards. Instantly, and for the first time in his life, he realised he was watching an English defeat. Apart from a steady group of men-at-arms and archers in the middle of Fastolf's line, men were running from the battlefield closely pursued by French cavalry and offering no resistance at all.

He ran back to his men and shouted, "Sergeants! To me!" Hawkswood, Skippon, ap Griffiths, and Fletcher gathered round him. "Something's gone badly wrong. A battle is being fought behind us, and we are losing. Get the men mounted, tell them to shoulder their bows, stow their arrows, and draw hand weapons. Today we fight as hobelars. Hurry!"

By the time Richard's force of three hundred and sixty improvised hobelars appeared on Fastolf's left flank, the situation had worsened.

Rempston's seven hundred veterans plus the few stouthearted remnants of the rest of the main guard were fighting hand to hand and taking a battering from a thousand or so of the French vanguard, all mounted knights and men-at-arms. Without a second thought or any attempt to form line, Richard yelled, "Charge!"

Normally combat between heavily armoured men-at-arms on large destriers and lightly armed hobelars on small horses and ponies would have been a complete mismatch, but by now the French were tired, their horses blown, and the attack on their flank came as a surprise. But even so, the French were elated by their success and fought back manfully when Richard's force struck them.

For a few anxious minutes, the outcome was in the balance, but Rempston's men, encouraged by Richard's unexpected help, found new reserves of strength and started to push the French back. Sadly, the hobelars were suffering grievously against their better equipped foe. Richard, at least, always wore his father's armour, which was now outdated, having too much mail and not enough plate, but he was still better protected than his men who wore only metal-studded brigandine jackets. Hoping to lead by example, he drove his horse towards a large French knight who was spreading carnage amongst his men with a huge mace. The knight saw him coming and raised his weapon, but at that moment, a voice behind him shouted, "Captain! On your right!" It was John Fletcher warning him of another Frenchman approaching on his blind side. Richard saw the danger out of the corner of his eye and swung his large sword to the right with a backhanded stroke that caught the Frenchman between his shoulder plate and helmet. The blow unhorsed his adversary, but the distraction gave the knight in front of him time to deliver a massive blow, which smashed into his shield so hard that his left arm went numb, and he lost all feeling below his shoulder. Even worse, he could not feel his horse's reins though he could still see them in his left hand.

The French knight did not follow up his advantage because around him, his comrades were falling back having given their all that day. Nor did the English pursue; they were unable to. They simply collapsed exhausted where they stood, allowing the victorious French vanguard to retire unmolested to the forest by the crossroads where they could take a well-earned rest.

* * *

V

"God's teeth! Am I glad to see you!" said a relieved Fastolf clasping Richard by the left shoulder.

"Aaah!" groaned Richard as he flinched from Fastolf's hearty embrace.

"Are you wounded?"

"I think so, Sir John, a mace blow just before the French withdrew."

"Well, get it seen to as soon as you can. Have you lost many men?"

"I believe so. Hobelars are no match for men-at-arms, but I had no choice."

"You chose well. Call the roll quickly so we can see how many fit men we've got left." Then pointing to the land south of the crossroads, which was now covered with armoured men, Fastolf added, "Yonder are the leading files of the French main guard. We need to get away from here before they join the action."

"But, Sir John, what of Talbot, Scales, and Rempston?"

"Well, they're not with us, so they're either dead or prisoners. They were lost when the rear guard fell apart."

The roll was called, and the sergeants reported back on numbers still fit for duty.

Peter Tallon

"Forty-seven for Yorkshire," said Skippon.

"Forty-six for Wales," reported ap Griffiths.

"And thirty-eight for Wiltshire," added Hawkswood.

"But where's Sergeant Fletcher?"

"I'm afraid he's dead," answered Hawkswood. "I saw him fall with his skull smashed by an axe blow just after he shouted a warning to you, Captain. I believe he was dead before he hit the ground. He would have felt nothing."

This was a shock for Richard. He had known John Fletcher longer than any of his other sergeants. "I am truly sorry to hear that," he muttered.

"As are we all, Captain," replied Hawkswood. "It's been a hard day. I took the liberty of calling John's roll. Just thirty-three for the Norfolk and Suffolk men."

"Thanks, all of you. Stay here while I report to Sir John."

Richard found Fastolf checking the roll of Rempston's men with Rempston's second-in-command, Sir William Shelford. "How many left in your companies, Richard?"

"One hundred and sixty-four fit for duty, Sir John."

"Damnation! That's less than half."

"And the losses have been especially heavy in the Norfolk company, which has only thirty-three left."

Fastolf swore again, "Damnation! It's been a bad day. Sir William Shelford here has four hundred and eighty left, so that's a total of six hundred and er…"

"Forty-four," added Sir William helpfully.

Fastolf looked at the French main guard, which had already entered the forest by the crossroads where Lord Scales's men had been undone less than an hour ago. "We must get to Janville and regroup tonight if we can. Sir William, get your men on the march as soon as possible. We will be just behind you."

Shelford replied, "Yes, Sir John," and ran to his men signalling the mount-up sign as he went.

This left Fastolf and Richard alone. "Richard, we need a rearguard action to keep the French off our tails. I want you to ride ahead and get to our vanguard as soon as you can. Then order the commander in my name to halt, dig in, and form a defensive line behind which we can round up as many of our men as we can while the vanguard keeps the French at bay. This will give us time to reorganise ourselves into something like an army again. I'll stay here with my own companies and delay the French as long as I can."

"I will do as you order, Sir John, but, with respect, you should go, and I will command the holding action here."

"Why?" frowned Fastolf, unaccustomed to having his orders questioned.

"Because whoever commands the vanguard will outrank me. By now, those who fled the field on horseback will already have reached the vanguard, which may take some persuading not to take flight too. Under these circumstances, the commander may choose not to obey an order coming from a mere captain even though I shall use your name. He may say I misheard or misunderstood you. You must go yourself so there can be no doubt."

"But I am a garter knight! I cannot leave the field of battle when other garter knights are still unaccounted for."

Richard tried to mask his exasperation. "Sir John, you may be a garter knight, but you are also now the commander of England's last field army in France. If you don't go yourself, we may lose the vanguard too—another thousand men in the French bag!"

Fastolf was silent for a few seconds, struggling with his conscience and his duty. Then he said, "You're right, Richard. I am not thinking straight. My duty as army commander must come first. I shall need half an hour, no more. That will give Shelford enough time to get clear and me the chance to turn back the vanguard."

"You shall have your half hour, Sir John."

"Good, but no heroics, Richard. Half an hour only. I need you safely back with me more than ever now."

"I understand, Sir John, but I will guarantee your half hour."

"Remember now," said Fastolf as he turned his horse's head northwards, "no heroics, and God be with you!"

Richard quickly lined up his companies on the crest of the hill, three in the front line and the battered Norfolk company in reserve. The French main guard was now emerging from the forest on the crossroads and fanning out right and left so its line would overlap Richard's. But Fastolf and Shelford had been gone less than ten minutes when John Stebbings of the Norfolk company shouted the alarm. "Captain! Behind us! Look!"

Everyone turned round. Richard felt as if his stomach had turned to stone. Screened until now by a fold in the landscape, a column of French men-at-arms had appeared from the west less than half a mile behind Richard's little force. They had just begun crossing the Janville road cutting off the English escape route.

"The main guard must have been much nearer than we thought," said Sergeant Hawkswood quietly.

The Angel of Lorraine

"How many do you reckon, Henry?"

"About six hundred, perhaps a few more."

"More than enough to bottle us up here."

"And now it looks like the main guard commanders have arrived to watch the fun, Captain."

Richard turned back to look at the crossroads and saw a group of banners, including the royal banner of France, emerging from the forest. "Sergeants, to me!" he ordered. "Hurry now!" He was quickly joined by Skippon and ap Griffiths. "Now listen carefully, there is not much time left. Sir John must have at least another twenty minutes before the French can be allowed to give chase because he needs time to reach our vanguard, turn it around, and form a prepared defensive line to cover what's left of our army. Although the French have just cut off our retreat, there is still an opening to the east, but it won't last long. I want you to mount up, take your men towards that gap, and encourage the French to follow you. Some will surely stay here to block us off from Janville, but the fewer the better. Sergeant Hawkswood, you will be in command."

"Yes, Captain, but—"

"No time for buts. The French are heavily armoured men-at-arms, so you will be faster than them, but you must make them think they can catch you to draw away as many as possible from here. When you've ridden for fifteen minutes as best as you can judge, accelerate to full speed, turn to the northwest, and keep going until you reach the Janville road. Sir John and the vanguard will not be far away."

"What of you and the Norfolk boys, Captain?" asked ap Griffiths.

"We shall remain here, Owain, and give the French something to think about. It will be risky, but it will give you time to get through that rapidly closing gap to the east. But you must go now, or it will be too late!"

Richard ran to the Norfolk company to explain what was happening. He had selected them to remain behind because he knew them all and most of their families well, but they had no sergeant now. Fastolf needed his half hour, and although Richard had ensured three companies would escape, he had not yet delayed the French long enough. There was a good chance that he and the men from Norfolk and Suffolk would die in the attempt, but he hoped that after shooting a few volleys, he might find a weak point in the ring of armour that was now surrounding them and break through to the Janville road.

While he was telling them about his plan, he was touched by the simple faith they had in him. He knew the chances of getting any of them back to Fastolf were slim, but the Norfolk company, veterans though they were, knew that whatever the odds, Captain Richard would look after them like he had always done. But this time he had deceived them and felt bad.

A Wiltshire voice from behind him said, "Captain, may I speak with you?"

"Sergeant Hawkswood. I gave you orders to leave!"

"That was one order I could not obey, and before you ask, I left Edward Skippon in command of the other three companies."

Richard signalled Hawkswood to move out of earshot of the Norfolk company. "Captain," continued Hawkswood, "I can see there's no way out for you and the Norfolks from here. After all we've been through together, I must be at your side if this is going to be our last battle."

Richard felt his eyes moistening. "Henry, I thank God you disobeyed me, for there is no one I would rather have beside me today than you. We'll face whatever is to come together."

As the English quietly watched the French preparing to charge, Richard noticed that amongst the enemy banners, the unusual one, the one that was not recorded in the Information Ledger when he had been counting the numbers at Blois, was present here. If this really was Joan's, he began to wonder how a woman whom the French were calling a saint could preside over so much slaughter. Yet he knew that she had given Glasdale every chance to surrender before the final attack on the Tourelles, and even then, she had allowed the last few English defenders to keep their lives. That sparked another thought in his mind, one that provided more hope than an unlikely breakthrough and would ensure Fastolf got his half hour.

"Henry, help me onto my horse. My left arm's been injured. I can't use it."

"It looks crooked at the elbow, Captain, broken I shouldn't wonder."

"And send John Hook to me with an English surcoat turned inside out so the Saint George's cross doesn't show. I'll need it tied to a poleaxe or a shortened lance so it can be used as a flag. I'm going to try and parley with the Frenchies."

With just seconds to go before the French launched their attack, Richard and Hook cantered towards the French lines with Hook carrying a white flag of truce. Richard was unarmed. He held his reins in his right hand while his left arm hung limply by his side and rode directly towards what he guessed was Joan's banner; hopefully he had not left it too late. French outriders galloped towards the Englishmen to block their way, but at a sharp order from one of the knights beneath the banner, who was mounted on a large bay destrier, the outriders let the English pass.

Richard rode towards the knight who gave the order and drew rein in front of him, but before he could say anything, the knight spoke first. "What is the meaning of this! We are about to charge your position, yet now you wish to speak. It's too late for words!"

"I apologise, Mon Seigneur. All our leaders are captured or dead. I am but a humble captain, and we have no guidance from above, but before you charge, I do wish to speak to you."

"Your name?"

"Captain Richard Calveley. I am Sir John Fastolf's man."

"We do not have Fastolf."

"And he is not with us."

"Captain Calveley, if you seek mercy, you are too late."

"I do not seek mercy, Mon Seigneur, and we will fight to the death if we must. I am here to offer ransom."

"How can you? You are not a knight."

"No, but there are thirty-four men with me, and I have the money to pay for their ransom and mine."

The French knight suddenly became more interested, and his voice softened a little. "Captain, your arm, you are wounded."

"Yes, Mon Seigneur," then noticing the coat of arms of the large knight sitting beside the knight he was speaking to, Richard addressed him directly. "A mace blow from you, Mon Seigneur, I believe."

The French commander said, "Your conqueror is Etienne de Vignolles, better known as La Hire, and I am Jean Dunois, bastard of the Duke of Orléans. Our leader the Duke of Alençon has ridden forward to cut you off from help."

"He has already succeeded, Mon Seigneur."

"On my left," continued Dunois as if Richard had not spoken, "is Jeanne, the Maid of Orléans, who guides all that we do."

"Your names are well-known to us, especially the Maid's."

La Hire said, "Captain, your armour is old-fashioned. My blow would not have caused you so much damage had you been wearing more plate."

The Angel of Lorraine

"It was my father's, I wear it out of respect for him." *So far, so good*, thought Richard; he had overcome the initial hostility and gained a little more time. At least the French were talking.

Turning to Dunois again, Richard began to bargain. "Mon Seigneur, I offer you ransom on the basis that my men and I are allowed to leave with our arms and horses."

Another knight who was sitting just behind Dunois said irritably, "This is ridiculous! We cannot trust a commoner. Kill them all and have done with it!"

"Not so fast, Gilles," replied his commander, who then addressed Richard again. "My companion makes a fair point. Do you have a knight who can vouch for you?"

"Only Sir John Fastolf, but he is not here. If you do not accept my offer, then we shall die, but not before we have taken many more than thirty-four French lives with us."

Dunois shook his head. "Brave words, Captain, but I am sorry I must refuse—"

"I will vouch for Captain Calveley!" It was the knight holding Joan's banner who interrupted his commander.

"But, Marcel, how can you do that?" demanded Dunois, not at all pleased by this infringement on his authority.

Marcel spoke to Richard, "Captain Calveley, I am Marcel, Sieur de Freuchin. You saved my life at Agincourt when I fought against you English without first fully discharging my ransom. You remember me?"

"Of course, Mon Sieur," answered a surprised and relieved Richard.

For the benefit of Dunois, Marcel added, "Captain, when I was a prisoner, you took pity on me knowing the fate that befalls anyone who fights while still on parole. You disguised me in an English archer's brigandine topped with a surcoat bearing the cross of Saint George and escorted me through the middle of the English camp to freedom. Without you, I would not be here today." Then speaking again to Dunois, he said, "Knight or no knight, I know Captain Calveley is a man of honour, and I have no hesitation in vouching for him."

De Rais growled, "Kill him."

"Wait a moment, Gilles. What is your opinion, Jeanne?" asked Dunois.

The young woman, who was only two years older than Richard's own daughter, looked hard into his face. She seemed but a child to Richard. "This man has, as we have heard, shown mercy, which is a true Christian virtue. He also has a kind face, and I do not believe that the life or death of thirty-four Englishmen will change the outcome of this war. My voices assure me we will win. Gilles, remember what you said to me at Orléans about winning this war at the lowest cost to French life so that more French mothers will see their sons come home?"

"I do, Jeanne, and I shall be content with your decision even though I already know what it will be. You have always been proved right so far."

De Xaintrailles, who was in earshot of this, marvelled at the change Jeanne had caused in de Rais. His friendship with the Breton lord had begun during the visit to Duke Philippe in Bruges, but de Xaintrailles had always held back because of de Rais's dark reputation concerning sexual promiscuity with children. But now the sinner seemed to be reformed by the light cast by Jeanne. Truly she must be an angel sent from God.

Jeanne said to Dunois, "I believe we should at least hear what Captain Calveley offers. If it is adequate, lives on both sides will be saved. There has been enough Christian blood shed today, and we already have the victory."

"Then let us hear your offer, Captain?" said Dunois.

"Two gold ducats for each of the thirty-three men, three for the sergeant and five for me—seventy-four ducats in all."

Dunois frowned. "But, Captain, that is nothing like enough. I am disappointed in you."

"Well then, Mon Seigneur, to save us wasting our breath, just tell me your price. If I cannot pay it, then we shall fight. I will not haggle."

"My price is five ducats for each man, including the sergeant, and ten ducats for you." The total of one hundred and eighty ducats was a huge sum, and Richard remained silent for a while wondering how he could pay it. He was also gaining time to meet Fastolf's half hour.

"Too much, Captain?" enquired Dunois.

"I think I may be able to find the money."

"All taken from us in the first place," muttered de Rais.

"Not so, Mon Seigneur. Our great King Henry forbade pillaging in France because he believed that would be stealing from subjects who were rightfully his." Then speaking to Dunois once again, Richard asked, "Mon Seigneur, will you give me two months to pay? I have good farmland in England which I can sell to meet your price, but it will take time to turn it into cash."

"Of course, and the Sieur de Freuchin will accompany you."

"Thank you, Mon Seigneur. He will need an extended pass from a senior English commander to ensure his safety."

"Well, it so happens we have quite a number of those at the moment." This caused a few sniggers amongst the French, then for the first time since the parley began, Dunois smiled a heartwarming smile. "Will Lord Talbot do?"

"Indeed he will, Mon Seigneur, Lord Talbot knows me personally."

"Excellent, then you shall be our guest while Lord Talbot writes and seals the pass, and your companion may return to your men and tell them the good news. Marcel, please prepare yourself for a visit to England."

Richard returned to the Norfolk company just as the sun was setting, this time accompanied by Marcel instead of Hook, but his elation was muted. Firstly, although he had secured well over Fastolf's required half hour, the French returned to Orléans instead of chasing after the English vanguard. When Richard asked Marcel about this as they slowly walked their tired horses back to the Norfolk company, he discovered that the French thought they had beaten the entire English army. They had no idea that the vanguard had escaped, so, ironically, Fastolf never needed his half hour after all.

Then, when they were only yards from the English position, Richard saw Will Potter's body lying stretched out between two Frenchmen. The head was facing him, and the grotesque teeth were exposed in the death grin. Poor Will had gone through all that dental pain for nothing. Now Margaret could go back to her saddlemaker in Wrentham if she wished, or with all Will's prize money, she could do whatever she liked. "Such is the fate of war," said Richard quietly to himself.

CHAPTER EIGHT

Georges de la Trémoille, Grand Chamberlain of France and the most powerful man in the country after the dauphin, came from a long line of nobility and was distantly related both to the Valois and Plantagenet dynasties. As a young man he had been captured at Agincourt, but the English considered him of little value, and accordingly his ransom was set low. Consequently he was soon released, and having had his fill of war, he joined the crown civil service as a clerk and administrator.

His talent was soon recognised by Arthur of Richemont, the future Constable of France, and through his patronage, Georges quickly rose through the ranks during the later years of mad King Charles VI's reign. But while all those at court lavished their attention on the Dauphin Louis, and after his early death, the new Dauphin Jean, both well-built, handsome young men, Trémoille was perhaps the only court official to recognise the intellectual power of Charles, the pale and puny youngest brother.

Fate was hard on the numerous brood of King Charles and Queen Isabeau, but when the Dauphin Jean followed Louis to an early grave at only eighteen years of age, Trémoille's farsighted, personal investment in the next dauphin paid off handsomely. Charles never forgot that the only man who helped him when he was less than nothing at court was Georges Trémoille, and as a result, he remained absurdly loyal to Trémoille, who became something of a second father to the dauphin as well as his personal confidante and adviser. This attachment remained firm long after it was obvious to everyone else that Trémoille had become a liability to both Charles and France.

But in June 1429, Trémoille was at the height of his power and influence, so it was no surprise that when Charles decided to leave Chinon to be nearer the heart of the war with the English, he chose Trémoille's moated fortress at Sully sur Loire, twenty-five miles upstream from Orléans, to be his temporary home. The grand chamberlain was delighted.

Patay was fought on the eighteenth day of June. In the evening of the twenty-first, three riders and a small entourage arrived at Sully to see the king. They were granted immediate entry, for the riders were the Duke of Alençon, commander of the king's army, Gilles de Rais, and the inspiration for the victory, Jeanne, the Maid of Orléans. Waiting for them in the high vaulted dining hall, which was also used as an audience chamber, was Georges de la Trémoille. He was now forty-one years old and had grown excessively fat on too much food and wine and not enough physical activity.

"Welcome to my humble abode," he said smoothly, knowing full well that his abode was anything but humble. "The king is in one of my paddocks inspecting the horses we captured at Jargeau."

"I have no love for the English, but I have to admit they do breed excellent horses," acknowledged Alençon.

"Which they waste as pack animals because they choose to fight dismounted whenever they can."

"You have experience of war?" asked Alençon incredulously as he looked at Trémoille's grotesque frame.

"I fought at Agincourt when you were a boy. You still look like one to me."

Although still young, Alençon was not at all overawed by this pompous creature. "I am a prince of the blood. I am not a boy, and you will use my title when addressing me."

"Of course, Mon Seigneur," replied Trémoille, labouring the word *Mon Seigneur*, "and I shall endeavour to remember you are not a boy." Then looking at Jeanne, he added, "You have not yet introduced me to this girl."

"Nor is this lady to be spoken of in that manner." De Rais was delighted with the way his commander was comporting himself in front of the insolent Trémoille. "You have the honour," continued Alençon, "to be in the presence of Jeanne, the Maid of Orléans, the architect and inspiration of all our victories."

"I am indeed honoured," said Trémoille, not bothering to keep the sarcasm out of his voice. "And what is your business with the king? I have already informed him of our victory at Patay."

"Our victory?" Questioned Alençon. "I do not recall seeing you there."

"France's victory. Are we not all French?"

Jeanne had heard enough. Male bickering irritated her, so she cut straight to the quick. "Mon Seigneur, we need to speak to the dauphin about the march to Reims and his coronation, which should take place as soon as possible."

"But the king is going to Paris next. It was decided at the Royal Council meeting this morning. This was considered the right step by more measured and mature minds than yours."

Alençon, who could feel de Rais bristling beside him, interrupted. "I must ask you to watch your tongue, Mon Seigneur, or my good friend standing here beside me will tear it out."

Trémoille looked at de Rais's dark, venomous eyes and became a little more conciliatory. "The Royal Council determined that the correct strategic move is to march on Paris and recapture the capital city of our beloved country."

"And were any of our military commanders present for this debate on strategy?" demanded Alençon.

"No, but—"

"Then how can you judge the right strategic move without the benefit of military advice?"

"Is it not obvious?"

"Was this your advice too?"

"Yes."

"Well, be aware that whatever your council has decided, we will be marching on Reims, not Paris, for the king's coronation with the holy oil of Clovis, thus making him the indisputable true King of France."

"But you cannot overturn a decision by the Royal Council. It outranks any military council."

"God can override any earthly council!" said Jeanne.

"How can you know this?"

"The voices from heaven have told me."

"Voices from heaven? Pah!" was Trémoille's response.

"Pah or no pah," replied de Rais, "Jeanne's voices have never failed us yet, and all in the army believe Reims is the right decision."

Alençon closed the meeting. "Trouble yourself no further, Mon Seigneur. We shall leave you now and inform the king ourselves. Good day."

The Angel of Lorraine

As predicted, Charles changed his mind after he spoke to Jeanne; and if ever Trémoille needed proof that he had a serious contender for the favour of the king—or the dauphin, as Jeanne still insisted on calling him—the evidence was now clear. This threat needed to be removed. The royal army began assembling at Gien, fifteen miles upstream from Sully sur Loire, ready for the perilous march through Burgundian territory to Reims; but Jeanne, unaccustomed to the vicissitudes of court life, had no idea that she had just made a deadly enemy, one powerful enough to become the instrument of her ultimate downfall.

The march to Reims did not go smoothly. To begin with, the towns and cities along the twelve thousand–strong army's path quickly changed their allegiance from Burgundy to the Valois King of France when they saw it approaching, until it reached Troyes. This was the city that gave its name to the notorious treaty that disinherited Charles from his throne. Here the city elders and the Burgundian garrison refused to surrender. For three days, the royal army sat outside the heavily defended city walls while deputations and letters went back and forth between the garrison and the French commanders, but the city elders remained stubbornly committed to the Duke of Burgundy. Food for the besiegers began to run low, and all the while they knew that their artillery train, which had been put together in haste, was inadequate to deal with the massive walls of Troyes. Voices in the Royal Council started to propose returning to the safety of the Loire valley where they could revictual and augment the siege cannon before trying again in the autumn.

But a retired old warrior who served in the Royal Council, Robert de Macon, felt differently. He had served under the renowned Constable of France, Betrand du Guesclin, who won back most of the land lost to England during the reigns of earlier French kings. This link to a more successful era ensured Robert was appointed to the council by Charles's father, and he had remained there ever since. He said the council should hear what Jeanne had to say, for she was the reason the army had already advanced this far.

So it was that on the morning of the eighth day of July, Jeanne and Dunois presented themselves at the king's campaign tent outside Troyes. Dunois was anxious, but Jeanne was not at all concerned about the status of the Royal Council or those within it, even though the king's tent was twice as large as her house in Domremy. Her confidence derived from her voices, not the trappings of men.

"Be careful, Jeanne," cautioned Dunois. "Trémoille will be at the meeting. He is the king's favourite, but to him, you are the greatest threat since Arthur of Richemont, and you know what happened to him."

"He was banished from court."

"Yes. After giving Trémoille the patronage he needed to climb through the ranks at court, that was the thanks he got."

"Jean, I do not care about such matters. I am on a mission from God."

"Then for God's sake, do not trust that man."

Jeanne and Dunois were welcomed to the Royal Council by Charles. Trémoille also provided an effusive welcome. "I am so glad you have come here, Jeanne. Your advice is much needed by this council. Some, the majority I dare say, propose we should retire to Orléans while others believe we should push on to Reims without capturing Troyes first." He was careful not to say in front of Charles which option he preferred. "So, Jeanne, what is your opinion?"

"Both proposals are wrong. Certainly we must not retire to the Loire, our credibility would be seriously damaged if we did, but nor should we leave an undefeated enemy behind us. We must attack Troyes at once. I will lead the army, and within a few days, our noble dauphin will enter the city as the victor. Of this I am certain."

"Did your voices tell you that?" asked Trémoille rather too innocently. The small, dark lizard-like eyes in the round, chubby face flickered back and forth as the chamberlain assessed the reactions of those sitting round the table, most importantly, the king's. Either way, Trémoille had ensured his credibility. If the assault failed, he would have backed the angel from Lorraine despite his better judgement, but her aura of invincibility will have been shattered, leaving him still the king's most reliable adviser. But if Troyes fell, he would take credit for backing the winner and would bide his time until he found some other way to bring Jeanne down.

"Mon Seigneur," answered Jeanne. "There is no doubt Troyes will fall if we attack. All our noble dauphin needs to do is give the order. After that, the army and I will do the rest."

Charles looked at Dunois. "What do you say, Jean?"

"I can speak only for myself, Your Majesty, but I believe the entire army, including me, will follow Jeanne's banner wherever it takes us, and we shall win."

That settled it. The Royal Council agreed unanimously to attack Troyes without delay, and Trémoille led the obsequious applause for Jeanne and the king when Charles gave the command to start preparing for the assault the next day.

There was much to do before an assault could take place, and the work began on the ninth day of July. In full view of the citizens, carpenters began constructing scaling ladders for the escalade, sappers dug approach trenches for the siege guns, and Jeanne, resplendent in her armour, led the common soldiers to the city walls and exhorted them as they started to fill in the deep ditch in front of the walls with earth and straw to provide a firm footing for the ladders when the dreadful moment for the escalade came.

The stiff backbones of the city elders began to soften as they realised there really would be an assault. Everyone knew that a city taken by escalade was at the mercy of the besiegers. The fear and tension felt by the assault troops caused by the most dangerous action in war always released itself on the citizens. They became the victims of wild soldiery out of control of their officers, free to indulge their basic animal instincts in savage revenge for the terror they had just undergone and exhilaration because they were still alive.

Jeanne had already written to the members of the city council assuring them the lives of all the citizens would be spared if they renounced Philippe of Burgundy and returned their allegiance to the dauphin, who would shortly be crowned in Reims. But ominously, she gave no warranties for their safety once the assault had started. This offer, ridiculed a few days before, now seemed attractive.

On the tenth day of July, Troyes threw open its gates and formally surrendered on the terms Jeanne had proposed. Once again, the Maid had pulled victory, this time bloodless, from the jaws of defeat. The miracle continued.

News of Troyes's surrender quickly reached Reims. Despite repeated requests for help, the prospects of a relief force coming from Burgundy or the English were negligible, so following Troyes's example, Reims sent a deputation to the approaching royal army offering allegiance to the true King of France. Charles entered the city as the merciful victor on the seventeenth day of July.

Reims, the sacred city where the fifth-century Frankish king, Clovis, had been converted to Christianity, was a special place. For a thousand years, French kings had been crowned here and anointed with the same holy oil that had supposedly been used for Clovis's conversion. Now the cathedral of Notre Dame, said to be the finest in Europe, put on a magnificent ceremony for King Charles VII's coronation despite the short notice.

Breaking with precedent, Jeanne was given the place of honour and was permitted to stand beside Charles throughout the ceremony. Her mother and father were invited to see their daughter's crowning achievement along with Father Front, and as the coronation ended to the deafening sound of a sublime trumpet fanfare rising in glorious celebration of the righteous King of France, so Jeanne's star rose too.

The Angel of Lorraine

This day was the zenith of her miraculous life.

* * *

II

"Well, Henry, it's time to go our separate ways," said Richard as he stood with Sergeant Hawkswood at the fork in the road outside Janville. It was the day after Patay, and while the French were celebrating at Orléans, Richard was collecting what English stragglers he could find to join his tiny, orderly column in a sea of chaos. But at Janville, his road, the road to Rouen, forked to the left while Henry and the rest of the Norfolk company needed to follow the main army on the right fork that led to Paris.

"Captain, are you sure you can trust this Frenchman?"

"Almost as sure as I can trust you, Henry. The Sieur de Freuchin just saved all our lives back there at Patay. He could easily have stayed silent but chose not to."

"Well, that's good enough for me. When will we meet again?"

"After I have gathered the ransom money in England and reported to Sir John, wherever he is, but I don't know when that will be…a couple of months perhaps."

"Very well, Captain. Give my compliments to your wife, and apologies for the death of John Fletcher. I know they shared the same beliefs."

"They did indeed, Henry, and I firmly believe that Lollardy will one day form the basis of the way we govern our people. Meanwhile, farewell, and may we meet again soon."

Richard and Marcel reached Rouen in the evening two days later. Mary's delight at the unexpected visit from her husband was quelled when she saw his wounded left arm, and her curiosity was aroused by the presence of Marcel.

Richard quickly reassured her. "There is nought to fear, Mary. Let's go indoors, it's getting chilly, and I will explain all."

"I have the honour to present Marcel, Sieur de Freuchin," said Richard to Mary and a wide-eyed Joan as they sat in the front room reserved for greeting important guests. "Marcel is my officer of parole and is here to make sure I pay the ransom I agreed with the French for the lives of the Norfolk company and myself."

"It is only a formality, ladies," said Marcel soothingly. "I know Richard will do this with or without my presence."

"Thank you, Marcel, and may I present to you the two most important ladies in my life—my wife Mary and my daughter Joan."

Marcel stood up and bowed. "I too am honoured."

Mary raised a coquettish eyebrow. "You two seem to know each other well for supposed enemies."

"We have known each other since Harfleur, fourteen years ago," replied Richard. "War is strange and can create unexpected friendships."

"So I see!"

Richard went on to explain all that had happened at Orléans and Patay, how he had been wounded and how he had managed to ransom himself and Fastolf's men. "So you see," he ended, "Marcel is here with a warrant for his protection signed by Lord Talbot, and will accompany me wherever I go until the ransom is paid. This means I must travel to England to sell my land, which I will do after I've reported to army headquarters here in Rouen. But I shall take a couple of days off before I do. I need a rest."

"But surely Sir John Fastolf will pay the ransom," said Mary indignantly. "It is his men you saved."

"I'm sure he will, but I did not have his permission to negotiate the ransom, so I will visit him before I go. It's quite possible I may not have to go to England after I meet him."

Mary sighed. "You obviously have not heard that Sir John has been sent home in disgrace. He's being blamed for the defeat and even accused of cowardice."

"What! But that's infamous! Nothing could be further from the truth. I was there and saw it all."

"Well, the Duke of Bedford is in Rouen, so maybe you should go to headquarters tomorrow and speak to him."

"I certainly will. Such slander must be quelled before it spreads, but this evening, Marcel is our guest. I apologise for springing this on you, but we need to take care of him until we can find him lodgings in Rouen."

"That won't be a problem. The tenant in our house near the river has just given notice of his departure, so the Sieur de Freuchin can lodge there."

Marcel jumped to his feet again. "Madame, please address me as *Marcel*."

"And you may call me *Mary*, and if my daughter pleases, you may call her *Joan*."

"Oh, yes, please," said Joan enthusiastically, "and I will help you cook dinner for our guest this evening, Maman."

"And for your father too, I presume?"

"Of course, Maman."

Next morning, with Marcel's permission, Richard went unaccompanied to army headquarters. One-armed Michael welcomed him at reception. "Captain Richard, what a coincidence! The Duke of Bedford was asking after your whereabouts less than an hour ago. He is eager to meet you."

"Can he see me now?"

"He's in a meeting at present, but I'll make sure he knows you're here. While you're waiting, why don't you visit our surgeon? Your arm looks in a bad way."

"Thank you, Michael. I've got Patay to thank for that."

"Then I'll take you to him."

The surgery was located at the back of the building where yells of pain could not be heard from the offices in the front. The surgeon, a small, insect-like man, reminded Richard of one of the officious clerks he had seen in the Ipswich customs office. When Richard removed his tunic, the surgeon raised his eyebrows. "Badly swollen, broken elbow I expect. Give me your left hand palm upwards."

"Ouch!"

"Stop fussing," said the surgeon as he put away the six-inch long needle, "at least you've still got feeling in your fingertips, so I do not recommend amputation just yet. But it may be necessary if the blood turns poisonous. Are you in much pain?"

"Only when you stab me with a bloody great dagger! The elbow hurts if I try to use my arm, but if I let it hang loose, there is only a dull ache which is bearable."

"Well, I can give you a compound of willow bark, which will ease the ache. The swelling should go down soon, and then I can reset the elbow if you like."

The Angel of Lorraine

"Reset?"

"Break it again and put it back in the correct position. If nothing is done, you'll never be able to use your arm properly again, and even if I do reset it, your fighting days are over. You're no longer a young man, so you cannot expect a complete recovery."

"You're a bundle of joy, aren't you."

"Do you want me to reset it or not?"

"Will it be painful?"

"Yes."

"Then I'll think about it. I have to go to England tomorrow, but I'll be back in a few weeks."

"Well, don't leave it too long. If the bone has time to set in its present position, it will be more difficult to carry out the remedial operation, and then it will hurt even more! Now drink this." The surgeon handed Richard an evil-smelling mug of disgusting brown liquid. "This is the willow bark compound I mentioned. I'll give you a flask to take with you, but only use it when you need to, and then no more than a small amount at a time."

When Richard left the surgery, promising himself never to go near it again, the Duke of Bedford was ready to see him. Michael took him to the same office he had used when he composed the letter he sent to Ruth. Now the Regent of England and France was standing there by the window watching the people of Rouen busily going about their daily lives. It was five years since Richard had last seen Bedford. They were about the same age, but when the duke turned round to greet him, he was shocked by the change in Bedford. His jet-black hair was now mostly grey, deep worry lines had developed round his mouth and across his brow, and bags had formed under his eyes. He had lost weight, and his neck was scrawny; he looked more like sixty than forty.

Peter Tallon

Bedford noticed Richard staring and smiled. "Yes, Captain Calveley, unlike you, time has not been kind to me. The effort of trying to manage two kingdoms has taken its toll."

"I don't understand how you are able to do it, my lord. The stress would be too much for a lesser man."

"I have my dear wife, Anne, to thank for that. She is my best friend as well as my wife."

"Then I am happy for you both, my lord."

Bedford pointed to the chairs around the conference table. "Let us sit down, Captain. What happened to your arm?"

"A present from Patay, my lord."

"Have you seen a surgeon?"

"Yes, I saw the one here, but I don't think I'll be seeing him again."

"Very wise. Amputation and the leech are all they know. It's said that the French surgeons are better than ours."

"But the surgeon who removed the arrow from your brother's face after the battle of Shrewsbury must have been skilful."

"Aye, he was exceptional. Strange, is it not, that surgeons can perform minor miracles like the one on my brother, yet there is still nothing they can do about the bloody flux which carries off so many including my brother."

"I cannot explain it, my lord."

Bedford put his hand on a rolled-up letter that was on the table beside him. "Captain, Patay was a bad business. This is a letter I've just received from Lord Talbot. The recriminations have started."

The Angel of Lorraine

"I'm surprised the French allowed him to send you a letter at all!"

"It's common practice between senior commanders on both sides, though I am sure the French will have read it before it was sealed, so Talbot could not say anything of a strategic nature. But before I let you read it, perhaps you would give me your account of what happened at Patay. You look as though you were in the thick of it."

It took Richard almost an hour to describe what happened. Bedford asked many searching questions, and at the end said, "Captain, you have made no mention of the size of the French army. We were heavily outnumbered, were we not?"

Richard paused, knowing that what he was about to say would not please the regent. "My lord, you may recall that I am a surveyor as well as a soldier. I personally counted the numbers of one of the two French armies that united to fight us, and Lord Talbot himself told me the size of the other one, so I know that the French had around seventeen thousand men at Patay."

"About three to one then?"

"Not really, my lord. The plain, unvarnished truth is that we were beaten by the French vanguard alone, no more than fifteen hundred men, before the rest of the French army reached the battlefield. Our own vanguard was never engaged, so we had about four and a half thousand present. Therefore, three to one is correct, but not in the sense you meant it. Most of our army was composed of raw recruits, and I am sorry to say that they panicked and ran when they saw our rear guard fleeing. Only Sir Thomas Rempston's men and Sir John Fastolf's own companies stood firm."

Bedford spoke quietly, "This makes difficult listening, Captain. Where was Talbot at this time?"

"He had stationed himself with the rearguard and was taken prisoner with Lord Scales and Sir Thomas at the beginning of the battle."

"I see. Now, Captain, I have something sensitive to put to you. This letter I have received from Talbot accuses Fastolf of fleeing from the battlefield like a coward and abandoning other garter knights as well as his own men. Do you have anything to say about that?"

Richard felt hot pinpoints of rage pricking his skin. He wanted to vent his own anger about Talbot but knew he must keep his temper and appear calm and measured in front of Bedford.

"My lord, I heard these rumours when I got back to Rouen and wondered who was spreading them. Now I think I know. The relationship between Sir John and Lord Talbot is not good. They quarrelled bitterly over strategy, but Talbot made the final decision because he was in command. I was on duty outside the farmhouse at Janville where this took place and heard every word. Sir John wanted the army to retire to Paris where it could regroup and replenish after our defeat at Orléans, but Lord Talbot wanted to head south again and attack the French before their two armies could unite."

"That sounds typical Talbot," murmured Bedford.

"That move proved abortive when Beaugency fell, so we turned round and went north again just as Sir John had proposed two days earlier. But by then, the French armies had managed to unite, our men were in low spirits, and the battle was fought at Patay as I have already described to you. How Lord Talbot could say those things about Sir John confuses me because Talbot was already a prisoner of the French and could not possibly have seen what really happened."

"Then what did happen, Captain?"

"When all was lost, Sir John asked me to ride ahead to our vanguard and order it to halt and turn about while he fought a holding action to try and salvage what he could of the rest of the army. It was I who suggested he should go himself because I doubted if the commander of the vanguard would obey an order from a captain when some of the fugitives would already have reached the vanguard spreading panic. Sir John said he could

The Angel of Lorraine

not leave the field because he is a garter knight, but I pointed out to him that now Lord Talbot had got himself captured, Sir John was in command of the remains of the last English field army in France, and therefore he should act as such. It is my firm belief that had Sir John not ridden forward to the vanguard and turned it around leaving me to command the holding action, the French would have bagged the entire army and not just half of it."

"Thank you, Captain, I thought it might be something like that."

But Richard had not yet finished. "Finally, my lord, to call Sir John Fastolf a coward is not only a gross defamation of his character, but also ridiculous. You fought alongside him at Verneuil as I did at Rouvray. There is no braver knight walking on God's earth than Sir John."

"Well, there will have to be an inquiry," said Bedford, "but with your evidence, Sir John will be cleared. I have sent him home pending that inquiry, but now I shall write to him today and ask him to return at once. What are your plans? You are in no fit state to return to the army."

"I shall go back to Suffolk, my lord, to raise the ransom money I agreed with the French for the remains of the Norfolk company."

"Good, and no doubt Fastolf will assist you with that."

"I hope so, my lord, but I have the necessary assets in any event."

"Then will you take my letter to him yourself? That will be the quickest and surest way to get him back here."

"Of course, my lord."

"I have one final question for you, Captain. During your account of the battle at Patay, you said you negotiated the ransom for the Norfolk company with Jean Dunois."

"That is so, my lord."

"Did you meet Joan the Maid?"

"Yes, my lord."

"Is she truly a witch?"

"No, my lord, more like an angel in my opinion, though I would not admit that to anyone but you. It was she who prevailed upon Dunois to show mercy. To me she appeared to be little more than a child, but she spoke with wisdom and maturity, and it is thanks to her that I am standing here today."

"If she is not a witch, then how do you explain her dramatic effect on French fighting prowess?"

"Her own unquestioning certainty of victory has given them confidence. They now fight like the French of old."

"But where does her certainty come from?"

"She says from God."

"So God has turned against us?"

"I cannot say, my lord, but it does seem to me that God cares precious little about the affairs of men one way or the other."

"Seems like Joan may have cast a spell on you too, Captain."

"I trust not, my lord. I am too thick-skinned for any witch to waste a spell on me."

"Perhaps, perhaps not. Anyway, Captain, I commend you for your actions at Patay and wish you a safe and speedy journey to England. Impress upon Sir John how urgent it is that he gets back here quickly. We are desperately short of experienced leaders at the moment. Now please wait while I write the letter to Sir John and his charming wife, Millicent."

"Richard, when must you leave?" asked Mary as they finished their evening meal with Joan and Marcel.

"A cog is scheduled to depart from Rouen for Ipswich on tomorrow evening's ebb tide. Marcel has given me permission to travel alone because he is averse to sea journeys. I do not expect to be away for more than a month, but it depends on how long it takes to sell my land and transfer the money here. There's a Lombard bank in Norwich and another here in Rouen, so it should be possible to complete the transaction by banker's draft rather than risk carrying so much cash with me, especially as I'm hardly in a condition to defend myself at present."

"It looks like your fighting days are over, Richard. What will you do now?" asked Marcel.

"I don't know. I might still find work with the army. I'm a trained surveyor as well as a soldier."

"And you're a good storyteller too, Papa," said Joan. "You never really said much about your adventure in the Holy Land."

Marcel put down the goblet he was about to drink from. "You have been to Outremer? Jesus Christ's own land?"

"About four years ago."

"But it's full of Turks, is it not?"

"Yes. They were not pleased when we arrived."

"I should like to hear that story too."

Mary put her hand on Richard's. "We would all like to hear it. You have only ever referred to it in passing."

The rest of that evening passed convivially, though Richard was careful to avoid any reference to Ruth. He often thought back to that happy occasion spent with two women he loved and a Frenchman who was fast becoming a firm friend, but there was yet to be another twist in his life, for he had not yet noticed how Marcel and Joan were looking at each other.

***

III

On the first day of July, Richard stood outside the walls of Dunwich priory looking at the graves of Ann, his first wife, and his two boys. It was early morning, the matins bell was ringing, and his long shadow touched Ann's headstone like a kiss from another, more simple time when he thought his destiny was to be a farmer working the land for his family in Westhall. He was pleased to see the graves were well tended, unlike some others in the graveyard, and he knew he had Father Hugh to thank for that.

Fastolf's manor at Caistor near Yarmouth was only half a day's ride away, so Richard had plenty of time to visit Hugh and see how his erstwhile steward was coping with monastic life. He had already taken a short diversion to look at his land at Westhall near Beccles and was satisfied that it was being well tended with wheat and barley growing in the fields while the green pasture near a small tributary of the River Blyth was being grazed by liver brown beef cattle. Fastolf's tenants were keeping the land in good heart, so it should achieve a good price at auction.

He waited for an hour to give the friars enough time to say their morning prayers and eat their breakfasts before he knocked at the heavy, oak priory doors. The prior, Father Simon, remembered Richard and took him to Hugh's chamber, which overlooked the garden. "I'll leave you two to reminisce," he said. "It's a beautiful morning. Why not take a stroll around our well-tended gardens? I know Father Hugh is especially proud of his excellent work in the herb garden."

When the prior left, Hugh said quietly, "Balls to the bloody herb garden!" After that, he seemed disinclined to speak. They walked silently past the rose beds and the delightful smelling rows of lavender until they reached the aforesaid herb garden. This garden was oblong in shape and divided into eight small squares separated by narrow stone paths. Each square was dedicated to a particular herb, and Richard recognised rosemary, chives, parsley, and thyme by their unmistakable individual scents. There were other herbs he could not identify. He tried to prompt Hugh to converse. "Hugh, the herb garden is truly a work of art, you are to be congratulated. How goes it here with you?"

The response was not immediate, but when it came, it was uncompromising. "Badly. I should not be here. I have no vocation, my life in this God-forsaken priory is pointless, I would be better off dead."

"Well, that's clear enough," replied Richard. "Can't you get your ordination rescinded and make your way in the outside world? You certainly have the skills to do that."

"Not without the authorisation of Pope Bloody Martin the Bloody Fifth!"

"Can't a bishop do that?"

"Apparently not, according to bloody Simon."

"Hugh, if you must keep swearing, keep your bloody voice down!"

"I would have to travel to Rome," continued Hugh, "see Pope Martin, and pay him a fee—all at my own expense, and even then, he could still refuse. Anyway, I have no money. Everything I earned as your steward was given to the priory."

Richard's mind began to whirl. Rome was not so far from Genoa where Ruth and Enrico lived. Maybe he could help Hugh shake off the shackles of the Church and at the same time work in a visit to Ruth and

Peter Tallon

Enrico. "What if I accompany you, pay your expenses to get to Rome and also the pope's fee? Would you make the trip then?"

"Certainly I would, but why would you do that?"

"For the moment, can we just say I have my reasons."

"All right, but Simon would find a way to thwart me. I have already suggested something along those lines involving a loan from the priory, but he refused saying it would set a bad precedent within the Dunwich community."

"But how could he stop you?"

"Easily. He could have me locked in my room or have me watched so that I cannot pass through the priory gate. There are many in this sad, inward-looking community who would be happy to carry out such duties as a break from the endless daily monotony here."

Richard thought for a few moments then said starkly, "Hugh, are you prepared to take a risk that could lead to your freedom?"

"Happily," came the immediate response.

"Then so am I. Much has happened since we last met, including a change for the worse in English fortunes in France as well as certain events in my private life which I will describe to you before I leave. I shall only tell you these things so you can understand how deeply committed I am to making a trip to Genoa, which is not so far from Rome."

Hugh's sullen attitude suddenly vanished. This sounded like the priceless currency within the barren Dunwich priory community: good quality gossip. All of a sudden, he was his old self again. "Well, don't keep me in suspense. Tell me now!"

Richard held nothing back and spoke freely of his adventure in the Holy Land, including his affair with Ruth and the birth of his son whom he had not yet seen. At the end of it all, he felt much better for sharing a secret he had borne alone for five years, though he had only recently discovered the existence of his son.

When he had finished, there was silence. Then Hugh looked at him with that impish grin he remembered from happier days. "So I'm not the only one who's been a naughty boy then?"

"Apparently not."

"You little devil!"

"Do you want me to rescue you from this hellhole or not?"

"Yes, please."

"Then stop being so damned smug!"

"Richard, are you really serious about getting me out of here?"

"Yes, but not by the front door. It will have to be at night." Then pointing to the priory's flint-and-mortar curtain wall where it was reinforced by a large stone buttress, he added, "That wall is about fifteen feet high. In exactly a week from now, during the night of the eighth of July, I shall be on the other side of that wall with a rope to help you to climb over it and a spare horse to get you away from here. The priory clock chimes on the hour, does it not?"

"And also on the half hour."

"Then at half past eleven on that night, I shall throw one end of the rope over the wall so you can climb over. The buttress should help you because it has small, horizontal ledges in it as it thins towards the top which you can use for handholds if you need to. What about clothes? A friar's habit is not ideal for this sort of work."

"I still have the clothes I used to wear when I was your steward."

"Perfect! But you will still need to bring your Franciscan garb for your meeting with the pope. Have you a bag or valise you can stow it in plus any personal items you wish to bring? Remember, you will never return here."

"I'm sure I can find something. The hemp vegetable sacks are usually thrown away after use, so are the flour sacks. I can use one of those."

"That will do for your escape, but I'll bring a smart, leather valise for you. We can't have you meeting the pope wearing a flour sack! The moon was a quarter full last night and waxing, so we should have enough light to ride to Ipswich without waiting for dawn unless there is too much cloud. Anyway, you will hopefully not be missed until matins."

"Or even later because I often sleep through that dirge."

"If there is too much cloud cover, we'll walk the horses as far as we can until dawn, then ride hard for Ipswich port. There'll be no sleep for either of us that night."

"What if there's no boat due to sail for the continent?"

"Father Simon will guess you've left with me. He knows I disembarked at Ipswich, I mentioned it when I arrived here, though now I wish I hadn't, so he'll probably send the Dunwich sheriff after us. Therefore, we'll take any ship leaving the port on the ninth of July wherever it's going just to get away from Ipswich. Hopefully there'll be something heading south even if it's only destined for another English port." Realising the enormity of what he was about to do, Richard looked hard into Hugh's large brown eyes. "Are you sure you want this, Hugh? I don't know what law we'll be breaking, but I'm certain that what I'm proposing must be illegal."

"More than anything. My life here has no purpose, but you have given me hope again, and whatever the outside world has in store for me, it cannot be worse than this."

"Very well, I shall go now and give Father Simon a generous donation for the priory as I leave, which he will no doubt spend on himself. You have a week to prepare yourself for another long overdue adventure!"

* * *

IV

Richard reached Caistor Manor at noon. His arrival at the entrance to the manor house was announced by Fastolf's two gigantic mastiffs who were roaming free behind the short drawbridge that spanned the moat protecting the flint curtain wall enclosing the manor buildings. The drawbridge was left down during the day, for there was no need to raise it while the two large furry custodians were present to protect the residents. Their deep throated barks reverberated around the courtyard, but at a sharp word of command coming from one of the manor buildings, both dogs immediately sat down and contented themselves with glaring quietly at Richard from the far side of the drawbridge.

Soon William, the grumpy steward, appeared. He was well into his seventies now and could barely see as far as the hand at the end of his arm, but Millicent Fastolf insisted that he should be retained on the manor staff because of the forty years of loyal service he had given to the Fastolf family. He had become painfully thin; his clothes hung from his body like a shroud around a skeleton, but fortunately the two mastiffs obeyed him as their pack leader. But even so, an accidental knock from one of their wagging tails would have sent him flying to the other end of the drawbridge.

William peered vaguely in Richard's direction. His voice crackled like dry, snapping tinder wood.

"Who's there!"

"Captain Calveley."

"Master Richard?"

"Yes, William, it's me."

The grumpy expression disappeared. "Master Richard, how good to see you after all these years, though *see* is not really the right word. Come across the bridge."

"Will your dogs allow me to?"

"The only danger from Cuthbert, the fawn one, is lick and slobber. The dark brindle with the black face is Wulfstan. Left to his own devices, he could give you a nasty nip, but he'll be fine as long as he's with me."

Richard crossed the drawbridge and took a closer look at the dogs as he shook hands with William. Cuthbert's large brown eyes seemed friendly enough, but Wulfstan's bright amber eyes staring out of his jet-black face made him seem like some evil terror from a dark, Norwegian folktale. Richard stroked Cuthbert's broad head. "How much do they weigh?"

"Difficult to say because you can't weigh an unwilling mastiff, but the last time they were weighed accurately was when the fair was in Yarmouth a couple of years ago. One of the stalls had scales for measuring the weight of horses, so we know they were both over two hundred pounds then with Cuthbert being slightly the heavier of the two. I dare say they may be a bit heavier now."

"I never saw such big dogs. They must be a great comfort to you and Lady Millicent."

"We are never troubled by intruders, if that's what you mean."

Richard stroked Cuthbert again and received a slobbery lick in return, which soaked his tunic sleeve. "Is Sir John at home?"

The Angel of Lorraine

"He's gone to inspect some building materials in Yarmouth, but he'll be back this afternoon. Lady Millicent is here though. She'll be pleased to see you. I'll take you to her."

Millicent was working in the herb garden, which was alive with honeybees and butterflies.

"My lady!" called William. "Master Richard is here."

Millicent Fastolf, who was on her knees weeding, stood up and tried to straighten her hair. Tall and erect, she was a stately figure for a woman of fifty-five; any man would be proud of her as indeed Sir John was. "Richard! It must be five years since we last saw you."

"Too long, my lady. I understand Sir John is in Yarmouth."

"Yes, is he expecting you?"

"No, my lady. I have a letter for him from the Duke of Bedford."

The smile left Millicent's face. "I was about to take a midday break, so let us share some bread and cheese together, and we can sit outside in this lovely weather. Would you see to that please, William?"

"Yes, my lady. Two goblets of wine to accompany the food?"

"A good idea, we should celebrate Richard's visit."

While William left to prepare lunch, Richard and Millicent sat together on a wooden bench overlooking a small pond full of white water lilies and busy brown dragonflies. "I know John was sent home from France under a cloud," she said, "but I hope Bedford's not hounding him. It's been a delight having my husband at home without the cares of war troubling him."

Richard handed her Bedford's letter. "It's addressed to you both. I think you'll find it will explain all."

Millicent read it quickly and sighed. "I knew it was too good to last. Bedford wants John back in Paris as soon as possible."

"And I thought I was bringing good news. I'm sorry, my lady."

"Don't be. John will see this letter as good news. His reputation is restored thanks to you. Yesterday he told me he intends to rebuild Caistor Manor as a castle befitting our status. It is to be constructed of a new baked clay material called brick and contain the luxuries he's seen in French chateaux such as constantly available hot water and rooms dedicated to bathing. I suppose all that will have to wait now."

"When your husband says he will do something, he always does. He's a man of his word, and I have no doubt you shall have your castle, bathing rooms and all."

Millicent watched the dragonflies hunting insects above the pond for a few quiet moments, then looked at Richard again. "I know John is not a popular man, but tell me about this bad blood that exists between him and Lord Talbot."

"They are both strong-willed men but very different leaders. Talbot is a heroic and charismatic commander who has the common touch without compromising his authority. The men love him and will follow him anywhere, and until Patay, he always brought victory even against the heaviest odds. He is a very self-confident and aggressive leader but not good at listening to advice that doesn't suit him and, in my view, not averse to risking his men's lives to feed his lust for glory."

"You don't like him, Richard?"

"Not after the scandalous remarks he made about Sir John, but there's no doubt he's a charming and dynamic battle leader, though his self-confidence sometimes spills over into arrogance. A touch of humility would make him an even better general. Your husband could not be more different. He is also a great commander as I saw for myself at Rouvray, but most captains would consider Talbot better. Your husband's men respect rather than like him, for

The Angel of Lorraine

he does not seek popularity from them nor does he court friendship from his officers. He is more cautious than Talbot because his mentality is more that of an accountant than a warrior. He sees his men as valuable assets that have cost time and money to produce, which should not be wasted on unnecessary risks. Replacements are expensive and difficult to acquire. Also, thanks to the rules of prize money, Sir John's success at securing plunder filters down through his officers to his men. We've all done well financially under him, which is why there is no shortage of volunteers wanting to join his companies. I know who I would rather serve."

"But you've not explained why Talbot accused John of cowardice."

"There was a big argument between them over strategy. As ranking commander, Talbot insisted on having his own way, but Sir John was proved right, and Patay was the result, which made Talbot's first defeat doubly bitter. His pride was hurt, and he needed someone to blame, but that is no excuse for attempting to destroy your husband's reputation."

"I understand, and thank you for your part in this, Richard. Bedford speaks well of you in his letter and asks John to assist you with the ransom payment for the Norfolk company, which," she added with a hardening in her voice, "I'm sure he will."

"Thank you, my lady."

"You will need to give John and me a little time alone together when he gets back from Yarmouth. Meanwhile, walk with me, and I shall show you how my herb garden is developing."

Richard met Sir John and Millicent in the reception hall in the manor house later in the afternoon. Fastolf was very pleased to see him. "By god! I'm right glad you're here, Richard. When we went our separate ways at Patay, I remember wondering if we would ever meet again. Millicent has told you about the contents of Bedford's letter?"

"Yes, Sir John."

"Well, in that case you know I am in your debt for saving my men and my reputation, and of course I will help with the ransom. How much is it?"

"One hundred and eighty gold ducats."

Fastolf raised his eyebrows. "That's a steep price."

"The French were in no mood to negotiate."

"How did you plan to pay it?"

"I have two houses in Rouen I can sell, which will raise about half of the money. The rest will be paid for by the sale of my land at Westhall, hopefully to you."

Fastolf thought for a moment. "Richard, are you sure about selling your land? There may be other ways to raise the money."

"The fact is that I cannot return to England with Mary until the laws against Lollardy are repealed. As you know, Mary is a convicted heretic with a death sentence by burning to face if she sets foot in England again, so the land at Westhall is no use to me anymore. My future lies in Normandy."

Fastolf gave Millicent a wary, sidelong glance and announced, "Richard, I always pay my debts, and as I just said, I'm indebted to you, so here's what I will do. In view of your wife's situation, I shall indeed buy your eighty acres at Westhall. The price I shall pay will be three times market value, which amounts to two hundred and forty pounds, less notary's fees disbursements and so on—" Millicent cleared her throat meaningfully. "Well, on second thoughts, I'll pay those costs as well. That means you won't have to sell your houses in Rouen, and you should have some cash left over to keep for yourself."

"Sir John, that is too much. I never expected such generosity."

"Oh, well, in that case—"

"John!" It was Millicent again. "Richard, take the offer while it's still there."

"Sir John, I am pleased to accept your most generous offer, and I know Mary will be grateful too."

Fastolf quickly recovered from his momentary lapse. "Richard, I am not a popular man, but you are the nearest thing to a friend I have. We will need to go to Norwich tomorrow to sign the contract in my notary's office and arrange the transfer of funds to Rouen."

"Sir John, you have been very kind, but I still have a favour to ask you."

Fastolf was immediately on his guard in case it was going to cost him more money. "Well, what is it?"

"It concerns Father Hugh."

Fastolf relaxed again. "Ah, the misbehaving Franciscan."

"I called on him at Dunwich priory on my way here. He's in a sorry state. His vocation has gone—"

"If he ever had one."

"Indeed. He hates monastic life. Father Simon, his prior, has informed him that there is no escape for him unless he gets his Sacrament of Holy Orders rescinded, which can only be done by the pope in Rome, where a donation to the Church will be expected. Hugh has no money of his own, so he has as much chance of meeting the pope as walking on water."

"So what can be done for him?"

"Are you still a magistrate, Sir John?"

"No, I gave that up years ago to concentrate on my affairs in France."

"Then I may speak freely in front of you?"

Sensing something interesting was coming up, Fastolf leaned forward intrigued. "You may. What are you planning, Richard? I know that look."

"In exactly a week from today, I am going to help Hugh escape from Dunwich priory." Richard went on to explain how it would be done, to Fastolf's amazement and Millicent's delight. She clapped her hands and said, "It sounds like a tale the storytellers recount to entertain audiences during long, winter evenings."

Fastolf laughed. "I'm not sure if assisting a breakout from a priory ranks as illegal or not, but the Church will doubtless have something to say about it."

"Hopefully we'll be long gone by then, Sir John, but we'll need to get to Rome quickly so that Hugh can be released from his vows before news of his escape gets there."

"Which it certainly will. How will you travel?"

"Because of the war with France, I think we'll take a ship from Rouen as soon as I've paid off the ransom."

"Overland might be quicker."

"But risky, and Rome is a long way south."

Fastolf asked, "But what about Pope Martin's donation—or should I say bribe?"

"Bribe would be more accurate, but that was the weak point in my plan because I did not know if I had enough money. Now, thanks to your generosity, I'm sure I'll have enough."

"Then what is the favour you want from me? You seem to have everything well planned."

The Angel of Lorraine

"Breaking Hugh out of his prison is one thing, but he will need work when he joins the outside world. He is fluent in Latin and French and was a notary's assistant in Yarmouth before he joined the Franciscan Order. He has experience in estate management because, as you already know, he was my steward at Calveley Hall where he served the estate well. Is there any chance that you, with all your contacts in Norfolk, could find work for him?"

Fastolf frowned. "I'll give that some thought, but nothing springs to mind immediately."

"What about William?" suggested Millicent. "He's forgetful, frail, and as blind as a bat though he pretends not to be. You have your castle-building project coming up, so you'll need someone to manage that for you, check you receive the correct quantities of materials you pay for, count the number of bricks used, and so on. Hugh could also cover for William's fading powers as his deputy and save you a great deal of money."

"How fortunate I am to have a wife who has all the answers," said Fastolf in a neutral voice.

"Well, that's settled then," replied Millicent sweetly. "Richard, you may tell Hugh that there will be work for him here when he gets back from Rome, and we'll find him accommodation in one of the estate houses."

"The rent for which will be deducted from his pay," added Fastolf masterfully.

"Of course, dear, that is only fair."

"He'll be delighted," said Richard, "as am I. Now he'll have something to live for and a means to pay his way. I'm sure you'll find him good value, Sir John."

"Doubtless, doubtless," agreed Fastolf half-heartedly.

Quickly changing the subject now she had got what she wanted as usual, Millicent asked, "And what about your arm, Richard? Do you get much pain?"

"Only at the elbow when I try to straighten it, and sometimes at night."

"Is there anything that can be done?"

"The military surgeon in Rouen offered to break it again and reset it, but even if I undergo that painful procedure, there is no certainty it will recover well enough for me to carry a heavy battle shield again."

"Then while you're here, I'll arrange for our physician to give you something for the pain. His surgery is in Yarmouth."

"Thank you, my lady. I can combine that journey with a visit to the horse market. I shall need to buy one for Hugh."

* * *

V

Under a clear, starry sky and a half moon that made nighttime travelling possible, Richard stood outside the Dunwich priory curtain wall waiting for the clock to strike half past eleven. The week at Caistor had passed quickly. Fastolf had left for Paris on the day after the financial matters for the ransom were completed in Norwich, which left Richard with a few days to make his preparations for Hugh's escape and enjoy long walks through the East Norfolk countryside accompanied by Cuthbert and Wulfstan, both of whom had now accepted him as part of the Caistor household.

Beside Richard were the two horses that would carry Hugh and himself to Ipswich port. Hugh's, a grey palfrey with a docked tail, was a sturdy beast, though considerably smaller than his own bay warhorse, but more than adequate to carry Hugh's lightweight frame.

The priory clock chimed half past eleven. Richard threw one end of the rope he had purchased in Yarmouth over the wall and waited. Minutes passed, but all was silent on the other side of the wall. He began to worry, but he could do nothing because his broken arm would not allow him to scale his side of the wall. The clock struck twelve. Something must have gone wrong. He had just decided to pull the rope back when he heard scuffling on the other side of the wall. Seconds later, a shadow appeared above him. "Richard! Are you there?"

"Yes. Is everything all right, Hugh?"

"No. How far is it to the ground down there?"

"About thirteen feet. The grass is long, and the ground is quite soft."

"But I can't see a bloody thing! Can you—" Suddenly there was a shout from somewhere inside the priory, and the church bell started to ring as if an invasion had begun.

"Hugh, you'll have to jump."

"What about the rope?"

"Just leave it, there's no time. Jump now, or it'll be too late!"

The shadow fell to the ground just by Richard's right hand side. "Ouch! I think I've twisted my ankle."

"No time to worry about that. Have you got your things?"

"Yes, all in this flour sack."

"Then get on the grey horse and follow me before the whole of Dunwich is woken by that bloody bell!"

They soon reached the Ipswich road and cantered for about ten minutes until they passed the town of Saxmundham. There Hugh begged Richard to stop. "I haven't ridden for five years, and my arse feels red raw. For God's sake, can't we stop for a while?"

Richard drew rein and halted. Hugh was about to speak again, but Richard whispered, "Quiet! Listen and don't dismount yet." The only sound they could hear was the panting of their horses and the light breeze gently moving the forest branches; other than that, all was still. Satisfied that the pursuit, if there was one, was still far away, Richard said, "I think we can risk a five-minute break. Dismount but keep your horse's reins tightly wrapped round your wrist. What the hell happened back there?"

Hugh slipped painfully from the saddle and rubbed his sore buttocks with his free hand. "One of the friars must have been having a bad night and kept wandering up and down the corridors mumbling prayers to himself. I waited for him to go to bed, but when the clock chimed twelve, I knew I had to leave or risk missing you. Inevitably I bumped into him just as I was about to open the gate to the garden, so I hit him with my flour sack and ran. He fell over, but instead of chasing me, he ran to the church and sounded the alarm. The rest, you know."

"Well, we must assume Father Simon will call out the Dunwich sheriff and his men, but I doubt they'll leave before dawn. He'll guess you've left with me, so he'll direct the sheriff to Ipswich. I think we've time to walk the horses for a while, but we must reach Ipswich by sunrise, before the port authorities are alerted. You'll have plenty of time to recover once we've embarked."

Richard and a very sore Hugh arrived at the north quay just as the sun was appearing above the North Sea horizon. They went straight to the office at the customs house, which was always open throughout the day and night.

"The tide begins to ebb at midmorning, and we have three ships scheduled to leave," said the bleary-eyed clerk who was just coming to the end of his shift.

"Destinations?" asked Richard.

"One is heading to Newcastle to collect recruits for the army, poor beggars, another is going to Wivenhoe to do some dredging in the port there, and the third is taking wool to Calais."

"The name of the last one?"

"*Sea Sprite*, Captain Robert Coombes from Portsmouth commanding."

Reluctant at first, Captain Coombes happily found space on his deck for the two fugitives and their horses when Richard offered him a silver florin on departure and another two on safe arrival at Calais, but there was a five-hour wait to be endured until the tide was right for *Sea Sprite* to depart. At last the captain ordered the ropes to be loosened and brought in from the quayside bollards. His ship slowly began to drift towards the middle of the River Orwell, where she would catch the tide and be taken downstream to the North Sea.

Richard looked back and saw eight rough-looking horsemen arrive by the port's north gate. They headed directly for the customs house office. He gave the somnolent Hugh a nudge. "Look! It seems we've escaped our pursuers by just a few minutes."

"Have we really," said the exhausted friar, and went back to sleep.

CHAPTER NINE

Monday, the eighteenth of July, the day after the coronation at Reims, King Charles and Queen Marie attended a meeting of the Royal Council in the archbishop's palace next to the cathedral. It was another beautiful summer morning, so Dunois, who had not been invited, decided to take a relaxing stroll through the beautifully manicured palace gardens. First, he walked through the vegetable garden, which was being watered by three well-groomed servants, then he stopped at the pond and observed the fish for a while. After a few minutes, his attention was drawn by a wonderful scent wafting from somewhere near the southern end of the garden, so he decided to investigate.

He walked towards a tall yew hedge, which had an arch cut into it, and went through. On the other side, he beheld a long arbour with pink, white, and red roses growing up the sides and over the top so that the wooden arbour frame was invisible to someone looking from the outside. This was the source of the scent. On such a lovely morning, he felt it would be good to give his senses a treat by strolling slowly down the arbour tunnel, but paused just before the entrance when he heard the sound of movement coming from within. Quietly, he peeped into the tunnel and saw Yolande, Queen Marie's mother, delicately holding one of the roses to her aristocratic nose.

"My lady, what a pleasure to meet you here."

Startled, and briefly annoyed that her private moment had been interrupted, Yolande's stern face broke into a pleasant smile when she recognised Dunois. "Jean, what a wonderful morning to follow the happiest day of my life."

"Everyone shares your joy, my lady, but especially me, for I know how hard you have worked to see the king crowned here in Reims."

"That is true, but we should all really thank Jeanne the Maid for that. It was she who made it possible. I have not seen her yet today. Is she attending the Royal Council?"

"No, my lady. Like me, she was not invited. I think she has gone hunting with falcons with de Xaintrailles and de Rais. La Hire is sleeping off a heavy night's celebration, which is why there is only you and I in the archbishop's garden this morning."

"I see, but I have not yet had chance to thank Jeanne for all she has done."

"You will certainly get that opportunity, my lady, because the army will not leave Reims for a day or two yet."

"Good. Jean, tell me, do you really believe in Jeanne's miraculous voices?"

Dunois had not expected such a direct question. He wanted to give Yolande the comfort of saying yes, but speaking the truth was more important. "My lady, the fact is I do not know, but I can say that I have never seen anything like Jeanne in my entire life. She is truly inspired and spreads that inspiration to all who meet her. The effect on our soldiers is amazing. I was at Rouvray where they ran like sheep from the English, but that was before Jeanne arrived. I was also at Patay where they fought like raging lions, and it was the English who ran. Some would call that a miracle, I am not sure, but no one can dispute the change in the fighting power of our soldiers."

"I have heard there has also been a change in our soldiers' behaviour too."

"Now that really could be a miracle because if anyone had told me five months ago that French soldiers would give up swearing, plundering, and agree to abandon the prostitutes who make up a large part of the camp followers, I would have called them mad. But it has happened. The biggest change known to me personally is in Gilles de Rais. Because of Jeanne, he seems to have abandoned his dark past, prays frequently, and goes to Mass whenever he can."

Yolande frowned. "I doubt you're right about that, Jean. Men with de Rais's sexual perversions do not change, because they cannot. If anything unfortunate were to happen to Jeanne, he will revert to his old ways. If he does not, then that will certainly be a miracle."

"No doubt you shall have the chance to see for yourself, my lady."

"I am uncomfortable in de Rais's presence, but I am more concerned for Jeanne. She has made a powerful enemy at court."

"Trémoille?"

"Yes. He hates me too, but he does not dare to challenge me openly. Jeanne threatens his influence over Charles without even knowing it."

"I have already warned her about the grand chamberlain, but I don't think she took it in. She is highly intelligent with a sharp wit and a dry sense of humour, but she has never come across a creature like Trémoille, who will pretend to offer friendship but plot her downfall at the same time."

"She is too unspoiled to comprehend Trémoille," agreed Yolande. "I am beginning to wonder if now would not be a good time for her to retire from public life while she still has an unblemished record of success. It is difficult to see what more she can achieve."

"I do not think she'll do that, my lady. Her voices keep driving her forward telling her she must expel the English from France. She will not rest until she has done that."

"Yet even now she is not invited to the Royal Council where Trémoille reigns supreme. Is that not a sign of things to come?"

"Perhaps. Until now, Jeanne has been ever present at the Military Council, which is chaired by me. There she is welcome, and her counsel is always invited. Decisions are made quickly and acted upon. But since the king and his Royal Council joined the army, things have changed. Everything has slowed down, even the speed at which we march. On the day of Patay, we marched nearly twenty miles before we caught the English and then fought a battle in the afternoon. Now we are lucky to achieve ten miles a day. Trémoille does not like to be woken too early, and the king does not relish campaigning at all."

"Don't worry, Jean, it won't last." Yolande laughed. "Charles will not manage without the comforts of court life for long. Because of his coronation, he feels he must be seen to lead his army for a while at least, but as soon as the weather turns, he and his Royal Council will return to Chinon as soon as they decently can. I love my son-in-law dearly, but he is not a soldier and never will be."

"Indeed, my lady, but he's turning into a great leader and understands strategy. He has now authorised a proposal put forward by de Rais a few months ago which will stretch the English. We will divide our forces so that while the royal army marches on Paris, two smaller, fast-moving armies commanded by leaders of proven mettle will attack the English elsewhere. The English have fewer men than us, so they will be faced with the choice of defending Paris and watching their other conquests fall to us, or abandoning the city and defending Normandy, Anjou, and Maine instead."

"They will never leave Paris unless they're driven out."

"That is so, which means we will make rapid progress recovering the rest of English-occupied France, especially since Talbot, their best general, is now our prisoner."

But Dunois could not have foreseen what the Royal Council was about to decide that very morning, and he soon discovered why he had not been invited to the meeting.

On the afternoon of that same day, the Military Council assembled for an emergency meeting at Dunois's quarters in a hotel located in the western suburbs of Reims. As well as Dunois and a notetaker, Jeanne, de Xaintrailles, La Hire, de Rais, and Alençon were present. An ashen-faced Dunois opened the meeting in the hotel dining room overlooking the small River Vesle.

"Jeanne, Mon Seigneurs, I have been asked to inform you of the decision made this morning by the Royal Council to agree a two-week truce with the English and Burgundians."

"Impossible!" exploded de Rais. "This is treachery!"

Dunois held up his hand for silence. "Wait, Gilles, there is more. It seems discussions have taken place without our knowledge since we captured Troyes. The truce will exclude Paris and the area immediately surrounding it, but will affect all other areas of conflict starting on the twenty-eighth day of August. We have been told to expect the truce to be extended certainly to the end of this year and probably till spring next year."

De Xaintrailles said, "Once again the king and his council have undone what the soldiers have achieved. Why are they doing this? The English are on the run, and Paris is there for the taking. Our army has never been stronger."

"It's not lack of men, Jean Poton, but lack of money," answered Dunois. "At least that is the reason given by Trémoille. Keeping a large army in the field since March has virtually broken the Exchequer, which needs time to source new funds. We can no longer afford to pay our soldiers."

The Angel of Lorraine

Alençon, although still young, was perhaps the most intuitive of the men present. "There must be more to this than lack of money, Jean. What do you think is the real aim of the truce?"

"I think it is nothing less than a full peace with Burgundy. Duke Philippe remains an ally of the English partly because of the influence of his sister, Bedford's wife, but above all, he seeks reparation for the murder of his father under a flag of truce on the bridge at Montereau ten years ago by supporters of Charles VI who was mad at the time. Our present king cannot be blamed because he was only fourteen when that happened, but he will have to pay the debt if there is ever to be peace with Burgundy."

"And what form will this debt payment take?" enquired Alençon.

"A public apology, penance, and a pilgrimage, but mostly money."

"Hah!" sneered de Rais. "So the treacherous Burgundian duke gets paid by the English to fight and by us to make peace. Philippe wins both ways while we and the English become poorer."

"And that is where our brave soldiers' pay is going!" said La Hire. "There will come a day of reckoning with the Duke of Burgundy," he added grimly.

"I hope so," agreed Dunois.

"But if the men are not paid, they will resort to plunder, and we cannot blame them for that," said Jeanne. "We have managed with great difficulty to stop their excesses, but all that will be wasted if we fail on our side of the bargain by not paying them."

"And what of the strategy of attacking the English with small, fast armies along numerous fronts?" demanded de Rais. "Has that come to nothing?"

"Not necessarily, Gilles," replied Dunois. "We have until the end of next month to do something. Paris is not part of the truce, and the English will send every man they can to defend it. One of the small, fast armies you mentioned is already starting to assemble just north of Chartres, where four thousand men have been preparing to invade Normandy."

"Who commands?" asked de Rais.

"You, Gilles. I want you to ride to Chartres as fast as you can and lead the army to Evreux. Our agents tell us the town is only lightly defended, so if you can take it quickly, all of southern Normandy will be open to us. Even Rouen, which is only two days' easy march from Evreux, will be threatened. The English will be obliged to defend Rouen, which will draw some of their forces away from Paris, but all this must be achieved in the six weeks before the truce commences."

"Then I shall leave today, capture Evreux, and return to you in time for the assault on Paris."

"And I shall rely on you, Gilles, to select a good commander to hold the town until we decide where next to send the army."

"It shall be as you wish, Mon Seigneur."

But it was not to be as simple as that because the situation in France was so serious that John, Duke of Bedford, decided to retrieve English fortunes himself rather than leave it to others, and was on his way to Paris accompanied by almost three thousand native-born English soldiers, all of whom were war-hardened veterans. Among them was Sir John Fastolf, victor of Rouvray, who was now restored to favour and aching to avenge Patay.

The French army began its ninety-mile march from Reims to Paris on the twentieth day of July. The journey should have taken less than a week, but it lasted more than three. This was not entirely the fault of the king's Royal Council because along the way, towns and cities previously under allegiance to Burgundy were throwing open their gates and welcoming the newly anointed King of France, turning the march into a triumphal procession. Town and city councils had to be greeted, celebrations attended,

The Angel of Lorraine

and awards made for the newly discovered loyalty of the citizens, which had been lacking until the approach of the powerful royal army. King Charles had never experienced such affection, and he revelled in it.

Chateau Thierry, Soissons, Laon, Compiègne, and even distant Beauvais offered their loyalty to the king, but as the march on Paris slowed to a crawl, Bedford had time to strengthen the city defences and advance up the Seine to offer battle at the village of Montepilloy, a few miles from Senlis on the fourteenth day of August. It seemed that a great battle was about to take place on the fifteenth, but neither side wanted to attack.

Jeanne was beside herself with frustration as was de Rais, who had returned from Evreux having extracted a promise from the English castellan that he would surrender the town if no relief force had appeared by the twenty-seventh day of August, the day before the truce was due to take effect. At Montepilloy, he joined Jeanne as they rode up and down the rows of sharpened stakes that lined the front of the English position challenging them to attack. But there was no response. The English, outnumbered as usual, did not want another Patay nor, thanks to Fastolf's advice, would they launch an attack on the French where a large number of Bureau field cannon were placed ready to sweep away any forward move from Bedford's army well before the longbow could take effect. But on the evening of the fifteenth, Bedford received news from his castellan at Evreux of his commitment to surrender on the twenty-seventh if no help came. This determined the next move.

During the night, the English broke camp and began the march back to Paris. Behind the formidable walls of the best defended city in Europe, Bedford could detach enough men to lead them to Evreux's rescue while leaving Paris under the nominal command of Duke Philippe's ally Duke John of Luxembourg, but in fact in the capable hands of John Fastolf. Meanwhile, the cumbersome French army slowly closed in on Paris, and finally, at noon on the eighth day of September, the feast of the nativity of the Blessed Virgin, the assault spearheaded by Jeanne and her banner began.

It was a complete failure; an unwelcome new experience for Jeanne. Despite the heroic efforts of the French, the attack on the Port Saint Honore, the gate that defended the Louvre palace, never got beyond partially filling the deep moat beneath the city walls. But worse was to come. The fighting continued throughout the afternoon, but when the sun was low in the western sky and the French effort was withering from exhaustion and discouragement, one of the Parisian crossbowmen, who were famous for their deadly accuracy, decided to take a carefully measured shot at the Maid. Jeanne had briefly laid down her banner to help carry more straw bales to fill the moat when the heavy bolt struck her. It was a close-range shot and penetrated her armour between the hip and knee. She was knocked to the ground, but without crying out from the blistering pain, she sat up and began to examine her wounded thigh. Her banner bearer that day was a young knight from Provence; he was deputising for Marcel, who had not yet returned from Rouen. He ran to her aid, knelt down beside her, and raised the visor of his helmet so he could see Jeanne's wound more clearly. Then a second crossbow bolt hit him in the middle of the forehead, and he fell dead beside her.

Gilles de Rais, never far from Jeanne in battle, saw what happened and ordered her to be carried from the battlefield despite her protests to remain. When news of Jeanne's injury reached Dunois, he immediately ordered the assault to be suspended and the army to return to camp. But next day, the Royal Council decided that the army had done enough fighting for one year and issued the order to retire to the Loire. The campaign of 1429 was over.

* * *

II

Richard and Hugh rode hard from Calais and reached Rouen on the afternoon of the seventeenth day of July, the same day as King Charles's coronation in Reims. They found Mary sitting alone in the small, walled garden at the back of the house reading the Lollard Bible Hugh had

The Angel of Lorraine

brought with him on his last visit five years ago. She was overjoyed to see them.

"Father Hugh, how wonderful you're here, and what a coincidence! I'm reading the English Bible Father Anselm gave me which you delivered all those years ago. How is Anselm? Does he still live?"

"Sadly no, we have a new prior now who is not worthy to lick Anselm's boots. Anselm cared for everybody, Simon cares only for himself."

"And how is it that you are not wearing the grey, Franciscan habit? You look more like a notary than a priest."

"It's a long story."

"Then I look forward to hearing it. Joan and Marcel will be home soon, so perhaps we should wait for them before you explain what brought you here. And now I must welcome my handsome husband," she added as she stood up and put her arms round Richard's waist.

"I'm glad you noticed me at last!" He laughed. "Where is Joan?"

"She went to the charcuterie in the market square with Marcel to bring back some ham and pies. They should be back any moment now."

"With Marcel?"

"Yes, he's making himself useful. It's hard to believe he's your officer of parole. Sit down, both of you, while I bring some wine to celebrate your arrival."

Mary had just enough time to place a jug and three goblets on the garden table before the front door of the house opened. "Maman! We're home!"

Hugh expected to see the child he remembered from his previous visit, but a little older, so his eyes widened when he saw an attractive young woman as tall as himself enter the garden. Behind her was a handsome black-haired young man. They were both smiling, but Joan gave a whoop of joy when she saw her father and threw herself into Richard's arms. "Papa! Did you bring anything for me?" She might have grown up, but she still expected presents from her father when he came home.

"Nothing this time, my dear, unless you count Father Hugh."

"Father Hugh! I did not recognise you. You are wearing proper clothes!"

"And I hardly recognised you. You are no longer a child."

Remembering her manners, Joan said, "May I introduce Marcel, Sieur de Freuchin. He is Papa's keeper until his ransom is paid."

"A pleasure to meet you, Father. Joan has a quaint way of explaining my role. I am Richard's officer of parole, but please address me as Marcel."

"Thank you, Marcel, and please drop the *Father*, and just call me Hugh. Richard, I think now is the time to explain why I'm in Rouen and how I got here. That will also explain why Joan has got me instead of a present."

Frequent interruptions, questions, and digressions meant that the story was not completed until the shadows had lengthened and the background bustle from the streets had quietened down. Mary spoke first. "I shall write to Sir John and Millicent Fastolf to thank them for their generosity. I must admit, I thought Sir John would be more parsimonious."

"I too was surprised," agreed Richard, "but Millicent was more than helpful in that respect."

"As you know, I've only met Millicent once, and that was briefly on that freezing night we escaped from the Beccles sheriff's men, but I could tell even then that she is a very special lady."

"That is true, Mary," said Richard, "and she is the only person on God's earth who can bend Sir John to her will."

Joan asked, "How long can you stay with us, Papa?"

"Tomorrow, Marcel and I will go to the Lombard bank to see if the ransom money has arrived. It should have because the documents were signed in Norwich four days before I left. If it has, that will enable Marcel to return to his duties with Jeanne the Maid and the French army. Meanwhile, Hugh and I must continue our journey to Rome as soon as possible so Hugh can have his interview with Pope Martin before news of his escape from Dunwich reaches the Vatican."

"So soon?" sighed Joan.

Mistaking the reason for Joan's disappointment, Richard said, "It will not be for long…a month, six weeks at most, then I shall return, and because of my wound, my fighting days will be over."

Mary was much happier with his response than Joan. "And I shall be able to sleep at night knowing I will wake up to see my husband who will no longer be in danger. It is what I have prayed for, though I am sad the price to be paid is a broken arm. Now it is time for Joan and I to prepare the evening meal. Marcel, will you stay for this?"

"Of course."

That night, after they had made love but before he blew out the candle, Richard said, "Mary, is it just me, or do Joan and Marcel seem to be rather friendly?"

"She's a young woman, and he's a handsome knight. What do you expect?"

"But Joan is not yet sixteen, and Marcel is over thirty."

"That is not such a big age gap."

"But he's a Frenchman and our enemy!"

"A Frenchman, yes, but not our enemy. Richard, you are jumping to conclusions. Marcel will leave after the ransom is sorted, so you have nothing to worry about."

Richard remembered guiltily that there was a bigger gap in age between him and Ruth. "Thank you, my love, you have set my mind at rest, so that's an end to it. Sleep well."

Next morning, Marcel and Richard went to the Lombard bank where Richard identified himself. They were both taken to an office where a grey-haired Italian welcomed them. "Mes Sieurs, we are honoured by your visit, but I must tell you we have not yet received notification of the transaction you say took place in Norwich on the third of this month. I do not doubt it happened, but I would normally expect two or three weeks to pass before such a notification reaches us from our colleagues in England, and you will understand that we cannot pay out such a significant sum until then."

"So it might be another week before you can pay?"

"I'm afraid so. You have made good time from Norwich."

"Yes, we did," admitted Richard. "Could I not leave written authorisation for you to pay the sum of one hundred and eighty gold ducats to my officer of parole in my absence? I am in a hurry to get to Rome."

"Regrettably that will not be possible for such a large amount. You must be here to authorise the transaction in person."

As they left the bank, Richard apologised to Marcel. "I'm sorry about this, but it looks as if you will have to wait a few more days before you can leave."

"A little longer will not matter," replied Marcel cheerily, "and you will still be well within the two-month payment period you requested at Patay."

"Then as we're in no hurry, let's go down to the docks and find out when the next ship departs for Rome. We still have a chance of beating the Dunwich news to the Vatican."

Somewhere amidst the forest of masts and spars that lined the docks on the Seine was the customs house where Richard would find the information he needed, but they had only just reached the quay where the seagoing craft were moored when he suddenly stopped.

"What is it?" asked Marcel.

Richard pointed to a sturdy-looking vessel that was being loaded with wooden barrels. "When I set out for the Holy Land, I first left England for Venice. Well, that three-mast cog looks very like the vessel that took Sergeant Hawkswood and me on the first leg of the journey. If it is, I know the captain. Let's find out."

Sure enough, the ship was *Morning Star*, and Captain John Skelhorn, easily distinguishable by his height, for he was well over six feet tall, and his entirely bald pate, was directing the loading operation from the deck of his ship.

Richard shouted, "Captain Skelhorn!"

Skelhorn looked up, frowned for a moment until recognition dawned, and called back, "Captain Richard Calveley?"

"Yes, Captain."

"Then come aboard and bring your companion with you."

Richard was welcomed with one of Skelhorn's vice-like handshakes, and Marcel was introduced, but as Skelhorn could only manage a few words of French, the conversation had to be in English.

"Your left arm looks none too good, Richard."

"A wound from Patay."

"A bad business that, I hear. Will your arm recover?"

"Not fully according to the army surgeon, which means my fighting days are over."

"Well, that can't be all bad. What brings you to the docks?"

"I need to arrange a passage to Rome for myself and two friends, including the one who is with me now, as soon as possible."

Skelhorn shook his head. "I think you may have a long wait. There was nothing destined for Rome when I looked at the departure schedule yesterday."

"A pity. Then we may have to risk the overland route. Where are you headed?"

"Constantinople. I'm taking French wine and English salted herrings, which, believe it or not, are considered a delicacy by the inhabitants of that great city. On the return journey, I've been chartered by a group of Suffolk businessmen to bring back to Ipswich a valuable cargo of Oriental spices and Chinese silks which are worth their weight in gold."

"But you will be travelling through Turkish waters and pirate-infested coastlines. I know because I was in the eastern Mediterranean a few years ago. We were attacked by Dalmatian pirates and lost our entire cargo. Aren't you taking a big risk?"

"Not as big as you might think," smiled Skelhorn. "We won't be sailing alone, we'll be travelling with a convoy."

"A convoy?"

"A group of trading ships protected by a naval escort, so although the risk will still be there, it will be considerably mitigated."

"Who will provide the escort?"

"Constantinople's oldest ally, the Genoese."

A thrill shot up Richard's backbone. "Then does that mean the convoy assembles at Genoa?"

"Yes, ten days from now, so I'll be catching this evening's tide provided these Rouen lubbers get on with loading the wine casks."

Richard's mind was racing, but outwardly he remained calm. "Captain, could you find room for three men and their horses as far as Genoa?"

"Not really, we shall be fully laden."

"I would pay you well."

Skelhorn sucked his teeth and glanced at *Morning Star*'s deck. "There's no room below, but if you were prepared to sleep on deck, I might manage three men, but definitely no horses. At least it's midsummer, so you should be able to cope well enough."

"Then we'll be here this evening. How much?"

Always a shrewd businessman, Skelhorn sensed the urgency in Richard's voice. "A gold ducat for each passenger."

It should have been silver, but Richard was in no mood to risk losing this unexpected opportunity. "Done!"

As they walked back through the dockyard, Richard explained to Marcel what he had just agreed and finished by saying, "I realise this means I may go over the two-month period I asked for to pay the ransom at the negotiations at Patay, but it won't be by much. Genoa is not so far from Rome, and I will still be in your custody."

Marcel responded quietly. "Richard, it is not the extra time that matters, that is of no consequence, it is the journey itself. The thought of being trapped on a vessel for weeks at a time on a voyage that will include the Atlantic Ocean does not appeal to me at all."

"But I must get Hugh to Rome, and you are my officer of parole."

"I realise that, so what if I were to give you leave to go without me while I await your return at Rouen? I know full well I can trust you to come back and pay off your ransom."

This offer could not have suited Richard better, for he could now make the diversion to see Ruth and Enrico without having to answer awkward questions. He tried not to sound too eager. "Well, if that is acceptable to you, Marcel, it's acceptable to me too."

"Very well, that's agreed then. I wish you and Hugh a safe journey and look forward to your return next month."

* * *

III

Morning Star made good progress, thanks to calm summer seas most of the way, so Richard's seasickness was less debilitating than the last time he travelled on Skelhorn's ship. Even Hugh managed to find his sea legs before the journey's end, though he ate almost nothing during the eight-day voyage. *Morning Star* berthed three hours after dawn in Genoa's well-sheltered port on the twenty-sixth day of July, a full two days before the convoy was due to sail.

Captain Skelhorn was in fine spirits as he bade the two travellers farewell. "I may even see you back in Ipswich because I expect to complete my voyage around the end of next month—leaner, fitter, and a lot richer!"

"And the best of luck to you," said Richard as he followed Hugh down the gangplank. "You'll certainly need it where you're going."

With the sun shining directly in their eyes, Richard and Hugh crossed the market area behind the dockyard where the stallholders were setting out their produce for the day and entered Genoa's bewildering maze of narrow streets flanked by tall tenement buildings. The smell of fish frying in olive oil coming from the small, family-owned taverns preparing the first meal of the day whetted their appetites, so they decided to enjoy their first breakfast on dry land since Rouen before seeking accommodation for a few nights.

While they waited for their food to be cooked by the large, matronly owner of a tavern near the spectacular, black-and-white striped, slate and marble front of the cathedral of San Lorenzo, Hugh said pensively, "Richard, have you thought about exactly what you're going to do when you find Ruth's home? You're hardly going to be welcomed with open arms by her husband."

"Not in detail. I think I may visit her father first and see how the land lies with him, but whatever the objections and obstacles put in my way, I shall see my son. Meanwhile, after we have eaten, we'll separate and meet again at this tavern at noon. While I go to the Jewish quarter, you find us suitable lodgings for the next two nights, possibly three." He felt inside his tunic for his money belt and handed Hugh three silver ducats. "This should be enough to get somewhere decent. I think we deserve that after eight nights on Captain Skelhorn's deck."

The Jewish quarter was small, just a few houses clustered round a simple, leafy piazza and hardly deserving the term *quarter* at all. It was not cut off in any way from the adjacent areas of the city, and Richard only realised he had entered it when he saw the Star of David above the entrance to a tiny synagogue hiding behind a typical Genoese frontage. He entered and was directed to an office at the side of the synagogue where the affairs of the Jewish community in Genoa were managed. There he asked how to find the home of Chaim ben Issachar, father of Ruth.

"And you are?" asked the black cloaked official in perfect French.

"My name is Richard Calveley. I am a captain in the English army."

"You are expected, Captain Calveley. Chaim's instructions are that you should wait here and he will come to you because he will not invite you into his house. I shall go and fetch him. You may wait in the office behind me where you can meet Chaim in private. I won't be long."

Not a promising start, thought Richard as he stood by the office window and watched the black robed figure walk across the piazza and enter a house through a dark green door. If Chaim knew he was coming, it meant that his letter to Ruth had probably been intercepted, in which case she would still be under the impression he had not answered hers. This was a crushing disappointment that he must put right.

"What do you think can be gained by you coming here?" were Chaim's first words when he entered the office.

"Has Ruth seen my letter?" responded Richard.

"No, and she never will. She's made a happy life with Paolo Dandolo. She has two more children now and does not need the past to be dredged up again. Your coming here is the height of selfishness."

"I always answer my letters. Ruth must think I've ignored hers."

"You took four years to answer!"

"You've read my letter, so you know why. It's wrong that she thinks I ignored her."

"I've sent a message to Paolo, who happens to be in Genoa at the moment. He will be here shortly."

"Good, then I shall say what I must say when he gets here."

It had been five years since Richard last saw Chaim on that dreadful day he left Ancona docks after his return from the Holy Land. The ringlets that bordered Chaim's round face were now entirely grey, and his right hand twitched involuntarily, though that might have been caused by the stress of the moment. The large, brown eyes had sunk into their sockets, and he had lost some teeth; the years had taken their toll.

The contrast with Paolo Dandolo could not have been more stark. The dashing Venetian captain arrived wearing a smart red doublet and green hose. He had been driven out of his home city by Doge Foscari and now worked for Venice's greatest rival, Genoa, as Chaim's business partner. He looked just the same as he did when he captained the ship that took Richard to the Holy Land except that there was no sign of the winning smile, just the set jaw of determination. Nor had his French improved.

"Why you come here, Richard?"

"To see Ruth and my son."

"Is impossible. Ruth is my wife, and we are happy together. Enrico calls me Papa. I am only father he knows. You abandoned him."

"I didn't know about him! I have no other son. I must see him."

"Enrico has brother and sister now. We are happy family now. You will destroy us if I let you."

"I don't want that, I just want to see Ruth and Enrico."

"And then what? You leave and take them with you? You desert your wife in France? No good can come of this. You must go."

"All right, if you allow me to see only Enrico, I will leave. He does not even need to know who I am."

"No! You no understand how I feel. I am proud man, but I know Ruth still love you. She no say nothing, but I know. You go now."

"I have not travelled a thousand miles just to be turned away," said Richard grimly. "I will at least see Enrico whether you like it or not."

"Over my dead body!"

"If it must be so, then so be it."

"Stop! Stop!" shouted Chaim as he stepped between them. "This is madness! You two were once close friends. There must be a better way to resolve this. Richard, would you please step out into the piazza and give Paolo and me a few minutes together. While you do this, try and open your mind to how Paolo must be feeling—everything he lives for is about to be shattered. I will come and get you shortly."

"Very well. Have you still got the letter I wrote to Ruth?"

"No, it's burnt and the ashes spread in the piazza. It would be cruel to let her know."

Richard sat on a bench under an acacia tree and watched multicoloured butterflies fluttering between flowers planted in a round, carefully tended bed. Now that the confrontation had taken place, the enormity of what he was trying to do at last began to dawn on him. In his single-minded, blind desire to see Enrico and Ruth, he was not only prepared to destroy a happy family, but he had just threatened to murder Paolo, the man who had saved him from certain death at the hands of the Turks. In the heat of the moment, Paolo had asked him the most important question: what would he do after he had seen Enrico and Ruth? Would he abandon Mary and Joan? That was unthinkable. And what if Ruth refused to meet him anyway? Five years had passed; she may have stopped loving him despite what Paolo thought. He desperately wanted to know, but was that worth the destruction of a family? He had now accepted he could not see Ruth, but Enrico was a different matter, for he was his only son. He'd had two sons by his first wife, Ann, but they had been murdered alongside her by the order of his cousin Geoffrey; that crime had still not been avenged, and it was now that Richard decided the time had come for that debt to be called in. He would visit his cousin as soon as he'd paid off his ransom and settle the score in the only way he could.

That thought gave him some comfort, but he felt ashamed and guilty, not of his intent to murder his cousin, but for not thinking through the consequences of his mission to Genoa. His failure to control his passion had blinded him to the damage he had been prepared to do to good people who deserved better. Even Hugh, that very morning, had tried to warn him, but he would not listen. Now he knew what he must do. It was time to go and complete his mission to Rome with Hugh. He would leave now, quietly, before he could do any more damage; but if only he could have seen Enrico, just for a few seconds.

It was too late. Chaim came out of the office and called him. "Richard, come, Paolo and I have thought of something which does not meet all your needs but may go far enough to prevent bloodshed."

"Chaim, I don't—"

"Say nothing until you've heard what Paolo is going to offer."

Paolo's first words were unexpected. "Richard, your arm?"

"Broken at the Battle of Patay."

"You gonna fight me with that?"

"I don't want to fight you at all."

"May not be necessary. Tomorrow morning, I take my family for walk to look at ships in the docks. Our route goes through Piazza Caricamento near Palazzo San Giorgio. We walk slowly through the piazza between eleven and twelve o'clock. Many places to sit in the piazza, but you must not speak or come near. Must disguise yourself too so family not know you are there. You can see but no speak."

Chaim said, "It seems a fair compromise, Richard."

Peter Tallon

"It is more than I expected or deserve, and I shall make sure I'm not recognised."

"Where you go afterwards?" asked a relieved Paolo.

"Rome. I need to get there as soon as possible."

Paolo looked at Chaim. "We have cargo waiting at Ostia. We could send small ship tomorrow afternoon and take Richard. Would be at Ostia next day. Would be quickest way."

"Would that suit you, Richard?" asked Chaim.

"Where's Ostia?"

"Is port for Rome," answered Paolo. "Is about four hours' walk upstream along Tiber to Rome. You could be at city in two days' time."

"Much faster than going overland from here," added Chaim.

"And I bring forward time for tomorrow's walk with family to nine o'clock. Then you meet me at docks at twelve noon. Ship's name is *Bella*, a small fast galley. Captain Angelo commands. He will take you, but I still have more to say. Before you leave, you see my surgeon this afternoon. Have best surgeons in world at Genoa who know everything about arm injuries because of experience with galley oarsmen. I take you there. Meet me at Cathedral San Lorenzo at two o'clock."

Richard was lost for words at the kindness these two men were showing him after his inauspicious arrival. "Thank you, both," he stammered, "for what you are doing for a foolish adventurer, but there will be two of us coming to Rome if that's all right. A companion of mine needs an audience with the pope."

Chaim raised his bushy eyebrows. "An audience with the pope is not granted to just anyone."

"I know, but my companion is not just anyone."

Sensing Richard did not want to speak more on the subject, Paolo said, "Is no matter, he can come anyway."

"I'll need to borrow your Franciscan habit tomorrow morning," said Richard when he met Hugh back at the tavern near the cathedral.

"Of course, but why?"

"I need a disguise, and I can't think of anything better. I'm going to be permitted to see Ruth and Enrico, but I must not communicate with them in any way."

"Is that sufficient for you?"

"It's more than I deserve. Have you organised somewhere for us to stay?"

"Yes," answered Hugh handing back one of the silver ducats Richard had given him earlier that day.

"Not a place full of beggars and drunken seamen I hope. I'm not in the mood for Franciscan self-sacrifice."

"It's no palace, but I think you'll find it adequate."

Richard shrugged. "Well, it's only for one night anyway. We leave for Rome by a fast galley tomorrow at noon. You'll enjoy that—very different to Skelhorn's tub. We'll be in Rome the day after tomorrow, so we should still beat Father Simon's letter to the Vatican."

"God be praised!" exclaimed Hugh.

"And Captain Paolo Dandolo," added Richard.

Peter Tallon

In the afternoon, Paolo left Richard in the hands of a short, round cheerful man called Pietro Andretti, Master Surgeon. Despite the grand title, the surgery was in a winding back street near the seafront where prostitutes plied their trade and contraband was bought and sold. It was only the respect accorded to Paolo that gave Richard a reasonable hope of escaping this place once the surgeon had done his work. Andretti spoke good French and was obviously a well-educated man, so understanding each other was not going to be a problem.

"Captain Dandolo informs me that you received your wound at Patay?"

"Yes, caused by a mace blow which brushed past my guard and broke my arm. My attention was on another opponent at the time."

"How long ago was Patay?"

"About six weeks."

"Any treatment since then?"

"No, except for some horrible liquid to ease the pain."

"Does it work?"

"No."

Andretti looked up to heaven for help, which he knew would not come, and said, "Take off your tunic." While Richard unbuttoned his tunic, he looked round Andretti's surgery. It was nothing like anything he had seen in England or France. The room was cluttered with strange objects that looked like something out of a torture chamber. Particularly concerning was a horizontal steel bar set into the ceiling with formidable-looking hooks and levers hanging from it, beneath which was a long table with an assortment of knives, scissors, and pliers laid out on it in a threatening array. Most nerve-racking of all was a metal chair with screws, levers, hoists, and other unidentifiable gadgets attached to it that would put the fear of God into the bravest soul.

"Sit down and give me your arm," said the surgeon, thankfully pointing to the only normal-looking chair in the surgery. Richard nervously did as he was bid, remembering that last time a surgeon asked him to do this, he had been stabbed with a six-inch needle. But despite his avuncular appearance and podgy fingers, Andretti's touch was reassuringly professional, and unlike the surgeon in Rouen, he inflicted no pain.

"Mmmm, you say your arm is broken?"

"Yes."

"You are wrong. It is only, how you say, *dislocazzione*."

"Dislocated?"

"*Si*, yes, at the elbow. I can deal with this now if you wish."

"Will I make a full recovery?"

"Maybe, but six weeks of no treatment since the injury means your recovery may not be quite complete. But unless you go back to war again, you will not notice the difference between complete and almost complete."

"Will the treatment be painful?"

"Yes, very, but I can give you something to combat that. Do you wish me to proceed?"

"How much will it cost?"

"Nothing to you. Captain Dandolo has already underwritten the charge."

"Then go ahead."

Richard guessed what would happen next even before Andretti pointed to the evil-looking chair with the hooks and levers. "Please sit." Then the surgeon went to a cupboard and took out a phial of reddish-brown liquid. "This is tincture of laudanum. It is a potion brought back by the Crusaders from Outremer, the Holy Land. It drastically reduces pain. I will give you some in a moment. When I do, drink it in one draught. Soon you will feel a little drunk and very content. When that happens, raise your right arm, and I shall begin."

Without any further comment, Andretti strapped Richard's left shoulder to the chair and his forearm to the arm support so that he could move neither. Then standing in front of him, the surgeon clenched both of his fists and pushed them together so that the knuckles interlocked. "Look at my fists, Captain." Andretti then slid one fist upwards against the other by about one inch and back again. "That has happened to your elbow. I am now going to stretch the joint and slide it back into its true position again. It will hurt, but it will be worth it." He took the lid off the phial and placed it in Richard's right hand. "Now drink this and give me the signal when you are ready." Richard knew nothing about laudanum, but he recognised alcohol when he tasted it. Within a few seconds, he felt the effect predicted by Andretti, so taking a deep breath, he gave the signal.

His howl could be heard halfway to Venice, but the shock soon passed, and the surgeon unstrapped him from the chair. "Can you hear me, Captain?"

"Yes."

"Good. Wait here for five minutes, and when you can walk properly, return to your lodgings and go to sleep. You will not awaken till dawn or thereabouts, and when you do, you may feel a little dizzy, but it will not last long. Do not try to do too much with your left arm for a day or two, then exercise it gently but allow your body to tell you when you have done enough."

"How will I know?"

"The pain will tell you because it will hurt if you do too much. You should be recovered enough in one month to use your arm normally, unless you put too much stress on it too soon. I will give you a small phial of tincture of laudanum to take with you just in case the pain comes back."

"Over and above Captain Dandolo's bill, I would like to pay to take two more phials with me to keep in reserve for the future."

"It's expensive."

"I can pay."

"Very well, but treat it with respect. I will write a short note describing how to administer it and how much to use. Never exceed the stated dose because too much will kill. Some have been tempted to enjoy the sensation rather than use laudanum for medical reasons and have paid the ultimate penalty."

"I understand, Surgeon Andretti. If ever you care to spread your knowledge, there are many I can think of in England who would pay well to learn from you."

Andretti smiled. "Thank you, Captain, but it's too cold that far north, much too cold!"

* * *

IV

At nine o'clock next morning, Paolo led his family to the Piazza Caricamento and began a slow promenade towards the dockyard.

"Why are we doing this, my dear?" asked Ruth as she walked arm in arm with him.

"I think it's time Enrico saw how his father earns a living. I spoke to your father yesterday about this, and he approves."

"But the piazza is full of old men playing dice and drunkards with a hangover."

"And retired seamen reminiscing about how much better things were in their day, but it would be good for Enrico to see one of our ships. *Bella* is in port at the moment, and Captain Angelo will make Enrico welcome, and you too of course."

"Will we go on board?"

"Certainly. Angelo will give you a conducted tour of *Bella*. She is lithe and beautiful, just like you, my darling."

"One day your silver tongue will get you into trouble, Paolo Dandolo."

Together the family, with little Enrico holding his father's hand, strolled along the main path, which bisected the piazza, a picture of contentment—exactly the image Paolo wished to convey. They were almost halfway across when Enrico pointed to one of the piazza benches facing the sea. On it sat three men. Two sat together at one end chatting, their weather-beaten faces suggesting they were almost certainly retired sailors, while at the other end sat a grey friar with his hood pulled over his head and a rosary clutched in his right hand.

"Look at that monk, Papa, his cloak is too short for him."

"He is not a monk, Enrico, he is a friar of the Franciscan Order founded by Saint Francis of Assisi. They all take a vow of poverty and so must wear whatever is given to them. Here is a silver half ducat. Go and give it to him and ask for his blessing."

Richard could not believe his luck when he saw little Enrico running towards him. Had Paolo relented about speaking to him, or was the disguise working too well? The boy stopped in front of him, held out the coin, and spoke to him in Italian. Richard could not understand the words though he still managed to catch the gist of what was being said because many Italian words are similar to French, but he could hardly speak anyway because he was looking into a pair of eyes as green as his own. He took the coin and said, "Bon giorno," one of the few Italian phrases he knew, and then added, "Mille grazie," which he thought was about right for "Thank you very much." The boy knelt down, clearly expecting a blessing, so Richard put his hand on his head and mumbled some Latin words that he thought sounded holy. The black hair felt soft; after all this time, he was touching his own son! It was a moment of unbearable happiness. Sadly, he quickly ran out of Latin words and forced himself to take his hand away. Enrico jumped to his feet, clearly satisfied with the unusual Franciscan blessing, and gave him a broad, generous smile, which Richard never forgot. He ran back to Paolo and his mother, who briefly looked back at the strange-looking friar; then the family resumed their walk through the piazza.

The two old sailors at the other end of the bench stopped talking for a few moments; the grey friar beside them was weeping.

"There was something odd about that friar," said Paolo when he reached the moorings where *Bella* was docked. "Did you notice anything?"

"Only the ill-fitting grey habit that Enrico pointed out," answered Ruth.

Paolo thought for a moment. "Yes, that must have been it," he agreed, and walked up *Bella*'s gangplank to greet Captain Angelo.

In fact, Ruth had indeed noticed something that Paolo must also have seen but without registering it; the friar was wearing military-style boots, not the customary sandals of the Franciscan Order. For some reason, she wanted time to think about this before divulging it to her husband. Then, just before she stepped onto the gangplank, she turned to Enrico. "Was there anything strange about the Franciscan you spoke to, my darling?"

"No, Mama, he was just a man," then he added as an afterthought, "except he had green eyes, just like mine."

CHAPTER TEN

"What an amazing place!" said Hugh as he stood on the balcony of the apartment Richard had rented on the fourth floor of a tenement building overlooking the River Tiber. "From this very spot I can see things I have only read about—the Colosseum, Trajan's Column, the Curia where the senate used to meet. I could go on and on."

"And don't forget the Pantheon. I must visit that before we leave," added Richard, who was standing beside him. "It's difficult to believe how the present-day Romans can walk past all these magisterial buildings barely giving them a glance."

Hugh sighed. "Familiarity I suppose, although I don't think I could ever stop being amazed by what the ancient Romans achieved."

"Well, today we'll find out what the modern Romans can do. Our landlord, who can't speak French, pointed to that castle just across the river when I said 'Vatican,' so we'll try our luck there this morning. You'd better wear your Franciscan habit just in case you get an interview sooner than we think."

Nothing seemed less likely when they arrived at the Vatican gate, which was located in the wall to the north of San Pietro, the old basilica, which had fallen into ruins when the popes abandoned Rome in the previous century and, under French pressure, relocated the papacy to Avignon. It had been half a century since the papacy returned to Rome, but despite their wealth, none of the popes since then had done anything about repairing the most important church in Christendom.

Richard and Hugh stood dumbfounded when they saw the huge crowd trying to attract the attention of only three priests who sat calmly at a table just outside the gate, seemingly oblivious to the noisy scrimmage going on just in front of them. There was no order, no neat queue like there would have been in England, just hundreds of yelling Italians clutching scraps of paper, which were their petitions for an audience with the pope. Some were obviously experienced at this, for they had brought long poles with a piece of thread at one end to which their petition was tied. They used their poles like fishing rods, which enabled them to pass their petitions over the heads of those in front and dangle their pieces of paper under the noses of the priests who barely looked up as they took the nearest petition and examined it against a long list laid out on their table.

"Looks like we should have made an appointment at another office before coming here," said a downhearted Hugh. "Richard, can't you speak to someone? You must have learned some Italian when you went to Venice and the Holy Land."

"Only a few words from the Venetian sailors, not enough to hold a conversation, and mostly unsuitable to speak with a priest."

"Well, we'll never get through this lot, and even if we could—" Hugh suddenly went quiet, then slowly the hint of a smile started to pluck at the corners of his mouth. "Richard, do you at least know the Italian for 'Please move aside?'"

"Try 'Scuse!' That's near enough. What are you going to do?"

"Watch and learn and stay close behind me."

Hugh pulled his hood over his head, placed his rosary round his neck, and bellowed, "Scuse!"

Peter Tallon

The nearest Italians turned, moved aside, and knelt down as Hugh gave them a blessing as he passed by. "In nomine patris, et filii et spiritui sancti. Amen." The impact of the holy Franciscan was remarkable. Hugh continued to repeat the blessing and move forward. The crowd squeezed aside and knelt down; those in range of the blessing crossed themselves as the devout friar and his acolyte passed through them. It was like the parting of the Red Sea before the Israelites. A couple of alert Italians tried to insert themselves between Hugh and Richard, but Richard unceremoniously pushed them aside; then another minor miracle. He suddenly realised he had used his left arm without pain. The work of Surgeon Andretti was beginning to make itself felt.

The middle priest of the three at the table looked up because of the unaccustomed silence that had just broken out and beheld a scruffy Franciscan standing in front of him. He said something in Italian that sounded hostile; the preaching orders were not popular in Rome, but Hugh responded in Latin, the language known to all priests wherever their origins.

"My name is Father Hugh from Dunwich priory in England. I wish to see the Holy Father."

The priest—a broad-shouldered man of about fifty, with short cropped, grey hair and large, sky blue eyes—stood up and said in English, "Father Hugh, we've been waiting for you. Your escape from Dunwich has been the talk of the Vatican for the past week." He held out his hand. "Father Robert Harrison, now a Vatican priest but originally from Derby, most pleased to meet you. May I shake your hand? You've done what many of us just dream about."

"You're English," said Hugh rather unnecessarily.

"As English as you are."

"But how could you have known about me so soon? We hurried here hoping to see the Holy Father before the news reached you from elsewhere, but you have known for a week!"

"The Vatican has couriers that travel faster than you can imagine. I am not at liberty to tell you more, but the Holy Father might if you ask him."

"So he will grant me an audience then?"

"Yes. His standing orders are that yours should be the last petition of the day. That way he will be able to spend more time with you. It is a great honour." Then noticing Richard at last, Father Robert asked with a twinkle in his eye, "And are you Father Hugh's accomplice in this heinous crime?"

"Yes, Father. Captain Richard Calveley at your service."

"Well, Captain, the interview with the Holy Father is only for Father Hugh, who will have to wait here all day, but I am off duty at ten o'clock, so if you care to meet me in half an hour at the bridge over the Tiber you have just crossed, I can show you around some of the places of interest in the Eternal City."

"The Pantheon?"

"We can certainly include the Pantheon if you wish."

"I would be delighted, Father Robert."

Richard remembered the rest of that day as much for the cheerful and knowledgeable company of Father Robert as for the monuments themselves. Father Robert also had a memorable day, for while he gave Richard an entertaining tour of ancient Rome, he in turn received that most precious currency in any closed institution—gossip. The inside story of the escape from Dunwich priory fed the curiosity of those dwelling inside the Vatican for weeks.

Meanwhile, Hugh was waiting all day becoming more and more anxious about what was to come. He was given liberty to wander through some of the imposing Vatican chambers where portraits of popes, cardinals, and bishops with obscure Italian names stared back at him from every wall; but at last, just after he heard a bell ring for five o'clock, a serious-looking cardinal dressed in red took him to the large, cedarwood double doors, which led to Pope Martin's private apartments. One of the two tall soldiers who stood guard opened the doors while the cardinal and a very nervous Hugh entered.

The contrast to the formality of the rest of the Vatican was striking. Here was a home. Instead of innumerable boring portraits of men who looked much the same as each other, skilfully woven multicoloured tapestries and beautifully painted pictures of nature hung on the walls. The chairs and benches were covered with soft cushions and quilts. Bright flowers of a type Hugh did not recognise were placed in vases on ledges at the base of tall windows on the west side of the room, which let in the afternoon sunlight. The marble floor was inlaid with small, coloured stones in the ancient Roman mosaic style, which were carefully placed to create geometric patterns that held the eye as it followed lines that turned back and forth, right and left, without crossing, ending, or coming back to the beginning again.

At the far end of the chamber was Pope Martin himself, the fifth of that name, reading a scroll through a clear piece of crystal that magnified the writing to help his ageing eyes. He was sitting beside a window wearing a plain, black robe without any of the pomp and ceremonial that was required in public; the only visible evidence of his status was a purple skullcap perched on the back of his head. Pope Martin's had been a successful papacy, restoring the unity and authority of an institution that had been divided and weakened for over a century, but the effort had taken its toll, and he appeared much older than his sixty-one years. Hugh swallowed nervously as he looked at the lined face that seemed very severe.

The pope dismissed the cardinal with a disdainful wave of the hand, but once they were alone, the formidable face relaxed into a smile as he held out his hand, palm downwards, for Hugh to kneel and kiss the papal signet ring. He gestured towards a comfortable-looking padded chair. "You may sit," he said in Italian.

Hugh easily guessed the meaning and answered in Latin, "Thank you, Holy Father."

"My conversational Latin is rather rusty. Do you speak French?"

"Yes, Holy Father," answered Hugh in French.

"Good, then we can relax. Have you been looked after since you arrived?"

"Yes, Holy Father," lied Hugh, who had not eaten all day but was far too nervous to begin now.

"So you are the notorious Father Hugh who gave the Franciscans the slip in England?"

"Yes."

"And now you want to withdraw the sacred oath you made when you were ordained?"

"I lost my vocation years ago, Holy Father."

"This is a serious matter, so you must tell me everything that has happened before I can make a decision about your future."

Hugh's life story from his ordination, the Agincourt campaign, and his stewardship of Richard's manor where he had a passionate affair with Annie Mullen, another man's wife, took about an hour. The pope sat silently through it, asking only a few questions when clarification was needed. At the end, he remained silent for a full minute, eyes closed in contemplation. Hugh began to wonder if his holiness had fallen asleep, then suddenly the old voice crackled into life.

"My son, I fully understand that the monastic life does not suit all those who enter it in good faith, but that does not mean you must give up the priesthood. I could arrange a transfer to something more suited to your undoubted talents, your own parish perhaps? But on second thoughts, that could expose you to temptations you have already failed to resist. Maybe you might like a secretarial role with one of your English bishops, or I could even find a place for you here at the Vatican if you prefer, though you would have to learn Italian? There is plenty of precedent for this sort of thing, and you are not the first priest to struggle with the vow of chastity, but releasing you from the vows you took at Holy Orders is another matter."

"Holy Father, I am indeed grateful for the opportunities you have just outlined, but after all that has happened, my heart is no longer with the priesthood. I would rather spend the rest of my life as a good steward or notary than a bad priest. I am now thirty-seven years old and can still live as a good Catholic, but not as a priest."

The pope sighed. "It seems your mind is made up. I can refuse your request, but that would only mean you would abandon the priesthood anyway, which means living your life in mortal sin and being condemned to hell for all eternity when you die. I do not want that any more than you do."

Hugh's heart skipped a beat as he began to realise that his quest was going to be successful. "But," continued the pope, "this will set a bad precedent and should not be encouraged. Therefore," the benevolent, old voice hardened, "there will be a price to pay. I shall require a significant donation to Mother Church for the poor example you will set."

"I understand, Holy Father."

"I wonder if you really do. Have you money?"

"None, but my companion who helped me escape and travelled with me to Rome has money."

"Then he will have to be a good friend indeed to pay the sum you will need."

The Angel of Lorraine

"He is, but I shall repay him from the salary I'll earn when I start work as a steward's assistant."

"Then I hope they pay good salaries to stewards' assistants in England because the donative will be twenty-five gold ducats."

Hugh fell silent. This was a huge amount of money; it would take him at least twenty years to pay back this amount even if he spent nothing on himself. He had no idea if Richard possessed that sort of wealth. His respect for this pope diminished somewhat as he realised, to use a market trader's term, he was being fleeced. "That is indeed a huge sum, Holy Father, will you accept fifteen?"

"I will not bargain. You will accept my price, or you will remain a priest for the rest of your life. Choose now!"

Hugh had no real choice. "I agree," he replied quietly.

"So that we understand each other, the release from your vows will not take effect until the money is paid in full. You may complete the transaction through Father Robert, one of your own countrymen whom you have already met."

"I understand."

The benevolent tone returned once more. "My son, you must also undertake penance for the remission of your sins. In addition to the donation, you will say a rosary each day at ten cathedrals and churches in Rome for the next two weeks. Father Robert will give you the list. Now would you like me to hear your confession?"

To be offered confession by the pope himself was something every Catholic Christian would want, so Hugh could not miss the opportunity. "Thank you, Holy Father, but it won't take long. I was confessed by Father Anselm, the previous prior of Dunwich, when I returned to the priory, so all my mortal sins were absolved then. For the last five years, I have lived a cloistered life, so the chance to commit sin, except in thought, has been severely limited."

The pope smiled; this could be an interesting confession. "You may go back in time as far as you like to give me the context which drove you to lose your vocation. If a sin is forgiven twice, it can do no harm. It may even reduce your time in purgatory!"

By the time the confession was done, the same bell that rang for five o'clock was now ringing for seven; Hugh had not noticed the one in between. As he stood up to leave, he said, "Holy Father, may I ask a question before I go?"

"Certainly, my son."

"My friend and I raced from England to Rome as quickly as humanly possible to make sure you heard about my escape from me before you were informed by the English Church authorities, yet Father Robert said you already knew of it a week ago. How can that be?"

At last, some genuine warmth entered Pope Martin's dark, southern eyes. The previous thin smile widened and removed the severity from the lined face. "The clue, my son, is in your use of the word *humanly*. Come, I will show you."

When the pope stood up, Hugh was surprised to see that such an authoritative figure was barely five feet tall, but he moved with the speed of a much younger man, and Hugh was hard-pressed to keep up with him as he descended a small, wooden staircase to an unguarded door that opened onto the Vatican gardens. Signs of neglect were everywhere; weeds taller than a man, overgrown box hedges, unpruned fruit trees, and uncut verges revealed these had once been fine gardens.

"I've not had the chance to spend much time or money on these gardens," said the pope apologetically, "but I will. At present, the fabric of dilapidated buildings must take priority. Otherwise, precious works of art will be at risk."

Hugh followed the diminutive figure up a small, overgrown path that passed a bog that had once been an ornamental pond. Then, after a sharp right bend, they entered a round clearing in the centre of which was a miniature, many-faceted house placed on top of a sturdy pole. The droppings round the base gave away the identity of the occupants.

"A dovecote!" said Hugh. "We had one at Dunwich."

"Close, but not quite right, my English friend," said the pope, knowingly tapping the side of his nose with his forefinger. "The occupants here are not doves but pigeons, special pigeons, sent as a gift from the patriarch of the Eastern Orthodox Church in Constantinople. These birds have been trained to fly long distances but always between the same places. They can carry short messages attached to their claws. We have relays of them throughout our communities in Europe and also links with what is left of the Byzantine Empire. One of the most used routes is between the Vatican and London." He pulled a slate-grey, cooing bird from one of the dovecote accesses and stroked its head. "These little feathered creatures can pass a message from London to the Vatican in just four days, so your Dunwich prior only had to deliver his message to London for it to reach here before you. He probably didn't know that, but the head of the Franciscan Order in England certainly would have."

"Thank you for showing me such a wonder, Holy Father. The world must be full of such wonders which I shall discover during my new life."

"You will no doubt learn many new things, but I would prefer you to keep this particular wonder to yourself. Our enemies in the east have already worked out ways to intercept our messenger pigeons with falcons. We don't want such ideas spreading into the west any sooner than they have to."

Hugh stopped on the bridge over the Tiber on the way back to his apartment and gazed at the river's slow-flowing, muddy water. It had been a day of mixed blessings. Most importantly, his mission to escape the priesthood had been achieved, but the cost was high, and it would take him years to pay off the debt. But he would be a free man after he completed

Peter Tallon

his penance, and thanks to Richard, there was a good job waiting for him at the Caistor Manor estate. He had no doubt that Richard would pay the twenty-five ducat donative; he was fortunate to have a true friend like that, but he was resolved to pay the debt in full, even if it took a lifetime to do so; it was the least he could do for receiving his freedom.

Meanwhile, back at the Vatican, Pope Martin V, alias Oddone Colonna from Genzzano, a poor town in southern Italy, was also satisfied with his day. Not only had he saved a troubled, wandering soul from eternal damnation, he had made the easiest twenty-five gold ducats in his life. Not bad for just two hours' work, even for a pope!

* * *

II

Due to Hugh's two-week period of penance, he and Richard could not leave Rome until the fourteenth day of August, and after a slow journey that involved changing ships at Cadiz and Bordeaux, they finally arrived at Rouen on the last day of August at six o'clock in the evening. They walked through the dockyard and headed for Richard's home between the market square and the cathedral. The ground was still damp from an afternoon thunderstorm, and the evening was pleasantly mild.

Hugh breathed in deeply. "This is glorious. Do you realise we have not experienced rain for over a month!"

"We don't appreciate it until we need it," agreed Richard. "It sharpens the mind, which perhaps explains why I have only just thought about what I am going to ask you."

"Which is?"

"Your name. You are no longer *Father Hugh*, but you cannot live the rest of your life being addressed simply as *Hugh*. What was your father's name?"

"I don't know. I was a child when my parents died, and like you, I was left at the gates of Dunwich priory, but I have already given consideration to my new name. My life did not really begin until that terrible day when I met you just after your family was murdered and your house destroyed. Your disaster was the beginning of my slow ascent from the drudgery of monastic life to freedom. We met at your property in Westhall, so with your permission, I would like to call myself *Hugh of Westhall*, or better still, *Master Hugh Westhall*."

"I would be honoured, Hugh."

"Then it shall be so. As soon as we reach Sir John Fastolf's manor, I shall go to Yarmouth and register my new name with a notary."

"Master Hugh Westhall! It has a certain ring to it. Then hurry up, Master Westhall, or we shall miss one of Mary's famous suppers."

"Richard! Father Hugh! Thank God you're safe," said Mary when she opened the door to the two weary travellers. "Joan!" she called. "Your father's back home!" It was a warm evening, so she ushered them into the walled garden, lit two candles, and brought some wine.

"Joan and I have already eaten, but it won't take long to prepare you something."

"If you don't mind, Mary," said Hugh, "I would prefer to go to bed. My stomach is still feeling the effect of the sea journey. A goblet of wine will be welcome, but I'm not ready for food yet."

Richard added, "We were obliged to wait at the mouth of the Seine until the tide turned. Anchored offshore in choppy waters is not easy even for the hardest stomachs, but this time I seem to have escaped the worst of it."

When Joan joined them, Richard was taken a little by surprise. Each time he saw her after being away for a while, she looked more like his first wife, Ann. This time she had changed the appearance of her black hair from a simple, pageboy cut to a more mature-looking style with the hair parted down the middle and no fringe, exactly like her mother's used to be. She looked radiant.

Richard smiled. "I remembered you're no longer a child, so I brought you both the same gift." He rummaged in his bag and placed two beautiful-smelling, decorated wooden boxes triumphantly on the table. "These are the latest items that fashionable women in Rome are using to enhance the appearance of their faces. They are not exactly the same because yours, Mary, is for fair-haired women while yours, Joan, is for dark-haired ones. There is also perfume too."

"You seem to have thought of everything, Richard, but I'm sorry to hear you think Joan and I need to enhance our appearance!"

"No, no, I didn't mean that! Sorry. I should have thought—"

Mary put her forefinger to his lips to quieten him and laughed. "It was only a jest, Richard. I'm surprised at how thoughtful you've become."

"And me too, Papa."

"Joan, I think one of the containers in your box may have been damaged on the voyage because my cabin began to smell like a lady's chamber. I got some strange looks from some of the sailors!"

After a full account of events in Rome had been given, Hugh retired to bed. Joan excused herself shortly afterwards, leaving Richard and Mary alone in the flickering candlelight. Richard sensed something was not quite right. Joan in particular had been uncharacteristically quiet, sullen almost. He pushed his chair nearer to Mary's so that he could put his arm round her. "Is there anything the matter, my dear?"

"Richard, you've just put your arm round me."

"So?"

"But it's your left arm!"

Richard had said nothing about his visit to Genoa, so he told Mary about Surgeon Andretti but was forced to lie by omission when Mary assumed the treatment had taken place in Rome. He knew he would have to compound the deceit by briefing Hugh in the morning to ensure nothing was said by accident. He hated himself; the pleasure of his return home was gone.

"Will you make a full recovery?" she asked.

"In time yes, but I must be careful not to hurry the process."

"Well, there is no hurry now that we have the truce."

"What truce?"

"Of course, you won't have heard. A short truce has been agreed between England and Burgundy on the one hand, and France on the other, but we are told it is likely to be extended into next year."

Richard's mind raced. This was unexpected news, and he was not sure how to respond.

"When did it take effect?"

"Three days ago."

"Does it apply to all areas of conflict?"

"I don't know, but you can find out at army headquarters tomorrow."

"I shall, and I will also go to the Lombard bank to check the ransom money has arrived, then Marcel can end my parole and return to the French army."

Mary remained silent for a few moments, swallowed, and said, "Richard, I need to speak to you about Marcel."

Alarm bells rang in his mind. "Go on," he answered guardedly.

"Well, without beating about the bush, he wants to marry Joan."

Unlike so many of his comrades, Richard had learned to maintain self-control when confronted with bad news, but this was too much even for him. He jumped to his feet. "Impossible! Marcel is the enemy!"

"I thought he was your friend."

"He is, but he's a bloody Frog!"

"Richard, sit down and calm yourself. Let us discuss this as rational people without swearing or tantrums."

Richard sat down and would have grabbed his wine goblet had he not knocked it over when he jumped up. Mary slowly picked it up, refilled it, and handed it to him. "Now, my dear, remember Marcel is a knight."

"A knight without land."

"At the moment, but Joan would still gain a title."

"I thought, as a Lollard, you do not approve of titles and the like."

"I didn't until now," answered Mary frankly. "You always said you wanted Joan to become a lady, well, here's your chance."

"Exactly how old is Marcel?"

"Thirty-one."

"That's twice as old as Joan!"

"An age gap of sixteen years is not uncommon between a man and a woman."

Mary thought she had made a telling point when Richard did not immediately bite back, but in fact his conscience was reminding him he was eighteen years older than Ruth.

"What have you actually said to Marcel?"

"Only that I would speak to you before he asks formally for Joan's hand."

"So you did not warn him off?"

"Why should I? He is a handsome, intelligent, young knight who loves Joan, and she loves him."

"And what happens when the war resumes? A truce is not peace, the war is far from over."

"I could not discuss such matters with Marcel before speaking to you. I know it will not be easy, but I suppose Joan will have to live in Marcel's home."

"I doubt he has one! He has no land, so his home will probably be with the French army. Do you want Joan to become a camp follower?"

"I'm sure you will be able to arrange something, Richard."

"Thank you very much! You expect me to sort out domestic family arrangements across an area of open war!"

Mary sighed. She knew her husband well enough to realise she had broken the ice, but there was still more work to be done. "My darling, we must think ahead not only for Joan but for ourselves. You have always been honest with me"—Richard's guilt hit hard when she said that—"so tell me now, who will win this war?"

"The French, not soon but in ten years, maybe fifteen."

"Then what will happen to us? I cannot return to England on pain of a heretic's death, and all your wealth is in Rouen."

"I know, I know, but I have not thought that far ahead."

"Well, perhaps now is the time. The only way you will be able to keep what you have here is through influence in the French court. Imagine how useful it will be to have a son-in-law who was Jeanne the Maid's banner bearer and who may, by then, have children who will be citizens of France and your grandchildren."

This was the sort of logic Richard could appreciate. There was nothing for him in England anymore. Everything he owned and loved, excluding Ruth and Enrico, was in Rouen. "You are sure Joan loves Marcel? This is not some childish infatuation that could disappear as quickly as it arrived?"

"She adores him. Ask her yourself if you wish."

"I will do, but not yet. Your judgement is enough for now. Will you get a message to Marcel to meet me here in this garden at three o'clock tomorrow afternoon, when I will listen to what he has to say? By then I will have collected the ransom money from the Lombard bank, so he will be free to stay or go as he pleases."

"What will you say?"

"That depends on him. No more talk now, my head hurts. Let us see what tomorrow brings."

Mary closed her eyes that night knowing she had won her husband round and loving him all the more for it.

"Marcel, welcome! You will be pleased to know there are one hundred and eighty gold ducats in the two bags on this table, so you may now release me from parole and return to the French army." Richard pushed the two leather bags across the garden table towards Marcel and said, "I understand you wish to speak to me about my daughter, who I love very much. Please sit." No need to make this easy for him, he thought.

Marcel cleared his throat. "I shall not insult you by counting this money. You are now fully ransomed, and your parole is ended."

"Thank you."

"With regard to Joan, I love her deeply, and I believe she loves me too. I humbly ask you for her hand in marriage."

"Do you indeed? We are at war, and although we are personal friends, we are also enemies. How do you propose to deal with that?"

"Of course it will not be easy, but I have enough money to buy a property in Rouen where Joan can live while I'm away. As you know, very little fighting takes place during the winter months, so I can return home then. Crossing the ever-changing boundary between true France and English-occupied France has never been difficult."

"Mmmm, I will not challenge you on your definition of France at this moment, but I would like to know how you will take care of Joan financially. Your land has been taken away by the Burgundians."

"As part of the coronation celebrations in Reims, King Charles awarded land and other gifts to his most loyal supporters. I was given a small demesne at Courville near Chartres, which is not so far from Rouen. The rents from this will enable me to look after Joan properly, and while I'm away, you and Mary will be able to see as much of Joan as you desire. Even when I am at home, you will always be welcome, and you will see your grandchildren whenever you wish. This war will end eventually, and we shall prove that strong family ties can outlast any conflict."

Richard was surprised and impressed by Marcel's response. "You have clearly thought much about this. Marcel, stand up please and give me your hand." Richard also stood up, creating an air of sacred formality. "Marcel,

Sieur de Freuchin, you have my permission to propose marriage to Joan, and if she accepts, you also have my blessing. But you had better make haste and arrange the marriage while the truce lasts because if—" He was interrupted by a screech of delight as Joan erupted from the house, ran to her father, and threw her arms round him.

"Thank you, Papa! Thank you, thank you."

"You've been listening! How much have you heard?"

"Every word," replied Mary, who was just behind Joan, smiling broadly. "Surely you can't think we would have missed that!"

Richard kissed his daughter on the head and looked at Mary. "Let's go indoors and leave these two in the garden. I believe this Frenchman has something to ask our Joan, which is best done in private."

Later that evening, Richard and Mary sat in the garden alone together until late, ruminating on the eventful day. "Well, Richard, you have made three people very happy today," said Mary.

"Four if you count me."

"What will happen now?"

"Sadly, Marcel should leave tomorrow with the ransom money and return to his duties because the truce does not yet apply to Paris. I have persuaded him to stay a little longer on the grounds that it will take a couple of days to arrange a suitable escort for him bearing in mind how much gold he'll be carrying. English soldiers are few and far between in Rouen at the moment. They're all needed to defend Paris."

"Will you be going too?"

"No. My arm is improving rapidly, but it is not yet ready for combat. I shall return to England with Hugh."

"But why? He's perfectly capable of going on his own."

"That is true, but now that my land at Westhall is sold, there is nothing left for me in England. I may never go there again. My home is here in Rouen with you. But there is a debt still to be called in, which is a matter of honour and revenge. I must deal with that before I can truly rest."

"Your cousin Geoffrey?"

"Yes. He's managed to escape justice all these years for the murder of Ann and the boys. He must pay. It is not just revenge for me but justice for my previous family."

"What will you do?"

"It's better that you do not know."

"Richard! Tell me!"

"I shall execute him."

"But that will make you a murderer in the eyes of the law."

"I shall be careful to cover my tracks. I know Calveley Hall well enough to gain access unseen."

"Then be careful, my love. I don't want to lose you, especially now that you've come home at last."

"You don't disapprove?"

"Certainly not! Geoffrey should not be allowed to escape punishment for what he did. He thinks he's avoided retribution."

"I confess I am both surprised and grateful."

"Richard, you've been away too long fighting the French. Have you forgotten there is fire in my belly too?"

"How could I ever forget the way you demolished the Bishop of Norwich at your trial."

"Yet I was still found guilty, which is why I don't have the same blind faith in the law as men do. It is only as good as those who administer it, none of whom are women."

"Thank God I still have you, Mary. Promise me you will never change."

"I promise, but I noticed a change in you even before you were wounded at Patay."

"How so?"

"You have mellowed. Perhaps it's something to do with getting older, but you listen more than you used to, and you understand better than most men that there are many shades of grey between black and white."

"I have no doubt it's mainly due to your influence, but there is something else. While I was waiting for Hugh in Rome, an English priest took me to see some of the monuments built by the Romans of old. There was one in particular that stands out in my memory above all the others. It is called the Pantheon. It's a temple dedicated to an ancient Roman called Agrippa. From the outside it looks impressive enough, but when you enter, it's like crossing over to a different world, a world where anything is possible. The roof is a huge dome with a circular hole in the centre to let in the light. It's impossible to understand what keeps it from falling to the ground unless it's held there by invisible powers from heaven. Even our great cathedral builders have achieved nothing like it. The walls are made of stone of many colours—green, red, white, and even purple, all carved so skilfully as to make you think that the ancient stonemasons must have had the power to mould the stone as if it was wet clay. All this was done more than a thousand years ago, and it is still in perfect condition despite

The Angel of Lorraine

the ravages of war and time. How much has the human race forgotten since then, and will we ever be able to learn it again?"

"I would love to see this place, Richard."

"Then I shall take you, but what I am trying to say is that such wonders help you see things in perspective. What seems important to us now often matters very little if you step back and think about it in terms of the ascent of man. Even this unending war between England and France is no more than a simple argument between two related families, Valois and Plantagenet. It would be far better for them and everyone else to settle the disagreement over a game of dice and save all the pain and suffering."

"But, Richard, you have done very well out of the war."

"That's true, and I know I sound like a hypocrite because for every man who has done well, thousands have done badly. I am ready to finish with war and would walk away now if I could, but it will take a few months to discharge my responsibilities first."

"War is all you know."

"I can still work for the army without being in the front line. For every fighting soldier, there is an administrator of some sort working behind the scenes to keep the military colossus functioning properly."

"Then we must pray that Marcel gets through the war unscathed. Have you thought about Joan's dowry?"

"Not yet, but I expect you have."

"There's no need for Marcel to buy a house in Rouen. We could give Joan the house by the river for her dowry. It has a pleasant aspect, and perhaps they may choose to live there when the war is over rather than at Marcel's new demesne near Chartres."

"An excellent idea," agreed Richard, "and then we shall see our grandchildren often. I shall arrange it with our notary tomorrow."

"Joan and I will start planning the wedding, church, guests, and so on. Any thoughts about a date?"

"Well, it must be before the truce ends. I will find out more about that when I visit army headquarters tomorrow."

"It looks like tomorrow will be a long day. We'd better go to bed."

"But I'm not tired yet."

Mary smiled impishly. "So much the better, neither am I!"

* * *

III

After a pleasant week in Rouen, Richard and Hugh left for England. They rode first to Calais where, as luck would have it, they found Captain Coombes and *Sea Sprite* in the harbour unloading a cargo of wool bound for the Flemish weavers. They were not in a hurry, so they waited for two days in the town while Coombes completed his business and was ready to return to Ipswich.

On the morning of the fifteenth day of September, in a moderate swell, *Sea Sprite* approached the Orwell estuary on a larboard tack. Richard and Hugh were on deck watching the small fishing boats spreading their nets in the shallow, coastal waters, when Hugh spotted a large ship anchored alone just off the Suffolk side of the estuary. "What do you make of that, Richard?"

The Angel of Lorraine

"I don't know. It seems a strange place to drop anchor when there's the shelter of Ipswich or Harwich nearby. I'll have a word with our captain when we get a bit nearer."

Half an hour later, the two ships were close enough for Captain Coombes to be able to identify the other ship from the shape of the hull and the number of masts even before the name of the ship became visible on the starboard bow. It was *Morning Star*.

"Don't like the look of this, Richard," said Coombes as he joined his passengers on the starboard beam, "don't like it at all."

A moment later, the lookout stationed on the foredeck shouted, "Captain! The black cross!"

Richard hardly dared utter the most feared word in the English language. He whispered, "Captain, is it the plague?"

"I'm afraid so," answered Coombes. "*Morning Star* is now a plague ship. We'll know more soon because here comes a pilot boat from Harwich on the Essex side of the estuary."

The pilot signalled *Sea Sprite* to heave to and climbed up the rope ladder hung out for him with practised ease. A short, middle-aged, weather-beaten man, he had that air of authority of an experienced sailor who had once commanded his own ship. "I am Captain Wix, deputy harbour master of the port of Harwich."

"Captain Coombes at your service," replied *Sea Sprite*'s captain.

"Captain Coombes, you are sailing too close to that anchored ship. You are ordered to go no nearer."

"I shall pull away immediately, Captain Wix. I recognise that ship as *Morning Star*, Captain Skelhorn commanding. How long has she been here?"

"She's done twenty-four days of her statutory forty, but I do not think there are any survivors now. No one returned our hail yesterday, so we must expect the worst."

"Poor Skelhorn," said Richard. "He thought this cargo would make him a wealthy man."

"What was he carrying?" asked Wix.

"Eastern spices and silk cloth from Constantinople."

"Then he picked up more than he bargained for. Plague always begins in the east. It also explains what happened two days ago. A small cutter approached from the Suffolk side of the estuary, but before we could intercept it, two fools had climbed aboard and started to unload cargo. They were there for twenty minutes before we drew near and made off before we could stop them. I'm glad they did because I would not want to get too close to men who had been aboard that ship."

Richard asked, "What will happen after forty days, Captain?"

"By then the plague should have exhausted itself, but we'll take no chances. We'll cut the cable, check there are no survivors aboard *Morning Star*, tow her out to sea, and sink her, cargo and all."

"And good riddance," said Coombes. "We've been free of plague for more than a generation, so let's keep it that way."

"Indeed," agreed Richard. "It was plague that carried away my mother and father. I pray it never touches my family again."

It was a late September afternoon. Richard and Hugh stood side by side watching the river traffic on the Bure drifting on the ebb tide towards Yarmouth.

The Angel of Lorraine

"Well, Master Hugh Westhall, it's time for me to go. I doubt I shall return to England, so we are unlikely to meet again, but I have the comfort of knowing you are settled into your new life at Caistor Manor."

"Richard, I can't thank you enough for what you've done for me, but I fully intend to repay you as soon as I can. You have spent so much time and money giving me a new life."

"It's only money, Hugh. Please regard it as a gift. When you have earned enough yourself to enable you to help others, you will understand that the pleasure is in the giving, not the receiving. The best way you can thank me is to write to me at Rouen once a year and inform me of your progress. I always answer my letters, so we can continue to correspond that way, and who knows, one day I may need your help."

"Unlikely, Richard, you are too well organised for that to happen, but tell me, are you going back to Rouen now?"

"Not quite, I will call upon my cousin on the way. I still must settle the outstanding debt he owes my family."

"How?"

Richard took a long, thin dagger from his belt and stroked the evil-looking blade. "This is an archer's dagger. It is sometimes called a misericord, and it is what I shall use to send my cousin Geoffrey to hell."

"Why an archer's dagger?"

"Because it is designed to kill a helpless enemy. After a battle, our archers patrol the French wounded searching for knights worthy of ransom. Ordinary men-at-arms are dispatched with these. The blade is strong but thin so that it can be pushed through the visor slit in a man-at-arm's helmet and finish him off without mess or fuss. It will be quite sufficient to end my cousin's miserable life."

"But, Richard, you will be taking a risk."

"Not really. You know Calveley Hall as well as I do, if not better. I shall not knock at the front door. Instead the deed will be done quickly and stealthily. I shall be long gone before anyone realises there is something amiss."

"Is your cousin worth the risk?"

"I have been a soldier for fifteen years. Calculated risk is my stock-in-trade. In this case, the risk is not great. I have hated only two people in my life, both Englishmen. One was Geoffrey's steward, Titus Scrope, who carried out my cousin's orders. You were present at his death five years ago, and even he made an attempt to compensate for his crimes. Repentance like that would never occur to cousin Geoffrey. He has managed to place himself beyond the law, so I must deal with him myself. Even Mary approves."

"Then so do I," said Hugh, "and may God go with you."

The two friends shook hands, then Richard was gone.

By the time Richard reached Calveley Hall, it was almost dark. Something seemed wrong as he climbed over the fence in the twilight and tethered his horse to a fence post at the rear of the hall. A single, flickering light lit the main upstairs bedroom, but other than that, the house was dark. Apart from the sound of the breeze in the trees, there was utter silence, not even the sound of a barking dog to announce the arrival of a stranger, yet it was far too early for the servants to have gone to bed. Carefully, he approached the door to the servants' quarters and drew his dagger to force the lock, but there was no need; the door was unlocked. Sensing a trap, Richard, now more alert than ever, paused to consider his options, but he could not believe Geoffrey had been forewarned because only Mary and Hugh knew what he intended to do.

Holding his dagger at the ready, his heart raced as he silently pushed open the door. He was greeted by the most disgusting, filthy smell he had ever experienced. As a soldier, he was familiar with the stench of death, but this was far worse. He stood still until he could compose himself; he dare not vomit and awaken the entire household. After a minute standing in the dark, he felt he was able to contain his heaving stomach, and holding his kerchief to his nose with his left hand, something his wound would not have let him do a month ago, he entered Calveley Hall for the last time. There was just enough twilight left for him to navigate his way through the once familiar surroundings, so he was able to pass through the servants' quarters and reach the main stairs to the upper floor. Still no one challenged him. The silence seemed almost tangible as if some huge unseen hand had placed a thick, black blanket over the entire hall. As he ascended the stairs, the smell got worse, and just before he reached the upper floor, he could not stop himself from retching.

"Who's there?" came a weak voice from the main bedroom. The bedroom door was open, but Richard did not answer and approached the door silently.

"Who's there I say!" This time the voice was a little stronger; it was Geoffrey's.

Richard entered the bedroom; this was the source of the foul smell. "It's your cousin Richard."

He found Geoffrey sitting upright on the bed, which was soiled with his own ordure, holding a lavender pomander to his nose. A candle burned on the small table beside him. "What a time to visit! Smells a bit, doesn't it. No servants to clean the mess up."

"Where are they?"

"Those who are left here are all dead. It's not just me causing the stink."

"What happened?"

"Plague."

Richard involuntarily took a step back. "But how?"

"Came with some merchandise from the east."

Peter Tallon

"On the *Morning Star*?"

"How did you know?"

"I should have realised it was you. I met the Harwich pilot a few days ago. It was you who sent those poor wretches to their deaths when they collected your goods before the forty days were finished."

"My steward, Luke Cotter, and his brother knew the risk they were taking and were well paid for it, though they never got the chance to spend their reward."

"Where are they now?"

"Dead, somewhere in the garden I think."

"And what about your wife and son?"

"Also dead. Everyone here caught plague. I'm the last to go."

"So they all died because of your greed."

"If you say so. Why are you here?"

"To take long overdue revenge for the murder of Ann, Robert, and John."

"You mean to kill me?"

"Of course."

"Well, get on with it then, you'll be doing me a favour."

"Hellfire awaits you."

"Perhaps, perhaps not. I shall soon know."

"Now at least, you have some idea of how I felt when you murdered my family."

"I never ordered that. Scrope let it get out of hand. I only meant to frighten you."

"You are still responsible for their deaths even though you didn't have the guts to do it yourself."

Geoffrey coughed; more stinking, brown ordure oozed out onto his bed. "I have a terrible thirst. Can you pass me that water jug beside the candle?"

Richard handed his cousin the jug, being very careful not to touch him, but when Geoffrey tried to drink from it, most of the contents spilled over his face because his skeletal hand shook so much. "Well, come on, Richard, I'm ready. Do your worst. I'll be dead by morning anyway."

Richard sheathed his dagger. "You're not worth it. Your own greed has brought this upon you, so I shall leave you to see it through alone." Then he turned and left. As he descended the stairs, he heard his cousin calling him to come back, no one wants to die alone, but Richard kept going and ran out of the servants' quarters, desperate to breathe fresh air again. He mounted his horse and cantered through the manor's open front gate, unaware of the large, black cross painted on it.

Later that evening, the residents of the nearby market town of Halesworth saw a red glow in the sky to the northwest. It was caused by Calveley Hall, which was burning fiercely. In his desperation to reach the water jug again, Geoffrey must have knocked over the still-burning candle. In the morning, all that was left of the hall was a pile of charred timbers and ash. Having destroyed the residents, the plague had, in turn, destroyed itself.

CHAPTER ELEVEN

Jeanne was sent to Bourges, sixty miles south of Orléans and far away from the war, to recuperate from the wound she received beneath the formidable walls of Paris. Yolande and Queen Marie placed a royal house near the cathedral of Saint Etienne at her disposal and ensured she received the best possible medical treatment, so by the time Dunois visited her on the twenty-fifth day of September, her body was almost recovered, though her spirit was still troubled.

He arrived at three in the afternoon. There was a chill in the air presaging an early autumn, so they sat together inside the house watching the crowds milling around the stalls selling souvenirs outside the cathedral.

"I'm gratified to see how quickly you are recovering from your wound, Jeanne," said Dunois. "You are very lucky it wasn't much worse."

"A combination of good treatment, a young body, and God's will, Jean. My armour absorbed most of the force of the bolt, so it did not penetrate too deeply. The surgeon said another half-finger width, and it would have severed the main artery."

"You know, Jeanne, you should be more careful. I realise that God is with you, but you should not test his patience too far."

She smiled. "That is exactly what Marcel says. I have agreed to do my best to take more care, but in the heat of battle, I always feel protected by the power of heaven. My life will only end when God wills it to."

Dunois knew he was wasting his breath but kept trying. "There is not only death to consider. Have you thought of the consequences should you be captured alive by our enemies?"

"No, because I will never surrender. I shall fight to the death rather than be taken."

"Of course. You must be pleased to have Marcel back at your side."

"Certainly. He brought the ransom money in full back with him, which will make a useful contribution to your half brother's release from captivity in England. He seems to have enjoyed his stay in Rouen and says that English morale is low."

"But with the Duke of Bedford back in France again in person, we must expect their morale to improve, at least until you take the field again."

Jeanne paused and stared out of the window at the crowd for a few moments. "What are people saying, Jean?"

"About what?"

"Me."

Dunois frowned as he gathered his thoughts. "The division between the Royal Council and the Military Council grows deeper. The English are saying that our reverse at Paris and your wound prove your voices come from hell, not heaven. While not going that far, there are some in the Royal Council, most notably Trémoille, who are still sceptical about your messages from heaven."

"What about the king?"

"He is becoming more difficult to assess. I thought I knew him, but now I am not so sure. In the spring, he seemed totally convinced about your mission, but at Paris he took advantage of your wound to abandon the siege before it had started in earnest. He speaks less of you now, though when he does, it is always in positive terms, but Trémoille's influence grows stronger. I am convinced he is planning something, but I have no idea what it is. I'm sure he resents you, though he does not say so openly."

"Was he responsible for the early retreat from Paris?"

"I believe so, but the fact is we were not properly prepared. We did not have enough siege artillery with us and relied too heavily on you providing another miracle. You still have the backing of the Military Council, which believes you were not properly supported at Paris, but your wound shocked everyone's confidence."

"I have been wounded before."

"But not so badly. At the Tourelles you fell but recovered quickly and returned to the fray, which only added to your reputation. The army's faith in you is still strong, but you must avoid another mishap."

"Were our soldiers paid in full, Jean?"

"Yes, but only because the king made up the Exchequer's shortfall from the finances of his own purse."

"He did the right thing."

"But he won't do it again. The truce will give us breathing space to finance the war properly next year and maybe even pay Duke Philippe his demand for reparation for the murder of his father. Tax revenues are starting to flow once more."

"When will the truce end?"

"April the sixteenth, Easter Sunday next year. It includes Paris now."

"It's a long time to wait."

"We need that time, Jeanne, to be certain that next year our brave soldiers are paid in full. I know you feel strongly about that."

"And pay off the Duke of Burgundy?"

"Hopefully, but the Duke of Bedford's influence is still strong, thanks to his wife." Dunois stood up and reached for his cloak. "I must return to Sully now, Jeanne, where the king is in residence with his court, but it has been good to speak with you."

"What will you do during the truce, Jean?"

"I shall spend some time with my family in Blois, relax, and do a little hunting. Then I shall return to duty. What will you do, Jeanne, go home to Domremy for a while?"

"I don't think so. I shall wait to be guided by my voices. They will advise me."

"Of course. Farewell, and may God be with you wherever you go."

Jeanne did not have long to wait, but it was not her voices that determined her next task. Three days after the meeting with Dunois, Georges de la Tremoille came to see her. Whereas Dunois had come alone apart from a squire, Trémoille arrived in the grand chamberlain's lavish coach drawn by grey horses and accompanied by an escort of ten royal household knights. In consideration of his bulk, Jeanne received Trémoille on the ground floor to save him negotiating the stairs, and sat him down in the reception room. He lowered himself slowly into the largest chair, which was made of finest French oak and did not buckle even under his weight. His dark, reptilian eyes flickered round the room inspecting rather than looking at it. "I trust you are being looked after adequately, Jeanne?"

"More than adequately, Mon Seigneur."

It was two hours after noon, so Trémoille asked, "Is there wine?"

"Bordeaux or Burgundy?"

"Bordeaux I think. Burgundy might appear a little disloyal." He smirked at his own weak joke.

Not wanting the meeting to last any longer than necessary, Jeanne asked as soon as the wine was brought, "How can I be of assistance, Mon Seigneur?"

"But it is I who hope to be of assistance to you, Jeanne. Although the truce is in place, there is still a campaign to be fought against an ally of Burgundy and England who is not part of the truce. You would be the ideal person to lead it. Have you heard of Perrinet Gressart?"

"Only in passing. I know nothing about him."

"He claims to be an ally of Burgundy and England, both of whom pay him to wage war against us, but he is really no more than a villainous mercenary who has carved out a small fiefdom for himself in the upper reaches of the Loire between La Charité and Saint Pierre. Both of these are barely a day's march from Bourges, which he could easily threaten if he thought there was profit in it for him."

"Then why has the king allowed this to happen?"

"Until now, the English were the greater danger, but now they've been driven northwards. Thanks to your great victories, the king is ready to deal with this threat from the east. He asks you to lead a small but well-equipped army to bring this Gressart to heel. He also gives you the services of my own dear half brother, Charles d'Albret, as your joint commander who will handle supplies and logistics while you lead the soldiers into battle."

"But I am here to fight the English and win Burgundy back for France."

"And you shall do that as soon as the truce, which we need to build up our strength, is ended at Easter. We shall be much stronger then if Gressart has already been dealt with. You do not have to accept, but it is your king's wish for you to lead this campaign. You would be doing a great service to him and our beloved France."

Jeanne was not taken in by Trémoille's flattery. A winter campaign amongst the remote hills of the upper Loire with none of the commanders she knew and trusted would be risky. There would be little glory to be gained by defeating a mere brigand, and if winter came early, there was the possibility of another reverse. Nor had her voices predicted this turn of events. On the other hand, she had nothing else to do until next Easter, and the thought of waiting for another six and a half months was even less appealing. At least Marcel would be with her.

"I accept," she said simply.

"Excellent! I will give the order for your soldiers to assemble here at Bourges together with the siege equipment you will need. Are you sure your wound has healed sufficiently to allow you to do this?"

"Yes, it was not as bad as it looked. I am young and from sturdy peasant stock. I heal quickly."

Trémoille left well pleased with his meeting with Jeanne. He had two motives for sending her on the Gressart campaign—one personal, the other political. Four years earlier, when he had been leading a delegation to Burgundy, Trémoille was captured by Gressart as he passed through La Charité. He had no choice but to pay Gressart's demand for a large ransom to secure his freedom, but such an insult and humiliation could not go unpunished forever. The political motive lay in Trémoille's desire to destroy Jeanne's influence with the king. By arranging and partly financing the Gressart campaign, the grand chamberlain would be demonstrating his loyalty to King Charles and his faith in the Maid of Orléans, even though he had none. If she was successful, he would be praised for his confidence in Jeanne and his good judgement for choosing her to lead the army. If she failed, which he believed was likely, a second defeat would degrade her credibility still further while Trémoille could claim to have done everything to help and be able to say, "I provided an army and gave the command to the so-called Messenger of God. What more could I have done?"

The Gressart campaign lasted just two months. Jeanne and d'Albret first surrounded Saint Pierre le Moutier, a fortified town at the southern end of Gressart's unofficial fiefdom, but after a week of ineffective bombardment, Jeanne lost patience and ordered an escalade. With Marcel holding her banner at her side, she led the attack on the fourth day of November. Remarkably, the defence collapsed after little hard fighting; the angel of Lorraine had regained her miraculous ways.

Next, Jeanne and her little army appeared before the walls of La Charité on the ninth day of November, but the weather was getting cold. This was a much more formidable obstacle than Saint Pierre, so there could be no question of an assault before the siege cannon had forced open a proper breach in the city walls. Food, powder, and shot were running low; no help came from the king, and by mid-December, no adequate breach had been blasted into the city's walls. The euphoria after the victory at Saint Pierre had faded away, and the men were discouraged. Jeanne decided that breach or no breach, an escalade would have to take place before Christmas, but she could not put her plan into action because orders came from the Royal Council in Bourges to abandon the siege and withdraw.

The Maid had met another defeat, Trémoille was quietly delighted, and Marcel could get married in Rouen before the truce ended.

* * *

II

January to March 1430 was a lonely and desolate time for Jeanne. Marcel went back to Rouen, and even the king's proclamation announcing the ennoblement of her family did nothing to lift her depression because the tone of the proclamation had an air of finality about it, thanking her for her past services and wishing her well for the future. She travelled between the towns and cities of her previous victories, but it was only the prospect of the resumption of war with the English that kept her going. Eventually she was able to rejoin the king at Trémoille's castle at Sully sur Loire to become part of the Military Council, which offered strategic advice to the king on how best to use the new armies that were now available to him to drive the English out of France.

But before the first meeting took place, Jeanne was visited by Dunois, Alençon, and de Rais at her private residence in the castle grounds. All three seemed agitated as they sat down together in the drawing room in the small dwelling near the west gate, which had once been a guardhouse.

Dunois, ever the loyal friend, began. "Jeanne, it's important we speak to you before the Military Council meets tomorrow."

"Why?"

"Because there has been a change in the council's membership. Arthur of Richemont has been permitted to return to his duties even though he is still refused access to the court. As Constable of France, he is the most senior soldier in the country and now chairs the Military Council by right. This has led to some strains in our relationships. For example he used to chase de Xaintrailles and La Hire up and down the country during their more unruly days, and even now, neither trusts Richemont. Since the reverse at La Charité last year, Richemont now questions your suitability for a direct military command saying your tactics are always the same. Attack! Attack! Attack! Regrettably even de Gaucourt supports this view. Both point to your failures last year, but especially Paris, where, according to de Gaucourt, we gave the English an easy victory."

"I followed the voices from heaven, but even by your own admission, I was left unsupported by the king at Paris as I was at La Charité. I cannot do God's work if I am not given the tools to carry it out."

"Richemont wants to make you no more than a figurehead, but those of us who know you realise that is not in your nature. The constable dresses this up by saying we cannot afford to lose you, but he is not yet sufficiently secure in his rank to insist against the majority on the council that you withdraw from the front line. If he did that, he knows I would resign. Consequently I am pleased to be able to tell you that you'll be given joint command of a small but well-equipped army to be sent to assist the defence of Compiègne, which, our agents in Bruges tell us, will be Duke Philippe's first target when the truce ends."

"Who will be the other joint commander?" asked Jeanne nervously.

"You need not worry, Jeanne, it will be de Xaintrailles."

"Hurrah! It will be good to have Jean Poton alongside me again. I was never sure about d'Albret."

Alençon said, "Unfortunately, Gilles and I cannot be with you because we'll be leading small, fast armies westwards to try and loosen the English grip on Anjou and Maine. Local resistance to the English is building, so now is the time to support it."

"And the wonderful Royal Council will remain here with the king in the south," added de Rais, "so we'll be able to fight the war properly without having that deadweight slowing us down. I have a good feeling about this year."

Dunois concluded the meeting. "Then we shall all meet again tomorrow morning at the Military Council when details of strategy will be discussed, and Jeanne will resume her place as the inspiration of France!"

But Trémoille was following his own strategy. When the Military Council met in his castle at Sully, he was at a covert meeting at Gien, fifteen miles upstream. Not even the king was aware of the grand chamberlain's assignation with Guillaume de Flavy, the castellan of Compiègne.

Compiègne, thirty-two miles north of Paris and half a mile downstream from the confluence of two great rivers, the Oise and the Aisne, was a small city that had been Burgundian until it transferred its allegiance to King Charles after his coronation at Reims. By the terms of the truce, it should have been handed back to Duke Philippe, but the citizens did not want this, so it never happened. That was why its capture became Philippe's first objective. He would then punish the citizens and make an example of the recalcitrant city councillors.

Compiègne lay on the south bank of the River Oise and was strongly fortified, but although the main city defences were on the south bank, the outer, curtain wall crossed the river to the north, which added an extra barrier of defence that was linked to the city by a stone bridge. At the beginning of May, Jeanne and de Xaintrailles arrived, but as usual, the king provided less than he promised, so there were only five hundred men with them. Even so, the mere presence of the Maid of Orléans lifted everyone's spirits, and a large crowd gathered to cheer her as she was welcomed by de Flavy at the city hall. Her arrival had been signalled well in advance, so there was time to prepare a fine reception for her and de Xaintrailles, at the end of which de Flavy, a courteous and fine-looking knight, made a speech praising Jeanne as the saviour of France.

But Jeanne was eager to take the fight to the enemy, so in the middle of the afternoon when the reception ended, she and de Xaintrailles met de Flavy in his private office near the Bridge Gate where they had a fine view of the river and the land to the north, the direction from which the Burgundian attack would come.

"With your five hundred, we now have two and a half thousand men fit for battle," said de Flavy. "Our latest estimate of the Burgundian strength is between five and six thousand plus a powerful artillery train."

"Who commands?" asked de Xaintrailles.

"Duke Jean of Luxembourg, though Philippe himself is accompanying the army. He is displeased with our citizens for not handing themselves over to him as required by the truce."

Joan asked, "How close are the Burgundians now?"

"Less than a day's march away," answered de Flavy. "Interestingly we've heard that English soldiers are marching from Paris to help them, but this has not been confirmed, so we don't know where they are or how many are coming."

"Then surely we should attack the Burgundians before the English get here. The last thing Philippe will expect is an aggressive move from a much smaller force."

"Jeanne makes a fair point," agreed de Xaintrailles "and if we can get behind the Burgundians, the surprise will be complete."

De Flavy, whose prime task was to hold on to Compiègne, demurred. "That would mean reducing the garrison to a dangerously low level. If Philippe and Luxembourg attack while you are away, the city could fall."

De Xaintrailles shook his head. "Very unlikely. Philippe won't have dragged his precious guns all the way from Bruges without wanting to try them out on your walls."

"It's risky," objected de Flavy.

"Not as risky as allowing the Burgundians and English to unite," responded de Xaintrailles.

"How many men will you want?"

"Fifteen hundred."

"Impossible!"

De Xaintrailles raised an aristocratic eyebrow. "I believe Louis of Bourbon, Count of Vendome, is here. Should he not be consulted?"

De Flavy went to the cabinet behind him, unlocked it, and brought back a small scroll. "This is my letter of appointment as Castellan of Compiègne. You will see it bears the royal seal and is signed by the grand chamberlain and chairman of the Royal Council, Georges de la Tremoille. Read it, and you will understand that my authority here is absolute."

De Xaintrailles quickly scanned the letter and handed it back to the castellan. "This does indeed confirm the nature of your appointment, and it is gratifying to see that authority is now being conferred on the basis of competence rather than rank." He flashed one of his best, most irresistible smiles and added, "I congratulate you, Mon Sieur."

De Flavy, who had been expecting an argument rather than a warm compliment, was surprised and flattered; the de Xaintrailles charm was working. "It might be possible to spare the Count of Vendome and his retinue to help with your plan," *and*, the castellan thought to himself, *get rid of a prince of the blood for a while who thinks he should be in command here.* "His retinue amounts to just under six hundred men-at-arms, which, with your own five hundred, is not so far off the fifteen hundred you requested."

"Thank you, Mon Sieur," replied de Xaintrailles, then turning to Jeanne, he said, "I think eleven hundred with the element of surprise will be sufficient. What is your view?"

Before Jeanne could reply, de Flavy, who seemed to be warming to the project, added, "If you ride east and cross the Aisne at Soissons, the castellan there, Guichard Bournel, may be able to spare a few more men to help you. Then you can turn west and take the Burgundian army in the rear. I shall be looking out for you and will support you with a sally from the Bridge Gate when you attack."

De Xaintrailles addressed Jeanne again. "Well, that seems to meet all our needs, does it not?"

Jeanne, whose instincts were warning her not to trust de Flavy, answered with a simple, "Yes, it does."

De Flavy said, "I do not know Bournel well, so I will write him a short letter asking him to support your venture."

The expedition departed on the eighteenth day of May, but from the beginning, nothing seemed to go well. As soon as they left Compiègne, the Count of Vendome rode up to de Xaintrailles and Jeanne demanding to take over command, which, as a prince of the blood, he claimed as his right. De Xaintrailles put the count firmly back in his place, threatening to hang him if he disobeyed orders, but when they approached Soissons, Vendome showed his displeasure by peeling off the column and heading southwest with his retinue to Senlis, leaving Jeanne and de Xaintrailles with just their original five hundred. Now, without support from Bournel, the project would have to be abandoned.

Guichard Bournel, Castellan of Soissons, was a man of few words and, as it transpired, even fewer principles. De Flavy's letter had no effect, for Bournel flatly refused to permit Jeanne's soldiers access to Soissons, which meant that the river crossing was barred to them. His excuse was the presence of Burgundians in the area who would take revenge on the citizens if they were seen to be helping the enemy of their lord, Duke Philippe. In the face of such hostility, Jeanne and de Xaintrailles were left with no alternative but to return to Compiègne. They chose a more southerly route than before where they could pick up a few reinforcements along the way.

They arrived under cover of darkness on the night of the twenty-second of May, but then, at last, their ill fortune seemed to change. Despite the loss of Vendome's contingent, de Flavy welcomed them, for he had received some important information from a Burgundian deserter who was quickly brought to the castellan's office where Jeanne, de Xaintrailles, and de Flavy awaited him. At Jeanne's request, Marcel was also present because his ancestral lands were nearby, so he knew the area well.

The Burgundian, a small, fair-haired man of about thirty, seemed terrified, but de Xaintrailles quickly put him at his ease. "You will not be harmed if you speak the truth"—De Flavy nodded his agreement—"but if you deceive us, we will know, and you shall be put to death. Is that clear?"

"Yes, Mon Seigneur," croaked the deserter.

"Bring him some water," said Jeanne. "He can hardly speak." De Flavy handed him a goblet and allowed de Xaintrailles to conduct the interrogation.

"Your name?"

"Laurent of Peronne."

"Well, Laurent, why did you desert?"

"I was notary to Duke Jean of Luxembourg, a very senior position, but I was accused of being drunk and unfit for duty, so I was sent to join the ranks of the fighting men. I have a weak constitution, and I know I could not survive the rigours of army life."

"And were you drunk?"

"Only a little, but five years of loyal, dedicated service was not taken into account when I was punished."

De Xaintrailles turned to Marcel. "You are from Picardy. Would you ask this man some questions to prove he is what he says he is?"

"Yes, Mon Seigneur. I can say now that his accent sounds genuine."

Marcel looked at the sorry creature in front of him. "You say you are from Peronne, so you must know the castle with the square towers."

Laurent frowned. "I am sorry, Mon Sieur, but the only castle I know has round towers."

"Then you must know the cathedral of Saints Peter and Paul at Noyon!"

The Burgundian grimaced in terror. "Mon Sieur, I am sorry, but I really am from Peronne."

"Answer my question!"

"The cathedral at Noyon is called Notre Dame."

Marcel addressed de Xaintrailles, "I cannot tell you if this man is or is not a deserter, but he is definitely from Picardy. His answers were correct even though I attempted to mislead him."

Satisfied with that, de Xaintrailles spoke to the Burgundian again. "Now, Laurent, you have passed the first test, so I want you to repeat to me exactly what you told the castellan here. He will be listening for any inconsistencies with your previous story. If your information has value, you will be rewarded. You already know what will happen if you try to deceive us. You may begin."

Laurent composed himself and spoke quietly but clearly. "You already know, Mes Seigneurs, that I was Duke Jean of Luxembourg's notary, which means I wrote down all the orders he gave to his commanders. Consequently I know the dispositions of the Burgundian troops around Compiègne."

"What of the English?" interjected de Flavy.

"I know nothing of them. I was not even aware they were near until you told me."

"Continue, Laurent," said de Xaintrailles, mildly irritated by the castellan's interruption.

"To the north of Compiègne is the village of Margny from where twelve hundred men are blockading your gate north of the Oise. About a mile to the east is another village called Clairoix where Luxembourg's main force is based. He has three thousand men, but the important thing is that most of them are camped on the far side of a tributary of the Oise called the Aronde. There is only one bridge, so if that was blocked or destroyed, Luxembourg would have to march north to Bienville before he could find another crossing."

Jeanne asked, "Can the Aronde be forded?"

"I do not know, but it is quite fast flowing and could not be forded easily or quickly by heavily armoured men. Duke Philippe is based at Bienville with the reserve of one thousand men."

"So, if I understand you correctly," said de Xaintrailles, "you are suggesting we could destroy the force in Margny before help could arrive from the rest of the Burgundian army?"

The Angel of Lorraine

"Exactly, Mon Seigneur! You would have at least four hours to achieve that."

"Thank you, Laurent. You will now be given food and wine but will remain under close guard until your information has been validated one way or the other."

When the Burgundian had left, de Xaintrailles said, "Well, what do you think?"

Predictably Jeanne replied, "God has sent us an opportunity, so we must grasp it. Attack Margny at first light."

"I agree with Jeanne," said de Flavy. "Even though we've lost Vendome's retinue, we still have nearly two thousand men, so we can spare half that for a surprise attack now that we know the garrison at Margny will be unsupported for four hours at least."

"Only if we capture and hold the Clairoix bridge," warned Marcel.

"Fifty bold men should be able to do that," replied the castellan. "The bridge is narrow and made of wood. We could burn it if necessary."

"But what of the English?" asked de Xaintrailles. "We don't know where they are or how strong they are."

"Or if they even exist!" said de Flavy. "Our Burgundian deserter had not heard anything about them. It may be just a wishful rumour. I am sure if they were near, we would have been informed by now."

The meeting went quiet for a few moments, then de Xaintrailles broke the silence. "I'm uncomfortable with this. It all seems a bit too easy."

"It's a gift from God, Jean Poton, we must not spurn it," urged Jeanne.

Marcel said, "You are well-known for your daring, Mon Seigneur, yet out of the four of us, you hold back."

De Xaintrailles hesitated, then made his decision. "Very well, we'll attack at dawn if you agree, Mon Sieur."

"I do," replied de Flavy. "I shall detach fifty good swordsmen to hold the Clairoix bridge by whatever means necessary and put five hundred of my own men under your command, Mon Seigneur, for the attack on Margny."

"Jeanne, will you lead the charge with me?" asked de Xaintrailles, already knowing the answer.

"Of course, Jean Poton, where else would I be?"

"Then let us warn the men to be ready at dawn."

"And make sure they are all confessed," added Jeanne.

* * *

III

The night was cloudless. Dawn on the twenty-third day of May broke cold and clear. As a thousand men-at-arms were quietly assembling behind Compiègne's Bridge Gate, an exhausted messenger arrived at the Soissons Gate on the southeast side of the city bearing the news that Guichard Bournel had sold himself and Soissons to the Burgundians the previous day.

"Not an auspicious start to this morning's action, Marcel," whispered de Xaintrailles. "I can't get rid of the feeling that something's not quite right. What is the name of the hamlet a few minutes ride to the west?"

"Venette, Mon Seigneur."

"Then select ten of our most reliable men to occupy Venette when the Bridge Gate is opened with instructions to keep a good watch on the road beyond. If the English do come, it will be from that direction."

"I will, Mon Seigneur."

"And stick to Jeanne like a leech. She's got that wild look in her eyes again."

"I shall stay closer to her than her own shadow, you can count on that."

"Good! It's time to go. Pass the word. No trumpets, no shouting. We want to catch the Burgundians while they're still in their beds if we can."

The thunder of four thousand hooves soon alerted the Burgundians, though not before the rampant French had trampled their pickets and overrun their advanced camp, but most of them were camped a little way behind Margny and were able to mount up and offer organised resistance before the French reached them. The sun was up now, and de Xaintrailles could see a second charge would be needed to break the stubborn Burgundians. He reined in his lathered horse beside Jeanne.

"Jeanne! Marcel! We must extend the line left and right to outflank them and cut off their retreat. You go left, and I'll go right! Trumpeter, sound the charge!"

There was no need for stealth now. The sound of the trumpet stirred the French as well as their warhorses, who also recognised the call and surged forward. Their riders cheered, "For France! For France!" and smashed their way into the ranks of Duke Philippe's horsemen who were still recovering from the first charge. All seemed to be going well, but as the enemy fled before him, de Xaintrailles saw another column of men marching towards the battle from the north; the banners identified them as Philippe's personal bodyguard. The Burgundian deserter had not predicted this. Then a call from behind warned of another more serious threat.

One of the picked swordsmen, who had been chosen to defend the Clairoix bridge, came galloping up to de Xaintrailles. "Mon Seigneur, the Burgundians were waiting for us on this side of the Aronde. We never got near the bridge. They are crossing in force as I speak. They will cut us off from Compiègne if we do not retire immediately."

"So it was a trap after all. Laurent of Peronne will not live out this day."

"The trumpet is sounding the recall, we must turn round," panted Marcel as he tried to keep up with Jeanne.

"But we have almost cut off the Burgundians, we must go on!"

Marcel grabbed one of her reins and forced her to stop. "Jeanne, no! We have a direct order. We must obey."

"I am in joint command."

"But you are not commanding, are you! While you cannot see further than the end of your nose, de Xaintrailles is trying to save the army from disaster. He would not have sounded the recall for nothing just when we are winning."

Reluctantly, Jeanne gathered her entourage together and led them back down the road towards Compiègne, leaving the shaken Burgundians free to join their comrades advancing from the north to their rescue.

Meanwhile, de Xaintrailles was fighting a managed withdrawal as more and more Burgundians crossed the Clairoix bridge. Despite being heavily outnumbered now, the withdrawal seemed to be progressing well until a messenger arrived from the scouts at Venette who Marcel had posted to watch the west road.

"Mon Seigneur, the English are coming!"

"Where are they now?" asked de Xaintrailles.

"They've just chased us out of Venette. They'll be here in ten minutes."

"How many?"

"At least a thousand."

The Angel of Lorraine

"Then we must break off immediately." Calling to his squire, de Xaintrailles issued his orders slowly and calmly. Now was not the time for panic. "Thierry, take my banner and personal bodyguard and form a defensive line fifty paces outside the Bridge Gate. Call for covering fire from the battlements. You will be the rear guard behind which the rest of our men can run for the gate. I will join you shortly. On no account allow the gate to be shut until I am with you." He peered up the Margny road. "Thierry, my eyes are not as good as they were. Can you see the Maid?"

"Yes, Mon Seigneur, and I can see her banner. She is riding hard with her men towards Compiègne."

"Thank God for that! Now off you go and send the trumpeter to me."

The trumpet sounded the urgent notes for retreat. De Xaintrailles's men needed no second bidding; they broke off the fight and ran for Compiègne with the enemy hot on their heels, but Jeanne had never seen this manoeuvre before and mistook it for blind panic.

"Marcel! Jean Poton is in trouble. We must help him!" Before Marcel could explain what was happening, she had waved her banner, left the Compiègne road and, calling her men to follow, galloped headlong towards the Burgundians. Marcel had no choice; he had to follow her, but fewer than half of Jeanne's men did because they had heard the trumpet sound the retreat, the gates of Compiègne and safety were still open, so they made their choice. As he tried to catch up with Jeanne, Marcel had a quick look round and counted about fifty men following; they were charging an enemy numbered in thousands. Maids and miracles seemed a distant memory now.

The clash was terrifying. The clang of metal on metal, screams of horses, and shouts of frightened men were mind-numbing, especially for the younger soldiers. But the more experienced ones knew that the greatest danger was yet to come. Casualties in the first stages of a clash were generally few because the men were alert, fresh, and heavily conscious of self-preservation; but as the seconds passed, the shield grew heavy, the arm dropped a little, and weak points in the defence became exposed. But

Peter Tallon

even then, mortal wounds were few and far between. The bloodbath really began when one side broke and turned tail to flee. Then the only defence for the vanquished was to gallop faster than the victors because their backs were exposed and they were helpless. Often shields and even swords were thrown away to lighten the weight on the horses so that the fugitives could outpace their pursuers.

The Burgundians were not expecting a spirited attack from behind and initially gave ground before it. Jeanne and her escort plunged deep into the enemy ranks, but soon resistance stiffened, and the fighting became harder. During one of the brief, unplanned lulls for rest that often happen in hand-to-hand fighting, Marcel caught sight of de Xaintrailles's banner close to the Bridge Gate. "Look, Jeanne, Jean Poton has reached the Bridge Gate. He's safe! Now let us try to do the same."

But with de Xaintrailles and his men escaping, the Burgundians closed ranks and barred Jeanne's route to Compiègne with a wall of horseflesh and steel. Meanwhile, de Xaintrailles, exhausted and slightly wounded in his left leg, heard Compiègne's Bridge Gate clang shut behind him. He raised his visor and spoke to the captain of the gate. "Is the Maid safe?"

The captain frowned. "I do not know, Mon Seigneur, I have not seen her."

"What! But you must have. I saw her riding for this gate less than ten minutes ago!"

"Mon Seigneur, I have been at this gate since the battle began. I can assure you she has not passed this way. If she had, I would have seen her."

"This is madness! I cannot believe it! Where is de Flavy?"

The captain pointed to the battlements above the gate. "Up there, Mon Seigneur."

"Then prepare to reopen the gate. I shall be back soon."

Despite his leg wound and still dressed in full armour, de Xaintrailles rushed up the steps to the battlements and confronted de Flavy. "Castellan, what is the meaning of this! You shut the gate before Jeanne returned!"

De Flavy answered calmly, "Because the Burgundians were about to rush it. I could not let that happen, else the city would fall."

"Nonsense! This is only the gate in the curtain wall. Our main defence is the other side of the Oise. Any Burgundians entering would be made captive before they even reached the river!"

"That is your opinion, Mon Seigneur, it is not mine."

"Open the gate at once!"

"Mon Seigneur, look," said de Flavy pointing to a scrimmage about a hundred paces outside the gate. "The Maid has just been taken and her entourage killed or captured. She is beyond our help now." Then pointing to another group of soldiers arriving from the direction of Venette, he added, "Take comfort from the fact that the English are too late to capture her."

De Xaintrailles could see it was now impossible to do anything to help Jeanne, but he was unable to contain his anger. "De Flavy, you could have done more to stop this. A quick sally would have saved her, she was so near to safety."

"My responsibility is the safety of Compiègne."

"So you keep saying, but you have not heard the end of this."

CHAPTER TWELVE

Under a warm, late spring sun, a small column of English soldiers was marching along the road from Paris to Rouen, a distance of eighty miles. They had left Paris at dawn, and although it was only two hours past noon, they were almost halfway to Rouen because they were all mounted; the truce had enabled the English to re-equip and recover from the disasters of the previous year. The column, which was returning to its home base now that the French threat to Paris had receded, was led by its newly promoted captain, Edward Skippon of Thirsk in Yorkshire. His troops were men of the Fastolf companies from Norfolk, Wiltshire, and Yorkshire, which were once more at full strength, thanks to an influx of native-born Englishmen during the truce. It was the last day of May in the Year of Our Lord 1430.

Riding beside Captain Skippon was his senior sergeant, Henry Hawkswood of the Wiltshire company. The two were firm friends bonded by facing many mutual dangers together.

"Henry, what do you make of that group yonder?" said Skippon, pointing to five men further along the road. They were stripped to the waist unloading something from a cart.

"Looks like a road maintenance gang," answered Henry. "God knows, there are enough potholes in it needing to be filled."

"Then ride ahead and check all is well. The truce is ended now, and we must all be on our guard, even in our own backyard."

The Angel of Lorraine

As Sergeant Hawkswood cantered towards the maintenance workers, one of the figures seemed familiar even though he had his back to the sergeant. He was tall and giving instructions to the others. He was also confident, for he did not take the trouble to look round as Hawkswood drew rein behind him. "Captain Calveley?"

The tall figure spun round. "Henry! How good to see you!"

"And you too, Captain." Henry signalled the all clear to Skippon, dismounted, and embraced his old captain, much to the surprise of the rest of the maintenance gang.

"We'll take a short break now," ordered Richard, and his men sat down by the roadside to enjoy a welcome rest.

"We've heard no news of you since Patay, Captain. It seems your arm has improved since then."

"It certainly has thank you Henry, it's almost as good as new, and there is much to tell, including a visit to Rome since I last saw you, but while we're alone, I have a few questions for you. Who commands Fastolf's companies now?"

"Edward Skippon."

"How's he doing?"

"Well. Sir John offered me the captaincy first, but I declined because I didn't want to get involved with the administration work. Edward is shaping up well. He doesn't say much, he's a typical Yorkshireman, but he listens, and the men respect him."

"And who commands the Norfolk company?"

"Young Hook. The Norfolks lost so many at Patay that Hook was really the only choice. It's early days yet, but I think he'll be fine. He is trying to model himself on you and takes great care about the welfare of his men, most of whom are older than he is."

"But what of you, Henry? You're getting quite old now for active service."

"I'm forty-five I think. I admit I sometimes feel my age first thing in the morning, but there are a few good campaigning years left in me yet. The army is my home. I have nowhere else to go."

"Then if there is nowhere in England, why not think about settling here in Normandy? Rouen perhaps? You have won enough prize money to buy a house with a smallholding, and we will be neighbours. You speak French well enough to get by, and there are plenty of local maidens who would regard a retired English warrior as a good catch."

The Wiltshire sergeant lifted his eye patch and rubbed the empty socket as he always did when he was thinking. "I will definitely consider that, Captain."

"Don't call me *Captain*. Edward is your captain now. I am just Master Calveley, surveyor to the king's army in France. I make maps and measure distances. Today my team and I are installing mileposts along the Paris to Rouen road."

"You will always be captain to me, Captain."

"Well, enough of that. Here comes Captain Skippon now."

Skippon rode up with the three Fastolf companies just behind, dismounted, and shook Richard's hand with his iron grip. "Good to see your arm is better, Captain."

"Thank you, Edward, but you are captain now. Address me just as *Master Richard*."

"I prefer *Captain* if you don't mind, Captain. Anything else doesn't feel right."

"As you wish, Edward."

"Have you heard the news from Compiègne?"

"No, what news?"

"Joan the Maid has been captured."

"Who holds her?"

"She is the Duke of Luxembourg's prisoner, but everyone knows it will be Duke Philippe who'll decide what's to be done with her."

"Thank God for that!" exclaimed Richard. "I don't rate her chances in English hands."

Skippon frowned. "But she's our enemy."

"Yes, Edward, but she is also the reason Henry and I are still alive. Without her intervention at Patay, there would have been no ransom agreement, and the Norfolk company, including Henry and I, would have been crow's meat."

"I did not know that, Captain. She is merciful then?"

"Yes, almost to a fault. She is also very young, just a year or two older than my own daughter who got married in January. We must look beyond the Maid for our defeats last year."

"Bad leadership for a start," said Henry bitterly. "Nothing went right after we lost the Earl of Salisbury."

"And overconfidence perhaps?" suggested Edward.

"Both powerful factors," agreed Richard. "We must hope the Duke of Burgundy sells her to the French rather than us, or she might encounter a heretic's death."

"Not burning?"

"I'm afraid so, Henry. That's the fate for a condemned witch, but Jeanne seemed more like an angel when I met her. Anyway, she was beaten at Paris, her reputation for invincibility has gone, so she can do us no more damage now."

"But surely the French will outbid us?" said Edward. "They'll want her back more than we'll want to burn her."

"That should be the case," acknowledged Richard, "but sometimes the French king can make unpredictable decisions. He is also said to be jealous of those who help him rather than grateful. Look what happened to Constable Richemont."

"The French seem to hate each other more than they hate us."

"And long may that remain so, Edward. If they ever reunite with Burgundy, we'll be hard-pressed to hold what we have, never mind conquer the rest of France."

"Do you think that might happen?" asked Henry.

"Not as long as My Lord Bedford and his good wife, Anne, Philippe's sister, remain in good health. I hear that the Burgundian duke is still very close to his favourite sister, and it's she who keeps the alliance between us firm."

Edward looked at the position of the sun in the near cloudless sky. "Well, we'd better be on our way and leave you to your surveying, Captain. Don't you miss the army?"

"At times like this, when I am chatting with old friends, I miss it greatly, but on the other hand, I now get to spend most nights with Mary and see my daughter, which compensates."

"Then give them both our best wishes and your new son-in-law too. His marriage to your daughter made news in our camp."

"I shall, Edward, though I will not see Marcel for a while. He's a French knight and Joan the Maid's banner bearer."

The two English sergeants were about to remount, but that comment stopped them in their tracks. "I knew he's a Frenchie, but not Joan's banner bearer. How did that happen?" asked Henry.

"It's a long story and goes back fifteen years to Agincourt. Where do you intend to spend the night?"

"Vernon," answered Edward.

"Then when we've finished here, we'll do the same. I'll explain all over a mug of ale this evening."

"And I'll pay," said Edward.

Henry laughed. "History's been made here today. A Yorkshireman's offered to pay!"

* * *

II

Sixty-one-year-old Pierre Cauchon was a man on a mission. A longtime supporter of the Burgundians even before the alliance with England, he was part of the Church's intellectual elite in what was now English-occupied France. He held many benefices and became Bishop and Count of Beauvais in the Year of Our Lord 1420 under the protection of the

Duke of Burgundy, but when the citizens of Beauvais declared for King Charles VII after his coronation at Reims, he was thrown out along with his English and Burgundian supporters and was obliged to seek refuge in Rouen.

The Duke of Bedford, who valued Cauchon's loyalty and intellect, compensated him for the loss of Beauvais, but the vengeful bishop blamed Jeanne for his humiliation and determined to work for her downfall. Now, thanks to Bedford's return to France, his opportunity came because he was given a special mission to negotiate with Philippe of Burgundy for the transfer of the Maid of Orléans into English custody, which would be followed by her trial for heresy and witchcraft. The chief prosecutor would be Cauchon himself.

Using his diplomatic immunity, Cauchon travelled through Compiègne, which was still holding out against the Burgundians, and presented himself and his small escort at Beaurevoir, one of Jean of Luxembourg's castles forty-five miles north of Compiègne, on the fourteenth day of July. Here Duke Philippe awaited him for the first of many discussions about the sale of his valuable prisoner. Apart from notaries, the two men met alone in Luxembourg's private quarters; not even Duke Jean, to whom Jeanne officially belonged according to feudal law, was permitted to be present. They made an interesting contrast—Cauchon, the high-browed, intellectual academician pitted against the spiderlike duke with the cunning of a fox. It was a gross mismatch, for there could never be any doubt as to who would come out on top.

"Welcome, Mon Seigneur Bishop," said Philippe, offering the proud cleric a seat at the head of the oak table in the office where the negotiations would take place. "It is now two hours before noon, which gives us plenty of time to set out our stalls before lunch." He could not help using the metaphor of a market trader because, at heart, he was one himself.

"Thank you, Mon Seigneur," replied Cauchon as he brushed some dust off the chair before placing his holy hind quarters on it.

"Are you here as a delegate or a representative?" enquired the duke.

"I do not understand the question, Mon Seigneur."

"A representative has the power to negotiate, whereas a delegate merely relays a message."

The proud Cauchon could only give one answer. "A representative, naturally."

"Good, that means we can have a serious discussion. As you asked for this meeting, it is for you to speak first and tell me what you want."

Cauchon cleared his throat. "England and Burgundy are allies with the same aim in mind, namely a strong Burgundy and a Plantagenet King of France. All was going well until last year when a witch in angel's clothing appeared and duped the French into following the path of Satan. But now, by God's mercy and the brave soldiers of your army, the witch known by some as Jeanne the Maid has been captured and awaits her just fate. I am here as a representative of your English allies, who have suffered much from the witch's enchantments, to ask you to hand over your captive to the Church, which will determine, after fair and scrupulous interrogation, the fate of one who has caused so much pain."

"It sounds to me that you have already decided her fate, Bishop Cauchon, and it is strange, is it not, that emissaries from the French king have already been here with the same request except that the French see this Maid as an avenging angel sent by God to save France. I thought we all believed in the same God, yet your Church says Jeanne is a witch while the French king's Church says she is an angel. Who am I to believe?"

"Mon Seigneur," said a red-faced and frustrated Cauchon, "do not toy with me. Both the Duke of Bedford and you fight for the same cause. We will pay you well to release this woman into our custody. And have no doubt that Jeanne is a witch. Since her capture, have not our fortunes improved? Charles's men are being chased out of Normandy by the English, and you are on the verge of taking Compiègne. Surely that cannot be a coincidence."

"Perhaps not," agreed Philippe, though in truth he knew the change in fortune was because he had fooled King Charles into thinking the truce would be followed by a full peace. Consequently Charles had disbanded his army to save money while Philippe prepared his for war and was ready to go on the offensive as soon as the truce ended. Jeanne's capture was simply a piece of luck.

All these considerations passed through Philippe's mind in a few seconds. "You do understand, I hope," he continued, "that Jeanne is a prisoner of war. The knight who captured her and his commander, the Duke of Luxembourg, will expect a good ransom for such an illustrious prisoner. The French are also prepared to pay for her and have already made an offer," lied Philippe.

"We will pay more than the French. How much have they offered?"

Philippe feigned an attitude of bored indifference. "It is unbecoming for men of gentle breeding to get themselves embroiled in a street market auction. If I were to tell you the value of the French bid, then I would, to preserve my honour, be obliged to tell them yours. That would inevitably result in an auction. Therefore, make your bid now or go home empty-handed."

Cauchon was out of his depth. He had no experience of bargaining and bluffing, but he could not contemplate returning to Rouen as a failure; his pride would not allow it. Beads of perspiration ran down the side of his face. Philippe knew he had his man hooked.

"Six thousand pounds in gold," blurted out the bishop.

The duke did not respond immediately, letting his victim sweat a little longer. Instead, he allowed an expression of pain to cross his face. "You insult me, Mon Seigneur Bishop. I thought you were here to make a serious bid, yet you offer me a paltry sum for a prisoner of higher value than the Duke of Orléans!"

The Angel of Lorraine

The look of shock on Cauchon's face told the wily duke he had hit home hard. The bishop stuttered, "I am sorry, Mon Seigneur, I did not mean to insult you. I thought six thousand pounds was a fair offer."

"Well it is not, far from it, but nonetheless I will be fair to you. I shall not tell you the French bid," which was easy enough because the French had not even bothered to make contact yet, "but I will give you exactly one month to return with your final and only offer. You will win or you will lose. There will be no further negotiations. I shall also give the French a chance to reconsider their offer on the same basis. I cannot be fairer than that, can I?"

"No, Mon Seigneur," agreed a humbled Cauchon. "I shall come back within a month with a revised offer."

"Good. Is there anything else?"

"Yes, Mon Seigneur. May I see the prisoner? It would help us to review our bid if I can report I have seen her with my own eyes and that she is in good health and fit to travel."

"Of course you may," answered Philippe graciously. "She is here in this very castle. You shall see her this afternoon after we have shared lunch together. Duke Jean of Luxembourg will join us if you agree."

"Certainly, Mon Seigneur."

With the negotiations temporarily suspended, Duke Philippe became the amiable host, a role he played well, so after a congenial lunch, Cauchon was permitted to have a private meeting with Jeanne. Luxembourg's elderly aunt, also named Jeanne, was the only other person present as the chaperon. After all he had heard about the witch, the bishop was surprised to see a slim, open-faced girl who looked younger than her eighteen years, but he was not pleased to observe that she was still permitted to wear men's clothing and have her hair cut in the fashion of a boy. Although she was a prisoner, Jeanne had been given a well-furnished, upper-floor room without bars at the window; the Burgundians seemed to have no consideration for her security. The interview was conducted with both parties standing and the lady of Luxembourg sitting between them.

"So you are Joan the Maid of Orléans?"

"Jeanne, Mon Seigneur. I am French."

Cauchon's ice-blue eyes bored into her. "It is said you are a witch."

"Only by the English, and I have not yet flown out of the window. I am a messenger from God. My victories prove that to be so."

"And what about your defeats?"

"I do not have to answer to you."

"But you will when you are handed over to the English. Has no one told you that the Burgundians and the English are regaining their losses of last year?"

"No, and I do not believe it to be so."

"But even now, the young King Henry of England is in Normandy and will soon be anointed King of France."

"Where will this ceremony take place?"

"In the cathedral of Notre Dame in Paris."

"Then it will count for nothing. Reims is the only place where a French king can be anointed, and in any event, we have a king already."

Cauchon was impressed and a little irritated that he could not overawe this slip of a peasant girl with a country accent. "You do not fear the wrath of God?"

"Of course I do, but I have no reason to. I am doing his work."

The bishop's grey eyebrows knitted ominously. "Then you should at least fear the wrath of the English. Do you not realise that a heretic's pyre awaits you?"

"And what of my right to a fair trial? You seem to have condemned me already, but I do not care. You cannot harm me, I have been assured of that."

"By whom?"

"That does not concern you."

Cauchon had heard enough. The prisoner was in good health and would face trial as long as the English offered more money for her than the French.

After the bishop left the room, Jeanne said to her chaperon, "That man does indeed frighten me. There is no mercy in him."

"Then you did well not to show your fear, my dear."

"I do not want to be handed over to the English."

"I will speak to my nephew. You are his prisoner, not Philippe's, and I already know he shares your wish."

"Thank you, my lady."

But nothing, not even the Duke of Luxembourg, could divert the implacable Cauchon from his chosen course of action.

* * *

III

Towards the end of August, a private meeting took place in King Charles's personal office at Chinon overlooking the River Vienne. It was late in the evening, but large candles banished the darkness to the corners of the office walls as Charles and Georges de la Tremoille discussed Jeanne's future.

"Duke Philippe will demand a high price for the Maid's ransom, but we need every ecu to pay for the army," said the grand chamberlain. "We've lost ground since the truce ended because of Philippe's lies about it leading to peace, while all the time he was getting ready to resume the war."

"The people think the English revival has happened because we have lost Jeanne."

"Let them think what they like, Your Majesty, they do not decide policy."

"But their view is shared by some in the Military Council."

"You mean Dunois and Alençon?"

"And La Hire, de Xaintrailles, and de Rais amongst others."

"The Military Council carries out the bidding of the Royal Council. Those you mention need to be reminded of that. They have fallen under Jeanne's spell."

"Spell! Are you too saying she is a witch!"

Trémoille saw the anger in the king's face; he had gone too far and quickly backtracked. "My apologies, Your Majesty, an unfortunate choice of words. I should have said *influence*, not *spell*. But the point I am making is that Philippe's demand for Jeanne's release will be exorbitant. Will she really be worth it? There is no doubt she was an important factor in our successes last year, but there were other factors too, most notably the improvement in the quality of our armies and their commanders. These were trends already in place before Jeanne first met you here, Your Majesty."

"There is something in that I suppose."

"Indeed, but since her failure at Paris, and then again at La Charité, she has achieved nothing, yet she still thinks she is the saviour of France."

"As do many others, Georges."

Trémoille struggled to keep the exasperation out of his voice with this vacillating king. "If Jeanne could only be made to understand she has done all she can, but now the time has come for her to retire from active service while the people still believe in her. You have already ennobled her and her family and exempted her home village from taxation, which is almost without precedent. We might still be able to find her a useful role as a figurehead travelling through France helping to raise men and money for the war."

"But that would still mean paying Burgundy for her freedom, would it not?"

"There are means other than money within your power to do that, Your Majesty. You are well aware of Philippe's desire to expand the boundaries of Burgundy. Perhaps a concession or two could achieve more than money alone."

"Are you saying give him French territory!"

"Only briefly. You can always take it back once the English are beaten."

Before Charles could answer, there was a firm rap on the office door, and without waiting for a response, Yolande entered. She was alone. Trémoille let out a loud sigh of annoyance that his private meeting with the king had been disturbed, but Charles just said amiably,

"Welcome, Mother, how may we be of service?"

Yolande sat down in a chair between the two men and pointedly turned her back towards the grand chamberlain as she spoke to her son-in-law. Not forgetting court protocol, she used Charles's formal title in the company of someone not of royal blood. "Your Majesty, I have heard that the English made contact with Philippe of Burgundy more than a month ago with an offer to buy Jeanne the Maid from him. Obviously you will not allow this to happen, but knowing Philippe's weakness for money, is it not time we made an offer ourselves? It may be you have already done that, but I would like some reassurance that we are taking positive steps to ensure Jeanne is returned to us as soon as possible."

"This is a matter of state to be determined by the Royal Council," said Trémoille, speaking to Yolande's back. "Our policy has yet to be decided."

The queen mother said icily, "Your Majesty, does that voice behind me speak for you? You have already had a month to decide your so-called policy, yet it must be obvious to everyone, except perhaps your grand chamberlain, that we must outbid the English and bring Jeanne home."

"Mother, it is not as simple as that. We must consider the cost, which will be high, and the future value Jeanne may have for us."

Yolande's pent-up anger began to show as her voice started to quaver. "Your Majesty, on the contrary, it is extremely simple. You owe everything you have to that young girl. Without her, you would now be a cowering exile in some remote, freezing, Scottish castle awaiting a call to return to France, which would never come. Even if Jeanne has no future value to us, which I very much doubt, it is a matter for your personal honour that you rescue Jeanne from the clutches of the English by whatever means you can."

"The king must think of France before himself," interjected Trémoille.

At last Yolande deigned to notice the grand chamberlain for the first time. She turned and gave him a withering look. "What is France if her king loses his honour? But I would not expect you to understand that."

The Angel of Lorraine

Then turning back to the king, she dropped the formality of his title and used his name as she began to realise Jeanne was going to be abandoned. "Charles, the English say Jeanne is a witch. If you allow her to fall into their hands, she will face a witch's execution: burning at the stake. Is that the thanks you will give her for saving you and your throne!"

"Mother, it won't come to that. I am certain of it. The English will not want to make a martyr of her. That would be self-defeating."

"But what if you're wrong? You were duped by Philippe into thinking the truce would lead to peace, and you are misled every day by the counsel of the creature sitting behind me. You cannot abandon Jeanne, your honour will not permit it. If you do, how could anyone in our beloved country ever trust you again!"

"Mother, matters of state sometimes require difficult decisions."

"How very convenient for you!" Yolande could contain her anger no longer. She stood up, walked stiffly to the office door, turned, and gave the king her parting shot. "That young girl is prepared to give her life for you, yet this is how you repay her. Doubtless you would have tried harder had she been a man! You are not worthy of her. Do not attempt to seek my advice again." The office door slammed shut behind her.

"Do not trouble yourself, Your Majesty, she is but one woman," said Trémoille unctuously. "If she had her way, the Angel from Lorraine would become the Liability from Lorraine."

"But, Georges, I am not comfortable with this. Surely we should at least make an offer to Philippe?"

"But what if he accepts? Then we'll have the problem back with us. Best to do nothing and let events take their course."

* * *

IV

On the twenty-fourth day of October, the siege of Compiègne was at last lifted when a royal French army arrived and drove away the Burgundians. During the fighting, some senior Burgundian knights were captured, so a prisoner exchange was quickly arranged, which saw Marcel released from custody. He was welcomed back into the French army and given leave to go home and recuperate, but with instructions to rejoin the army after the customary Christmas truce, which would end on the sixth day of January, the feast of the Epiphany. It was during this time that Richard's first grandchild was conceived.

When Jeanne was informed she had been abandoned by the French king and was to be handed over to the English, she tried to escape by jumping from the window in her room at Beaurevoir. Her captors had thought it was unnecessary to bar her window because it was twenty-five feet above ground level. They were right. Instead of escaping, she badly twisted her ankle and knee and lay prone, unable to move, until the Burgundian guards found her. Shortly afterwards, she became ill, the ailment most probably caused by the heavy rain that soaked her while she was waiting to be carried back to the castle.

Meanwhile, Cauchon relentlessly closed in on Jeanne during a series of meetings in which the wily Philippe kept dangling the objective of his mission under his nose until November, when agreement for the ransom price was finally reached. Ten thousand pounds in gold was a huge sum, worthy of a king. Philippe was delighted with the result of his negotiating skills, playing off the intelligent but impractical Cauchon against an imaginary French offer.

Consequently, Jeanne was handed over to the English in Rouen on Christmas Eve in the Year of Our Lord 1430.

CHAPTER THIRTEEN

The conditions of Jeanne's confinement at Bouvreuil castle, just outside Rouen, were grim. Richard Beauchamp, thirteenth earl of Warwick, castellan of Bouvreuil, and a member of the King's Council was not a vindictive man by nature; indeed, he was the epitome of knightly chivalry having fought for young Henry VI, his father, and grandfather, but he was aware that Jeanne had twice attempted to escape whilst in Burgundian custody, so he was taking no chances. In contrast to her comfortable confinement at Beaurevoir, she was placed in the castle prison, which was located close to Warwick's personal quarters, and attached to the prison wall with leg irons. Worse still, she was under constant observation, a task for which five guards were appointed, any two of whom would always be present in the same chamber as her; she would have absolutely no privacy. But her spirit remained undaunted, and she continued to refuse to wear women's clothes, which was understandable due to the nature of those who kept her company.

"Don't you think you should visit Jeanne?" said Mary as she and Richard sat by a cheerful log fire on the first evening of the Year of Our Lord 1431. "She is alone and friendless amongst her enemies. A visit from you might raise her spirits a little to face what lies ahead."

"I was already considering that," answered Richard. "She probably won't even remember me, but I'll gladly go and see her."

"Then I'll prepare some victuals for you to take and a few small things that any woman will need for a long stay."

"Thanks, and I'll take her a Bible too. I don't suppose she's been provided with anything to help pass the time."

"What's going to happen to her?"

"I don't know. No one's saying much, but the rumour is she will go on trial for heresy and maybe witchcraft too."

"We both know only too well the penalty she faces if she's found guilty."

"It would be a Church trial," said Richard, "so she'd be found guilty for certain because unlike civil courts, the accused is presumed guilty unless he or she can prove otherwise."

"Typical!" snorted Mary.

"But hopefully the Duke of Bedford, who is a fair and reasonable man, won't let it get that far." Richard felt far less confident about that than he sounded, but there was still time for common sense and, if necessary, mercy to prevail.

Next morning, Richard went to Bouvreuil castle and was taken by one of the guards to the Earl of Warwick's quarters on the upper floor. A clerk was sitting outside the door scratching some notes with a quill. He made Richard wait while he was finishing his sentence, then looked up. "Appointment?"

"I don't have one," answered Richard, "but I have brought some supplies to ease your prisoner's stay here. I have met her before at Patay."

"Have you indeed. Name?"

"Richard Calveley, recently invalided out of the army after an arm wound. I was the captain of Sir John Fastolf's companies."

The name *Fastolf* had an immediate impact. The clerk stood up and said, "Wait here. I'll find out if the earl will see you."

A minute later, Richard was ushered into the presence of Richard, Earl of Warwick. A tall, greying man in his midforties welcomed him. "Captain Calveley, we have not met before, but I have heard of you. I understand from Peter, my clerk, that you have brought some provisions for Joan, or Jeanne as she prefers to be known, whom you met at Patay."

Richard gave a brief account of how Jeanne saved his and all the survivors in the Norfolk company's lives at Patay, at the end of which the earl rubbed his chin and said, "I hope Sir John was suitably grateful to you."

"Sir John Fastolf was most generous, my lord."

Warwick replied with a twinkle in his bright blue eyes, "Well, I can honestly say that is the first time I have heard the words *generous* and *Fastolf* mentioned in the same sentence." Richard tried to smother a smile. "Of course you may see the prisoner," continued the earl, "I will escort you myself. I'm afraid you'll find the conditions harsh because she refuses to give her word that she will not try to escape. She made two attempts while in Burgundian custody and nearly succeeded the second time. The prison here is on the same upper floor as this, so at least it's not damp and enjoys daylight from a barred window, but Joan is wilful and resourceful, so she must be watched constantly."

It was but a short walk to Jeanne's prison. The earl acknowledged the guards who unlocked the heavy, wooden door, which had a viewing panel cut into it. The security afforded the small, slim girl sitting near the window with her legs clamped in irons seemed incongruous. The chamber was large and circular because it was located in one of the castle's round towers. The furnishings were sparse, just a wooden bed and chair for Jeanne, and two chairs for her guards. There was a small area near the window that was cordoned off by a grubby curtain where Jeanne could wash and relieve herself, but other than that, she was under constant observation.

"Joan, you have a visitor who's brought you some provisions," said Warwick. "I will have your irons removed while he is here." He nodded to one of the guards who unshackled her ankles.

Richard's first reaction was anger, but he knew he must restrain himself if he was to be of any use to Jeanne. "My lord, is there not a danger that the prisoner might be violated in these conditions? Two guards against a lone woman?"

"The guards have been warned not to touch her on pain of death except for locking and unlocking her irons. I am a man of my word, and they know it, but Joan only needs to give me her word about not escaping, and I would move her to a properly furnished room and give her the freedom of the castle."

Richard turned to Jeanne, who was rubbing her ankles, which had been badly chafed by the leg irons. "Jeanne, you won't remember me but—"

"Captain Calveley! We met at Patay, did we not?"

"Where you saved my life and my men's. I shall always be grateful to you for that."

The gaunt, little face smiled. "I am glad to hear it and pleased to see you. You have brought me something?"

Richard welled up with emotion. This child could so easily have been his own daughter speaking to him when he used to return home after a campaign. He swallowed hard. "Just a few things, Jeanne," he replied as he put down a leather bag beside her. "Some food and ladies' things packed by my wife, Mary, and a Bible from me. It's written in Latin of course, but it has a French commentary at the end of each chapter."

"I thank you and your wife for this. I do not read well, but now I shall have the chance to improve."

"Jeanne, why not give the oath that My Lord Warwick asks for?" implored Richard. "Any prisoner of war awaiting ransom would do the same. It's customary."

"Captain, I am not awaiting ransom but something far less pleasant. Even if I were expecting ransom, I would not give the oath. My voices have already told me I shall come to no harm, but neither have they authorised me to accept imprisonment. Will I see you again?"

Richard glanced at Warwick. "With My Lord Warwick's permission." The earl nodded approval.

"Good," said Jeanne, "then I have something to look forward to."

Back in Warwick's office, Richard asked, "Will she go on trial?"

"Yes, a Church trial headed by Pierre Cauchon, Bishop of Beauvais. He is a hard, implacable man."

"There can only be one outcome then?"

"Unless Jeanne recants, but you have seen for yourself how wilful she is."

"Just like my own daughter, Joan. I would like to see Jeanne again, my lord."

"I will not permit that because you are clearly emotionally involved as I would be in your place."

"That is hard, my lord."

"It is for the best, but what I can do is arrange a pass for you to attend the preliminary interrogation, which will take place here in the castle chapel. The interrogation is when the most serious work is carried out, and as it will be done here, arranging a pass for you as a military observer is within my gift. Then you will at least see her, and so keep your word, but you will not be allowed to speak to her."

"I am most grateful, my lord. At least Jeanne will see one friendly face amongst the battery of hostile clerics confronting her."

Pierre Cauchon was now in his element. His dedication and eye for detail were ideal for the preliminary tribunal, which would gather the evidence needed for Jeanne's trial. Everything would need to be done strictly by the internationally recognised procedures of the Church. Statements would be taken from as far away as Jeanne's home village Domremy, no mean task while a war separated Rouen from Lorraine, and no stone would be left unturned to ensure that the so-called Maid of Orléans was given a fair trial before she was found guilty of heresy. Cauchon's ideal result would be a conviction for heresy followed by a recantation from the victim so he could spare Jeanne the flames, appear merciful, and sentence her to life imprisonment, but he knew his English masters wanted her to burn, so burn she must if he was to be rewarded with, he hoped, promotion to an archbishopric.

But despite the diligence of Cauchon's agents, and after six weeks of painstaking research, no evidence was found to implicate Jeanne in any form of heresy or witchcraft. On the contrary, the chief agent reported that all the evidence supported Jeanne's own contention that she was a good Catholic and had lived a chaste and wholesome life. He added, somewhat unwisely, he had found nothing that would shame even his own sister. Cauchon promptly sacked him, called him a traitor, and withheld the salary due to him. Now the Bishop of Beauvais knew he had a problem. Breaking biblical law by wearing men's clothing was a self-evident charge against Jeanne but not a heretical offence; she could not be burned just for that. The justification for a conviction of heresy would have to come from her own mouth because there was no supporting evidence. This was going to be tricky; he would need a top-class inquisitor.

Unsurprisingly, Cauchon struggled to find anyone willing to take on the case. Jean Graverent, the Inquisitor of France, said he was too involved

The Angel of Lorraine

with another case. His deputy, Jean Lemaitre, was equally unwilling to become involved but reluctantly accepted, giving a long list of conditions that must be agreed first. But his lack of enthusiasm forced Cauchon to look elsewhere, and in Jean Beaupere he at last found his man.

Beaupere, who was one of those men who smiled a lot but without warmth, was a priest who could not celebrate Mass. He had lost the use of his right hand in an encounter with highway robbers who had left him for dead some years before, so he could not bless the Eucharist. But his mind was unaffected, and he saw the interrogation and trial of Jeanne as a way to advance himself by appeasing the English-dominated French clergy in Rouen who were determined to see her burn. His mind was deep and subtle; he was able to pose questions in a way that tired the victim, who would begin to give answers that conflicted with previous statements causing confusion and unintentional admissions, but he was not needed for the first day of Jeanne's public interrogation because Cauchon, as presiding judge, had decided to handle it himself.

Jeanne appeared before her judges on the twenty-first day of February in the Year of Our Lord 1431 at eight o'clock in the morning. She was just nineteen. Facing her were forty-four important clerics including theological academics, bishops, and lawyers expert in both religious and civil law. They occupied long benches on three sides of the chapel at Bouvreuil while she stood alone with no lawyer to defend her, which was in direct contravention of the inquisitorial process. At the end of the bench on her left sat Richard, but he could not tell if she had seen him. He need not have worried, for two months of incarceration seemed only to have hardened her heart. The interrogation lasted for just under three hours, at the end of which she was sent back to her prison and Richard went home elated.

"I've seldom seen a broader smile," said Mary. "I take it that all went well then?"

"Forty-four of the highest intellects in the land against a single, poorly educated peasant girl, yet she wiped the floor with them. I wanted to jump up and shout *hallelujah*! The Bishop of Beauvais, who was in charge of the proceedings, tried to get her to swear an oath requiring her to tell the whole truth to any questions posed to her. She refused and said she would not answer questions on matters private between herself and God or the French king. Most of the morning was taken up by arguments about the oath taking, but in the end, Jeanne won. She's remarkable."

"Will you go again tomorrow?"

"Yes, but I think the interrogation will go on for many weeks, and I have work to do mapping the land between Falaise and Anjou."

"Do you think Jeanne has any chance of being found innocent?"

"Yesterday I would have said no, but now I'm beginning to wonder."

"But if she's found guilty?"

Richard sighed. "I am only a retired captain, but I know the Duke of Bedford personally. He has the power to show mercy, but even he cannot stop an ecclesiastical trial. But if things go badly, I shall appeal direct to Bedford to use his power to commute the inevitable sentence."

"Can you not help her to escape? You did that for me and Hugh."

"If I could, I would, but even I cannot take Bouvreuil castle alone."

Mary kissed him. "I know you will do all in your power. I am glad you're my husband. I wouldn't have anyone else, be he as high and mighty as the emperor of ancient Rome."

The second day of interrogation went very much the same way as the first, but Richard left feeling less comfortable because he sensed the threat behind Beaupere's smooth questioning, which was absent from Cauchon's loud but ineffective bluster. On the third day, he was obliged to return to duty and was away for a week and a half. By then things had changed.

The Angel of Lorraine

It was a rainy spring morning when Richard returned to Rouen from his surveying tasks around Falaise. He went first to Bouvreuil to visit Warwick, but the earl was elsewhere, so he left the castle, though not before Peter, Warwick's clerk, had updated him on events during his absence.

But it was an anxious Richard that arrived home later that morning. "Things have taken a turn for the worse. It seems that Jeanne was doing rather too well, so Cauchon moved the interrogation from the public chapel to Jeanne's own prison. The rest of the interrogation will take place in private."

Mary took Richard's wet cloak, hung it up near the fire to dry, and sat down opposite him. "So they can report and edit how they like. Jeanne has no chance now. Is it not time for you to visit the Duke of Bedford?"

"Not quite. I will only get one chance, so I must make sure I have my facts in order. The trial will be in public if it is going to maintain any semblance of credibility. It will only take a day or two because the verdict is already assured. I will wait for the charges to be read out, and then I shall find Bedford wherever he is."

"Will you have time? What if he's in England?"

"He'll be no further away than Paris. The seven-year-old King Henry VI is in France for his French coronation, which is scheduled for December this year. That means Bedford will be in France at least until Christmas."

Mary was not convinced. "But will he have enough time to stop Jeanne's execution?"

"Certainly, if he has the will to do it. It is my task to ensure he has!"

The conclusion of Jeanne's interrogation and trial was delayed because she fell ill due to a bout of food poisoning, but Warwick sent his personal physician to minister to her, and gradually her health returned. But as soon as she had recovered, she was assailed with more questions, accusations, and threats, yet her dauntless spirit held firm, though her responses were becoming confused, repetitive, and contradictory; she was exhausted.

On the twenty-sixth day of March, the interrogation ended and the formal trial began. Cauchon ensured that this too was held behind closed doors in Bouvreuil castle; he had no intention of allowing this wilful girl to undermine his case in public. Jeanne faced seventy charges, which took two days to read out, but in essence, everything came down to whether she would or would not accept the authority of Mother Church. If she would, this would be demonstrated to all by her return to wearing women's clothing. If she would not, she would be found guilty of heresy and sorcery and handed over to the civil authority for the ultimate punishment of death by fire.

But Jeanne remained firm and was condemned.

* * *

II

News of the verdict quickly spread throughout Rouen. Now Richard knew he must act. On the morning of the twenty-fourth day of May, he went to see one-armed Michael at reception in army headquarters. "Michael, I need to see the Duke of Bedford urgently. Do you know where he is?"

"You're in luck, Captain. He's upstairs in a meeting with young King Henry and the Royal Council, but I don't know how long they'll be."

"Michael, it's a matter of life and death. Would you please ask him to speak to me now? It will only take a few minutes."

Michael returned with the duke. "The front office is vacant, my lord."

"Thank you, Michael," replied Bedford, who beckoned Richard to join him.

"Captain Calveley, I know you would not drag me out of a meeting with the king and his Royal Council for a minor matter, but I bid you to be quick."

"I will be, my lord. You may not yet know that Joan the Maid has been found guilty of heresy, demonic possession, and other fatal charges. She is to be handed over to the civil authorities to be burned to death."

"Go on," said Bedford in a neutral tone.

"The interrogation and trial were a travesty of justice. I attended when the process was open to selected members of the public. She was not even permitted a defence counsel."

"That was certainly out of order," agreed Bedford, "but I cannot just overturn an inquisitorial verdict."

"I understand that, my lord, but you could at least suspend the sentence until a review has taken place concerning the procedures permitted by the Bishop of Beauvais."

"Perhaps."

"My lord, there is not much time. Only you can prevent a gross miscarriage of justice."

"Was not Joan convicted of witchcraft too?"

"She was convicted of everything those complacent, arrogant clerics could think of. If Joan's a witch, then I'm the pope!"

"Captain, you are letting your emotions run away with you. I shall put two plain facts before you. Before Joan appeared, we English were all-conquering, but suddenly, from the evidence you yourself gave me in this very room at our previous meeting, the French changed and beat our previously invincible lads when the numerical odds were heavily in our favour. Then Joan was captured at Compiègne, and just as suddenly, we started to win again. Even as we speak, Sir John Fastolf has driven the French further away from Paris and we have regained most of our losses in Normandy. Do you think these two facts are unrelated?"

"I'm sure they're related, my lord, but not by spells and witchcraft. The loss of Joan was bound to have an impact on French morale. If she were truly a witch, she could have escaped by casting a spell on her guards while she was still in Burgundian custody."

Bedford nodded. "Actually, I have also wondered about that last point you make. Captain, I must now return to the King's Council, but I will think on what you have said, and I promise you I will contact you again before anything happens to Joan."

"Thank you, my lord, that is all I can ask."

Bedford was, as always, as good as his word, for that very evening a page arrived at Richard's house from army headquarters with a message from the duke. "Captain Calveley, I bring news for you from My Lord Bedford, Regent of England and France. Joan the Maid has recanted. Therefore, the sentence of the Church court will not be carried out."

* * *

III

While Richard had been talking to Bedford, Jeanne was led out of Bouvreuil castle to be confronted with the scene of her impending execution in Rouen. This event had not been made public, so only a small group were present at what was to prove to be a dramatic and decisive moment in the Maid's remarkable life. Despite the pretence that she had been given a fair trial, the pyre for her death by burning had already been constructed. After viewing the place of her imminent death, she was taken to the nearby cemetery of the church of Saint Ouen where Cauchon and her judges were waiting for her, together with a select group of their English masters. His work done, Beaupere had moved on, and it was left to the fire-eating young canon of Rouen, Guillaume Erard, to preach a final sermon at Jeanne. In truth, the sermon was no more than a litany of insults and exhortations to submit to Mother Church. If she refused, she was to be burned immediately.

Alone, unwell, and mentally unprepared for death, for she had expected a few more days yet, Jeanne's will finally broke. "What is it you want me to do?" she asked.

A short document was read to her, and she was told to sign it. "If I sign this, do you promise to take me to a Church prison to be supervised by women?" Cauchon nodded his assent but did not speak. He, like everyone else, was wrong-footed by Jeanne's sudden change of heart. She was about to deny the reality of her voices, admit to heresy, and agree to wear women's clothing, thus publicly submitting to Mother Church in all matters. Then believing Cauchon had agreed to transfer her to a Church prison, she signed the document by placing a simple cross at the base of it even though she was perfectly capable of signing her own name. This document was never seen again and was subsequently replaced by something much longer and damning in the official trial transcript.

This was something Cauchon neither wanted nor expected. He could see his English masters were angry. They wanted Jeanne dead, and no doubt they would not allow their expensive captive to be transferred to a Church prison where her opportunities to escape would be far greater than in Bouvreuil. His vision of an archbishop's mitre was fading fast. In the confusion, he was asked where Jeanne should go. He replied brusquely, "Take her back to where she came from," then after a moment's reflection, he added, "I shall also come to Bouvreuil. Bring the senior prison guard to me."

Peter Tallon

Jeanne was back in her prison before noon knowing she had been betrayed. What she could not see was the brief exchange between Cauchon and the senior prison guard, which took place out of sight of everyone else and left the guard two gold ducats richer. In the evening, she was brought a woman's dress to wear, but after putting it on, she found it was filthy and asked for it to be washed. Her request was approved, and her men's clothes were returned with the assurance that the dress would be ready for her to wear the next day. But it was not, and she was forced to wear men's clothes again because she had nothing else. Thus it was, that when Cauchon and some of her judges returned to her prison four days later, they found her wearing men's clothes once more. She was immediately declared a relapsed heretic, and the death penalty was reimposed.

The English had got their way.

The first inkling Richard had that something was wrong occurred when he left home to visit army headquarters to find out where his next surveying project would be. His route took him through Rouen's busy marketplace. Jeanne's pyre had only just been cleared away the day before, but the executioner had returned and seemed to be rebuilding it.

Richard walked over to him and said, "What are you doing?"

"And who might you be?"

"My name is Captain Calveley, commander of Sir John Fastolf's companies." There was no need to say he had retired, and the name *Fastolf* made the usual impression.

"I am building the pyre for the burning of Joan the Witch."

"But she recanted! The sentence was quashed."

"Don't ask me, Captain, I just obey orders. Sometimes the powers that be don't seem to know what they want. First I'm told to build a pyre, then to take it down again. Now, this morning, I'm told to build it again. It doesn't make sense."

"When is the execution going to be?"

"Tomorrow morning, Captain."

"Your name?"

"Geoffroy Therage."

"Thank you, Geoffroy. I shall see you tomorrow. I may have a favour to ask."

Richard ran to army headquarters and met one-armed Michael in reception. "I must see the Duke of Bedford at once!"

"But, Captain, he left with the King's Council for Paris."

"When?"

"On Saturday morning."

"God's teeth! Today's Tuesday. I'll never make it."

"Can I help, Captain?"

"Not this time, Michael, I'm not sure anybody can."

He ran to Bouvreuil castle, which was now full of men-at-arms preparing for another offensive against the French. At the gate between two tall towers, he was stopped by the captain of the guard, a new face Richard had not seen before.

"I am Captain Calveley, commander of Sir John Fastolf's array," panted Richard, "I must see My Lord Warwick immediately."

"Wait here, Captain, I will inform him of your request."

The wait seemed interminable, but at last Peter, Warwick's clerk, arrived and took Richard to the guardroom inside one of the towers beside the gate.

"The earl was half expecting a visit from you, Captain, but he will not see you."

"But he must!"

"Captain, please understand that the only thing he must do is obey orders as must we all."

"You are his clerk, what are his orders?"

"In the matter of Joan, he is to defer to the orders of the Bishop of Beauvais during the Duke of Bedford's absence from Rouen."

"So it is Cauchon who has changed the verdict?"

"It would appear so."

"Why will Warwick not see me?"

"He is no happier with what must be done than you are, Captain. The last thing he needs just now is to be lectured by you."

"So there is no hope for Jeanne?"

"I'm afraid not, Captain. The order has been made, and there's an end to it."

Richard returned home to Mary with his devastating news, the elation of the last few days now just a bitter memory. He sat down with his head in his hands. "I don't know what more I can do. If Bedford was still in Rouen, I would appeal to him, but he is two days away in Paris, and the execution takes place tomorrow."

The Angel of Lorraine

Mary could not keep the anger out of her voice. "You place too much faith in Bedford. He could have saved Jeanne if he'd wanted to."

"He's probably frightened of her. He really believes she's a witch."

"Cast a spell on him do you mean?" snorted Mary.

Richard thought back to that day in Rouen when he met the duke a few days after Patay. Bedford said something then about him being under Jeanne's spell. Richard had shrugged it off, but maybe the duke really meant it. "Well, Bedford is the only man who could have saved Jeanne," he said.

"You're wrong there. The other man is the most despicable of them all."

"Cauchon?"

"No, he is just a minor player in this game of power. I mean the French king. He abandoned the person who gave him his throne and turned round the fortunes of France for him. From what you've told me, he made no effort to pay off the Duke of Burgundy."

"That's what I've heard from reliable sources in the army."

"Then he is beneath contempt. Some might claim that Bedford acted from superstition or ignorance, but there is no such excuse for Charles of France."

"At least we can agree on that. Will you come to the market square tomorrow?"

"No. I could not face the crowd of gloating, stupid men. I know exactly how Jeanne must be feeling at this moment."

"Having gone through it yourself of course. I shall go because I must give something to Jeanne to ease the pain a little."

"The laudanum you brought back from Italy?"

"Yes. Jeanne will be well guarded, but I shall find a way to get it to her whatever it takes."

"I know you will. I realise I must sound angry, but it's not at you. If only more men were like my dear husband, the world would be a better place."

* * *

IV

The morning of Wednesday, the thirtieth day of May, in the Year of Our Lord 1431 dawned cloudless and bright. It was too good a day to die. Pierre Cauchon was up early updating his diary for the previous day. He knew he had again broken inquisitorial procedure by handing Jeanne over to the executioner before getting formal approval from the civil authorities for the reimposition of the death sentence, but pleasing the English was more important, so he omitted the procedural irregularity from his diary record. He looked out of his window and watched the early morning mist being burnt off by the sun and wishing this day, the day that would see the end of the arduous five-month process of trying and convicting Jeanne, could be over as soon as possible. But his private musings were abruptly disturbed by a sharp rap at his office door.

"Come in," he called, then added under his breath, "if you must."

In walked the assistant of Friar Martin Ladvenu, the Dominican priest who had been charged with comforting Jeanne in her prison during her last hours. "Mon Seigneur Bishop, Jeanne the Maid has asked to receive Holy Communion before she dies, but my master asks you in turn if it is permissible to give an excommunicated heretic the Holy Eucharist."

The Angel of Lorraine

In a rare moment of compassion, or maybe conscience, Cauchon answered, "Tell your master that Jeanne may have whatever she likes."

Just after eight o'clock, Jeanne was led under close English guard to her execution in Rouen's marketplace. A large crowd had already gathered, amongst which were many English soldiers with orders to ensure no disorder broke out. It was an extraordinary sight; a small, slim, teenaged girl flanked by burly warriors nervously looking from side to side ready to spring into action against any rescue attempt. The dismal procession approached the pyre where the executioner had made a ramp in the firewood so that Jeanne could easily climb to the wooden stake placed at the top. There she would have the last rites read to her by Father Ladvenu, then be tightly bound to the stake to undergo her sentence.

Some of the English soldiers in the crowd were yelling insults and hooting derision at this helpless child who seemed bewildered by all that was happening around her. One particularly objectionable character, who was standing in front and a little to the left of Richard, was calling Jeanne a slut and a whore to the evident delight of his compatriots. Richard had just decided he could take no more and put on his brigandine gloves ready to deal with the Englishman, when he was pushed aside from behind by a familiar figure who dealt the uncouth soldier a blow to the jaw, which felled him instantly. "Shut your bloody mouth! You know nothing about this, you idiot!" The Wiltshire burr confirmed it was Sergeant Hawkswood.

"All right, all right," replied the floored soldier. "I'm just wondering whose side you're on."

"Henry!" shouted Richard. "What are you doing here? I was never more glad to see you than today."

"Captain! I might have guessed you'd be here. We've just returned from campaigning in the south. Thank God, Sir John and the Norfolk company are still on the march, or there'd be a riot here."

Before Richard could respond, Jeanne, who had now reached the ramp in the firewood, cried out, "A cross! A cross! Does anyone have a cross!"

Peter Tallon

Richard picked up two pieces of kindling at the base of the pyre and formed them into a rough cross. "Henry, have you got any hemp or string with you? I must make a cross for Jeanne."

"I've got a spare bowstring, Captain. Will that do?"

"Yes, yes, cut a twelve-inch length off, and hurry, we don't have much time."

Jeanne called out again, but her executioner began to lose patience and urged her up the ramp.

"Geoffroy!" called Richard. "Wait! I have a crucifix."

The executioner remembered Richard from the previous day and beckoned him forward. "Captain, you must be quick, my masters are watching."

"I understand, and I shall be quick, but would you avert your eyes for a few seconds?"

"I will, Captain."

Richard turned to Jeanne. Her clear blue eyes were swollen; she had been crying. His heart went out to her. "Jeanne, it's Captain Calveley. Here is your cross."

He handed it to her. Her little fingers gripped it as if it could save her, and she held it to her heart. Her voice was hoarse with terror. "Thank you for your kindness, Captain."

He took the phial of laudanum tincture from his sleeve. "Quick, drink this, it will reduce the pain." He held it to her lips.

An English voice in the crowd shouted, "Hey! What's he doing?"

The Angel of Lorraine

But Jeanne turned her face away from the phial. "My voices have told me I will not be harmed."

"Jeanne, do this for me, not for yourself. My faith is not as strong as yours. Quickly now."

"Come along, time to move on," said Geoffroy, but by then, Jeanne had swallowed the contents of the phial.

"I will be with God soon, Captain," she said. "He and I will watch over you, but for now, I would like you to stay close by."

Richard's eyes were watering as he replied, "I will, Jeanne." He could not see clearly as he made his way back to a slightly different place in the crowd from where he could watch the execution. He stayed there for Jeanne's sake; he would far rather have gone home. Beside him stood a hooded Dominican friar.

The executioner knew his job. As soon as Father Ladvenu had read Jeanne the last rites, he quickly strapped her to the wooden stake and began to light the kindling at the foot of her pyre. The wood was dry and seasoned and took fire quickly; there was very little smoke. Jeanne's suffering would be kept to the minimum possible.

The friar beside Richard spoke. "You weep, Englishman. Why are you here?"

"To witness the murder of a saint. Why are you here?"

"To witness a miracle. Jeanne's voices told her she would not suffer. I believe she will be proved right."

As the heat began to burn, Jeanne cried out, "Sweet Jesus!" The flames began to consume her feet. Again and again, she cried, "Jesus!" but the flames started to spread around her, and the pitch of her voice rose as the pain became unbearable until all that could be heard was a prolonged scream. Suddenly her head fell forward; the screaming stopped. Apart from the crackling of the fire, there was utter silence in Rouen's market square.

A moment later, the English lout who had been jeering at Jeanne, the one that Henry had felled so effectively, said to anyone who would listen, "God save us! We're all damned! We've just killed a saint!"

Others in the crowd murmured approval of this sentiment, and Richard turned to the hooded friar beside him. "What of your miracle now, friar!"

The friar was slow to respond, but when he did, there was a surprise in store. He threw back his hood and said, "I am not a friar, and I remember you, Captain Calveley. I was with Jeanne at your parley after Patay. My name is Gilles, Baron de Rais."

"You were the one who wanted us all killed!"

"Yes, it would have been so much simpler."

"Then why have you identified yourself? I could have you arrested and held for ransom."

"True, but unless I am mistaken, you will not." De Rais was not mistaken.

"Then what of my question? Your miracle did not happen," said Richard bitterly.

De Rais sighed. "Alas, it did not. I hoped against hope that it would. My life before I met Jeanne was shameful and debauched, but she was such a bright light I reformed and believed in her and her message. I really thought she was an angel sent by God to save France. Now I realise it was all just an illusion, but nevertheless a powerful one which changed the course of our war. Now I no longer believe there is a God nor some sort of magical afterlife called heaven or hell. If there is a God, then I do not wish to know him if he is capable of allowing such an injustice as we have just witnessed. Heaven with him would be hell for me."

"What will you do now, Baron?"

"I shall act as if there is no afterlife and no God. I shall revert to my old ways, my old sordid pleasures, and indulge myself safe in the knowledge that there is no reckoning after death. I won't have to spend eternity with the monster who let Jeanne burn for him."

Richard saw Henry making his way through the dispersing crowd towards him. "Mon Seigneur de Rais, pull up your hood and leave now. English soldiers are coming." De Rais slipped away just as Henry arrived. "Captain, it's over now, thank God."

"Indeed, Henry. I need a drink. Are you on duty?"

Henry looked from side to side and shrugged. "I think England can manage without me for an hour or two."

"Good. Then we'll go back to my house, collect Mary, and go to a tavern for some wine for her and some strong ale for you and me."

"Sounds good to me, Captain."

Richard put his arm round his old comrade's shoulder. "Come on, Sergeant, I've had enough for one day. Let's go home."

EPILOGUE

In the Year of Our Lord 1453, twenty-two years after Jeanne's death, two great battles were fought at the opposite ends of Europe. First, in the east, Constantinople fell to the Turks at the end of May. It had long ceased to be a true bastion against Islam, but its significance as the last temporal link with the Roman Empire was huge, and its fall sent shock waves throughout Europe.

Then, at the end of July, came the Battle of Castillon ten miles from Bordeaux. Once again, a small English army was pitted against a large French one, but this time the dice finally fell in favour of the French. In his sixties but still fighting for England, John Talbot, now Earl of Shrewsbury, had another one of those rushes of blood to the head when he led his men forward to attack three hundred entrenched field cannon commanded by Jean Bureau himself. Inevitably the English were swept away, Talbot and his only son were killed, and England's last army in France was destroyed. The war was over even though no formal peace was agreed.

On the day news of Castillon reached Rouen, Richard, now sixty-six years of age, was at home enjoying an evening with Joan, Marcel, their three children—all of whom were adults ranging in age from eighteen to twenty-two, and two grandchildren, who were playing alongside them. They sat in the garden watching the summer sun go down as they had done on this day for the last two years to mark the passing of Mary, who had died nearly three years before.

"You still miss her," said Joan.

Peter Tallon

"Every day, but especially at times like this. I feel I have lived too long. Most of my contemporaries have died. Hugh still writes from his home in Yarmouth, but when Henry passed on last year, I began to feel ready to go."

"Nonsense, Father," admonished Joan. "You still have your health and your family, and you often see Henry's children too. I know you feel lonely at times, but Marcel and I are nearby, and you know you can come and live with us whenever you want."

"And we can bore the children with stories of the war like old men do," added Marcel.

Richard smiled. "That would be good, and I will accept your invitation soon, but there are still too many memories here for me to leave just yet. I often think back to the day Mary told me you and Joan wanted to get married, and I am forever grateful to her for making me see the sense in it. Her prediction about the advantages of having a French son-in-law when the war was lost, or won in your case, Marcel, was proven correct. Without your influence, we would have been booted out of France to end up who knows where. We could never return to England because of Mary's Lollard conviction."

There was a knock at the front door. "Who can that be?" asked Joan. "The Grand Horloge has just chimed eight o'clock."

"I'll go and see," said Marcel.

A few moments later, he returned accompanied by a tall, weather-beaten man of about thirty.

"You had better introduce yourself," said Marcel.

The stranger drew himself up to his full height and spoke in heavily accented French. "My name isa Enrico Dandolo. I have come to see Capitano Richard Calveley."

Richard's heart pounded. He dared not hope this could be the man he thought he was. "I am he," he answered cautiously.

"I bring message for you. All isa explained in this letter." He gave Richard a rolled, sealed scroll. Richard's hand trembled as he broke the seal and unrolled the letter. "Er, would you give me a moment with this messenger? I will take him to the front room where I shall read this."

The two men left the garden, and Joan looked at Marcel. "Did you see the colour of his eyes?"

"Yes, jade green. And I remember Richard when he saved me at Agincourt. It could easily be the same man but forty years ago!"

Richard took Enrico to the front room and, as he prepared to read the letter, asked, "How did you find me?"

"Mama say go to Rouen and ask at Town Hall. Was easy."

Both men remained standing as Richard slowly read the letter.

Date July 2nd 1453
Genoa
To the grey friar whose vestments were too short

My Dear Richard,

I do not know if you are alive or dead. You did not answer my last letter but I know you must have received it because I knew it was you that day twenty three years ago on Genoa's sea front. I did not recognise you at first, even though there seemed to be something familiar about the figure within the grey friar's cloak as we passed by. But when Enrico came back after giving you a silver half ducat for charity and said, as an afterthought, that your eyes were the same colour as his, I knew it was you. I wanted to run to you and give myself to you again, but with a family of my own it was not possible.

I sincerely apologise if this letter causes you embarrassment. If your wife still lives then read no further, destroy it at once and send Enrico home. If she does not, then know this. I still love you, I always have. Paolo made a fine husband and as well as Enrico we had two more children together. I loved him too but he never spoke of what happened when you came to Genoa, nor did my father. That day I saw you was terrible for me, I could not sleep properly for weeks, but it must also have been difficult for Paolo so I never asked him about it.

Paolo died early this year, he was sixty one, a good age for any seafaring man. Since then I have had many suitors. I am forty eight and am told I'm still beautiful. Be that as it may, I want to be sure you know how I feel before I make any decision here. Enrico knows the truth, I told him just before he left. He seemed quite composed when I explained who his true father is; he's relaxed about that sort of thing, just like you!

If you still love me please come to me my darling. We could have many years together but, even if we only have a few, I shall be grateful for what we have.

You will soon realise if you don't already, that Enrico is a fine man, a son you can be proud of. Come to me if you can.

My fondest love,
Ruth

Richard rolled up the letter and looked at Enrico. "It says here that you know the truth about your father."

"I always know there's something different about me. I grow big, but everyone else in family is small. My eyes are green, but no one else in family has green eyes. When I ask, Papa says he has northern blood in ancestry. I accept, but years later when Papa dies, Mama tells me truth."

"Are you angry?"

The Angel of Lorraine

"With Mama? Never! Maybe good thing I do not know when I am younger, but now I am twenty-eight. Understand more about life now."

"Then you forgive me?"

"Isa nothing to forgive. Two people fall in love, it happen all the time. To me, Paolo Dandolo will always be Papa, but you will be Father."

Richard held out his arms, and the two men embraced in silence, then Richard pulled back and looked into the green eyes that were at the same height as his. "I don't know what I have done to deserve this, but I thank God you have come, Enrico. Do you remember when we first met?"

"Of course! You were the friar at Genoa."

"I thought that would be the last time I saw you, and now here you are."

"You have no wife now?"

"She died three years ago."

"Then you can come home with me? I know Mama wishes it. She still beautiful lady."

"Spoken like a true son. Yes, of course, I'll come, but I have some explaining to do first. Wait here, you shall stay in the guest room tonight. I shall bring you something to eat and drink because I may be a long time."

It took Richard an hour to tell Joan and Marcel the story about his trip to the Holy Land and how he and Ruth fell in love. He left nothing out, even the precious moments when he and Ruth made love thinking they were about to die on the day of the final Turkish attack.

When he finished, Marcel was silent, but Joan said, "So that's why you never said much about your adventures in the Holy Land."

Peter Tallon

"Yes, I am ashamed to have hidden that secret all these years."

"Father, you should not be. You are human like everyone else, though, as your daughter, it does come as a surprise. What will you do now?"

"Tomorrow, I shall visit our notary and put my affairs in order so that your financial future is secure. Then, the next day I shall leave with Enrico for Genoa. I do not really know what to expect, it has been such a long time, I may even see out the rest of my life there. But I will promise you that whatever happens, I shall return within two years to see you all, and I shall write every year so you get a letter just before Christmas."

"We shall miss you, Father, and so will your grandchildren and great-grandchildren."

Richard looked at them all talking and playing in the garden and began to have second thoughts, but Marcel intervened. "Richard, you must follow your star. You have lived honourably, and you have a chance to live out the rest of your life in the company of the woman you love. We shall not stand in your way."

Richard did remain in Genoa, but he came back to visit his family within two years and exchange news. He kept his word and wrote every year until the Year of Our Lord 1471, the year in which the Wars of the Roses flared up again in England but seemed, after battles at Barnet and Tewkesbury, to have ended at last in victory for the Yorkists. But in peaceful Rouen, no Christmas letter came.

In early January 1472, the snow was knee-deep in Normandy. A letter arrived from Genoa but in a different hand. It was addressed to Joan. She was sitting with Marcel in the same house they were in when Enrico so unexpectedly arrived all those years ago. Now they were entering old age, and the house that Joan grew up in was sufficient for their needs.

Date: December 8th 1471
Genoa
Dear Joan,

We have not met, but Richard told me so much about you I feel I know you. I am very sorry to have to tell you that Richard died two days ago. He was eighty three and retained his wits until the end. I am making arrangements for his body to be sent to a priory called Dunwich in England where his first wife and two sons are buried. It was his wish.

I was so happy when he returned with Enrico eighteen years ago. I never expected so much time with him, but I must tell you what happened on the night he died.

He had been very tired and quiet for the previous few days, then on that dreadful night, after we had eaten a small meal together, he said "Ruth, I think my time is near. I am in no pain but I feel a deep sleep approaching. I will go to bed now. Will you come and sit with me for a while?" Of course I did, and pulled up a chair beside our bed and held his hand. He looked at me, his green eyes were brighter than ever. He smiled, "I shall soon know. I love you Ruth." Then he closed his eyes and went into a deep sleep. I sat with him for a while then fell asleep myself.

I must have slept, slumped with my head on the bed beside him, for many hours. Then I was woken with a start because something touched my cheek. It was dark but there was enough moonlight to see Richard's outline. I put my ear to his heart; it was no longer beating but he was still warm and our hands were tightly clasped together. I am convinced that what I felt on my cheek that night was his spirit touching me as it left his body. I know that spirits are not supposed to be able to communicate by touch but I'm sure it was him.

I have told Enrico, who is a great comfort to me because I see Richard so strongly in him, and now I have told you. I shall not speak of this to anyone else, not even our priest or rabbi. It is just for the three of us to know. It will bind us together even though we are separated by many hundreds of miles.

May God protect you Joan. We both loved the same man in our different ways and I am sure we will meet, if not in this world, then in the next.

Ruth

Marcel had been watching his wife. "Is everything all right, my dear? Was that a tear I saw running down your cheek?"

"Papa has died. Read this letter. I know you will respect the confidentiality at the end." She handed him the letter and said, "I just need a minute or two alone." She slowly walked through to the kitchen and offered up a little prayer for her father. Then she looked through the kitchen window and watched her own great-grandchildren playing in the snow for a few minutes. *What would Papa say now?* she thought. A voice in her mind seemed to speak, "Joan, life must go on."

She wiped her eyes, smiled, and whispered as if he was there, "Thank you, Papa." Then she turned, straightened her hair, and went back to her husband.

The End

The Angel of Lorraine

What Became of the Major Nonfictional Characters?

The French

King Charles VII, 1403–1461. After the most inauspicious start, King Charles became one of the most successful kings in French history. Inheriting a divided kingdom on the verge of defeat by the English, he passed on a wealthy, united nation, which was once again the pre-eminent power in Europe. He gave himself the title King Charles the Victorious, and nobody could argue with that because he had finally defeated the English, the ancient enemy of France.

Despite his ultimate success, Charles was never loved by his people. His cold, calculating personality was needed for the times, but his lack of loyalty to those who helped him was not endearing. Late in his life, he even fell out with his son, the Dauphin Louis, causing a brief, but worrying split in the kingdom; but when he died, aged fifty-eight, he could turn his face to the wall satisfied that he had reunited his nation and left his people more contented than they had been for hundreds of years.

Yolande of Aragon, 1384–1442. Undoubtedly the most influential woman of the time and an early supporter of Jeanne the Maid, Yolande was the mother of Queen Marie, wife of Charles VII. When she died aged fifty-eight, she had ensured her bloodline would remain on the throne of France through the Dauphin Louis, her grandson. Her relationship with her son-in-law Charles was sometimes strained, and she managed to cause the downfall of Charles's favourite adviser Georges de la Trémoille, two years after Jeanne's death. She worked tirelessly behind the scenes to protect the Valois inheritance and even managed to persuade the Duke of Brittany to break his alliance with England and join France, which finally enabled Arthur of Richemont, a Breton noble and one of the best generals of the time, to return to his rightful place as Constable of France.

Georges de la Trémoille, Grand Chamberlain of France 1385–1466. Georges de la Trémoille, archenemy of Jeanne and Yolande, managed to hold on to his position as the king's closest confidante until 1435, when he was kidnapped and held to ransom by Arthur of Richemont, the reinstated Constable of France. King Charles typically abandoned him and left him to fester in internal exile until his death in 1466 at the remarkable age of eighty-one. He was suspected by many of betraying Jeanne to the Burgundians, but de Flavy remained silent and nothing could be proven.

Jean Dunois, Bastard of Orléans, 1402–1468. Charles's most reliable and loyal supporter, Jean Dunois gave a lifetime of service to his monarch. Showing true gratitude for a change, the king made him grand chamberlain on Trémoille's fall from grace in 1435. In 1440 and at great cost to his own purse, Jean finally collected the ransom money of 120,000 ecus of gold for his half brother, Charles of Orléans, the king's uncle, who had been held by the English since Agincourt. The king made Dunois Count of Longueville, thus ensuring his family line would become legitimate. Apart from Jeanne, no one did more to ensure final French victory than Jean Dunois.

Jean Poton de Xaintrailles, 1390–1461. Apart from a setback three months after Jeanne died when he was defeated and captured by the Earl of Warwick at the Battle of Beauvais, Jean Poton continued to live his charmed life. On payment of his ransom, he returned to the fight, and even though he never really abandoned his piratical behaviour, he was made a marshal of France in 1459. The only disappointment was that he never had any legitimate children, so his line ended with him at the good age of seventy-one.

Etienne de Vignolles, La Hire, 1390–1443. Perhaps the nearest of all the French leaders to Jeanne in terms of his aggressive spirit, La Hire was a formidable battlefield commander. Like his close friend de Xaintrailles, he never quite lost his appetite for private piracy, but the English were particularly respectful of his fighting prowess. He lived long enough to see the beginning of the end of the war but died of a fever aged only fifty-three.

Gilles, Baron de Rais, 1404–1440. A dark though interesting character, de Rais seems to have reformed as a direct result of Jeanne's influence. He was her most outspoken supporter and believed utterly in the truth of her claim to be a messenger of God. He must have been devastated by her execution, and disillusioned, he quickly returned to his sordid private life. He is said to have abused and killed between one hundred and two hundred children. Such crimes were as deplorable in the fifteenth century as they are now; consequently he was executed in Nantes at the age of thirty-six. Being of noble blood, he was garrotted before he was burned, a privilege not afforded to his evil companions in crime.

Duke Philippe the Good of Burgundy, 1396–1467. One of the most remarkable characters of the age and certainly the most successful, his only disappointment being his failure (just) to turn his dukedom into the Kingdom of Lorraine. This was the price he had to pay when he terminated his uncomfortable alliance with England and ended the civil war with France at the Treaty of Arras in 1435 (see below under the Duke of Bedford). At the end of his forty-eight-year reign, Burgundy was stronger and richer than it had ever been, but this was all to be squandered by his son, Charles the Rash, in his fruitless wars with the Swiss.

The English

John, Duke of Bedford, Regent of England and France, 1389–1435. Eldest of Henry V's younger brothers, Bedford spent his later life working to ensure that his nephew succeeded to the thrones of both England and France. He was utterly loyal to the wishes of his great brother, but the effort of trying to run two fractious kingdoms exhausted him, and he died aged only forty-six. Seen as a fair, reasonable, and merciful man, he was loved by the English and respected by the French; but like his elder brother, he had a strong loyalty to the Church, which made him hard on any form of heresy. He could have saved Jeanne, but along with the rest of the English establishment, he wanted her dead and discredited because he blamed her for the reversal of English fortunes and his life's work. His marriage to the Duke of Burgundy's sister Anne turned out to be a love match; the couple were devoted to each other. Anne was the bond that kept England and Burgundy together, but when she died of plague in November 1432, the unnatural alliance soon fell apart. Despite Bedford's best efforts, he could not stop the rapprochement between France and Burgundy, which was concluded at the Treaty of Arras in 1435. If Jeanne had turned the tide of war, Arras began the united French march to victory. Bedford died in Rouen just before the treaty was signed. Without Bedford's steadying hand, the latent rivalry between the houses of York and Lancaster began to develop unchecked, so just as France was reunited, England began the descent into the bitter dynastic conflict that later became known as the Wars of the Roses, and ended the Plantagenet dynasty.

John, Baron Talbot (later Earl of Shrewsbury), 1387–1453. Undoubtedly the best English commander in the latter stages of the Hundred Years War, Talbot was the darling of the English and earned respect from the French for the honourable way he conducted war. He won many small victories, but the days of huge battlefield successes were over. The remorseless French tide became unstoppable after the Treaty of Arras, and the most Talbot could do was delay the inevitable. He was captured again by the French when Rouen fell in 1449, but in order to secure his liberty after his ransom was paid, he was required to take an oath that he would never bear arms against the French again. He kept that oath, and when he was finally killed at the age of sixty-six at the Battle of Castillon, he wore no arms or amour and rode a small grey palfrey that was felled by a cannonball. Talbot was pinned to the ground, making him an easy target for a French man-at-arms to dispatch him with a battle-axe. Although recognised as a hero by both sides, he let himself down because of his personal feud with Sir John Fastolf, whom he unfairly blamed for his first defeat at Patay.

Sir John Fastolf, 1380–1459. Thanks to Shakespeare, who represented him as the fat, comical coward Falstaff over a century after his death, Sir John Fastolf is one of the most maligned characters in English history. The unjustified vendetta waged against him by Baron Talbot, the hero of the English, left a stain on Fastolf's character long after he was officially cleared of any wrongdoing by the inquiry into the Battle of Patay. It was Talbot's version that melded itself into the deep subconscious of the English, and thus into the quill of the great bard. In fact, Fastolf spent all his best years between 1415 and 1439 striving for an English victory in France, not only participating in many battles, but also lending money to Henry VI's government, most of which was never paid back. On his final return to England, he settled at his new castle at Caistor near Yarmouth with Millicent, his beloved wife, but she died in 1446, aged seventy-eight, leaving him a widower for the last thirteen years of his life. After her death, Fastolf cuts rather a sad, lonely figure litigating to the end, arguing with his stepson Stephen and becoming increasingly bitter with life. While he was honourable and brave, it has to be admitted that his reputation for parsimony was largely justified. He died aged seventy-nine but had no children of his own, so his line ended with him.

Pierre Cauchon, 1371–1442. Although a true born Frenchman, Cauchon began his political career as a supporter of the Burgundian cause, so when the English and Burgundians became allies after the murder of Duke Jean the Fearless at Montereau in 1419 by supporters of mad King Charles VI, it was natural that Cauchon should side with the English. He was well rewarded by the Duke of Bedford for his management of Jeanne's trial and execution, and later became a diplomatic envoy for England, amongst many other honours, though he never received an archbishop's mitre. He died at home at the height of his fame and power aged seventy-one, which just goes to show that in the real world, the bad guys don't always lose.

ACKNOWLEDGEMENTS

I would like to thank Stephen Cooper, author of *The Real Falstaff*, Pen & Sword 2010, for permission to use his original work in which he relocates the battle of Rouvray from the accepted location of Rouvray-Saint-Denis, north of the English base at Janville, to Rouvray-Sainte-Croix, a much smaller village south of Janville. This at once clarifies the seemingly bizarre behaviour of the English before the battle who supposedly marched south from Paris, passed Janville on their way to Orléans then turned round and marched north again to fight the battle, then turned round yet again and marched south once more. But Stephen Cooper's relocation eliminates the need for all this backtracking and simply keeps the English on a steady route south before being intercepted by the Franco-Scottish army.

I am also grateful to Neil Amos, whose map drawing skills yet again converted my spiderlike scribbles into an easy-to-understand map, and my two proofreaders/editors, Lawrence Tallon and Nick Meo, for their valuable contribution correcting and smartening up the script.

Also by Peter Tallon

The Lion and the Lily (AuthorHouse 2016)

Part 1 of the Richard Calveley Trilogy

The Templar Legacy (Book Venture 2018)

Part 2 of the Richard Calveley Trilogy

Printed and bound by CPI Group (UK) Ltd, Croydon, CR0 4YY